D0960718

THE CURSE OF
JACOB TRACY

THE CURSE
OF
JACOB TRACY

HOLLY MESSINGER

THOMAS DUNNE BOOKS

ST. MARTIN'S PRESS ✹ NEW YORK

This is a work of fiction. All of the characters, organizations, and events portrayed in this novel are either products of the author's imagination or are used fictitiously.

THOMAS DUNNE BOOKS.
An imprint of St. Martin's Press.

THE CURSE OF JACOB TRACY. Copyright © 2015 by Holly Messinger. All rights reserved. Printed in the United States of America. For information, address St. Martin's Press, 175 Fifth Avenue, New York, N.Y. 10010.

www.thomasdunnebooks.com
www.stmartins.com

Library of Congress Cataloging-in-Publication Data

Messinger, Holly.
    The curse of Jacob Tracy : a novel / Holly Messinger. — First edition.
        pages cm
    ISBN 978-1-250-03898-2 (hardback) — ISBN 978-1-4668-3431-6 (e-book)
    1. Curses—Fiction.   2. Saint Louis (Mo.)—History—19th century—Fiction.   3. Ghost stories.   I. Title.
    PS3613.E78927C87 2015
    813'.6—dc23

                                                                        2015034667

ISBN 978-1-250-03898-2 (hardcover)
ISBN 978-1-4668-3431-6 (e-book)

Our books may be purchased in bulk for promotional, educational, or business use. Please contact your local bookseller or the Macmillan Corporate and Premium Sales Department at 1-800-221-7945, extension 5442, or by e-mail at MacmillanSpecialMarkets@macmillan.com.

First Edition: December 2015

10   9   8   7   6   5   4   3   2   1

For Tony, without whom this story would
have had a very different ending

ACKNOWLEDGEMENTS

Much gratitude is extended to my writer's group, for their advice, enthusiasm, and eagerness to debate the etymology of obscure colloquialisms. Special thanks to Aly for composing Sabine's Latin spells, and Micah for providing just the right insight at a particularly rough point in the revision process.

Thanks to my mother, who gave me some of my best early writing advice ("Nobody enjoys reading present tense, dear"), and Dad, who has always had the most unwavering faith of anyone I've met, and taught me not to be swayed by the world.

And thanks to Sit, who taught me to wait.

A SHORT TRIP
TO SIKESTON

CHAPTER ONE

Miss Fairweather's Chinese butler showed Trace to the library, which was dark and cavernous, surprisingly masculine. Stuffed animals and birds loomed from the gallery, backlit by the skylights and the rose window at the head of the room. A fire helped dispel the early-March gloom, but Trace was careful not to look into any dark corners. These big old houses tended to hold nasty surprises for him.

"Miss Fairweather will be with you soon," the Chinese said, bowing.

"Thanks." Trace worried the brim of his hat in his hands and hoped he wasn't wasting his time. Usually by this time of year, he liked to have himself and Boz hired on with a supply train or party of settlers headed west, but the railroads stretched out further every year, and there just wasn't that much wagon traffic headed out of St. Louis anymore. He and Boz had been scratching for work all winter, and this spring looked to be more of the same.

John Jameson at the Seed and Livery hadn't been able to tell Trace much about Miss Fairweather or what she wanted done. "All I know is she's English and she's got money to burn. She bought that old Mannerson place, the one built by the railroad man before he went bust? Renovated the whole thing, but never has anybody in. Doesn't go out in Society, but I hear she's got some doings with the medical college. Trying to make them take female students, if you can beat that."

A glance around the library told Trace something else about her: she was a scholar. The books had a used look about them—cracks in the binding and papers stuffed between the pages. He stepped closer to the nearest shelf, squinting to read the titles, which were wide-ranging and impressive: history, theology, philosophy, medicine. A whole shelf on Spiritualism.

Trace's mouth curled in distaste. He'd met more than a few tricksters who made their living staging séances, preying like vultures on the emotions of the bereaved. Trace figured if a real dead person ever showed up to one of those productions, the so-called medium would just piss himself, and after that he wouldn't be so welcome in the fancy parlors.

Light footsteps sounded in the hall, accompanied by the rustling of silk, and Trace turned to see a porcelain doll of a woman enter the library.

She was young, was his first thought. He'd been expecting a withered spinster in black crepe, but this woman was maybe thirty, and seemed younger because of her small stature. She was thin to the point of frailty, with fair hair scraped back from an intelligent, sharp-featured face. Her silk morning gown was steel blue, her eyes as pale and chilly as a November sky.

"Mr. Tracy?" She crossed the Persian carpet and extended a hand to him—palm sideways, like a man. "I am Sabine Fairweather. Thank you for coming on such short notice."

Trace clasped her hand gingerly, conscious of his rough boots, his oilcloth coat over his one good shirt, and the fresh razor scrapes on his jaw. He was used to looking down at people, being well over six feet himself, but she was a dainty little thing—the top of her head barely reached his shoulder. "Pleasure, ma'am."

"Please, be seated." She indicated the big leather club chairs on either side of the fireplace, and crossed to the liquor cabinet. "Would you care for a Scotch?"

"That'd be fine, ma'am," he said, mildly surprised at being offered liquor by a lady at eleven in the morning.

She poured each of them a half inch and handed a glass to Trace before perching on the chair opposite him. "Mr. Jameson tells me you were at seminary before the war?"

"Yes, ma'am, that's right." The whiskey was wonderful, smooth and spicy, and against his better judgment he imagined what a pleasure it would be, to spend an evening in this library with a glass and a book.

"That must make you unusually educated, among your fellows," she said. "I suppose you read Latin?"

"It's been awhile, but yes ma'am, I do. Latin and French, a little Greek, a little Hebrew."

"How many trips to the west coast have you made?"

"Only got out to the coast a couple of times—once to Portland and once to Tacoma. Most of the trips I make are shorter—Montana, Santa Fe."

"As a guide?"

"Guide, trail boss, security." His smile twisted. "Most of the folks goin by wagon these days are headed off the beaten path. They're payin for protection more than my knowledge of Latin."

"Protection from what?"

"Indians. Outlaws. Their own foolishness."

That was perhaps not a tactful thing to say, but Miss Fairweather seemed amused. "And do you find it rewarding, championing fools?"

Trace shot her a wry glance. "Well, it doesn't pay as well as you'd think."

She acknowledged that with a smile, which lent a fey quality to her sharp features. "Mr. Jameson mentioned you had a young sister at St. Mary's. Is she your only family?"

If a man had asked him that question, Trace would have asked why he wanted to know. But he supposed a woman in her position—alone, interviewing men like himself—found it reassuring to know she was hiring a family man. "Pretty near. Got a brother in the army, but he's looked out for himself, since our folks died." Warrick was a captain at Fort Leavenworth, last Trace had heard. They hadn't spoken in eight years.

"Well, Mr. Tracy." Miss Fairweather turned to set her glass on the end table. "I'm sure you would like to know why Mr. Jameson referred you to me."

"Jameson's good for throwin work my way."

"Indeed. I told him I needed a trustworthy man to fetch some property for me. It amounts to a glorified errand, but I need someone reasonably intelligent, capable of discretion."

"Pleased to be at your service, ma'am." His curiosity had turned cautious; he hoped she didn't mean to involve him in some sort of swindle.

"I received a letter, from the solicitor of a dear friend of mine who passed away last year. In her will she made reference to a keepsake she wished me to have, but unfortunately my health prevents me from traveling to retrieve it."

"How far is it?" He didn't want to get too far away from St. Louis; he still hoped to get on with a wagon party for the year.

"Sikeston, Missouri. Not far by your standards, perhaps. I'll pay you two hundred dollars, half in advance and half upon completion."

Trace nearly choked on the Scotch. Two hundred dollars was five or six months' pay for the average cowhand. His half would pay Emma's board and tuition for another term, square him with the livery, and give both of them a little pocket money. "I'm agreeable, ma'am, so long as you give me the particulars of what I'm bringin back, so I can rent a wagon if need be."

"Oh, no, nothing like that. It's a box. A trinket box, such as we ladies keep things in. I believe I left the letter on my desk, here . . ."

She rustled away across the long carpet, toward the monumental desk under the rose window. She returned with a folded packet in her hand. "The particulars, as you say, are in there. Would you care for a cigar?"

"Ah, no, ma'am, thank you." That was an odd question, in his opinion; he hoped he didn't seem so uncouth that he'd smoke in the presence of a lady. He took the heavy, smooth papers from her hand and folded them open to reveal a fine copperplate script: *To whom it may concern . . . be it herewith known by these . . . bequeath to Miss Sabine Fairweather . . .*

"Oh, please don't demur on my account." She walked to the cabinet again and picked up a wooden casket, inlaid with ivory. "I have always enjoyed the aroma of a good cigar. And these are very fine, I understand. My father's colleagues always appreciated them."

Now he couldn't refuse without offending her. Trace glanced into the velvet-lined box and the sharp smell of tobacco teased his nostrils. They *were* good cigars. He took one, allowed her to trim the end of it, and let his attention fall back to the paper as she turned to the fireplace for a light.

. . . One rosewood box by description five inches in length by three inches in breadth by three inches in depth . . . To be collected by Miss Sabine Fairweather or her appointed agent—

She was coming back with a small iron salamander in her hand, the tip of it glowing hot. He raised the cigar, smiling politely; she was smiling politely, but there was something in her gaze, curiosity perhaps, and she opened her mouth to ask a question at the same time as the iron dipped in her hand—

Pain seared the inside of his wrist. He jerked and dropped the cigar, just managed not to swear out loud. Miss Fairweather started back with a cry of dismay as the smell of burnt flesh rose between them.

"Oh my goodness, how *could* I have been so clumsy! Mr. Tracy, I do so apologize!"

She set the salamander quickly on the hearth and spun back to grasp his palm in her own, pushing back his sleeve to examine the burn. It was a small, sizzling half circle below the butt of his thumb, angry red and stinging like a bastard.

"I am so very sorry. Please, let me call for Min Chan to treat that." She crossed to the doorway and pulled the bell cord.

"It's nothin, ma'am," Trace said, annoyed but trying to be gracious in the interest of employment. "I've had worse brandin calves."

"But not at *my* hand," she said. "Please, let me fetch some salve. I won't be a minute."

She hurried away. Trace got up and paced, shaking his hand and folding back his coat sleeve so the oilcloth wouldn't rub it, amazed at the carelessness of the woman. He'd had the impression she wasn't half stupid, but now he wasn't so sure.

He sensed a presence enter the room and spun around, expecting Miss Fairweather or the Chinese, but the new visitor was a pretty colored girl in a white apron and cap. She dropped a curtsy. "Can I get you anything, sir?"

"No, I don't need anything," Trace said irritably, and then stopped cold, his throat thickening with revulsion.

The girl was semi-transparent. Trace could see the brass gleam of the doorknob through her chest. She smiled at him, but her features were vague and blurred, as if he were seeing her through a warped pane of glass. She clearly had no idea she was dead.

This was why he didn't like being in town too long. Too many old houses, too many buried secrets that wouldn't stay down. Even the harmless ones, like this slave girl, made the hair stand up on his arms and neck, as if the devil were breathing down his collar.

He touched the crucifix that hung against his breastbone, through his shirt, and muttered under his breath, "Ecce Crucem Domini, fugite partes adversae . . ."

She didn't seem to hear, but they often didn't. She stood there smiling, hands twisted in her apron, becoming more transparent with every thud of Trace's heart, until she was gone.

He took a deep, slow breath, and worked his shoulders to ease the tension of fear up his neck. His burned wrist scraped against oilcloth. "Damn it," he hissed, more in embarrassment than pain.

Miss Fairweather's silk skirts rustled in the hall. She came into the room carrying a small jar and a bit of white cloth. "I hope you will trust my nursing skills. I make my own salve and I find this to be quite beneficial . . . Why, Mr. Tracy, whatever is the matter? Are you unwell?"

He flinched at the sound of her voice, which was far too bright, as if she'd walked in on a tea party instead of a surly would-be employee.

"I'm fine," he said shortly. "I'd be appreciative of that salve, though."

She came closer, pale eyes keen on his face, her whole frame intent on some devilry. "You weren't disturbed at all, while I was gone?"

Trace stared at her. For half a heartbeat he wondered if she'd *expected* him to see . . . but no, she couldn't have known about his curse. Everybody who'd had that knowledge was long dead.

But then, everybody knew *somebody* who'd seen a ghost or visited a haunted place. The Spiritualist craze only encouraged that kind of nonsense. She might well know her library was home to something unearthly, but that didn't mean she knew about *him*.

"No," he said. "Didn't see a living soul."

"THANKS FOR PASSIN my name along to Miss Fairweather, Johnny." Trace slapped a quarter on Jameson's countertop and helped himself to a bottle of flavored soda from the barrel in front.

"My pleasure," Jameson said, "but it wasn't me referred her. She sent that Chinese of hers in here to ask for you."

"Asked for me by name?"

"Not Jacob Tracy, but he wanted to find the man called 'Trace.' She sniffed you out from somewhere else." Jameson handed him two dimes with a twinkle in his eye. "What's she look like? Old maid? Crotch-faced old boot?"

"No. Young. Leastways, not older than me." Trace sometimes had to remind himself he was almost thirty-eight. "Thin and pale, though, like she's sickly." He took a thoughtful pull of sarsaparilla. "Boz out back?"

"Yeah, he's just moving those bags of seed I got in."

"Gimme another of those sodas. Can you do without him for a few days? Just for the week it takes us to get to Sikeston and back."

"No, no, s'fine with me. Work'll still be here when you get back."

Trace thanked the shopkeep and took the open bottle of soda out through the stockroom and down the back steps, out to the yard where Boz was lugging bags of wheat and seed potatoes off a wagon.

Boz was a hard, rangy colored man, tall except when he was standing next to Trace. He'd been a supplies sergeant in the Tenth Cavalry after the war, and he had outfitted every wagon party Trace had bossed for the last five years. Trace had hired him because he could figure better than Trace could, and grew to like him because Boz had a handle on reality like no one else. Boz thought about how things looked, tasted, weighed, and packed. He planned ahead, was rarely caught unprepared, and knew how to fix things when they broke. He worried about nothing more abstract than how long the coffee would last, and his attitude toward religion was strictly live and let live.

Also, he made the best corncakes Trace had ever eaten.

"Take a breather," Trace said, holding out the soda bottle. "Hear the news."

Boz wiped the back of his wrist under the brim of his hat and took the bottle. "Got the job from the Englishwoman?"

"Yep. She's payin us two hundred dollars to ride down to Sikeston and back."

Boz coughed as soda fizz went up his throat instead of down. "You're lyin."

"Hell I am. She gave me half in advance." Trace pulled back his coat lapel to show the wad in his vest pocket.

"She crazy?"

"Maybe. But I took the job, so what's that make me?"

"What'd you do to yourself?" Boz gestured at the fresh bandage on Trace's wrist.

"She burned me tryin to light me a cigar."

"Usually takes women a week or two to come after you with a fire iron."

Trace grinned. "For another hundred I may bend over and let her brand me." He quaffed the last of his soda. "Easiest money we'll make this year, that's for sure."

CHAPTER TWO

Sikeston, Missouri, was about a hundred and fifty miles south of St. Louis. It could be reached in three days of easy riding on horseback, in a day or so via riverboat, or in an afternoon train ride.

Speed wasn't everything, as Trace explained to potential customers. Yes, rail travel had gotten cheaper in the last few years. But that was only the cost of a seat—an uncomfortable, bare wooden seat in most cases—packed into a dirty, airless, noisy car with dozens of strangers. And forty dollars one-way across the country didn't cover the cost of transporting animals, or household goods, or basic foodstuffs—all of which would be needed at the end of the line. Traveling west by rail might get you to one of the jumping-off points faster, but outfitting a homestead or a wagon in Missouri or Utah could cost twice as much as it did in St. Louis, because goods were more scarce and vendors stood to make higher profit off unprepared emigrants.

It was a matter of time versus money, Trace always told those wide-eyed homesteaders, implying that his own fee was well-earned in keeping them safe from the unscrupulous.

As for himself and Boz, it made no sense to buy train tickets to Sikeston when they had two perfectly sound horses in need of exercise, and little else to their names this spring other than time to spend.

Unfortunately it rained, from the moment they left St. Louis. A chill, miserable March rain—not cold enough to freeze, just enough to make the roads treacherous to the horses' legs and drag out the trip twice as long as natural. They camped on the road, in the rain—Trace steadfastly refused to sleep in any unfamiliar barn or outbuilding, no matter how deserted it appeared to be, much to Boz's ongoing annoyance.

By the time they got to Sikeston they were both tired and irritable. They found a place to board the horses and then asked the stable manager for the nearest lawyer's office. He sent them to the printer's, and although there was in fact a shyster working out of that business, he had never heard of a man named McGillicuddy. The printer had a city directory, but there was no McGillicuddy in it, either, at least not in a professional capacity.

So Trace asked for the sheriff's office, figuring if anyone knew the whereabouts of a lawyer, it would be another lawman. But once they'd waded through the semi-flooded streets and the washes of mud, they found the sheriff's office dark and vacant.

"Well, hell," Trace said, peering at the sign propped inside the glass.

"What's it say?" Boz asked, scraping mud from his boot on the top edge of the porch steps.

"Sheriff's out of town for a trial. Won't be back til Tuesday."

"You *sure* Miz Fairweather said McGillicuddy?"

"Didn't just say, I saw it printed on the letter. Here! Mister! Father, I mean," Trace amended as the man on the street tilted his black umbrella to reveal a round hat and clerical collar. Trace took off his own hat. "Pardon me, Father . . ." The older man stopped in the mud, on the other side of the moat running in the street, and looked up at him calmly. "We're lookin for a man named McGillicuddy, supposed to be practicin law in this town."

"I assume you mean the business aspect of law," the priest said. "The only lawyer in Sikeston keeps his offices at the printer's."

"We've been there, Father. They never heard of him. It's about the estate of a lady by name of Lisette DuPres—"

"DuPres?" The priest cracked a smile. "She was hardly a lady, but if you're looking for her estate, it's over there." He raised one dripping black wing to point across the street at the saloon, brightly lit and inviting in the misty gloom.

"I don't think I catch your drift, Father," Trace said.

"Son, Madame DuPres was not only a practitioner but a purveyor of the world's oldest profession. Any assets she left behind would most likely be found in there. I believe the current proprietor is named McGillicuddy, though I've never met him personally. And while I don't mind standing and chatting with you lads, if I don't move soon I shall be permanently mired in this spot, so if you wish to continue this conversation—"

"No, no, Father." Trace tipped his hat. "Sorry to keep you."

"Not at all," the priest said, and splashed along his way.

Trace looked at Boz, who shrugged, but there was a gleam of mischief in his eyes. "Maybe Miz Fairweather heard about your former callin and feared you wouldn't take the job."

"If that's the case, she was mistaken," Trace said.

They waded across Main Street to the saloon. The place was handsome and prosperous-looking on the outside—brightly painted with gold-leaf lettering on the windows, offering meals, liquor, and rooms at a nightly rate. The lights inside were burning bright and from the porch they could hear the din of voices and music. It was suppertime and falling dark, and in weather like this, Trace knew, the place would be packed.

This was the sticky bit—although he and Boz knew which places in St. Louis would serve them both without fuss, walking into a new establishment in a strange town was always a bit of a gamble. Trace tried not to patronize his partner, but he also didn't like watching Boz get harassed by men who had half his class.

"You comin?" Trace said, their customary code.

Boz snorted. "I ain't lettin an innocent like you in there alone."

Trace allowed a grin and pushed through the gilt-painted doors.

It was lucky Boz was behind him. As soon as he crossed the threshold, something cold and vicious and distinctly feminine sank its claws into him and shoved. *Non!* the voice sounded distinctly in his head. *Non, non, vous n'êtes pas le bienvenu!*

He grabbed for the swinging door but it scraped past his fingernails.

He would have gone down flat if Boz hadn't caught him and wheel-barrowed him forward into the saloon. It was like being pushed through a briar hedge, but as soon as both feet were through the door he was loose of it. His lungs were left chilled and aching like the time he had slipped in a Colorado river and swallowed half of it.

"You all right?" Boz said.

"Yeah," he said gruffly, trying to catch his breath. "Just hit a slick spot, there." He had a stitch in his side, a pain where the old scar was. Some of the faces near the door turned toward him with varying degrees of curiosity and ridicule, but beneath the bright gas lamps and the beaming drunken faces he glimpsed something feral and mad, twisting in the shadows under their eyes and between the chair legs.

"Stay close," he muttered to Boz.

They made their way to the bar, careful not to step on any toes. Their quarry wasn't hard to spot: a short, ugly, Irish fellow in a striped vest stood at the corner of the bar, watching over the room and swinging a black-lacquered cane. He was surrounded by river hands, all drinking whiskey and laughing at his jokes.

Trace worked his way through the crowd until he could commandeer a spot near the Irishman. Boz took up a space at his back, not crowding anyone, keeping his own face to the room.

"Evenin," Trace said, when the proprietor broke from his posturing to notice their intrusion. "I'm lookin for a man name of McGillicuddy. Heard I might find him here."

The Irishman's piggy little eyes slid over them both. "I'm McGillicuddy. What can I do for yez?"

"It's a bit of private business," Trace said. "Don't suppose we could step into a corner somewhere?"

"Private?" McGillicuddy repeated. "Can't be anything shameful. I have no secrets, have I, lads?" This last was delivered over his shoulder, with a grin for the river hands, who lifted their glasses and declared their support for good ol' Gill.

"Suits me." Trace shrugged. "Has to do with the estate of Lisette DuPres—"

"Miss DuPres died more'n a year ago, boyo, and the sheriff's inquest ruled it a suicide, so if yer nursin a grudge or a broken heart . . ."

"I was sent here to retrieve some property of hers," Trace said. "I was given to understand you were in possession of it."

"And so I am. Left me the whole damn place, bless her little poxy heart." McGillicuddy swept his arm toward the ceiling of the saloon, buoyed by a fresh gale of laughter. His sleeve pulled free from the white starched cuff, baring a few inches of wrist and a glimpse of puckered scar, like a brand.

Trace felt an ugly jolt at the sight of it. He was still wearing a bandage on his own wrist. Miss Fairweather's salve had kept the wound from festering, but it also kept it from crusting over. "It's a rosewood box. Bout the size of a fist. Was told you had the whereabouts of it."

McGillicuddy's hand spilled the drink he was pouring, although Trace was probably the only one who noticed. The river hands were still jeering and joshing each other, but McGillicuddy set the bottle down and stared at Trace, the flush of drink standing out against his pallor. "I don't believe I caught yer name, friend."

"Sure you didn't. It's Jacob Tracy. And this is John Bosley."

McGillicuddy looked over Boz with the same strained curiosity. "Well then. We're all in the service of the Master, ain't we?" His left hand strayed to the opposite forearm and clenched around it. "Of course I'll fetch it for ye. Ain't I kept it safe all this time? It's just I'll have to make the proper preparations, being the time of the moon an' all."

"Of course." Trace matched McGillicuddy's smooth, bullying tone. "We're not in a rush."

"In the meantime you lads'll stay on as my guests, won't yez?" The Irishman twisted his thumb and forefinger around his right wrist as if trying to unscrew the hand from his arm. "Course I'll have to see the mark, ye ken, just to be sure . . ."

Trace hitched up the sleeve of his coat and held out his forearm. The sight of that grimy bandage made McGillicuddy shudder.

"It's still healin," Trace said.

"Hurts like a bastard, don't it?" McGillicuddy managed a strangled grin. "Even now . . . Well, then. Ye'll just have to stay the night, won't yez? You and yer man, here." He beckoned to a little red-haired whore near the stairs. "Sadie! Come here, girl. You lads'll have to tarry a couple days, while I make the arrangements—"

"Just don't let it take too long," Trace said, wondering what on earth Miss Fairweather had sent him into.

"O' course, o' course! We mustn't keep Mr. Mereck waitin, eh? Let me buy you lads a drink."

"That's mighty hospitable of you," Trace said insincerely. The last thing he wanted was to get drunk in this place. Even stone sober he could feel hostility prowling the bar, sniffing along his boots and collar like a cold draft. There was something nasty in this bar, far worse than any dead parlormaid. Something bitter and vindictive.

Meanwhile McGillicuddy was putting away whiskey as if preparing to have something amputated. Whatever he was afraid of, it was making him pugnacious; by the third or fourth shot the Irishman had some of his color back and his tongue was sharpening. "Hafta say I'm surprised ta see ye so soon. Mr. Mereck gave me to understand our arrangement was for the long term."

"I don't question the Master's orders," Trace said.

"Quite so, quite so." McGillicuddy eyed Trace shrewdly, though he seemed oblivious to the black tendrils of smoke coiling around his neck and limbs. "I'm not surprised he'd send *you*—he favors the ones with the Sight."

Trace managed not to flinch. He pushed his glass toward McGillicuddy, holding the Irishman's eye. "You must have a touch of it yourself, then."

McGillicuddy shook his head. "Naw, me dear ol' mother was the one with the gift. Me, I got just enough to make me lucky at cards." Trace watched in repulsed fascination as a tendril of black smoke looped around the glass in McGillicuddy's hand. "Can't say I regret it, seeing as how it made both Ma and Miss Lisette mad as hatters—"

The glass was wrenched from his grasp. It shot five feet down the bar and smashed into a bottle the bartender had left sitting. Glass and alcohol exploded in a stinging patter. The men sitting close yelped in surprise and then laughed uneasily, pointing out the mess to their friends who had missed it.

"That happen a lot?" Trace asked.

McGillicuddy looked like he'd swallowed something the wrong way. "Barman's trick!" he said, with ghastly false cheer. "Used to be able t'tip the bottle and make it pour, ha ha!"

"Think you've had enough, boss." Boz's hand landed heavy on Trace's shoulder, and Trace took the cue, feigning more wobbliness than he felt as he pushed away from the bar. "We'll take that room now, mister."

"Surely, surely!" McGillicuddy summoned the red-haired Sadie again. "Take them up to Miss Lisette's room. She don't need it, and sure she won't mind the company, eh?"

Aw, hell, Trace thought. He had to lean on Boz more than pretense required, to go up the stairs: the black smoke twined around his legs, so he couldn't see where his feet were landing. He looked up, through the darkness that swirled among the dancing and groping couples, and saw a little girl peering between the railings of the gallery. She was about five or six, with black curls and a full, pouting mouth. She was so solid Trace wouldn't have known she was dead except she had no eyes.

Trace tripped onto the landing. "Careful, there," Boz said.

Skinny little Sadie led them to the end of the gallery, where a corridor opened up and turned down the back of the building. "That's your room." She pointed at the door in the corner, then dropped her arm and scuttled back along the wall a few inches.

"It ain't gonna bite us, is it?" Boz said.

"N-no. I don't like goin by there, that's all. Miss Lisette died in there."

Better and better, Trace thought sourly. He eased off Boz's support, put a hand on the wall, and grabbed the doorknob. There was no feeling of cold, nothing pushing him away. The scrolled knob opened easily.

The room was large, and richly furnished. The curtains at the window and bedposts were wine velvet. There was a large mahogany wardrobe, a breakfast table, and a gilt mirror over the dressing table. No blood dripping down the walls, no flying furniture, not even a tormented moan.

Boz flipped a coin at Sadie and closed the door in her face.

"What in blazes did you get us into?" he asked, in a tone that would have made a prairie wife proud.

"If I had to guess," Trace said, "I'd suppose Miss Fairweather left a couple things out of her story."

"All that business with the mark, and servin the Master—that's talk I don't like at *all.*"

"Me either," Trace said, but not for quite the same reasons. He unwrapped a corner of the bandage and peered at the weeping wound. There was nothing special about it, just a raw semi-triangular patch out of his hide. McGillicuddy's scar had been curved, elaborate, but he hadn't seen enough of it to make out the pattern. "I shoulda known this wasn't an accident. Nobody's that clumsy."

"You're thinkin she branded you, and sent you here, cuz that little potato bug is expecting a messenger from *his* boss?"

"Appears to be the case, don't it?" Trace fought his way out of the sodden oilcloth coat and went to work on his boots. The mud was half-dry and sticky, getting up his sleeves and pant legs despite his best efforts. "Wonder if the hospitality extends to a bath."

"We passed a water closet, comin up." Boz prowled the room, inspecting the large gilded mirror and the cluttered dressing table. "Miss DuPres must've had some money." He opened a door of the wardrobe and ran a hand over the opulence of silk and ruffles inside. "They didn't clean out her things."

"Girls are afraid of this room. McGillicuddy, too. You saw that look he got. Sure bet she died bad, short odds he had something to do with it."

"Probably haunted," Boz said, with a sidelong glance Trace pretended not to notice.

A few years ago, during a campfire exchange of ghost stories with the drovers on the trail, Trace had told about the abandoned farmhouse he'd stayed at in Oklahoma, and how he'd heard screams in the gray dawn and woke to find a dead man standing over him, blood running down his face, shrieking and clasping his scalped head. Trace guessed he had told it with a little too much conviction, because the drovers' laughter had been uneasy, and Boz had looked at him speculatively for some time after that.

"You believe in spirits, right?" Boz had asked once.

"Sure," Trace said. "Scripture says they exist."

"But you think you seen some yourself, right?"

Trace had learned the hard way not to answer that question. "Aw, hell, Boz, everybody's had somethin happen they can't explain. Most of the time folks forget it come sunup. I don't try to explain it."

That had shut him up, for a while. Boz knew he'd been wounded at Antietam and in hospital for a long time after—although Trace had never told him the exact nature of that hospital—and he probably thought Trace had a case of soldier's melancholy. Or maybe he thought soft-headedness was the inevitable result of a Catholic education. Trace didn't care, so long as Boz didn't realize how often and intimately he saw the spirits.

"Flip you for the bed?" Boz offered.

"You can have it," Trace said.

CHAPTER THREE

He dreamt of the battlefield.

Artillery rent the air and clawed up the dirt around him, but he lay naked on the bleeding earth, skin flayed off and nerves exposed to every scream and stab and bullet. Horses pawed the air and groaned, legs broken and lungs collapsing. He soaked it all up as the ground did the blood of the fallen; as his life seeped out of him the souls of others bled into him and he was powerless to stop it. His eyes fixed on the blackened sky, found an opening in the clouds and he tried to get to it, but his dead and dying comrades dragged at him, crying they couldn't make it, they hurt too bad, they were missing limbs and heads and torsos and he had to carry them. They were pulling him down, he was skidding and sliding through loose earth into a mass grave, and he thrashed to break free.

The thrashing woke him to a strange bed—soft, perfumed—and a fire blazing on the hearth, which was fortunate because he had not a stitch of clothing on.

Hot, dry, smooth palms landed on his thighs. He jerked, tried to sit up, but he was just as immobilized as he had been on the battlefield. He could see only a silhouette against the firelight—a bright nimbus of sable curls, the slim line of a shoulder and hip. Soft laughter touched his ears. The hot, smooth fingers slid up his thighs to his groin, lingered a moment, and continued upward to the scar, above his hipbone on the right, which a bayonet had started and the surgeons had finished.

You were the lucky one, non? the voice said, husky and sensual, but with a disturbing guttural quality in the laughter.

"Wouldn't call it luck," Trace gasped. Sweet and soft and searing, skin against skin—

Mais vous avez le Vision, n'est ce pas? You speak with the lost souls. You can uncover tous les mystères de l'universe. Stroking, stroking, the hot pointed fingers found the seam of his scar and pushed deep into it. He screamed. Scarlet lips peeled back from teeth, grinning while she twisted his guts. *Quel est le problème? Voulez-vous le boît, ou non?*

Trace jolted awake, twisted in his bedroll on the floor, the old scar throbbing as it had not in years. "Jesus," he muttered, half-prayer, turning on his side to relieve the crushing sensation on his chest.

It was bright morning. Late, by the look of the light. The bed was empty, Boz's boots gone from the hearth. Trace rubbed the grit from his eyes. His mouth tasted like brine, the metallic tang of blood.

Someone was humming.

He turned his head, across the room to where the breakfast table sat beneath an eastern window. Pale sunlight slanted in, laying a golden halo on the sable curls of the little girl who sat there. She was playing tea party, with a doll and two shot glasses, humming happily to herself. She looked up at him with her empty eye sockets and then looked to the door as it opened.

"Bout time you woke up." Boz sidled into the room with a covered plate in his hand. He crossed to the now-vacant breakfast table and set down the plate and two steaming mugs. "Sounded like you were bein gutted or rutted, couldn't tell."

"Some of both," Trace grunted, getting his knees under him. His side still hurt, and his neck and shoulders felt kinked. So much for sleeping on the floor to keep the haunts away.

"I found out about our dead lady." Boz flipped back the flour-sack towel over the plate and uncovered all sorts of good things: cornbread and ham and slices of fried grits.

Trace limped to the table in his longjohns and took up one of the mugs. Coffee could save a man's life, sometimes. "What about her?"

"She owned this place, all right—had it passed down from her mama. Pair of 'em came up from N'Awleans when Miss Lisette was a girl. Miss Lisette run it by herself about three years after her mama died. Kitchen help says she was a good boss, paid fair, took care of her girls. Business was good. Then a year ago fall, this traveling carny comes through town, had one of those hocus-pocus men with it— what're they called, when they put you to sleep, but they can still make you move around and stuff?"

"Mesmerists."

"Yeah. Name o' this one was Mereck. Foreigner. German, maybe."

Un Russe, whispered a voice near Trace's ear.

"Russian," Trace said aloud, and reached for a slab of cornbread.

"Anyway, he moves in here with Miss Lisette and the pair of them start up a Spiritualist racket—tellin fortunes, callin up the dead and such. Got to doin regular performances—even the respectable people in town comin to see the show. Fore long, the town preacher comes to visit, objectin to the ghost-raisin, but Miss Lisette has Mereck throw him out. Couple weeks later, she turns up dead and he turns up gone. They say he left her and she killed herself."

Mensonges, the voice whispered again, seductive and venomous. *Lies.*

Trace shrugged, as if nagged by a mosquito. "McGillicuddy said that name. Last night. 'Mustn't keep Mr. Mereck waitin,' or somethin like that."

"I remember."

"Reckon that's the Master he was talkin about."

"What I thought, too, but the girls downstairs say they didn't have much to do with each other. McGillicuddy was the bartender here, before Miss Lisette died. She didn't leave no will, or if she did they lost it. McGillicuddy just kind of took over the place."

Trace tucked a piece of ham into his cheek and sucked the salt out of it. "Don't like it. Don't like any of it."

"Hell no. McGillicuddy finds out you ain't workin for his boss, he's liable to send those roughs of his after us. I know you don't like leavin a job unfinished, but this . . ."

"Don't like bein lied to, either," Trace said. "Even if McGillicuddy's got this box, he don't look willin to hand it over. Fellow acts like the devil's lookin over his shoulder."

Boz snorted. "White folks *is* the devil. Don't need no red sombitch with a hayfork. No offense to you or your former callin."

"None taken." Trace cradled the coffee mug against his chest, pensive.

"You reckon that's why she wanted you?" Boz said.

Trace looked at him. "How d'you mean?"

"Well she sent us here to fetch somethin don't belong to her, but she don't tell you somebody else won't wanna give it up. If she just picked any two idjits to ride down here and get a knife in their guts, I'd say she was stupid or mean—but Jameson said she came lookin for you special, so there's got to be a reason *why.* Maybe cuz you're Catholic? You reckon McGillicuddy's got any respect for a former man of the cloth?"

"I never was that." This line of questioning was cutting dangerously close to bone. Trace shook his head and stood up. "Got to take a piss."

Miss DuPres had evidently believed in investing her money in her business: the bath-room upstairs had flush toilets and piped-in water.

Trace had availed himself of the bathtub the night before, and went there now to do his morning duties.

He knew *why* Miss Fairweather had sought him out. What he couldn't figure was *how*. He'd told exactly seven people about his curse in the past eighteen years, and every one of them had died not long after. The most recent had been his father and stepmother, together with Trace's wife, Dorie, and their unborn child. Cholera had taken them, but Trace knew in his heart that their deaths were on him, because he had broken the covenant he'd made with himself, to never again tell a living soul that he could see the dead ones.

But evidently Miss Fairweather had not needed to be told. McGillicuddy had glimpsed what he was, because he had a hint of the Sight himself. So might not Miss Fairweather also . . . ?

He felt a sudden surge of hope, the old stupid conviction he'd thought was dead and buried, that finally, *finally* here was someone who knew the spirits were real and he wasn't crazy . . . but the hope flickered and drowned in the cold of rising anger. He remembered the fervent look on her face, after he'd seen the spirit in her library. Damn right, she'd known about his curse. And she'd packed him off to deal with a murdering pimp and a vengeful ghost without so much as a by-your-leave.

Trace stood before the bowl, unbuttoned his johnnies, and had just let loose a stream of water when a small voice asked, "Who are you?"

Trace flinched. Hot piss pattered the floor, and then the whole flow dried up. "Damnation," he breathed, and cautiously turned his head to see the little dead girl standing behind him. She held her doll by the hair and tilted her head curiously at him. The black pits of her eye sockets seemed to look into the back of her skull.

"Vraiment, you are not Mereck's man, n'est ce pas?" the little girl asked.

He glanced at her again, from the corner of his eye. He knew, from reading far too many Spiritualist newspapers, that spirits were supposed to feed off the medium's energy, and Trace had often suspected the same—he often felt a prickling along his neck and arms, as if there was an electrical storm in the air. This spirit was unusually forceful, summoning up a near-shameful caress of power along his skin, as if she knew exactly where to stroke. "I don't know any Mereck. You run along, now."

"I do not have to leave. It is my house."

"Who are you, then?" He rebuttoned his johnnies, trying not to

think about what he was talking to, figuring he'd go outside and finish his business behind the barn.

"Je m'appelle Lisette DuPres, *idiot*."

Trace turned full around, but she was gone.

He finished up in the bath-room, then went thoughtfully back to
his room—*her* room. Boz was sitting by the fire, rubbing grease into his
boots. Trace dressed without a word, got into his boots and vest, and
then fetched his saddlebag from the hearth and opened it on the bed.
He ran his hand down the side to retrieve the coil of leather he knew
was there, drew out a wide cowhide gunbelt and holster that sheathed
an army-model Colt.

Boz said mildly, "Got an appointment I don't know about?"

Trace wrapped the holster and belt around his hips, cinched it
snug. He didn't usually walk around heeled this close to civilization,
but folks were lying to him and this helped even the advantage. "I
ain't quite done here yet. I want to know Miss Fairweather's stake in
all this."

"Seems reasonable."

"You can come with me or not." Trace swept up his heavy oilcloth coat and settled it over his shoulders. With the coat on, the gun
wasn't obvious, but he felt comforted by its weight, more anchored
to reality.

"Where you goin?"

"Church," Trace said sourly.

CHAPTER FOUR

The church was quite small. There were twelve rows of benches in the
sanctuary. The tiny narthex at the front had barely enough room for
Trace and Boz to crowd in and close the door.

"Hello?" Trace called into the silence.

There was no immediate answer, but a moment later a door opened
behind the altar and a man stepped out, the same priest who had directed them to McGillicuddy's the night before. He was about sixty,
the perfect picture of a Christian pastor, lean and dignified, with a
strong jaw and a thick white shock of hair. Trace took off his hat.

"Well, good morning," said the priest. "Did you find your lawyer?"

"Found the man I was lookin for," Trace said. "The lawyer bit was misrepresented. I wondered if you might tell me a little more about Lisette DuPres."

"Ah yes," the priest said. "I wondered when you might come to inquire about her. Please, come join me."

They followed the man back through the narrow door behind the altar, to find a small living space. It had a stove and a table and chair. A bed was pushed against the corner, and books lined the wall across from the stove.

"Have a seat." The priest gestured at the bed. "Coffee?"

"Thanks," Trace said. "So you knew Miss Lisette?"

"I did." The priest handed each of them a hot tin cup. "Her mother raised her in the faith. They were quite devout."

"And you let them attend here?" Boz said.

The priest quirked a smile. "Our Lord ministered to prostitutes and lepers."

Trace wished his own priest had been as liberal-minded. "How old was Miss Lisette, when she died?"

"Twenty, I believe. I never knew her exact age."

"What did she look like?"

"Very pretty, especially as a child. Black curly hair, green eyes, honey-colored skin. Her mother was an octoroon, and the Negro blood was apparent in Lisette if you knew to look for it."

"What happened to her?" Trace asked.

The priest gave him an approving look, as if Trace had said something clever. "You're not asking how she died. You've heard the story, then, of her supposed suicide? Her involvement with the man who called himself Mereck? The séances? Yes. What you may not have heard is that Lisette DuPres had heard voices from the beyond all her life."

Trace dropped his coffee cup. "Sh—Sorry, Father. Hands're still cold."

"Not to worry." The priest handed him a towel. "It isn't a commonly known fact. Lisette didn't share her gift with people, until Mr. Mereck came along to exploit it."

Trace, mopping, looked up at him sharply. "You call it a gift?"

"Any natural ability is God-given; what else would it be? Of course, you're thinking of the Scriptural injunction against consulting soothsayers—"

"'The soul that turneth after familiar spirits, to go whoring after

them, I will set My face against him, and cut him off from his people.'"
Trace did not try to keep the bitterness from his voice.

"Ah, but, 'to one man is given the word of wisdom; to another the
working of miracles; to another prophecy and discerning of spirits' . . ." The priest smiled and shrugged at Trace's expression. "I prefer
the New Testament outlook on things. And I'm not one to see the
devil's hand in every unexplained happenstance. The Lord makes
mysteries, too."

Boz made a soft *hrrumph,* and the priest's eyes shifted toward
him. "Skepticism can be a gift, too, friend. I'd rather see more like
you, accepting the world as it is, instead of turning to mesmerists or
Spiritualists to lull them with platitudes and blind them with false
promises. I always thought that was the more accurate interpretation
of prostituting oneself to mediums," the priest added musingly. "In
Miss Lisette's case it was certainly accurate."

"Er, what do you know about Lisette's . . . gift?" Trace asked.

"As a child she had many invisible companions. Her mother believed she was seeing angels. I spoke to the girl several times, and while
I was never convinced her playmates were divine in origin, I found
no mischief in her. In time she realized her ability frightened people
and she stopped speaking of it. I never heard of her telling fortunes or
consulting spirits for clients, until Mereck found her." The priest
paused, frowning into his coffee cup. "It sounds like cheap melodrama
to say, but that Russian was the nearest thing to pure evil I've encountered in a man. And yet you'd be hard-pressed to put a finger on what
it was about him . . . He had a courtly manner, a sort of noblesse oblige.
And yet that very manner could seem threatening—as if the rest of us
were little more than ants he might crush at a whim.

"He moved into the saloon after only a few days in town, and they
began inviting people to Spiritualist services. For a while they were all
the rage. Several of the more prominent families in town—respectable
wives, who previously would not acknowledge Miss Lisette—suddenly
became devotees of hers."

"I guess you weren't real chirked about that," Boz put in.

"I can't say I was pleased to have that charlatan fleecing people,
but I've seen his type before—they blow in, reap the low-hanging
fruit, and then slink away in the dead of night. I can caution against
them, but certain types will always be drawn to hand-flash and empty
promises."

"Was Miss Lisette that type?" Trace asked.

"I would not have thought so, but once he began exerting his influence over her, she stopped coming to services or to confession. For several months she was only seen in Mr. Mereck's company, and near the end she never left the saloon. I began to hear rumors she was ill. A few weeks before her death, I took one of the deacons with me to the saloon, and insisted on seeing her.

"She came into the barroom with Mereck following close behind. I was shocked at her appearance—Miss Lisette had always been a vibrant girl, but now she looked as if she was dying of some wasting illness. Her hair and clothes were loose and unkempt, like a madwoman's, but she came skipping toward me like a little girl. She said I mustn't worry about her, her spiritual training was well in hand and all the mysteries of the universe were being revealed to her . . . And then she tried to embrace me, in the most lascivious manner. The deacon and Mr. Mereck intervened, but as soon as the Russian touched her she fell away, clinging to him and laughing like a wanton." The priest's mouth pinched at the memory.

Outside in the sanctuary, the front door creaked open and banged closed. Trace heard boots in the aisle, a cheery whistle, and then the rattle of the coal-hod.

"Deacon Scanlon," the priest explained.

Trace nodded. "So Mereck killed her."

"I believe he did. But not with his own hands. She was found dead in her room, throat cut, razor in hand, and a good-bye note from Mereck on her breast. The servants swore she had quarreled with Mr. Mereck and he had departed from town at least a day before. Sheriff Brocius ruled it a suicide, and I can't fault him for it. But I knew Miss Lisette for a number of years, and she was a bright, lively, pious girl. She would never have taken her own life." He looked at Trace. "You know your Scripture. What does a mark on the wrist call to mind?"

"'I saw another beast coming up out of the earth,'" Trace said, without hesitation, "'and he exerciseth all the power of the first beast before him, and he causeth all to receive a mark in their right hand or in their foreheads.'"

"Yes," said the priest. "That's what I thought of, too."

Boz had been still for some minutes, but now shifted restively on the cot. "So where's McGillicuddy fit into all this?"

"I suspect Mereck deputized him to carry out the murder, with his reward being ownership of the saloon. Mereck made sure he was well away before her death, so no suspicion could fall on him."

"Why?" Boz insisted. "What's in it for him? And what's this box everybody's so hot to have?"

"I think," the priest said, "evil men are like locusts. They can only stay and feed in one place for so long until the soil is barren to them, and they must move on or starve. But I think they leave seeds in the earth, to lay fallow until the land is again ripe for plunder."

Boz sucked his teeth. "Um-*hm*," he said, and leaned forward to set his tin cup on the table. "Thanks for the visit, Padre, but I got to tend to my horse fore we ride out of here, so I'll say good mornin."

"Hey," Trace said, but Boz walked out through the narrow door into the sanctuary. Trace went after him. "Hey! Where you goin?"

"Stables," Boz said. "Figure on doin somethin useful."

"You don't—" Trace began, but was interrupted by the man arranging hymnals on the front pew, who looked up at the two of them in affronted amazement.

"Can I help you gentlemen?" he said.

"Just talkin with the Father, here, Deacon," Trace said.

"The pastor won't be back until Thursday," the deacon said. "That room is off-limits to—"

"It's all right," Trace said, "he invited us."

"*Who* invited you?"

"The priest," Trace said patiently. "Father—what was his name?" He looked at Boz, but Boz was staring past him with a slack-jawed expression. Trace turned around.

The room was empty. The bed slats were naked, the table clear, the stove cold. There was a damp place on the floor beside the bed, where Trace's feet had rested.

Trace blinked. And then an odd feeling of exultation swelled his chest, as if he'd just been absolved of all kinds of things. He glanced at Boz, whose eyes were showing the whites all around, like a spooked horse. "Older feller. Snow on top. Long and tall. Dignified-lookin."

"That's Father Barrett," the deacon said, looking likely to faint. "He died three months ago."

"YOU ALL RIGHT?" Trace asked after a while, stirring the chaff on the barn floor with his boot heel.

Boz lifted his head from between his knees. His face was darker than usual, from the blood running to his head, but it was an improvement over the ashy color he had been upon leaving the church. "Just tell me one thing," he said. "Did you *know* that old fella was . . . was—"

"Dead?"

"—*not real*—when we went in there?"

"He was real. He was just dead. And no, sometimes I don't know right off."

"So they just do that? Pop up and talk to you when they feel like it?"

"On occasion. More often they don't know where they are or who they're talkin to. They're just echoin what they did when they were alive. The ones around here seem to have more of an agenda."

Boz stood up, jerkily, paced a few steps away. His eyes were troubled and far-seeing, and Trace guessed he was revisiting the craggy badlands of their relationship, certain questionable events of the past five years had been cached and marked but never discussed. "So all this time . . . those stories you told about the fella who saw ghosts in the hospital . . ."

"Yeah," Trace said unhappily.

"And that time out at Hell Creek—"

"Uh-huh."

"And that business about bein wounded at Antietam . . . ?"

"That was true, Boz. It was all true. It just wasn't the whole of it." Trace felt the cold around his nostrils, the sick-fearful relief of telling this story again, after eight long years of silence. "Lyin there in that ditch was the first time I saw 'em . . . I guess it's common for folks close to death to see those who've crossed over. But then when I woke up in hospital, they were still around me." He'd thought he was in Hell, at first. Then he'd thought he was crazy. Then he'd sunk down into morphine purgatory and stayed there for a couple of years.

Boz ran a hand down his mouth. "Does *she* know? That Englishwoman?"

"I think she does. I think that's why she came lookin for me."

"*How?*"

"Damned if I know."

"And you think she knew about this dead lady, and that little potato bug, and his Master?"

"Boz, I told you what she told me—"

"Yeah," Boz relented. "You did. So what d'you reckon is her business with these folks?"

That was the least of Trace's concerns at the moment, and he shrugged irritably. "I don't know. She could be tellin the truth about Miss Lisette leavin the box to her. Prob'ly McGillicuddy stole it along with the rest of her property."

"Maybe you should ask her."

"Miss Fairweather?"

"Miss Lisette. You said you saw her, right?"

"No," Trace said, repulsed. "I mean yeah, I saw her, but I ain't gonna call up some crazy woman's ghost."

"Why not? Sounds to me like she got somethin to say."

Trace almost choked on the lunacy of that proposal, and its source. "Ain't you soundin like a true believer!"

"Look, I ain't sayin I believe none of this—but hell, Trace, I rode across this country with you ten times. I seen some weird shit in the time we been together, and now you tell me this . . ." He gave a shaky laugh. "This actually makes some things make *more* sense. And I know you ain't any more crazy than I am, so if this is real, if you think it's real . . . then it seems to me, the sensible thing is, you go ask Miss Lisette what happened."

"I can't do that."

"Why not? We just sat in there and talked to some dead holy man—"

"I can't help it if they come to me, but I ain't gonna start callin up spirits and demons."

"Who said anything about demons? Just one poor dead crazy lady."

"Because people tend to die bad when I let it out," Trace shot back. "It's in the Bible, a curse against anyone who calls up the dead."

"Well *that* dead holy man came to you, and *he* called it a gift."

"Evil spirits can speak prophecy, too," Trace said, but the words felt phony, even as they passed his lips. The shade of a dead priest had visited him in a church and told him not to be afraid. Messages from God didn't come much clearer than that unless you were Moses.

"Christ on a crutch!" Boz hollered. "Don't it say in your Bible all niggers is cursed? Ain't you heard the one about Ham's sons bowin down to white folks cuz Ham's old man got drunk and left his pecker layin out? Now you tell me you believe that one, I'll head back to St. Louis and find myself a new trail partner."

"You know I don't."

"Damn right. You got the sense God gave you and that's worth a helluva lot more than some dead folks' words in a book. So quit feelin sorry for yourself and use that gift to find out what the hell we're doing here."

Trace looked at him for a long moment, trying to weigh the situation rationally, instead of see-sawing between the fear and that guilty throb of excitement in his brain and guts. Talking to the spirits had always given him an uneasy thrill, like some imp sitting on his shoulder whispering *Go ahead, live a little—no one will know.*

But Boz's argument made sense. He had never deliberately *tried* to summon a spirit and talk to it. All his years of keeping a lid on this thing didn't seem to have saved anyone; maybe it was time to try a different approach. Miss Fairweather and that dead preacher and Boz himself were pushing him to *act*—and was that allowing himself to be influenced by others, or God sending him so many signs he was a fool to keep ignoring them?

He drew a deep breath. "All right. But you got to come with me."

"What d'you expect *me* to do?"

"You can hold the damn guns, in case McGillicuddy comes around."

CHAPTER FIVE

Miss Lisette's room was just as they had left it, not even the little girl sitting at the breakfast table as Trace cracked open the door and waved Boz inside. But he thought there was an unnatural stillness about the place, as if something was listening. He hung his hat on the bedpost and slid out of his coat, ran a hand through his hair. His heart felt fluttery and sick. "You still got that bottle in your bag?"

Boz fetched his saddlebag from the hearth. "Nerves touchy?"

"Damn right they are." Trace took the whiskey bottle, pulled the cork. Two long draws and he was gasping.

"You sure you wanna do that?"

"This was your idea." The liquor hit his stomach like hot tar and spread. "Keep by the door. Make sure nobody comes in. And take this." He pulled the Colt from his hip and passed it over. "In case I'm not in my right mind."

Boz looked alarmed. "What d'you think's gonna happen?"

"I don't know," Trace admitted. "I don't know what the hell I'm doin." He eyed the breakfast table, with the two empty coffee mugs, and got an idea. He rearranged the dishes, placing a mug before each chair, and poured a small measure of whiskey into the other one. "No, stay there," he said, when Boz started forward. "Don't interfere, and don't come close or try to talk to us."

"Us? Is—somebody there?"

"If you'd quit yappin for a minute—"

"Sorry." Boz fell quiet. Trace continued to drink, faster than was good for his stomach. The sun was golden on the empty chair opposite him. Trace cast his eye around the room, got up and went to the dressing table, brought back the silver hand mirror and a small round velvet box that proved to be full of jewelry. Aware of Boz's anxious gaze, he pulled out a tangle of chains, rings, eardrops. Most of it was brass or silver, but here was a pair of garnet earrings that looked like real gold, and a signet ring, sized for a man—

"Those are mine."

Trace looked up, shoulders tensing despite the whiskey. The little girl sat across from him, empty black eye sockets accusing.

"These are yours?" Trace held up the earrings.

She nodded.

"What about this?" He lifted the signet ring.

"Maman say it belong to my papa. He was the soldier."

"So was I," Trace said. "Bayonet almost took my leg off."

She wrinkled her nose and looked at his wrist. "How do you hurt yourself?"

"Burned myself. Had an accident. Do you have a burn there, too?"

She made a queer hopping motion that made him think she had sat on her hands. "Not now. I take it off."

"Did Mr. Mereck put it there?"

"I take it off. Mereck, he leave. I tell him to go." The face and diction were childish, but the mannerisms, the voice, were disturbingly adult. Her brow was furrowing, and Trace began to feel violence prickling around the edges of his alcohol-diluted senses.

"Was he angry?"

"He want me to keep his box. I tell him no. I tell him to go. *Murderer! Liar!*" Her face contorted with the force of her shriek, and Trace could see the blackness inside her, all the way down the back of her throat. The childish shape was merely a shell, a vessel for that dark rage.

"Where's the box now?" He knew he was playing with fire, he

sensed the danger in provoking this thing, but oddly enough he wasn't fearful of it. On the contrary he felt strong, bold, the way a greenhorn might feel after a few drinks. But this wasn't bottle courage—he was clear-headed and sharp. His mind flashed back to Seminary, when he and the other students had been forced to kneel before the altar cross for hours, and a sort of swooning release had come over him, as if he was simultaneously leaving his body and being filled with holy fire—

A crafty look crossed the child's face. "Tu comprendes," she said, baring her teeth in a grin. "You know how it feels . . . so good . . . so sweet . . ." She ran her hands over her arms and throat, gurgling with pleasure. "I can teach you . . . show you. M'sieu say you need a spirit guide—I can show you tous les mystères . . ."

"Of the universe, yeah, I heard. I'm only interested in the one mystery, thanks."

"La boîte damnable! *Idiot!* You want to be the dog, the slave for this witch?"

"I'm nobody's slave and neither are you. Mereck lied to you, didn't he? Did that Irishman help him?"

She clawed at her throat, mouth agape, wailing. *"Murderer . . ."*

Despite himself, Trace's heart filled with pity. Evil men left their seeds in the soil, and watered them with the blood of innocents. Although perhaps the flesh of the less-than-innocent yielded a better crop, ripe as it was for corruption. "The Irishman's got the box, don't he? Where'd he put it?"

There was a sudden rattle at the door. Trace's attention jerked toward it, Boz flung out an arm to hold it closed, and a heavy charge of menace swelled the air. All the hairs on Trace's arms stood up.

"Mr. Tracy!" called an Irish brogue from the hallway, and the breakfast table trembled under Trace's hands. Lisette raked her nails down her face, grinning and drooling black rage down her chin.

"I show you," she cooed. "Show you the power—"

There was a heavy thud on the outside of the door. Boz set his shoulder against it, but a violent shove threw him into the center of the room. The door swung wide and struck the wall.

The apparition flew apart in a murder of black smoke. Trace stood but staggered; either he was drunker than he'd thought or talking to that spirit had taken the juice out of him.

"Well then." McGillicuddy's brogue rolled across the threshold, but the man did not. He stood in the hall and rocked on his heels while four of his boys pushed into the room. Boz moved quick—Trace saw him tuck the Colt into the back of his trousers before he lifted both hands in surrender. One of the rivermen sidled up to Boz and pulled both his pistols from their holsters.

"Well then," McGillicuddy said again, as another of the boys leveled a shotgun on Trace's midsection. "Seems we had a wee misunderstanding last night, eh?"

"Did we?" Trace dropped back into his seat. One of the rivermen came close and lifted Trace's right arm from the table, stripped the bandage off. They all looked at the burn on Trace's wrist, but McGillicuddy came no closer. He began rolling up his own sleeve.

"Aye, seems we did. Else why would yer man here be askin questions in my kitchen this morning, eh? About me an Mr. Mereck?"

The table vibrated under Trace's hands. He glanced down at it, saw threads of black swirling around the dishes and streaking the sunlight on the other chair.

"Mr. Mereck *knows* I'm a loyal servant—ha'n't I kept his treasure safe all these months? Didn't I pledge with my own flesh?" McGillicuddy shook his fist, and Trace saw for the first time what the brand was supposed to look like—a circle with curved lines cutting through it. "He told me he'd send for it one day, but that day ha'n't come, and you aren't the one, boyo. So what I want to know, lad, is who sent yez?"

The blackness was spilling across the carpet, over and around the men's boots, gathering near the doorway and piling into a seething malignant thunderhead. It shadowed McGillicuddy's face, but he didn't seem to notice.

"Took five of you to come ask me that?" Trace said.

McGillicuddy bared his teeth. "I take no shame in assumin' the advantage. Particularly against a man of yer stature."

The table gave a violent heave, tossing dishes and jewelry into the air. The man with the shotgun startled back and Trace grabbed for the whiskey bottle before it could spill.

They froze, round-eyed, staring at him. "No sense in wasting it," Trace said, and took a strong pull. "Go ahead, honey, now you can have it."

The breakfast table tipped up and flung itself at the man with the shotgun. The blast went up and over Trace's head, peppered the man standing behind him. Trace dropped out of the chair to his knees, heard gunshots and saw the man near the door double over, clutching his stomach with bloody fingers. Colt in hand, Boz grabbed

McGillicuddy and yanked him into the room, using his body for cover. The Irishman tripped on the rug and fell to all fours.

"Get *down*!" Trace yelled, and Boz crouched to his heels as the logs in the fireplace exploded. Sparks and cinders flew over their heads and pummeled the other rivermen. One of them was driven into the wall, the other took a clip on the shoulder and fell against the dressing table. Swearing, he straightened up and leveled his gun on Boz.

Trace clouted him across the head with the whiskey bottle, and down he went.

"What in the *hell*—" Boz said into the following silence. He still had his hand on McGillicuddy's collar, and the little Irishman was panting, wheezing, clawing at his throat and the buttons on his shirt.

"Stop that." Trace crossed the floor and bent over him. "Quit your blubberin and tell me where that box—"

"AAARRRGGGHH!" McGillicuddy screamed, his face going purple. He reared backwards, on his knees, and Trace saw the black smoke surge up his chest and pour into his open mouth. He batted with his hands but the blackness swirled around them, undeterred.

The front of his shirt bloomed bright red. He clutched at his guts, which were heaving and roiling beneath his shirt like the belly of a horse about to foal. McGillicuddy screamed again, and Boz backed sharply away, hand held out as if to ward away the sight before his eyes.

Buttons popped off like bullets. The fabric parted across McGillicuddy's straining gut, revealing a small hard shape like a fist, pressing the skin from the inside, and the ropy edges of a long scar splitting like leather before the strain.

Something ripped out of the Irishman's belly and shot across the room, striking the wall before it dropped to the floor and rolled a few inches back across the rug. McGillicuddy made a repulsive gurgling sound and flopped forward onto his face. A gush of blood poured from the wound, and wisps of black smoke rose up from it, eddied away across the floor.

"Faithful," he croaked. "Master . . ."

A red bubble swelled between his lips and burst. He sagged limp into the carpet.

Trace looked at Boz, saw the whites of his eyes all around; his own vision was starry and wet. He looked around the room, at three dead men and another wounded, and a small black object on the floor near the hearth.

"Is that it?" Boz said harshly.

Trace stumbled across the carpet, stooped to grasp it. The coating of blood and grease squished under his fingers and he had a brief, maddening idea that it was the Irishman's heart.

But no. It was a wooden box, egg-shaped and stained dark.

Voila, Lisette murmured in his ear. *I am the good servant, non?*

"Let's get out of here," Trace said.

CHAPTER SIX

It was about the size of Trace's fist, carved in a rough pattern of crescents and triangles. The opening seam was coated thickly with some white waxy substance, but underneath they could see what looked like ordinary brass hinges, and a latch.

Trace didn't like handling it. It felt warm, even after he had washed it under the pump in the chill March air. He held it in a piece of flour sacking cradled between his knees, sitting on a hay bale opposite Boz.

"You got to be some kind of sick pup to let somebody sew somethin up in your guts," Boz said.

"Miss Lisette wasn't that crazy," Trace said. "She refused to keep it for him. Told him to get out. So he killed her, found somebody else. Somebody dumber and greedier."

"That was *her,* who tried to knock you down when you first set foot in the door, wasn't it? And she broke the bottle at the bar."

"Yeah."

"So why didn't she kill him sooner?" Boz's eyes widened. "Did *you* tell her to—?"

"No! She was showin off. She thought I was gonna be her new master. She didn't give a damn about the box, she got it for me like a . . . love-token." He didn't like the way Boz was looking at him. "*That's* why I don't talk to them, Boz. Talkin to them makes them stronger, makes them come around more. Then they get mad if I don't pay attention. They start bargaining. Beggin for things, offering me things. Like imps of Hell. Christ, I'm never sure if some of them *aren't* demons. And I don't care what that preacher said—certain mysteries aren't meant to be known by men." Trace folded the sacking over the box, wrapped it around, and stood to stash it in his saddle pack.

A knot of worry appeared between Boz's brows. "Then what you reckon Miz Fairweather . . . ?"

"Don't know." Trace pulled the flap down, knotted the ties. "Don't care. Don't plan to ask."

"You just gonna hand it over?"

"Why wouldn't I?"

Boz stared at Trace as if he were a stranger, and a crazy one at that. "These folks are *killin* each other over that thing. You don't know nothin about Miz Fairweather except she's a liar and prob'ly as bad as the rest of 'em—"

"And that's why we're gonna hand it over and not say a word about where it was or how we got it." Trace slung his bedroll across the saddle skirt and turned to face his friend, keeping a hand on the horse's flank. "If we don't, how long you think we got before one of them comes lookin for it?"

"YE GODS, YOU found it," Miss Fairweather said, almost before she had entered the library. "Show me. Is that it?"

Trace rolled the wooden egg out of the sacking and put it into her hands. She seemed to flinch at the touch of it, her mouth tightening with the same repellence he had felt, but she looked it over carefully, inspected the wax seal with her fingertips. "You didn't try to open it."

"Not my business what's in it," Trace said. "Just my job to fetch it back."

"My goodness. A paragon." Her brows lifted slightly, as if he were something rare and intriguing. "May I ask how you were able to locate this?"

"Just lucky, I guess." He could not quite keep the hostility out of his voice, and he guessed she heard it, because her cool blue gaze flicked up to his, lips curling cynically.

"You will forgive me if I doubt that claim, Mr. Tracy." She tossed the box on the map table with such alarming disregard that Trace had to stop himself from diving after it. "I spent months trying to be certain you possessed the necessary talents, before I ever learnt your name or how to find you. I am quite certain *your* methods were no less deliberate."

Trace stared at her for a moment while her words sank in. He had not expected her to lay down her hand like that. She eyed him right back, with interest and a certain covetousness, as if he were a prize thoroughbred.

"How did you *know*?" he demanded.

"The spirits, of course. I've been watching them cluster about you for months." She cocked her head. "You're afraid of them, are you not? I suppose you take the Christian view that all spirits are evil. I expect you believe your power comes from the devil."

Her matter-of-fact dismissal of his entire creed was as shocking as a slap.

"Everyone I told is *dead* because of it," Trace said sharply.

"Due to your negligence?"

"Negligence?"

"Did you perhaps summon some malevolent spirit beyond your control?"

"I *don't* summon them. They come to me. I tell them to go away."

"And do they obey?" Her slight smile implied she knew the answer.

And Trace knew, completely and without doubt, that she had *all* the answers. Her eyes fairly gleamed with eagerness to educate him, just as Eve had Adam, and all he had to do was take that first bite.

He was more tempted than he would have believed. In the early years he'd sought out Spiritualists and faith healers and even a Voudou queen down in New Orleans, but all of them had been frauds or fools. This woman was neither.

But he didn't like being driven like a mule. And clearly Miss Fairweather was messing with some very dark forces. Whatever her purpose in seeking him out, he doubted it was wholesome.

"If you can see them," he said at last, "why didn't you go yourself?"

"I cannot see them. Not as you do, at any rate—my gifts are of a different persuasion. Besides, I could hardly visit an establishment of that ilk, now could I?"

If she had been a man, he might well have taken a swing at that damned smug smirk. "So this whole job—had you any claim to that box at all? Or was this just a ruse to flush me out?"

"I have as much claim as the man who held it, as you must realize. And I needed to be sure of your qualifications."

"Qualifications." He laughed, harshly. "And just what else were you plannin to have me do for you, lady?"

For the first time her expression sobered. And even as she opened her mouth again, Trace knew there'd be no truth coming out of it. "As I mentioned, my health prevents me from traveling. I have a rare condition—not contagious, but debilitating. Most days I cannot safely leave this house."

He looked her up and down. Pale and thin she might be, but she was no wilting flower. "Consumption?" he said dubiously.

She made an ironic sound behind her nose. "Nothing so plebian."

"Somethin darker," Trace guessed. "Havin to do with the spirits. Somethin you summoned, beyond your control."

She didn't like that. Her nostrils flared in annoyance. "In any case, I need someone of your talents to aid me in my search for a cure." She turned a step away, indicating dismissal with a wave of her hand. "Your payment is on the table beside the door."

Trace figured that was the right direction for him to be heading. There was a paper envelope on the small reception table. He picked it up, thumbed through the bills inside, and tucked it into his vest pocket. And he looked back at her.

She was watching him. Dainty and refined at first glance, but with something . . . *hungry* in her expression and in the clenching of her hands at her waist. Immediately she relaxed her posture and resumed her cool poise.

"I guess you know about this Mereck fella the Irishman was so afraid of," Trace said.

"Do you?" she countered.

"No," Trace said. "Can't say I'd welcome the acquaintance."

"No, I don't expect you would. The Russian Mesmerist, as he bills himself of late, makes a practice of trapping useful spirits in small vessels, and caching them with his dogsbodies until he has need of them again." She waved a hand over the box, resting in the open pages of a large atlas. "Would you like to see who or what is in this one?"

"Thanks, no," Trace said. "What're *you* gonna do if he comes lookin for it?"

"Please don't concern yourself about *me,* Mr. Tracy." The corners of her mouth curled in a frosty smile. "I shall send word via Mr. Jameson when I have need of you again."

Trace let out an explosive gust of humor. "Ma'am," he touched his hat sardonically, "it'll be a cold day in hell."

He let himself out of her house. The sun was out, melting the last patches of snow in the low places. Tufts of green stood up and waved from the mud.

Trace patted the envelope in his breast pocket and went to find Boz.

MARCH 1880

PRINTER'S DEVIL

CHAPTER SEVEN

Temptation, like guilt and grief, was an emotion that never really went away. He could tamp it down and cover it over and try not to think about it, but like a campfire buried too shallowly, it could flare up and singe a man's boots if he wasn't careful.

So naturally, Trace spent several days after Sikeston in a smoldering snit.

It was bad enough Miss Fairweather had tricked him into revealing himself. But far worse that she had fanned the flames of that old hope—the childish, arrogant hope that God had laid this curse on him for a good reason.

In the early years he'd supposed it was divine retribution, for defying his father and leaving seminary to enlist. Aloysius Tracy had been a staunch abolitionist, and while the nineteen-year-old Jacob had had no love for slavery, he'd subscribed to the more moderate view that the institution would die out on its own. He'd felt much more strongly on the issues of State's Rights and Throwing Off the Yoke of Oppression.

It had taken him a few years to realize whose heavy hand he'd been looking to throw off.

By the time he left the hospital he'd acquired a certain stoicism toward the curse. Plenty of men had lost their limbs or nerves or minds on the battlefield. He was better off than most. Plus he was on his own in the world for the first time, working ranches with the type of rough men he had never been allowed to associate with in his youth, men who drank and swore and fornicated and got along just fine without God, thank you very much. It was impossible not to notice that good and bad fortune were distributed among the ungodly in the same portions as the righteous, but on a cattle ranch folks didn't spend as much time wringing their hands and wondering why.

He read the Bible cover to cover in those years, then moved on to St. Augustine and Thomas Aquinas and even delved into some real heterodoxy—Martin Luther and Maimonides and Aristotle. Gradually he'd admitted to himself that he'd never wanted to be a priest. He'd even come close to declaring himself apostate, but only in his own mind. He wasn't given to dramatic gestures, and anyway he and his father were still estranged at that point so the rejection of his faith only gave him an uneasy feeling of anticlimax. But then he'd met Dorothea, and he'd begun to believe, again, that God still loved him and had a plan for him.

Which just showed he had not been as old or wise as he'd supposed.

He couldn't afford to start thinking that way again. Eighteen years now, he'd been carrying this curse around, and all it did was accumulate more carnage, every time he indulged it. Trace could not stop seeing McGillicuddy's fat florid face, blood bubbling between his lips, knowing it could have been Boz.

He *hated* not knowing what triggered the destruction surrounding his curse. He hated lying awake at night and puzzling over that dead priest's words—*to some men are given the gift of discerning spirits*—First Corinthians, chapter twelve, where Paul was describing the different spiritual gifts that were allotted to the faithful. What did that mean, to *discern spirits*? Did it mean merely being able to see them, or did it mean telling the good ones from the bad? Because he'd never seemed to have much success with that . . . But that train of thought led him inexorably to Miss Fairweather's smirking observation: *I suppose you take the Christian view that ALL spirits are evil?*

What was the distinction? What did she know that he didn't? What was God trying to do to him, bringing all these disturbing events and questions into his life just now, when he had enough trouble trying to keep himself and Boz in room and board?

"What're you stewin about over there?" Boz said, pacing along on his own horse at the other side of the road.

Trace pulled his mind out of its grim spiral and into a beautiful spring morning—birds singing, air rich with moisture and freshly turned earth. Damp green-and-black fields lay out on either side of the road.

They were riding south to Judd Herschel's farmstead in Carondelet. This was the fifth day of their contract to cut and cord the timber from Herschel's woodlot. It was make-work, but at least it was something.

"Nothin," Trace said. "Work. Did Jameson say if he'd heard back from the Baptist?"

"You ast me that already, and no he didn't. You sent him a note, right?"

"I wrote to him." Kingsley was the Baptist's name: leader of a group of missionaries who had the idea to move to Butte, Montana, and straighten out all the godless folk in the wilderness, because apparently there weren't enough around here to merit the effort. Montana was about the last of the Promised Lands not yet accessible by rail, though those who could afford it rode out to St. Joseph or Ogden, and outfitted there. The Baptists must be very poor or very devout to be undertaking the whole trip by wagon, and Jameson estimated it was both; Kingsley had been keen to hear that Jacob Tracy, trail guide, was a former seminarian.

"He told Jameson he'd get back to me this week." Trace hated when people dangled a lure for work and then never followed through on it.

"Well, we're gonna be another week clearin this lot, in any case," Boz said. "And we still got that money from what's-her-name. That's enough to pull up for the season and head out to Wyoming. You oughtta wire that horse-breeder you keep talkin about—"

"Miller."

"Yeah. See if he'll have you back."

Trace grunted. "I'm too old to be playin cowboy."

"Speak for yourself, young'un." Boz had a good five years on Trace. "Sides, you start askin around, you'd get on as foreman somewhere, easy."

That was probably true, and Trace knew it. But he found himself dragging his feet, just the same. He'd been working for Miller nine years ago when he'd met Dorothea, and he didn't relish the idea of going back to Wyoming and seeing how much things had changed . . . or not.

The limestone wall along the road gave way to split-rail fence at the edge of Judd Herschel's property. It was a prosperous-looking spread: two-story clapboard house, a wide wrap-around porch, and a fashionable turret at one corner. Herschel owned and rented out several properties in this part of town; he had been instrumental in getting Carondelet annexed to St. Louis and was now well poised to take advantage of the new city services. He'd already sold off one parcel of land to be used for the new Jewish cemetery.

For the past five days, Trace and Boz had arrived to find Herschel already at work in the barn, usually with one of his daughters, Anna or Leah, helping with the milking or feeding the chickens. But this morning they could hear the cow lowing to be milked, and the chickens were still shut up in their coop.

With a worried exchange of glances, the men hastened their horses' pace, rounding the side of the house to the yard. It was hard to say what caught the eye first—the kitchen door standing open, or the trampled and roughed-up look of the yard, which Mrs. Herschel always kept so neat and swept. There were dark splotches on the stone steps leading into the house.

Boz didn't say a word, just dismounted and marched over to the door. Trace followed, pausing to loop the horses' reins around the post. They were already huffing and laying their ears back, disturbed by the smell of death. Trace could feel it, too, an afterimage of violence permeating the air like swamp gas, and though he steeled himself before he stepped up on the back stoop, a vicious miasma rolled out of the house and grabbed him by the throat, almost knocking him down.

He choked, gagging, grabbing the doorframe for balance, and saw Boz stop a few paces into the kitchen and turn back. He'd been alert to Trace's every twitch since Sikeston, and now he looked spooked. "What is it? You all right?"

Trace nodded, breathing deeper as the stench loosened its grip on him. It was acrid and vile, like burning hair, but the aftertaste it left on his tongue was metallic.

"Is there somethin *in* here?" Boz demanded.

"No. I think there was, but it's gone." Trace edged past his partner in the narrow kitchen, walking lightly, feeling the house listening back at him. The stove was cold. A greasy pan containing a few popcorn hulls sat on top. A jar lay near the doorway into the living room, spilling paprika across the threshold and onto the rug. Small footprints tracked through the red powder.

The living room looked like an abattoir. Boz swore softly as they stood in the doorway, eyeing the soaked and sticky rug, the slings and drips on the walls and ceiling. A fireplace poker, matted with blood and hair, lay beside the door to the yard, and it was clear by the marks on the floor that a body had been dragged that way.

They followed the marks out the back, to Mrs. Herschel's garden. The well was back there, and as they got closer Trace could see the cover was off and there were bloody streaks smeared over the old bricks. A long-handled ax lay dropped across the path like a warning sign.

"Oh Jesus," Trace said, quickening his step despite the fact that he had absolutely no desire to look down that hole. He said it again when he realized that the small turd-looking things scattered around the base of the well were a man's amputated fingers.

Boz looked first and then turned away with a low, almost ironic sound, the back of his hand rubbing hard across his mouth.

The womens' skirts had ballooned up in the bloody water, making it look as if Herschel himself lay on a feather bed dyed turkey-red. He might've been resting comfortably except for the gash that had bashed in his nose and cheek, obliterating one eye and leaving the other to gaze sightlessly up at the sky.

"AND WHY DID you call on the Herschels this morning?" the detective asked, for what Trace guessed to be the fifth time.

"We were comin to cut timber," Trace said yet again, rubbing a hand over his face. The shock had long since worn off and he just felt tired and queasy. "Herschel hired us to clear that woodlot."

It was almost noon. The clear morning had given way to a sullen, overcast day that seemed occasionally to spit from the clouds upon the scene below. A score or more of people roamed the yard—policemen, neighbors, sightseers. Trace had no idea how word had spread so far, so fast. The police had arrived before he and Boz could decide if one of them should stay while the other went for help.

Apparently they had not been the first to discover the bodies. Anna Herschel, the younger daughter, had somehow escaped the slaughter, and stumbled a mile down the road to the Lombards' door, where she'd been found, bloody and hysterical, at sunup. Lombard and his son had come to the farm and seen the carnage more than an hour before Trace and Boz were due to arrive.

Nevertheless, it had looked bad that they were mounting up when the police arrived. They were detained and questioned several times over, but what was worse, in a way, was having to watch Mrs. Herschel's yard and pretty house get trampled by bored, drunken patrolmen and smug sightseers in fine hats and morning suits, who began to arrive in buggies not long after the police.

The detective in charge, whose name was Whistler, at least appeared to have a brain in his head. He was unassuming in appearance—medium-sized and balding, with sparse mutton-chops the same bleached color as his skin—but he had a dead-eye gaze that missed nothing. Trace had twice seen the detective snap his fingers at a patrolman and get him to run off some tourist who was trying to pocket a souvenir from the house or yard.

"Had you any other dealings with Herschel?" Whistler said to Trace, as they stood in the living room, and the detective's broad, blunt fingers glided over a half-played game of checkers, not quite touching anything, almost as if he were divining messages from the game board. "Did you rent property from him?"

"No and no," Trace said. "Me and my partner rent a room up on Bell Street."

"And how many days have you worked for Herschel?"

"The last five, excepting Saturday and Sunday."

"Anybody else who can vouch for that? Any other folks around here you've worked for? How'd you get this job?"

So Trace explained, yet again, how John Jameson allowed folks who frequented his store to post bills for labor, and how they occasionally bartered work with him in exchange for keeping their horses at his livery, and on and on. The only thing Trace couldn't describe was how they'd gotten the job with Herschel, because Boz had arranged that on his own.

"Detective?" one of the patrolmen called to Whistler, and the latter excused himself, but not before telling Trace to stick around.

Trace was not likely to go anywhere for a while, since Boz had been press-ganged into helping with the winch over the well. He went out into the yard again, noticing as he went that two more wagons had joined the circus: glossy black hearses with tasteful gold letters that read ROTH FUNERAL HOME. He had the morbid thought that Judd Herschel was going to be one of the first inhabitants of that new cemetery he'd sold to the city.

He rounded the corner of the house in time to see Mrs. Herschel hauled up out of the well, dripping wet and dangling from the hook that had caught under her arm and neck. Her head was thrown back, her stringing hair partially covering the gaping wound at her throat. There was so little blood left in her that the flesh was white as a trout's, though her hair and skirts were stained from the saturated water.

"Get her down!" one of the men snapped, and two of them reached to catch the body and the line from which it hung. Together they wrestled the sodden corpse over the lip of the well and lowered her to the ground. The small crowd of spectators shuffled and clucked amongst themselves.

Trace looked away. His gaze lit on Herschel's corpse, now laid out on a stretcher and covered with a sheet. The sight of those black boots protruding from beneath the shroud called to mind other visions, equally awful: rows of uniformed boys waiting for burial; his own father's boots, extending across the threshold of the house, where the cholera had dropped him.

Trace gave himself a shake. He dropped to one knee in the grass, crossed himself, and peeled the sheet back.

The wound to Herschel's face was clean from the water, and though Trace saw more than he wanted to of the bones in the man's head, it didn't look deep enough to have killed him. Knocked him senseless, maybe, and then he'd drowned. The angle of the wound was odd—near-horizontal, suggesting the ax had been swung at waist-level. Which meant Herschel had been kneeling, or maybe clinging to the edge of the well, trying to claw his way out . . . which would explain why his fingers were chopped off.

Trace glanced over his shoulder. Nobody was paying him the slightest attention, so he reached out and pressed on the chest of the corpse. Water surged out of the mouth and the nose wounds, along with a swarm of black, tadpole-looking animalcules.

"Shit!" Trace startled back, then leaned closer. They weren't tadpoles. They evaporated as he watched. He wiped one of the oily-looking black things from Herschel's cheek.

A ghastly sensation washed over him, the instant paralysis of nightmare. For a second his vision was gray, cloudy, and then he was looking out through an unfamiliar pair of eyes, feeling strange hands grasping a cudgel, beating something red and mewling—voices of women screaming and strange, maniacal laughter heaving his own chest—then the tables were turned and someone was beating *him*, the laughter had left him and he was only terrified—bloody hands scrabbled for purchase on slick stone, and the ax swung at his face—

A hand landed on his shoulder. Trace fell backwards on his butt in the grass, his throat raw, and realized he had been screaming. Boz was gripping him by both shoulders and people were staring.

"You're all right," Boz was saying, his voice tight with anxiety. "You're all right, Trace, it ain't real—"

"I'm all right." Trace repeated hoarsely. His heart was hammering, but the vision was as fragile as a dream and receding quickly. "It's over, it's done."

"Cripes, you scared me," Boz muttered, and hauled him to his feet. Trace clung to Boz's arm a moment longer, head bowed as if he were overcome with grief. Better to be thought unmanly than crazed.

"What'd you see there, friend?" said a nasal voice from a few feet away. "Was it the killer?" A dapper redheaded dude in a plaid suit stood just out of reach, pencil and notepad in hand, peering at Trace with a keen and knowing air.

"What's it to you?" Boz said.

The dude glanced at Boz and touched his hat with the stub of pencil. "Rex Reynolds, *St. Louis Times*. I heard the new chief of detectives had a medium on his payroll—are you it?"

"No," Trace said, brushing off his pants.

"You're Jacob Tracy, right? This your partner?" Reynolds jerked his chin at Boz. "You friends with the whole family or just the old man?"

"We just worked for them," Trace said, yet again. "We came up here to cut timber."

"I gotcha, I understand. How well did you know Miss Anna? You hear of any trouble between her and her folks, might prompt her to take after 'em with an ax?"

"Are you kiddin me?" Trace said, and rounded on Detective Whistler, who was striding toward them. "You ain't sayin Miss Anna did this?"

"That's none of your concern," said Whistler, and turned his dead-eye gaze on Reynolds. "I told you I didn't want you at my crime scenes anymore."

"Didn't know it was your crime scene, did I?" Reynolds said. "But since I'm here, Detective, can you confirm you're holding Miss Anna Herschel at Four Courts? And you don't have any other suspects at this time?"

"Get off this property before I have you removed," Whistler said. He cast a ruminating eye over Trace and Boz. "You two can go, too. Stay in town where I can find you."

Reynolds sucked his teeth as Whistler walked away. "Always makes you feel welcome." He turned back to Trace. "So how long you been communing with the Spirits?"

"I ain't no Spiritualist!"

"Hey, fella, neither am I, but I've attended a séance or two, and I don't mind saying I saw some things I won't forget my whole life long. And just now I saw you lay hands on that corpse before you started hollering." Trace stared at him, caught, and Reynolds half-shrugged, as if to say he couldn't help being right all the time. "You oughtta let me do a story on you. Whistler might give your opinion more weight if he thought you had some, er, *insight* on the matter."

"Why'n hell would he do that?"

"You'd be surprised who-all believes in Spiritualism," Reynolds said dryly.

"They really got Miss Anna locked up?" Boz interrupted.

"They really do," Reynolds said. "I hear they brought in one of the bailiffs' wives to sit with her, but make no mistake—they ain't likely to let her out except to the gallows."

"What in hell's the matter with you?" Trace demanded. "That young girl didn't kill anybody."

"Hey, I don't decide whether she's guilty or not. But you might wanna keep in mind, the court of public opinion has a lot of . . . swing." Reynolds looked back and forth between the two of them, making sure the pun sank in. "Fact is, *I'm* the best advocate Miss Herschel could have right now, and you could do worse than tell the public you sensed evil spirits about the place. People'd rather believe *that* than admit their own precious daughters could turn on Mama and Papa with an ax."

The reporter nodded at Trace's incredulous look. "Think about it. Reynolds. *Times*. Leave word. I'll find you." He nudged the brim of his hat with the stub of his pencil, and made for the road.

"Damn vulture," Trace said to his retreating back.

Boz shot him a worried look, but before he could start clucking like a mother hen, the young man with the camera barged into their midst.

"Excuse me, fellas. Sorry bout that." They backed away as the photographer parked the tripod by the corpse's feet. He was a very young man, maybe eighteen, but very intent and businesslike with his equipment. His hair was black and so were his fingernails. He glanced up and saw Trace watching him. "You oughtta stay away from that reporter, mister."

"Thanks for the tip," Trace said tartly.

The kid looked embarrassed. "I don't mean to tell you your business. It's just I know the guy. He's the dirtiest ink-slinger in town."

"Ain't you one?" Boz said.

"Um . . . not really. I'm just the printer's devil, but I was the only one in the office this morning, and I figured my boss'd crown me if I didn't check out this murder. Will you pull that sheet down for me?"

Boz exchanged a disgusted look with Trace and bent to pull the shroud back from the body. Trace touched the crucifix around his neck, muttered a quick benediction for the dead.

The photographer glanced around again. "You friends of the Herschels?"

"We knew him," Trace said. "Why?"

"Didn't figure you were from the neighborhood," the young man said. "But I meant to say, the Roths are progressive—they'll let Gentiles attend memorial services, if you wanted to pay your respects."

"Thanks," Trace said. It was about the nicest thing anyone had said to him all day.

CHAPTER EIGHT

"So what'd you see," Boz said, as they were finally riding away from the Herschel farm, "made you holler like that? You have some kind of vision?"

"Guess you could call it that. First I saw these . . . black things comin out of the body, kinda like when McGillicuddy died—"

"I don't remember that."

"You probably couldn't see it. But to me it looked like somethin nasty beatin a retreat. And when I touched one of 'em, I saw—it was like I got pulled into Herschel's skull, and I saw him beatin down the girls like I was doin it with my own hands. And laughin while he did it."

Boz looked shocked, but not incredulous. "You think somethin got into him and made him take after the girls with an ax?"

"You said it, not me."

"Makes as much sense as Miss Anna doin for 'em."

"Amen."

Boz chewed on that for a while. "You notice the living room, how neat it was?"

"Aside from the blood, you mean?"

"If they were fightin in there, whalin on each other with axes and pokers, they shoulda been staggerin about, knockin into things. None of the chairs was knocked over—the *rug* wasn't even out of place."

It was true. Trace remembered Whistler's blunt fingers gliding over the checkerboard, the undisturbed bowls of popcorn and cider mugs beside the game. Mrs. Herschel's needle woven through the fabric of her embroidery, the way a woman would if she had to get up for a moment. It was as if, at some prearranged signal, the family had set aside their peaceful evening activities in order to murder one another.

Trace shivered and passed a hand over his face.

"You all right?"

"I'm *tired,*" he complained. "Seein them all dead like that, and then standin around for hours gettin worked over by that detective, tryin to make out whether we'd been involved in it somehow, and then havin that vision on top of it—"

"Was their spirits in there?"

"No," Trace said, which was surprising, now he thought about it. Usually people who had died bad tended to haunt their deathplace, screaming and clawing at him as soon as he got near. "No, they seemed to have gone on, at least."

"So how was it you saw what Herschel saw?"

"I don't know. I never had that happen before." This questioning was making him acutely uncomfortable. He'd always had the sense of his curse being a private thing, not only because of the nasty events connected to it, but also because it was so tightly tied to his faith. Boz was not in the habit of respecting the unseen, and so tended to go at the subject like he was killing snakes. "Everything's been so quiet, the last couple weeks . . ."

"You mean you ain't been seein things?"

"I *always* see them," he said, though that was half the truth. The spirits *were* always there, but for the past fortnight or so they had been less inclined to come near and demand his attention. It was as if the misadventure in Sikeston had burnt out a pocket of bad air in his brain, and left him feeling clear and relatively unburdened.

Boz was quiet for a moment. "You reckon that Fairweather woman knows anything about this business?"

Trace turned his head so abruptly that Blackjack snorted and side-stepped in the road. "You ain't sayin *she* did for them—?"

"Naw, I didn't mean *that,* but you said she knows about spirits and such. She's still sendin you notes, right?"

Trace grunted. She had sent him three notes in the past two weeks. The first two had been brief and high-handed: she had another job for him and looked forward to discussing it at his earliest convenience, et cetera. Trace had burnt them both, railing to Boz about the sheer gall of the woman.

But yesterday there had been a third message, a single line in elegant copperplate script:

Have the spirits been less troublesome, since last we spoke?

He wondered how she could know that. And what else she knew. And what it would cost him to find out.

"You think I should go see her?" Trace asked, half-hoping Boz would advise against it.

"I dunno," his partner said, after a moment's contemplation. "I was thinkin maybe if she could tell you somethin—if there was some way you could prove Miss Anna didn't do it . . . but I don't know what. And I don't reckon you want to be beholden to her at all."

"No," Trace agreed.

"*THERE YOU ARE!*" Jameson bellowed, as Trace walked in from the back of the store. "Lawd a'mighty, boys, I was starting to think you'd been copped."

"Whyn't you announce that a little louder?" Trace said, glancing around to see the place was empty but for Miss Fairweather's pet Chinese, keeping company with the wooden Indian in the corner. "What the hell is *he*—?"

"Been here an hour or so," Jameson said, lowering his voice. "I told him you were out working all day and he insisted you'd be back soon. Then I saw this and I started to wonder if you were coming back at all."

Jameson reached for the stack of newspapers on the end of the counter, snagged a *Carondelet Citizen,* and thrust it at Trace. For a second Trace wondered why he was being handed a page of want ads. Then the print in the third column brightened from black to crimson and began to ooze down the page.

Trace smothered a grunt of revulsion and dropped the paper on the counter. The text instantly reverted to orderly black rows. THREE MURDERED AT LOCAL HOMESTEAD, proclaimed the headline.

"Is that true?" Jameson asked.

"Yeah, it's true." Trace rubbed his hand on his shirt. "We just came from there."

"Jeezly Crow," Jameson swore. "I mean I hardly knew Miss Anna, but Herschel's a good sort, and he doted on those two girls . . ."

"What's it say?" Boz asked.

"'A trio of grisly murders occurred in the late hours of Monday evening,'" Trace read, "'at the small but prosperous farm of landowner Judd Herschel, who with his wife and eldest daughter were hacked to pieces and their bodies thrown into the family well by an unknown assailant.'"

The piece went on to describe, in lurid detail, the scene at the house and yard, lingering over the image of Herschel's mangled face gazing up from the waters of the well. It also gave a lengthy recounting of Anna Herschel's story to the police:

> . . . Miss Herschel claims an argument between her father and sister, Leah, escalated to bludgeoning each other with a stick of wood and a fireplace poker. Anna and Mrs. Herschel attempted to intervene, and the mother was struck down in defense of her child. Mr. Herschel then vented his rage upon Leah, and battered his elder daughter about the head until she fell senseless.
>
> Then, seeing what he had done, Mr. Herschel sought to dispose of the bodies by tipping them into the family well. Anna, believing her father to be "possessed or mad," tried to dissuade him, but he swore he would kill her, too, and Miss Herschel ran for help. She claims her father was still alive when she left him, though "not in his right mind" and can offer no explanation for how he was killed or ended up in the well.
>
> Anna Herschel is being held at Four Courts jail pending further questioning.

"I can't believe it." Jameson shook his head. "I'd hate to think any child could turn on her parents like that."

"You can't think Miss Anna did it?" Boz said.

Jameson looked uncomfortable. "Well, you gotta admit it looks funny—her being the only survivor, and blaming her old man when he ended up dead like the rest of 'em. Herschel was worth some tin, you know. It wouldn't be the first time the heirs thought to inherit early."

"It wasn't Anna," Trace said, folding the paper. He looked at Boz, inclining his head slightly in the direction of the waiting Chinaman. "I'm gonna . . ."

"Yeah," Boz said. "I'll see you at home."

CHAPTER NINE

Miss Fairweather's neighborhood was genteel but aging, built by well-to-do German families before the war. It was not a street where roughnecks typically rode up in work clothes and left their shaggy quarterhorses on the curb. But Trace had not been raised in a barn, either; he touched his hat to the two young ladies who dawdled on the sidewalk, looking him over with a mixture of terror and fascination. Their mother gave him a well-bred eyeballing herself, before hastening her charges along.

The Chinese, who had trotted the whole way uptown like a hound at Trace's stirrup, let him into the house. He took Trace's coat and hat, said, "Miss Fairweather will see you in the laboratory," and set off across the foyer.

Trace followed the man up the grand staircase, past the quiet and richly carpeted second-floor landing, to the narrow and dimly lit third-floor hallway. The place was eerily quiet—not even the muted bustle of servants at work. The silence made him uneasy, as if the house were holding its breath, listening back at him.

At the north end of the hall was a rough stair leading up, and a trapdoor opening into the attic. The Chinese gestured for Trace to go ahead. He had to duck to avoid the trapdoor, and the sudden onslaught of daylight made him blink.

The back half of the attic rolled out before him, as big as a ballroom. The entire north face of the roof was glass, braced by girders and sealed with lead between the panes. The clouds rushing overhead teased his balance and he grabbed the nearest cabinet for support.

There were a great many cabinets and shelves along the wall, all of them packed to bursting with intriguing objects: jars of preserved specimens, bins and boxes, glassware and iron armatures and rubber hoses. There were several large trestle tables, most of them painted black, but one was a solid slab of white marble, and another supported a tin basin the size of a wagon bed. The wall behind the trapdoor was stacked with cages and tanks, in which small creatures flopped and fluttered and whistled.

In spite of himself, Trace was impressed. He'd seen Miss Fairweather's library, and he'd guessed she had a capable and curious mind, but this was no mere dilettante's parlor. This was a place of serious work. He moved farther into the room, trying to look at everything at once.

Built into the central wall of the house was a massive fireplace, onto which was grafted a network of ovens and ductwork. Copper pipes ran down from the roof to a large heating drum, and from there more pipes snaked overhead to feed valves above the tin basin and the marble table. Above the water drum, a vent opened every few seconds to let out a puff of scalding vapor.

Trace eyed the water line leading to the tin basin. He touched a porcelain valve handle marked HOT with the tip of one finger and it turned easily, letting a spill of water into the tin basin beneath it. He felt the heat of the steam against his hand and closed the valve again, marveling at the luxury of hot water anytime one wanted it. The water sped down a series of grooves and vanished, gurgling, through a tube in the floor.

The floor, he noticed then, was chalked with an elaborate diagram, full of esoteric symbols—alchemical, some of them, and a few Hebrew characters he recognized from his seminary days. He felt a lurch of excitement, and wrongness, as he realized that yes, the woman was working in magic, and yes, she wanted him to know it. She wasn't just granting him audience, she was . . . enticing him. Offering him a glimpse of things he'd always suspected existed, and been afraid to find.

A throat cleared gently behind him, and Trace turned guiltily, as if she had caught him peeping in her window.

She looked more like a schoolmarm today than a fashionable society lady. Her cornsilk hair was scraped back in a ruthless chignon that did nothing to soften the gaunt bones of her face. She wore a sensible nurselike apron, and her hands were in the pockets of it.

"What a pleasant surprise, Mr. Tracy." Her voice was lower than he remembered, and there was a hint of mockery in her cool blue gaze. "I was beginning to think you had taken a dislike to me."

Trace bit his tongue. It wasn't in him to insult a lady to her face, whatever he might think of her in his mind. "This is a . . . uh, interesting place you got here."

"I find it so," she agreed. "Are you interested in the study of natural science?"

Oh, is that what you call it? he thought, but he considered the question at face value. "Can't say I ever studied the sciences much. In seminary they were more concerned with preparin us for the next world than studyin this one. But I don't suppose I'd be much of a trail guide if I didn't know a bit about the beasts of the field."

"Well put, Mr. Tracy. Very sensible of you."

The civilities thus acknowledged, they regarded each other with curiosity, and a certain caution.

"So I guess you—" he began.

"May I ask—?" she said at the same time. They both broke off, and Trace yielded the floor to her with a nod.

"What made you change your mind about calling on me?" Miss Fairweather said. "Has it something to do with that newspaper you are clutching?"

"Matter of fact, it does." Trace moved to the nearest table, and laid the *Carondelet Citizen* on it so it faced her. He stabbed a finger down into the appropriate headline. "What do you know about that?"

"'Three Murdered at Local Homestead.'" Her fine brows lifted in surprise. "This is *today's* paper?"

"Well it wouldn't be last week's," Trace said, not sure what she was getting at.

"But the murders only occurred last night." Miss Fairweather circled the table to the writing-desk, which was piled high with books and papers. "I shouldn't have thought the bodies would be discovered yet."

"So you *did* know about this."

"It is why I sent Min Chan to fetch you this morning." She teased out a sheet of foolscap and held it out to him. Trace declined to take it. She rattled it at him impatiently. "I had been seeing an increasing concentration of spirit activity around you for the past few days, and—"

"Hang on—you been *watching* me?"

Miss Fairweather lowered the paper and gave him a patronizing look. "Mr. Tracy, I monitor spirit activity in and around this city for my own purposes. *You* are an unfortunately bright and distracting beacon in the area. It is quite impossible that I should *not* notice your whereabouts. However, I gather from your reaction that you were unaware of the menace in your proximity—"

"You might've warned me if there was!"

"I tried," she said crisply. "I sent you a card four days ago and you chose to ignore it."

That indictment was hardly calculated to increase his charity toward her. But his ire was held in check by the guilty fear that had been clinging to him all morning. "Are you sayin . . . you think *I* brought this down on them—?"

"Not in the least." Miss Fairweather's brows drew together. "Why would *you* suspect that to be the case?"

"Because it's happened before!"

"Under what circumstances?"

"I *told* you, everyone I've told about my—about this thing in me, tends to die from it, and not long after."

"Did you unburden yourself to these latest victims?"

"No, but . . ." It sounded like madness, spoken aloud. "That job I did for you, down to Sikeston—my partner Boz found out I could see things. And I been fearful ever since . . ." He made an embarrassed gesture. "I just thought, if not him, maybe somebody else."

"Have you any idea what precipitates these deaths? Do you notice an increase of spirit activity around the person in question? *Have* you noticed an increase, these past—?"

"No. You asked me that in your note. The answer is no. I still see them, they just ain—they haven't been comin close or makin such a nuisance. And I never saw *anything* out at the Herschels' farm, not even today."

"So the victims were known to you?"

Trace nodded, once. "Good man. Good family. Three of 'em chopped up with an ax and thrown in the well."

"Ye gods." Miss Fairweather actually looked shocked, which eased a suspicion in Trace's mind he had not quite acknowledged. "By someone in the family? That is, did it *appear* to have been done by a family member?"

"They're sayin the younger daughter did it. And *that's* why I came up here today—not cause you sent for me, but because the detective and everybody else seems to think that poor girl's a murderer."

"Clearly you disagree."

"I think it's hogwash. Anna Herschel ain—she's not much bigger than you. There's no way she overpowered her father."

"Where is the girl now? Have you seen her?"

"No, they said she'd already been taken to the jail. But they were still haulin the bodies out."

"Then you have been to the scene of the crime."

"Yes ma'am. Just came from there." He drew a short, sharp breath, and so did she, as if they both knew what his next words would be.

"And you saw something sinister," she finished for him. "And you came here seeking explanation for it."

"Yes, ma'am. For Miss Anna's sake."

It was hard to read the look she gave him. There was recalibration in it, for sure. "Perhaps you would like to join me downstairs for tea, Mr. Tracy, and you may tell me what you saw there."

The next hour was one of the strangest of Trace's life. Not because there was anything peculiar about sitting in a lady's library and drinking tea—he wasn't *that* far lost to the refined side of life—but because he had never before related such strange events to such a receptive audience. Miss Fairweather listened avidly as he described the unnatural neatness of the Herschels' living room, the paprika on the floor, the black tadpoles that swam out of the corpse and evaporated. She only interrupted once or twice, to request clarification, and she showed not a flicker of disbelief, either in the events themselves or in Trace's perception of them. That alone was worth the tea he choked down. He despised tea, but talking was thirsty work.

"There are several points that interest me," Miss Fairweather said, when the bulk of it was told. She pursed her lips, not quite touching the rim of her cup. "You are quite sure you saw no evidence of spirits at the farm?"

"None."

"Only the black emanations from the corpse. And the stench in the house."

"That's right."

"And the spilled pepper in the kitchen."

"Yes, ma'am. Though I'd say one of the girls did that—there was a woman's shoe-tracks through it."

Miss Fairweather set her teacup down with a click. "Well. I do have some theories, but before I jump to conclusions, I believe we should speak to the girl."

"I'll be surprised if they're lettin her have visitors."

"Visitors, perhaps, but they cannot prevent her from conferring with her barrister. I believe the law of this country entitles her to legal representation?"

"I believe so, yes ma'am."

"And dare I hope you have a more presentable coat than the one on your back?"

Trace looked down at himself. He was clean enough, though dressed in his usual coarse work clothes and boots. He had, he remem-

bered distantly, expected to be cutting wood today. He had one frock
coat left from his married days—it was several years old and too small
for him now, but . . .

Miss Fairweather did not wait for his answer. She spoke a few sing-
song words to the Chinese, who came forward and bowed to Trace.

"Go with Min Chan. I took the liberty of having some suits tai-
lored for you, in preparation for such an occasion."

"What occasion is that?" Trace asked, with a twinge of alarm.

"In case I needed you to look presentable," she retorted. "Pray do
not delay further, we may not have much time."

"SHE DID *WHAT* now?" Boz paused in his solitaire game, one hand
poised on the card he'd just played, frowning at Trace as if he'd lapsed
into Greek.

Trace plucked irritably at the stiff new collar and tie. "She waltzed
into Four Courts, hollerin about women's rights, and bullied the con-
stable into lettin Miss Anna be visited by her *lawyer*."

"Meanin you."

"Meanin me." He wriggled out of the tight wool coat and threw it
on the bed. "She bought *suits* for me to wear, Boz, three of everything
so one would be sure to fit. Just hangin there in an upstairs wardrobe,
waitin for the time when she'd need me to parade around—"

"Hang on," Boz interrupted. "She went *with* you to the jail? I thought
she didn't like to go outside."

Trace paused in the act of pulling off a boot. "I'd say for sure she
doesn't."

He'd ridden his horse to the jailhouse; she'd ridden in a shiny black
rickshaw pulled by the Chinaman. The rickshaw had deep black curtains that hid her completely from view, but Trace had gotten a glimpse
of the inside: it had arcane-looking symbols painted in red all over
the walls and curtains.

She'd seemed hearty enough at first, as she marched into the courthouse adjoining the jail, and demanded to know who had seen to
Miss Anna Herschel's rights and well-being. None of the answers satisfied her, and Trace had to admit they were pretty flimsy—there were
no matrons in the jail to tend to women prisoners, and no separate
holding cell for women. On account of the girl's hysterical condition
she'd been put in a sickroom and left there, without food or clean
clothes, since seven o'clock that morning.

"The funny thing was, I think she actually *cared* how Miss Anna was treated," Trace said. "She spent almost an hour getting her set to rights before she let me come in."

"And they just let *her* in?"

"She knew just who to talk to, and just what to say. She threw down the names of the police commissioner and the jail trustees and some judge she said was a friend of hers. I don't think she was lyin, either."

"Rich folks tend to know each other," Boz allowed.

By the time Trace was admitted to the infirmary, Anna was dressed in a plain, clean dress—also provided by her benefactress—her face washed, her hair brushed, and a little beef broth put into her. Miss Fairweather was busily packing away the things in her satchel, but Trace thought she looked whiter than usual, and her hands were shaking.

"You all right?" he asked her.

"I am not the one you should be concerned with," she said, through a jaw held stiff with control. "Please proceed with your questioning."

Miss Anna sat on the edge of the rough plank bunk, staring at nothing. She gave no reaction when Trace pulled up a folding chair and sat in front of her. She was wringing her hands in her lap, rubbing them over and over each other. There were terrible bruises developing on her wrists, the marks of a man's hard grip.

"Anna?" he said. "My name's Jake Tracy. You remember me? I been out to your house cuttin timber this week."

She stirred, and made a slurping sound as she breathed in. "Papa's dead . . ."

"I know, button. I'm sorry for that. Do you wanna tell me what happened?"

She looked away.

Trace touched a gentle finger to the puffy bruises on her wrist. "Who grabbed your arm, Anna?"

She clutched the hands closer to her body, shuddering. "That *thing* did."

"What thing was that?"

". . . in Papa . . ." Her voice was very small.

"Tell me about that thing, Anna."

"It killed Mama and Leah. It killed *him*. But it wasn't him. It wasn't!"

Miss Fairweather stepped around Trace and took the girl by the shoulders. The embrace was brisk, not maternal, but it had the desired bracing result. "We believe you, Miss Herschel. We want to find this thing and stop it."

Anna looked at her, then slowly around at Trace for the first time. It was impossible to know if she recognized him, or cared.

Trace folded his hands, summoning up the manner of every kindly-but-stern priest he had known. "Tell me what it looked like, Anna."

"Dead," she said listlessly. "Like he was sleepwalking."

"Was he behaving strangely?" Miss Fairweather asked. "Did he perhaps speak in an unfamiliar language? Or behave in a . . . an immodest manner toward you or your mother or sister?"

"No . . . he read the paper after supper, as always."

Miss Fairweather glanced at Trace and lifted an eyebrow. "What paper was that?"

"He took the *Carondelet Citizen*."

Trace remembered the words on the page turning to blood, in Jameson's store. He had attributed the vision to his curse, rather than the rag the story was printed in, but perhaps the two factors were dependent on each other.

"What were the rest of you doing after supper?" Miss Fairweather asked.

Anna shook her head wearily. "Leah and I were playing checkers. Mother was sewing. I got up to get some paprika from the kitchen. I like paprika on my popcorn. Then I heard something crash out in the living room, and Papa yelling—O Lord, it was an awful sound—like he was being ripped apart and strangled at the same time. I ran back to the living room and Papa was beating Mama. I saw Leah catch up the fireplace poker and start hitting him with it. But then he turned to strike Leah and I saw it wasn't him at all."

"How do you know it wasn't your pa?" Trace asked.

"It wasn't *any* of them," Anna wailed. "They were all beating each other, but not as if they were angry. They might've been cutting down grass, they were so . . ." She groped for a word. "They didn't even *say* anything—except for Papa crying out at the first they hardly made any sound. They just beat each other down, and the whole time Papa wore this grin . . . as if the thing inside him enjoyed the sight." She held out her hands in supplication. "How could it get us? My papa was a good man—he attended prayers every week . . . we kept a kosher house . . ."

Trace cupped her hands gently together. "There's evil things in this world, Anna. Some of them set out to destroy good people who'd stand in their way. In a manner of speakin, your Pa was a soldier, went down in battle."

Miss Fairweather's lips pressed together skeptically. "Is there anything else you can tell us about the intruder? Did you notice any unusual sounds in the place? Or smells?"

"There was a stink—like rotten eggs." Anna's nostrils flared. "It was there when I came back from the kitchen. I was almost sick . . . and then—" She recoiled, hands raising like claws to ward off the memory.

"Easy," Trace murmured, capturing her hands and holding them tight.

"I pushed it into the well," she said, her voice cracking. "It tried to throw Leah in . . . she woke up. She looked scared for a second. She caught at him and he lost his balance and I—I pushed him. Leah fell, but he caught on the edge. And then it laughed at me. Its eyes were all black, it was spitting black out its mouth, and it started saying all these things it would do to me. I chopped off its fingers, but it clawed up out of the well on bloody stumps." She began to sob. "I had to do it. I didn't have a choice. I swung the ax up and it saw what I meant to do and the black thing went away—but I couldn't stop—it was too heavy. It was Papa's eyes . . ." She put a hand over her mouth as if to hold back the awful truth. "It was Papa I hit with the ax. *I couldn't stop it.*"

She folded over, sobbing. Miss Fairweather stood and went to the table where she had left her satchel. She withdrew a small packet of paper and picked up the tin cup of water from the supper tray.

"Miss Herschel, I'm going to give you a preparation." She handed the cup to Trace, wedged a hand under the girl's chin, and forced her head back. "It will taste bitter, but it will help you sleep. You won't dream, and nothing will be able to harm you in your sleep. Do you understand?"

Anna didn't answer, but she didn't fight, either. Miss Fairweather poured a small measure of powder onto her tongue, and then followed it with a generous drink of water. Anna made a terrible face and swallowed as if it hurt her, but afterward she blinked back tears and gave her thanks.

"Do you have a Seal of Solomon—that is, a Star of David pendant?" Miss Fairweather asked. "No? Well, I want you to wear this one." Again she rummaged in the satchel, then draped a silver chain over the girl's neck. "It will keep evil spirits away. Never take it off while you are in here. Do you understand?"

Anna nodded.

"Good girl. Now go to sleep."

Anna lay down obediently. Miss Fairweather pinned her hat on her head, gathered up the satchel, and indicated Trace should follow her.

She took Trace's arm as they left the building, and not merely for form's sake; she was staggering with fatigue. He supported her as they descended the steps to the sidewalk, feeling through the heavy cashmere dress how frail her arm and shoulder were. Min Chan met them at the curb and helped her into the rickshaw. Once underneath its roof she revived enough to flare her nostrils and inform Trace that she had a theory, and if he would call on her tomorrow morning, she would discuss it with him.

"I must return home," she said, "and I have research to do. I do, however, have a question for you: Was the newspaper you brought to my house this morning recovered from the Herschels' house?"

"No, I got it from Jameson's store this morning."

"And it was today's edition? Not an extra?"

"No, it was today's regular weekly, as best I could tell. And there's more—when I first saw that story in the paper this mornin, the letters turned to blood and started to run down the page."

"Ye gods!" Miss Fairweather's voice cracked in indignation. "And you did not think to mention it?"

Trace's brows snapped down. "Lady, if I told you every strange thing I see in a day, you'd never get me out of your library!"

The thought seemed to arrest her for a moment, but then she shook it away. "Never mind. Tomorrow, I think it would be well if you looked into Judd Herschel's business of the past few days. Especially find out if he paid a visit to the *Carondelet Citizen* newspaper office."

"But that's where I ran into him last week," Boz said, breaking into Trace's recounting.

"It was?"

"Yeah, I was comin out of the barber shop there, and he came out of the printer's. I said hello, asked what he was up to, and he said he was puttin an ad in the paper for somebody to cut his timber. That's when I said we'd do it."

Trace pulled his suspenders over his shoulders.

"You think somebody at the printer's did this?" Boz asked.

"Well, I don't know anything about printing, but you gotta admit it looks funny that the story was on the street before the bodies were found. Hell, it had to have been printed the night *before,* if Jameson was to have a copy of it in his store this morning."

"What does *she* think did it?"

"She ain't told me yet."

"She tell you anything useful, or just parade you round town like a prize rooster?"

Trace cocked an eyebrow at him. "You got somethin to get off your chest?"

"I dunno . . . You spent two weeks tellin me you weren't ever havin nothin more to do with that woman, and now you come back in a new suit squawkin bout women's rights and Miz Fairweather said this, that, and t'other—"

"Uh, *you're* the one said she might know something about these deaths, and I'm tellin you what she said."

"She say anything about payin you for this job? Cuz you might recall we lost out on two weeks' pay, now that Herschel's dead."

Trace started to argue he wasn't working for Miss Fairweather, this time, but then she *had* asked him to consult with her, and she *was* taking up his time to escort her places. And *he* had been so caught up in the novelty of being able to talk to someone about his curse he had forgotten about practical matters like paying the rent and eating occasionally. "I'll make mention of it next time I go up there. *After* we go to the printer's tomorrow."

CHAPTER TEN

Like many small papers, the *Citizen* was kept afloat by its proprietors taking in job printing: calling cards, handbills, and other small items the public might require. Upon entering the shop, Trace and Boz were confronted with a long wooden counter and a rail, separating the reception area from the pressroom. Beyond the rail squatted a number of heavy, sinister-looking machines, long low tables, and rough-edged clutter. Everything had a coating of black over it.

At the back of the room, a young man labored over a job press the size of a small bison. He pumped a treadle with one foot, driving a large iron wheel, which in turn drove the cast-iron elbows to flex and straighten. Rollers licked red ink across a wide circular platen, then darted back inside before the jaws closed with a clang. The pressman's hands swiped in and out of the machine with casual daring, left hand snatching a freshly printed handbill from the gaping maw while the right laid a blank sheet of paper on its tongue. His movements were easy and unhurried, despite the apparent danger of losing an arm in the thing.

"C'n I help you?" A tall, balding man in spectacles got up from the bench at the corner, wiping his hands on a rag already black with ink.

"You the owner?" Trace asked.

The man jerked a nod. "Bob Avery, owner and editor."

"I'm Jacob Tracy, this is my partner. We were hopin to get some information about Judd Herschel, who I hear came in your shop last week."

"Is that right? Herschel, you say?"

"Yessir. The one who was murdered yesterday."

"Murdered! Well, I don't know anything about *that*."

Trace stared at the man for a moment, trying to gauge whether this was genuine denial or a poor joke. "Er . . . there was a story about it in your paper yesterday, if I recall correctly."

The editor gave him an odd look over his spectacles, and reached under the counter, to come up with a copy of the paper. "Tuesday, March twenty-third," he read, looking at the masthead. He scanned the front page carefully, turned to the second page and scanned some more. "Nope. Doesn't look as though we did . . ."

"May I?" Trace said, and the editor handed over the paper. Trace thought he remembered where it was, but in that space was merely a column of advertisements. One caught his eye:

Two or three able-bodied fellows wanted to clear timber lot. Daily wages plus dinner. Contact news office or see Judd Herschel, Seminole Lane, Carondelet.

As Trace read it, the ink began to blur and turn rusty. The paper buzzed in his hands, like a wasp's nest that wasn't quite empty.

He dropped it on the counter. "Must be my mistake. Though I see here, Herschel did put in this ad for work."

The editor peered at the page. "That's right."

"Did anyone contact the office here about the job?"

"Not that I talked to—Danny!" the editor hollered over the clanking of the press. "You talk to anybody about the Herschel ad?"

The press operator turned, and did a sharp double-take when he saw them. As well he might, Trace thought, hearing Boz suck his teeth meaningfully. The black-haired printer's devil was the same young fellow who'd been photographing the Herschel crime scene.

He threw a lever at the side of the press and came over to them, warily. "What about the Herschel ad?"

The newspaper editor repeated his question. The pressman claimed not to recall anyone asking about the ad. He looked Trace in the eye and said, "I'll take care of them, Mr. Avery, you go on back to the type."

When the editor had turned the corner and sat down, the young man said in an undertone, "You here to make trouble?"

"Just want to ask you a few questions," Trace said.

The pressman hesitated, then nodded. "Wait for me around back." Then, louder, he added, "Sorry I couldn't help you, sir."

A few minutes later, Trace and Boz were standing in the alley behind the newspaper office, watching the streetcars go by. The printer's devil came out the back door with a freshly rolled cigarette in his hand and a box of safety matches. He held his free hand out to Trace and then to Boz. "I'm Danny," he said. "Danny Lewis, he calls me." He jerked his head toward the interior of the building, and his boss. "My real name's Daniel Levy."

"The old man don't take to Jews?" Trace said.

"Rather not take the chance," Danny said. "And anyway, I got other reasons for changing my name. My brother was the assistant reporter and printer's devil here three months ago—Isaac Levy. He said the old man was all right, never gave him any trouble. But then Isaac turns up dead. Hanged by the neck in the press room."

"Hanged himself?" Trace asked.

The kid shrugged eloquently, hands cupped around his smoke.

"And you don't want the old man knowin there's a family connection," Boz guessed, "til you figure out why your brother died."

"Something like that." Danny exhaled. "I also don't want him knowing I was out at the Herschel farm yesterday. The *Citizen* doesn't print pictures. We don't have the money or manpower to make lithographs. So I moonlight. The photographic equipment's my own—at least it was Isaac's, and our father's before that. I take pictures where there's a story, and sell them to the big magazines when I can."

"How'd you know about the Herschel murders?" Boz asked.

"I got a friend at the funeral home. He tips me off when they get called to a murder scene." He cocked an ironic eyebrow at their expressions. "Hey, we all got to make a living."

"That's all well and fine," Trace said, "but it don't explain how the story got in your paper before the bodies were even out of the well."

Danny's eyes went wary. "A story in *my* paper? When was this?"

"Yesterday morning. Saw the new edition less than an hour after we left the Herschel farm. Best I can figure it had to have been printed up the night before—"

But Danny was shaking his head as the words were leaving Trace's mouth. "I'm sorry, but you couldn't have. I did the proofreading Sunday night. All we put in there about Herschel was his ad."

"There must've been another edition. A special."

Danny spread his hands. "Who would've run it? *I* sure didn't. And anyway, there wasn't *time*. Mr. Avery set the type, Friday and Saturday; I proofed it Sunday and printed it Monday. There was just time to wedge in Herschel's ad at the last minute, and only space because Mr. Avery dropped a couple of ornaments. I'm telling you, a full-length article on a murder—what was it, six or seven inches long?"

Trace measured with his fingers to show what he remembered, and Danny nodded. "Yeah, that's about six hours of work." He dropped his cigarette and scuffed it out. "I'm sorry, fellas, but you must've seen it in another paper."

"Must've," Trace agreed. "Tell me somethin—you work here pretty late nights, sometimes?"

Danny's eyes were on his shoe, making sure his cigarette was all the way out. "All ink-slingers do."

"You ever see anything . . . weird after dark? Like your eyes are playin tricks on you?"

"Only if I get too strong a whiff of Mr. Avery's breath," Danny said. "By nightfall he's pretty well corned."

When he had gone back inside, Boz said, "He's lyin."

Trace nodded. "Yup."

JAMESON'S STORE WAS on their way north, so they stopped by to check for messages. The place was busy, and Jameson was occupied with a customer, so Boz headed to the back to help load wagons.

There were several copies of the *Citizen* on the front counter, and Trace helped himself, wanting reassurance in his own mind that he had read the story there. But the first copy he picked up only had Herschel's want ad in it. As did the next. And the next. Trace went through the whole stack of them, astonished, excited, frustrated. He'd had that other copy—he'd left it with Miss Fairweather yesterday—but other than that he had no proof that the Herschel story had appeared in the *Carondelet Citizen* at all.

By contrast, all the daily papers made screaming mention of the murder, and several of the smaller papers had issued specials. Some of the stories appeared to be copied verbatim from the *Citizen's* original story; others had lifted the basic facts, but rearranged the words.

The *Times*, at least, showed evidence of firsthand reporting, and the reporter had not shied from making his own analysis of the case:

An examination of the scene of the crime, and the grounds surrounding the house, does not suggest the presence of anyone other than the family, and indeed Miss Herschel makes no claim of an invader. But the question remains, could a sixteen-year-old girl, of slight stature and gentle disposition, assault her grown father and two adult female relatives with murderous intent?

The answer may lie in intimations made by one Jacob Tracy, a local day laborer who was employed by Mr. Herschel. Upon entering the crime scene, Mr. Tracy appeared overcome by the ghastly sight, and when questioned he professed to be disturbed by the psychic malevolence of the place. "Great evil took place here," he said, and then withdrew into reticence when pressed for details.

"Son of a bitch!" Trace breathed, and then looked up to see Jameson and his lady customer staring with raised eyebrows. He felt his neck getting hot. "Sorry, ma'am." He took himself and the paper out through the back room, to the loading dock.

Boz came after him. "What's the matter?"

Trace read him the offending part of the article, and what followed:

The police admit to being baffled, and it would not be without precedent for detectives to resort to consulting with psychics in such a case. Although Mr. Tracy denies association with the Spiritualists, he was adamant in his assertions of Miss Herschel's innocence. Could some otherworldly knowledge be the source of his certainty?

"Could it be that reporter buggers goats?" Boz murmured.

"Or was fathered by one." Trace wondered whether Miss Fairweather took the paper, and whether her fascination with him was stronger than her apparent need to keep hidden.

"Now, now," said a nasal voice. "No need to get personal."

Trace and Boz looked up. Rex Reynolds stood in the back doorway of the shop, hands in his pockets, rocked back on his heels as if he had not a care in the world.

"You got plenty of nerve," Trace said.

"*I* got nerve?" Reynolds retorted. "How's Miss Anna's case coming along, Counselor?"

"What?"

"I hear you and that hoity-toity Englishwoman from Quality Hill swanned into Four Courts yesterday on false pretenses. You pass the bar when I wasn't looking?" Trace stared at him, and Reynolds grinned. "Son, you'll find there's little newsworthy in this town that I don't know about. I got sources in every police station, at every saloon and barbershop—hell, I got half the laundresses uptown willing to slip me a dirty word about the missus' sheets, if it's a slow news day. And I know you spent *your* morning, you and your pal here, down at the *Carondelet Citizen,* trying to find out how they scooped every other paper in town. And I'd give a pony to know that myself." Reynolds opened back his jacket lapel and pulled out a sheaf of folded news pages. "Take a gander at those."

They were five issues of the *Carondelet Citizen,* spread out over the past nine months or so. Each one had a headline screaming bloody murder in the third column, where the want ads should have been.

"The Herschels weren't the first to get advance coverage in the *Citizen,*" Reynolds said. "Back in January, a woman drowned her baby in the laundry tub. Husband said she'd been melancholy ever since the birth. November, an old man fell down the stairs and broke his neck in the middle of the night. Family claimed the daughter-in-law pushed him, cause she was tired of takin him to the necessary. Five other deaths in the last year, all inside homes on a Monday night, all reported by the *Citizen* on Tuesday morning, sometimes before the police got to the scene."

"How come nobody's noticed this?" Boz asked.

"Cause there ain't that many copies with the murder story in it," Trace guessed, looking at Reynolds to see if he was right. "I just went through that whole stack in there, and none of them have it."

Reynolds laid a finger alongside his nose. "Give the man a cigar . . . I been able to find plenty o' folks who claim they read the story in the *Citizen,* but precious few who can produce a copy with the text."

"Then how'd you know?" Boz said.

"When it comes to print, not much happens that I don't know about." Reynolds fetched out a second set of papers. "Once I wised up to that Levy kid beating me to all the murder scenes, I started buying off a patrolman on the south beat. He makes sure to save me any newspapers he finds on the premises. And when a, uh . . . *precognitive* issue does turn up, I go down to the *Citizen* office and get me a copy of the official edition."

Reynolds handed over five new pages, all folded open to the third-page classifieds. "See the connection?"

Trace could already guess, but he glanced through the pages, to be sure. "Every time there was a murder, there was an ad placed by the person who was murdered. Or kin to 'em."

"Big winner here, folks."

"You think that's how they were chosen? The victims went into the *Citizen* office to place an ad, and the killer picked them out, then and there?"

"Seems to be the pattern, huh?"

"But that Levy kid said there wasn't *time* to run a second edition," Boz pointed out.

"I don't think they're bein printed at all," Trace said, and described how he'd seen the ink change on the page. "Somethin's alterin the pages after they're printed."

"Awright, so how come nobody's noticed *that*? The Levy kid, or the old man—"

Reynolds snorted. "I'm fair sure you could march Sherman's army through that place most nights, and old man Avery wouldn't notice. As to Danny Levy's involvement . . ." The reporter spread his hands.

"So what're you sayin, the kid is committing murders to sell more papers?" Trace said.

"Or take his photographs," Boz suggested, and Reynolds cocked an approving eyebrow at him.

"I couldn't say who's doing it, or why they'd want to." Reynolds checked his watch, and dance-stepped down the stairs to the yard. "My advice is, take those up to Miss Clever-puss and see what she makes of it."

"You know Miss Fairweather?" Trace said.

Reynolds touched a finger to his hat in a mockery of good manners, all the while backing toward the edge of the yard and the sidewalk. "The gray space is smaller than you think, son." He winked, and disappeared around the corner of the building.

"Gray space?" Boz repeated.

"Don't look at me." Trace tapped the papers thoughtfully against his hand. "Guess I'm goin up to Hyde Park though."

"What, cuz *he* said so?"

"Well, no," Trace said. "I told Miss Fairweather I'd report back after we talked to the printer. And she's gonna want to know about this." He brandished the stack of papers again.

"Hrmph," Boz said. "Well, don't forget to ask about the money." He mounted the stairs to the back door, and added before he turned into the shop, "Don't forget to come back."

It put a sour taste in his mouth, that remark. Why should Boz suppose he *wouldn't* come back? He hadn't forgotten how she'd thrown him into that hornets' nest down in Sikeston, but at the moment, it seemed more important to find the Herschels' killer than to nurse a grudge.

But it made him uneasy, in the next breath, to realize he was looking forward to meeting with her again. He was caught up in the hunt, now, eager to pour this latest news into her willing ear and hear what she had to say.

He grimaced. To hear her approval, more like. Just like a damned bird-dog.

He made for the street, tracing Reynolds's footsteps, then turned the corner toward the front of the building where he'd left his horse. At the mouth of the alley he skirted a small pack of children who were gathered around a makeshift puppet stage. A gangly youth was manipulating the strings above the backdrop.

Trace glanced at the roughly built stage . . . and then looked harder, disbelieving what he saw. A red-faced male puppet was beating on two flaxen-haired girl puppets with a stick—no, it was an ax, with a realistic-looking blade that glinted in the sun. The puppeteer was clever; he voiced the high-pitched shrieks of both girls without pausing for breath, and little shots of red fluid squirted from the curtains to flick the children and make them squeal.

Appalled by this show of poor taste, Trace raised his gaze above the backdrop to the puppeteer, and it was Reynolds, wearing that shit-eating grin, but the flesh was worn away from the bones and the sack suit hung loose over a skeleton—

A hand clapped on Trace's shoulder and he nearly screamed.

"Cripes," Boz said. "Take it easy. Jameson said give this to you, since you were goin up there."

He handed over a parcel with Miss Fairweather's name on it— books, by the feel of them.

"Thanks," Trace said, stealing another glance at the puppet show.

The puppeteer was an unfamiliar pimple-faced kid, and the play was a couple of darkies trying to catch a squealing pig.

Boz peered at him. "You all right?"

"Yeah. Yeah, I just . . ."

Boz's mouth drew into a thin line. "What was it this time?"

MISS FAIRWEATHER SHOWED signs of a restless night—bloodless lips and bruised-looking around the eyes—and she did not get up when Trace entered the library. She waved him into the chair beside hers and offered tea or coffee.

"Coffee," Trace said, relieved that tea was not compulsory. "You feelin poorly?"

"Yes," she said. "Tell me about your investigations."

He told her about the trip to the *Carondelet Citizen*'s office, and Reynolds dropping by the store, and how the weasely reporter had poured kerosene on his suspicions about the *Citizen*.

"Rather conveniently, though, don't you think?" Miss Fairweather said.

Trace had to agree. "Especially since . . . I saw somethin peculiar this morning." He described his vision of Reynolds—a ghastly, ghoulish Reynolds—manipulating the Herschels like puppets. He heard Miss Fairweather suck in her breath, and glanced over to see she had sunk her teeth into her bottom lip, eyes bright on his face. "I guess you approve."

"I am impressed, Mr. Tracy. Is this the first time you have had such a waking vision?"

It was hard to say. There had been plenty of times he'd gotten feelings about things—to steer wide of an outcropping because there was a rattlesnake nest behind it, or the odd dream that had come true. But everybody had those. These visions *were* like waking dreams—a glimpse through dirty mosquito netting into another layer of reality.

"I think it's maybe the third or fourth in the last few days," he said slowly. "Worst one I remember was at the Herschels' farm, when I touched the body. I saw those black tadpoles coming out of his face, and then I *thought* a saw a vision of the family killin each other."

"But you claimed you saw no spirits at the farm."

"This wasn't spirits. I was . . . it was as if I saw through the dead man's eyes."

He had not told her that particular detail the first time. He heard her breath hitch again.

"Another first?" she guessed.

"Yeah," he said grimly. "It's like this thing in my head is all riled up . . ."

"From your proximity to the spirit activity. That is very likely the case."

Trace just managed not to swear out loud. "But that's what I didn't *want*. I was afraid if I started doin this work for you they'd start comin around more—"

"You said they had not."

"No, but these new things—" He shook his head in despair. "I don't *want* this power, lady. If you know any way to get rid of it—if I could *give* it to you, I would, believe me."

Miss Fairweather's face drew into harsh lines. "Do not say such things. Do you hear me? *Never* will your power away. It is a part of you, no different from your eyesight, and more precious because of its rarity. Anyone who succeeded in taking it would remove a piece of your soul with it, and leave you hobbled. Do you understand?"

He didn't, but her vehemence was sincere enough. He nodded.

"No, I don't think you do," she said. "But believe me, your power is a shield, not only against the spirits but against your enemies, if you would learn to use it."

"I don't have enemies," Trace said, spooked. "And anyway it don't sound very Christian to smite them—"

"Did I say smite? I said *shield*. And telescope and microscope, for that matter. Let's have those papers Mr. Reynolds gave you."

He spread the pages on the table but Miss Fairweather would not touch them. She had the Chinese examine them closely, in pairs. They exchanged a few words, and then he bowed and went away.

"Min Chan is going to fetch some supplies." She used the sugar-tongs to turn two of the newspapers around so Trace could read them. "In the meantime, please tell me what you see on these pages, Mr. Tracy."

He followed her example and bent over the pages without touching them. Two identical pages of advertisements, Judd Herschel's solicitation for work on both . . . "All the headlines about the murders are gone. They've changed again."

"Place your hands on them and see what happens," Miss Fairweather suggested.

He did, warily. As before, he felt the shiver of something alert under his fingers. The ink in the advertisement columns began to reshape itself into a blazon of blood, and Trace heard a faint, hateful whine in his skull.

He took his hands off the table. "Are they *alive*?"

"No," Miss Fairweather said. "They are the instruments of a demon. Having served their purpose, they revert to an innocuous state, to hide the demon's work. But your power reveals them for what they are."

"The work of a demon." A shiver went down his spine—excitement and dread all at once.

"You sound dubious."

Trace licked his lips, hoping his eagerness was not as obvious as hers. "I was raised to believe that demons are real. But I been walkin around my whole life and never . . . even after I started seeing the spirits . . ."

"You have never seen empirical evidence of demonic activity?"

"I once saw a Voudou woman down in New Orleans wavin chicken bones over a child to drive the evil spirit out of him. All the neighbors pointed and shouted when the spirit flew away, but I saw nothin, even with my . . . power, I saw nothin. I've also seen men, ordinary men whose minds don't work quite like everybody else, and people sayin they had a demon out of stupid ignorance . . ."

"I suppose you had that accusation leveled at you, after your powers became manifest."

He shot her a sharp look, but her face was expressionless. He thought of that confrontation with his father, when he'd finally come home from hospital—twenty-two years old, thin as a scarecrow, with a weeping wound in his side and a barely subdued addiction to morphine. "There were . . . some who suggested it."

There was a slight pause. "I trust the doctors at Richmond Sanitarium were more enlightened?"

Trace went cold. "How the hell did you—" For a second he couldn't breathe, and then heat flooded his face and neck. He came half out of his chair. "You god-damned harpy. What gives you the right—"

Miss Fairweather did not so much as blink, but Min Chan moved subtly into Trace's peripheral vision, reappearing out of the shadows like a bad dream.

Trace stood there, his fists clenched, washing over with shame and fury.

"That was my first recourse in locating you, Mr. Tracy," she said calmly. "Mental wards are one of the best resources for finding true psychics and mediums. Half the time the poor sufferers consider *themselves* mad. How else to explain why they can see things no one else can?"

That was a second shock to his sensibilities. He really *had* doubted his sanity for the better part of a year—careening between the delirium of morphine and the torment of going without it. The presence of the spirits had been constant that first year, probably *because* of the opiates poisoning his brain.

"A great many soldiers came away from the war with an opium addiction," Miss Fairweather said. "Far more than the general public realizes. It is a testament to your strength of will that you were able to overcome it. Did any of the doctors believe your story of seeing spirits?"

"One." His own voice threatened to choke him. "Hardinger. He was a Spiritualist."

Miss Fairweather gave a short nod. "Basil Hardinger was quite a brilliant psychologist, I understand, if prone to bouts of depression. He died shortly before you left the hospital, did he not?"

"He shot himself," Trace said. "But I guess you already knew that."

She tilted her head ambiguously. "I would hazard a guess, then, that during your stay at Richmond, none of the attending physicians suggested you were possessed by demons."

"Course not."

"Rather, they supposed your ailments were the result of overtaxed nerves, brought on by your injury and the stresses of war? And although you were raised to believe in demons, and in more recent years have been able to see and hear the spirits of the dead, you don't entirely believe that demons exist, is that right?"

"I . . . guess not."

"And why is that?"

"I suppose because . . . all the things that demons are supposed to cause can be caused by something else. I've *seen* the causes."

"Drugs, and madness, and war."

"Yeah."

"And you know *you* are not possessed by a demon—you merely fell victim to the mundane evils of the world."

Trace felt his jaw tighten.

"Let me tell you something about demons, Mr. Tracy," Miss Fairweather said. "Unlike the spirits you see every day, which are pale reflections of once-living persons, demons are whole, sentient entities. They are not *of* our world, but they are drawn to the empty places *in* our world. They can take the form of ordinary things—animals, people, or other, benevolent, spirits. Many so-called Spiritualists, who have not the sense or experience to discriminate, are unwittingly calling up demons in the guise of a patron's loved ones."

The thought appalled him. "I knew there was something fishy about that table-rappin'."

"Indeed. And now you have reason to believe that a malicious entity—we shall call it a demon, for the sake of brevity—has been infecting households in south St. Louis and dispatching their inhabitants."

"I guess so."

"Why would you doubt it? You yourself can testify to the innocence of the victims. You saw the black emanations from his corpse. You have seen reality rearrange itself"—she waved a hand over the newspapers—"in order to conceal the work of this entity. What further evidence would you require, before you accept the reality of something you claim to believe in? Ye gods!" Her voice cracked in exasperation. "Is it so threatening to your tiny Christian mind that you must deny the possibility, rather than accept it, and learn to fight it?"

Trace raised an eyebrow. He was too old to get into arguments over his faith, and far too old to rise to insults that sprang more from a woman's bitterness at the world than any inadequacies in himself. And she knew she had overstepped; he watched the color flood her cheeks and her eyes lower to the tabletop.

After a moment she said coolly, "I trust you were taught the Roman ritual of exorcism?"

"I learnt the words. But it has to be a priest who says 'em. An *older* priest, secure in the faith."

Her face smoothed out into careful neutrality. "In your case, I suspect raw talent will suffice in place of experience. Our primary problem at this point will be to locate the demon's hiding place."

"I like the looks of that newspaper office."

"I quite agree, although this Mr. Reynolds has also piqued my interest."

"D'you know him? He seemed to know who you were."

"I am not familiar with the name," Miss Fairweather said. "However, I am active in various philanthropic societies in this city. If he reports on social issues it is quite possible he may know who I am."

Trace shook his head. "No, he knows somethin about *this*. He knew enough to bring me the papers. And I had that vision of him manipulating the Herschels."

"But he doesn't work for the *Citizen*?"

"The *Times*, he said."

"Hmm," said Miss Fairweather. "Well, let us concentrate on the *Citizen* office for now, since we have direct evidence of activity there. Demons are not necessarily exclusive in their instruments of destruction, but they do tend to show a preference for a particular *type* of weapon, and this one appears to hold domain over the printed word."

She rose from her chair and crossed to the library table, on which lay a heavy tome nearly as big as herself. She leafed through it carefully. Many of the pages had tattered remnants of older pages pasted down on them, and there were a great many loose sheets in the middle. "Here. There was a case in 1608, in Germany, of a demon possessing a bookmaker and causing him to enact violence against his neighbors. An exorcism was performed by the village priest, however one deduces the attempt was unsuccessful, because the townspeople burned the bookmaker alive in his shop."

"Did that kill the demon?"

"Fire will drive them out, in most cases." She turned a few more pages. "There are many records of demons possessing books or being suspected of inhabiting books. As I said, they are drawn to empty spaces, which is why medieval monks filled the pages with ornamentation. It occurs to me that a printer's shop would appeal to a demon's sense of mischief. The press can be an effective means of manipulating the masses, and our trickster seems to have honed the technique to a needlepoint." She put her finger on the page and looked up at him thoughtfully. "In your training, were you taught a method of detecting demons?"

"Uh. No. I guess a man of God's supposed to recognize them when he sees them."

"An older priest," Miss Fairweather suggested blithely. "One strong in the faith."

Trace looked at her suspiciously.

A corner of her mouth curled. "Well, this is one area where experience counts for something." She beckoned to Min Chan, who approached the table and handed her a leather pouch. She worked open the strings. "I will show you a simple method of detecting the demon's presence. It's a folk method, but a reliable one. This demon's modus operandi suggests it is a minor entity, unable to manifest directly or maintain long-term possession of a human host, but I will caution you to be wary. Its powers of influence are quite strong if it can compel a family to murder one another."

"So what do you want me to do when I find it?"

"I will show you that, also," she said, and began to take items out of the pouch.

CHAPTER ELEVEN

It was late afternoon when Trace made it back to Jameson's store, and the place was busy. Boz was weighing out seed for old man Niels. Jameson was waiting on three customers at once, as usual, but as soon as he spotted Trace, he threw his hands in the air.

"It's the all-seeing wonder himself!" The shopkeep pressed his palms together and sketched an Oriental-looking bow. "Back from your travels in the spirit world, ready for more adventures in the great unknown. Come on in, Swami, and tell us what the baseball scores are going to be."

The lady customer gasped. "Are *you* the psychic I read about in the paper? The one who's helping to solve that awful murder?"

"Uhm," Trace said.

"He don't look like no psychic to me," said a red-bearded man, whom Trace knew vaguely, and disliked. "He looks like a gussied-up lawyer."

Jameson shook out a folded sheet of pink paper and read in a tremulous falsetto, "'Dear Mr. Tracy, I am desperately in need of your advice. Whose proposal should I accept? Mr. Barden is wealthy and promises me a life of luxury and pretty clothes, but I do not love him. Mr. Thomas is dear to my heart, but he has no prospects and I—'"

"Give me that." Trace snatched the paper and glared at it, thinking—hoping—Jameson was making it up, but no, he had read the words true, and skipped over a great deal of pap in between. "Where'd this come from?"

"They've been trickling in all day." Jameson held out a rainbow sheaf of pages, all addressed to Mr. Tracy or Tracey or Trayce. One simply said *to the sykic helping the polees.* "I was about to set aside a bushel basket for you."

The lady customer leaned her heavy bosom against Trace's arm. "Good sir, you *must* call on me as soon as possible. My dear husband left a *fortune* in bonds—only I have been unable to locate the copy of his will that left it all to me and now his family is squabbling over the estate. You *must* help me contact my late Henry."

"Why'nt you leave your card with Mr. Jameson here," Trace suggested, avoiding her clinging hands. "He'll keep me informed."

Trace hid in the back of the store until Boz had finished up with old Niels. The two of them slipped out the back and headed for their boarding-house on the next block.

"Well?" Boz said as they walked. "What'd she say?"

"She said thanks for the service and here's the next week in advance." Trace handed over the envelope Miss Fairweather had given him.

Boz rifled through the bills inside and whistled. "And, uh . . . what *service* did you do for her, all afternoon?" He leaned close to sniff at Trace's collar, and cackled when Trace shoved him away. "You *do* kinda smell like a whorehouse."

"It ain't me, it's this." Trace took the leather pouch from his coat. It had been badly cured, with bits of hair still on and the suggestion of a toe or two.

"What is it?"

"A demon-detecting kit." There was indeed a strange bouquet coming from the bag—rose oil, lavender, frankincense, sulphur, and something brown and dry that Miss Fairweather had called "mummy." The last two were what stank, giving the whole a perfume like some old lady's boudoir.

Boz wrinkled his nose. "So what're you supposed to do with that?"

But Trace held off the telling until they were back in their room. As he'd expected, Boz was not happy to hear that Trace had agreed to hunt down the demon and exorcise it.

"*Why?*" he kept saying. "Why'd you want to do that?"

"Because there's somethin nasty out there killin folks," Trace said. "If it were a mad dog or a bear or some lowdown cut-throat—"

"But it *ain't*. Do you even know you *can* exorcise this thing?"

"Miss Fairweather showed me—"

"Miz Fairweather ain't *here*. She's shut up in her big white house sendin you out to do her dirty work. Again." Boz cocked his head, exasperated. "She got some dirt on you I don't know about?"

"No," Trace said shortly. "I ain't doin this for her. I'm doin it cause it's the right thing to do."

"Bullshit. That is pure-thee-well bullshit, partner. Ever since we got back from Sikeston you been mopin around, checkin in at Jameson's every day, hopin to get a note from uptown—"

"Now hang on. We got *three* notes from uptown, and I didn't answer *one* of 'em."

"No, but you sure did like to talk about 'em, and how you weren't ever goin back there, til somethin strange happened, and up-a-daisy—"

"*You* told me I should go ask her. We both agreed she might know something. And she did. And this is what she said to do about it. So you got any better ideas, let's hear 'em."

Boz put a hand on his hip, scratched his nose. "Y'know, I grew up around hoodoo women, and witches. Before the war we had this neighbor lady was a Voudou queen. And she told me right out, folks had no call messin with demons. Said that anyone who did was a fool or a proud fool."

"The priests taught me the same thing," Trace shot back. "And they taught me anybody who saw ghosts and demons was devil-spawn and not fit to live among righteous folk. So I spent the last eighteen years stayin away from righteous folk and keepin my head down and tryin not to see 'em, and it hasn't done me a lick of good. Not one. I lost everybody I ever loved, soon as they found out about my curse. So now I meet this woman—maybe not a Voudou queen, but a witch, I bet— who not only wants to help me with this power but wants to pay me for it—" He paused for breath, and saw by the way Boz's head went back, his brow smoothed out, that he understood, finally. "I gotta do this, Boz. You and Emma are all I got left in the world. If somethin happened to you cause of my curse—" He locked his jaw up tight, shook his head. Looked out the window.

"Well," Boz said at length. "I don't reckon anything's gonna happen to *me*, cuz I don't believe in curses. But so long as you do it for *you*, Trace. Don't let that woman jerk you around just cuz she bats her lashes."

"Believe me, that ain't her manner *at all*. She's like a . . . a nun. No nonsense."

"Well, that explains the appeal." Trace shot him a foul look and Boz half-grinned, holding up his palms in surrender. "All right, I'm done . . . You want some supper? Or you gotta starve yourself before your holy mission?"

"Sandwich," Trace said dangerously.

Boz left the room. Trace sat where he was for a while, chewing over his own words. Yes, he admitted, he had been looking for an excuse to visit Miss Fairweather again. But he certainly wasn't pursuing this exorcism for her sake. Nor because it was the right thing to do, although he believed it was. He was, he realized, feeling a bit fatalistic. Either the demon would kill him or he would exorcise it. Either way, he'd be done wondering why this power had been laid on him.

With a sigh, he began to empty his pockets, preparatory to stripping off this tight black coat and getting back into his own clothes. He put down the leather pouch full of exorcism supplies, some change, some matches, and the embarrassing sheaf of notes addressed to "Mr. Tracy, Psychic."

He stripped down to his drawers and decided he could do with a wash—he *did* smell like Miss Fairweather's house. It wasn't unpleasant—books and coffee, overlain with something musky-sweet, like herbs or perfume. Strange that he knew her scent without ever having noted it on the woman herself. Disturbing, as if she had laid some kind of claim on him along with the new suit. He took off his crucifix and laid it alongside the letters.

At last, scrubbed and dressed more like himself, he sat down to sort through the mail. Another few handwritten notes had been shoved under the door of their room. There was also a printed notice from the boarding-house, reminding everyone that prostitution and gambling were forbidden on the premises, extra guests had to be cleared with management, and room 24 would shortly be available for rent, since its occupant, Jacob Tracy, had shot his Negro companion and then himself, leaving the room vacant.

Trace stiffened. "*No*," he whispered, and then found he could not inhale. A band of power was closing around his chest and throat, holding him immobile. He grabbed for the crucifix near his right hand, but his hand only strained, the tendons standing taut with effort.

The ink on the boarding-house notice began to run down the page, pooled at the edge of the paper, and then spilled over. It ran in a trickle to where his hand lay glued with sweat to the tabletop. The cold that spread through his hand and arm was indescribable. His heart clenched at the stabbing ache of it, but he was powerless to stop its climb up his arm, around his throat, and into his brain.

It crowded him out, chased him down into a murky well in his mind, a place near sleep where he could still hear and see what was happening, but only at a great distance and without reaction. He saw his hands grasp the table's edge, felt his knees flex and stand. He watched himself open the chest at the foot of the bed and take out his Colt. He dropped the holster to the floor.

It was not long to wait. Boz had only gone to the kitchen downstairs. The house's cook was sweet on him and always dropped whatever she was doing to fix him a treat.

Boz's bootheels sounded in the hall outside the door. From way down deep in the well, Trace thrashed and tried to cry out, but the blackness had hold of him, and raised his arm to train the gun on the doorway.

The doorknob turned. Trace's thumb pulled back the hammer. He managed a low grunt from his throat, but he couldn't move or even turn his eyes away. The door swung open, with Boz's brown hand attached to the knob.

What happened next was very fast, but from his far-off vantage point, Trace saw it all at the measured pace of a waltz.

The gun went off just as Boz's shoulders moved into the doorway. He had a tray in his hand, and a crockery pitcher on the tray, level with his chest. The bullet hit the pitcher and exploded it, spraying milk everywhere. Boz startled but leapt forward instead of back; in the time it took Trace to swing the gun after, Boz threw the tray at him.

It clipped Trace's gun hand and blocked his vision for a second. In the next instant Boz caught his wrist and hit him hard in front of the ear. The pain was distant but the force knocked Trace down. He was glad of it. He struggled against the blackness just as the thing used his body to struggle with Boz. It didn't seem to have a lot of fighting prowess but it was very strong and kept trying to bring the gun around. Boz knocked the gun hand against the ground but could not break Trace's grip. Trace's body tried to sit up and Boz punched him between the eyes. He put one boot on Trace's wrist and a knee on his chest. He took a fistful of Trace's hair and looked into his eyes. Whatever he saw there curled his mouth in disgust. He thrust his free hand into his vest pocket.

"Sorry about this, partner," he said, and spilled a handful of stinging red powder into Trace's face.

The blackness boiled under Trace's skin and shrieked in his head, trying to get away from the burning in his eyes and nose. He choked and sneezed and gagged, and Boz lifted off his chest, snatching up the Colt as he went. Trace rolled on his elbows, hacking up black tadpoles that hit the floor and wriggled away between the boards. In another moment he was in full possession of his senses again, a mixed blessing given the pepper in his sinuses.

"Here." Boz's hand slipped a basin under his chin; it was full of milky water. Trace plunged his face into it, sucked some into his mouth and nose and blew it out again. It helped immensely.

He lifted his head with a gasp to find a towel dangled in his vision. He took it and wiped his eyes, blew his nose. At length he shook damp hair out of his face and peered at Boz, who dropped to his haunches.

"Gone?" Boz said.

Trace nodded. "How'd you know?"

"Your shootin at me kinda tipped it off."

Trace snorted laughter, then had to work through another coughing fit.

"Far as the pepper goes," Boz continued, "I been told since I was knee-high to a grasshopper, red pepper drives off evil spirits. Never had much reason to believe it, til I saw Miss Anna's footprints in the paprika. *She* was the only one it didn't get. So I figure it protected her. I asked Miss Lucille down in the kitchen for some yesterday, and she said cayenne was best. Said the hotter the pepper the better it works."

"And you been carryin it around in your pocket?"

"Don't thank me or anything." Boz put out a hand and hoisted Trace to his feet.

"I mean, what made you think it would get *me*?" Trace went to the table, scooped up his crucifix, and dropped the chain over his neck, vowing to never take it off again.

"We went in the print shop this morning." Boz's tone was smug. "It knows we're lookin for it. You gave 'em your name, not mine. And this thing gets into people when they read words on a page. I don't read, so it had to be you."

Trace stared at him. "Y'know, as much as you bellyache about this stuff, I sure as hell wouldn't be alive now if you weren't so damn clever about it."

"Yeah, well." Boz shrugged. "I led you cross this country, what— ten times? Ain't let nothin kill you yet. How *did* it get you? One of those letters?"

"This." Trace pointed to the boarding-house notice. Sure enough, the words had rearranged themselves again—now it said that room 23 was available to let. There was no mention of his name or anyone being shot.

Just then their elderly landlord, Mr. Laufer, knocked on the open door. "Everything all right in here, boys?"

Trace and Boz glanced at the spilled milk and broken crockery, then at the bullet hole in the door.

"Fine," Trace said. "Why wouldn't it be?"

"Folks are saying there was gunfire coming from this room," Laufer said.

"One shot," Trace said. "Just an accident. No harm done."

Laufer put his finger through the hole in the door. "Look, lads, I can't have bullet holes put in my walls."

"Perfectly understandable." Trace went to the envelope of cash he'd left on the table, teased out a couple of bills, and held them out to Laufer. "Look, that ought to cover the damage. Won't happen again, my word on it."

Laufer was a mealy-mouthed sort, and probably would have let it go, but at that moment his overbearing wife crowded into the hall-way behind him, pushing a policeman in front of her. Mrs. Laufer was shrill and indignant, proclaiming to all within earshot that this wasn't a cowtown in Kansas, and decent people didn't shoot off guns in a crowded house. She wanted Trace and Boz both arrested, which the patrolman was reluctant to do, but when he heard their names he got more interested.

"Tracy, eh?" the cop repeated. "You wouldn't be the Jacob Tracy who worked for Judd Herschel, would you?"

Something in the way he said it made Trace suspect there was no good answer, but he said, "That'd be me . . . why?"

"I think you'd better come along with me, lad," the cop said. "The chief has some questions for you."

CHAPTER TWELVE

"I understand you came to visit Miss Anna here at the jail yesterday," Detective Whistler said.

"That's right," Trace said. "My regular employer is a Reformer. She heard about Miss Anna's case and wanted to be sure she was fairly treated. I escorted her here."

"Your regular employer?"

"Miss Sabine Fairweather. Englishwoman, lives up in Hyde Park." If she insisted on employing him, she could damn well provide his alibi.

"And what work do you do for Miss Fairweather?"

"Fetch-and-carry," Trace said carefully, having no idea what business Miss Fairweather advertised to the world at large. He thought of all the caged and preserved critters in her laboratory. "She's a—uh, naturalist. I get specimens for her."

"Specimens?"

"Animals. Beasts and insects, mostly."

Whistler sat back in his chair. "You're an educated man, aren't you, Mr. Tracy?"

"I was at seminary before the war."

"Did you study law?"

Trace felt a sinking sensation in his bowels. "No."

"So neither you nor your employer are fit to represent Miss Herschel in court?"

"I'm not," Trace said. "I can't say for sure about Miss Fairweather. She's an unusual woman."

"The bailiff thought *you* were Miss Herschel's lawyer."

"He must've misheard. Miss Fairweather said the girl had the *right* to a lawyer, and said she would pay for one, but I don't recall anyone saying *I* was the lawyer, because I'm not."

"And what is Anna Herschel, to Miss Fairweather?"

"I couldn't say they ever met, before the jail."

The detective's colorless eyebrows lifted. "She's mighty concerned about the welfare of a stranger."

"She's interested in her *causes*," Trace corrected. "She knows you don't have matrons here at the prison and wanted to see the girl was well treated."

"What about you? What is Miss Anna to you?"

"The daughter of a good man I knew."

"Not, maybe, the daughter of the man you worked for? Who maybe thought you weren't good enough for his daughter?"

Now Trace's eyebrows went up. "You got the wrong idea, Detective. I scarce said more than how-de-do to Anna Herschel."

"You must've said more than that, because she keeps telling me you're the man to talk to about this case." Whistler's dead-eye gaze fixed on Trace. "She says you know what really happened."

Trace looked at the man for a long moment, remembering Reynolds saying, *You'd be surprised who-all believes in Spiritualism.* "Lemme guess: she says a demon got into her pa and chopped up her mother and sister."

Whistler's face drew long in a non-expression that could've masked credulity or contempt.

"And of course you don't believe her," Trace said. "Who would?"

Whistler reached for a stack of papers at the edge of the table. "You happen to see the paper this morning?"

"Which one? They're all talking about the murder."

"But the *Times* is talking about *you,* Mr. Tracy." Whistler folded over the newspaper and pushed the relevant page toward Trace. "Someone got the idea you were a psychic with valuable information for us."

"I read that, too," Trace said, "and I sure would like to get my hands on the buzzard who wrote it."

"So you didn't tell that reporter Reynolds you were a Spiritualist."

"Hell no. I told him I wasn't."

Whistler pulled toward him the embarrassing stack of letters, collected as evidence by the cop who'd brought him in.

"'Dear Mr. Tracy,'" Whistler read from the topmost. "'I know that you are helping the police in the matter of the Herschel murders and I believe I have information that may be of value to you.'" Whistler glanced at Trace as if to say, *See? I told you so,* and tossed the note aside.

"'Dear Mr. Tracey, do you hold private séances? I assure you I can pay for your time, but I am desperate to receive word of my beloved Alice, dead now these three years . . .'

"'To the sykic helping the polees—'" Whistler paused to show Trace the laborious scrawl on the page, "'if you contac the ded you ar dammed to HELL you brot down punishmint on that famly and all yor eforts will be in VAIN VANITY is the mark of the BEIST . . .'"

"Look, I don't claim to be a psychic," Trace said, "and I sure didn't ask these folks to bring me their troubles."

Whistler shook out a folded page and read, " 'Sprinkle salt and ash or earth into the vessel. Make a trail of blood leading to the vessel, and surround with lights to draw the entity . . .' "

"Lemme see that." Trace plucked the sheet from the detective's grasp. He knew what it was—the instructions Miss Fairweather had written out for trapping the demon after he found it. He'd tucked it away with the other papers, and forgotten it in the wake of getting possessed and then arrested. She had not put her name on it, nor his, thank God.

"If you ask me, there's the fella you oughtta be questioning." Trace flipped the page back onto the table. "World's full of sick minds, but I ain't one of 'em. And I know you don't have anything to tie me to the Herschels' deaths, or you wouldn't be fishin the way you are. The evidence doesn't show there was anyone else there, and you can't find that Judd Herschel had a quarrel with anyone."

"How do you know that?"

"I saw the yard and the house, same as you. I know how to track. Believe me, if I knew who the bastard was did this, I'd hand him to you."

"I believe you might," Whistler said. "But that's *my* job, not yours, and I can't have you impeding my investigation."

"How have I impeded it? I was mindin my own business at home—"

"The city of St. Louis can't have you discharging firearms in a public boarding-house, either." Whistler stood, scooping up the sheaf of papers, and said to the waiting bailiff, "Throw him in the drunk tank for the night."

"This is horseshit!" Trace said.

"Take a lesson from it," Whistler said blandly. "Don't carry a round under the hammer."

CHAPTER THIRTEEN

They took him through the polished, still-new hallways of Four Courts, to the jail access deep at the heart of the building. They went through two locked gates and onto a walkway that circled a large, empty amphitheater. It was suppertime, the men had all been returned to their cells, and a couple of trustees were circulating with a cart.

"You had supper?" one of Trace's escorts asked.

"No," Trace said. "Kinda got interrupted."

"You'll get a plate." The guard turned his key in the cell door and swung it open. It was dim inside, just weakening daylight from the narrow window, but Trace *saw* something writhe in the far corner of the room—a sick and twisting movement like a nest of worms turning over on itself.

He stopped in the doorway, grabbing the jamb as nausea washed over him. Chill sweat prickled his neck and armpits. "What's in there?" he whispered.

From the corner of his eye, he saw the guard exchange a glance with his partner, and then the two of them struck like wolves—pinned his elbows back and applied a kick to the small of his back so he stumbled across the threshold. The door slammed shut and the lock clanked into place.

"Hey!" He slammed a fist against the door, face pressed to the window, but they walked away without a backwards glance.

Trace turned to face the room, breath coming in short pants of anger and dread. He forced himself to calm, to think. To feel, cautiously, with his extra sense.

He wasn't alone in the cell. He couldn't see the coiling horror anymore, which in a way was worse than seeing it. A ragged fellow hunkered on the bunk against the wall, head on his knees. There was a chamber pot in one corner and a wooden bench running the perimeter of the room.

Trace's heart slowed, but the prickle of unease, of *awareness* along his arms and spine did not diminish. He could feel something prowling the wall near the other prisoner, like a coyote guarding its kill.

"Hey there," Trace said to the shivering man. "You all right, mister?"

There was no response. Trace ventured into the middle of the cell. The darkness retreated from him, but not very far. Trace steeled his nerve and reached to touch the man's shoulder. "Hey there, fella. You all right?"

The prisoner jerked back flat against the wall, eyes rolling like a panicked horse. "What? What d'ye want?" His face was streaked with snot and sweat, his skin the color of whey. "I don't have any—they took it all. They took it all!"

"It's all right, friend, I'm not after your dope." Trace's mouth curled in distaste, but at the same time a tendril of memory bloomed in his mind: the warm, dreamy sensation of being wrapped in comfort—no worries, no responsibilities.

It had been years since he'd had a resurgence of that old craving, and he knew immediately it hadn't come from inside himself. He backed hastily away from the bench, groping for his crucifix.

"Hail Mary, full of grace, pray for us sinners now and at the moment of our death . . ." The words came easily to mind, blotted out the sick craving with thoughts of righteousness and sanity. The Rosary was one of the first prayers he had learned, at his mother's knee; saying it in times of crisis was one of Hardinger's tricks, one they had devised together, once Trace had accepted that the spirits *weren't* his imagination, they weren't going away, and the dope was making things worse.

Remember who you were. Hardinger's voice was as soothing as the prayer, in memory. *Before the sickness and madness and pain. When the craving or the voices become too much to bear, go back to an earlier place . . . a quieter place.*

But Trace had forgotten—or perhaps never noticed, given his drug-addled state at the time—how the stillness in his thoughts heightened his senses, gave him an awareness of the world beyond what his eyes and ears could perceive. His mind flashed backwards, to the meditation sessions he and his fellow seminarians had been forced to do: forty young men kneeling for hours in various states of boredom and ecstasy. He had taken to it better than most, frightened and exhilarated by the swooning sense of leaving his body. It was one of the few times he'd really felt at one with God and with the calling his father had picked out for him.

On the other side of the cell, the coiling horror paused in its circling to regard him with interest and enmity. He could hear it whispering to the dope fiend on the bench.

Because it can't get to YOU. The words sounded like Miss Fairweather's, but the realization was his own. *The power is a SHIELD, you fool. Hardinger tricked you into using it.*

The altar-boy in him shied from the thought, but his older, worldlier self was intrigued. That feeling of safety and security *did* seem to come from within, maybe even from that well in the back of his mind, where his soul had retreated while his body was possessed. He didn't have to think about it—the power swelled out of him in response to the demon's proximity. He could stretch inside it and push it to the outside of his skin and maybe—Yes, he could extend it outside of himself.

Experimentally, he pulled it back. Felt the tendrils of temptation and fear begin to crowd close again.

Let the power out. Felt safe. Strong, even.

Miss Fairweather knew, he thought. She *knew* he had this in him. *Is it so threatening to your tiny Christian mind that you must deny it, rather than learn to use it?*

Damn right it was threatening, when everything he'd been taught for thirty-odd years promised damnation as the price of acceptance.

Out in the corridor, someone was whistling a jaunty tune, heels snapping along on the iron floor.

Trace moved to the door, keeping that new sense trained toward the dope fiend. "Hey, out there!"

The footsteps halted, backtracked, and the whistle drew out in a long trill of surprise. "Why, Jacob Tracy!" Rex Reynolds said cheerfully. "Ain't you come down in the world?"

Trace recoiled from the window. "What're you doin here?"

"Following where the story leads, as always," Reynolds said. "Guess that lawyer act caught up with you, huh?"

"*You're* the reason I'm in here," Trace said. "I told you I wasn't a damn psychic, and now that detective's sore I'm messin with his investigation."

"Well, that don't seem fair, do it?" Reynolds bared his long teeth in a grin. "Tough break, I gotta say—although having you in *there* wasn't quite what I had in mind. How're you enjoying the company?"

"Charming," Trace said. "There's talk of startin a literary society."

Reynolds laughed good-naturedly. "Gotta be a special hell for someone like you."

"I reckon I can handle one pissant dope fiend."

The reporter's grin darkened. "But we both know he ain't the *real* danger, don't we?" He leaned closer, waggling his eyebrows. "Fact is, that tank has a reputation for being haunted."

"Naw!" Trace said.

"Yeah! Six men have taken their own lives in there since this place opened in '71. And that doesn't count the ones who were murdered by their fellows. Or had heart seizures. Or choked on their own puke. Hell, I heard one kid got a chicken bone caught in his throat and went thataway." Reynolds cocked his head. "I'd almost wonder if the chief put you in there hoping you'd clear out the place."

"I don't suppose someone gave him that idea?"

Reynolds shrugged. "*I* sure didn't. Whistler hates my guts."

"Can't imagine why," Trace said.

"Aw, now there's no need to be hurtful. And after I came all the way down here to give you this." The reporter held up a half-full whiskey bottle, with a piece of paper wrapped around it.

Trace reached out and palmed the bottle into the cell. The note came away in his hand and he recognized it immediately. It was Miss Fairweather's instructions on how to capture a demon—which he had seen moments ago in Whistler's hand.

"How'd you get this?" Trace asked, but when he pressed his face to the window again, the corridor was empty. Reynolds's brassy whistle echoed back from places unknown.

Trace looked thoughtfully at the brown glass bottle and the note. This was twice now Reynolds had appeared out of nowhere, bearing unlikely but useful information just when it was needed.

Over on the bench, and at the edges of Trace's awareness, something stirred. "What's that?" said a raspy voice. "What's that you've got there?"

Trace glanced at the ragged dope fiend, who was staring with beady interest at the bottle. "Nothin you're interested in."

He unfolded Miss Fairweather's instructions. They were longer than he had realized, when she was describing the process. The first section made him groan—paired-off lines of square Semitic characters. Hebrew had never been his best subject. But the second part was easy:

> *In the names of the Angels command the demon to leave his victim. Watch the victim carefully to determine which names or words cause the demon discomfort. Repeat those words to increase the punishment.*

That was the part he was familiar with, the Catholic rite of exorcism. Fragments of Latin came to him, though he doubted he remembered all of the prayers.

The last bit was new:

> *Thus bound, command the demon to tell you its name. You can then adjure it in the name of Angels to do your bidding. Order it to enter a bottle or box and close the vessel and seal with white wax.*

The Church definitely did not encourage the exorcist to talk to the demon or ask it questions. But Miss Fairweather said to trap the thing, and at this point Trace thought he'd rather be guided by her experience than the say-so of some priests who had likely never seen a real demon. And she'd even sent him a vessel to trap it in. Trace worked the cork out of the bottle and drew a healthy pull.

It wasn't whiskey.

He spat the vile bitterness across the cell, and looked at the bottle in alarm. It *said* whiskey, but the label was old and smudged. It was laudanum, probably homemade. The familiar taste clung to his tongue and nostrils, and craving leapt alive in him like a rabid badger—the queasiness, the shivers, and the wretched desire for another drink to make it all go away.

"Hey." His cellmate was gathering his feet up under him, licking his lips. "Hey-hey. Gimme some of that. Gimme some."

"You just stay where you are," Trace said, holding out the bottle at arm's length, one finger lifted warningly. From somewhere far away Hardinger's voice was urging him to dump the bottle, get rid of the temptation, but something else was scratching and plucking at the edges of his self-control, urging him to take another drink, whispering that he wanted it, he needed it, everything would be all right—

With a grunt of revulsion, Trace flung the bottle at the wall. His cellmate moved with preternatural swiftness and batted it down. The bottle bounced off the wooden edge of the bench and landed in the straw with a muffled *chink*. The dope fiend dived after it, snatched it up, and began sucking and licking at the spilled fluid on his fingers with the avarice of a pig at the tit.

Trace's legs and back cramped fiercely, dropping him to his knees. *Now you've done it,* whispered a voice in his ear. *Quick, take it back before it's all gone. He's a bantam, no trouble at all—just snap his neck and take it for yourself—*

Trace put his hands over his ears and gabbled the first bit of Latin that came to mind: "Sancte Michael Archangele, defende nos in proelio, contra nequitiam et insidias diaboli esto praesidium!"

The sly writhing thing in the cell with him sniggered, pawed at him with its clammy hands, but Trace thrust it away, summoned up his shield, and pushed it into place. The pounding in his head cut off so abruptly that he gasped. He heard the suckling stop, and sensed the intruder swarming away from him, surrounding the other man in the cell, settling into him.

The dope fiend shuddered and slumped, hitched his shoulders and wiped a grimy fist across his mouth. He raised his eyes and looked balefully at Trace. "Yer a pitiful sight," the addict said.

"You should talk," Trace said. "Looks like you've about used up that vessel."

The thing in the addict bared rotting teeth. "There's always another. Your kind are always lookin' for a way to ease the pain. Just like you, always runnin' away." The demon held out the bottle, waggled it invitingly. "You useta *love* yer medicine, din't you, altar-boy?"

"I never loved it," Trace said. "I hated the stuff. I hated bein out of my head and pukin like a dog, but the pain was worse, and then the visions were worse. The morphine made them stop."

"But now they started up again," the demon said slyly. "Cuz of *her.* An' you let her do it, cuz the *power* is what you really crave. Well, I got news for you, altar-boy. She means to feed you to somethin' much worse than lil ol' me. Better to snuff that power out, make it useless to her."

Knowing what he was talking to, Trace could hardly take such a warning seriously. It was no news that Miss Fairweather wanted to use his power. And at least she had told him *how* to use it. The words were coming back to him, welling up alongside the power, where they had been stored down there all this time. "Exorcisamos te, omnis immunde spiritus, omnis satanic potestas, omnis infernalis adversarii—"

"Aw, c'mon!" the addict jeered. "Issat all you got, altar-boy? Mumblin' prayers and shakin' gimcracks. All you shamans is the same."

But Trace could feel something building in himself, a spark of brightness, of *rightness* that had always been there, banked and waiting, and now was flaring in reaction to this threat. He felt a shiver of excitement and looked down to see all the hairs on his arms were standing up.

A shield, hell. This was a battering ram. A thunderhead. A hurricane.

He felt, rather than saw, the addict recoil. But then it sneered at him. "Big deal. You got a bit of glimmer. You don't know what to do with it."

"I don't think it takes much smarts," Trace said, rocking to his feet. "I been wrestlin with the likes of *you* for sixteen years."

The demon's eyes widened. "You don't have the bollocks."

Trace laughed. "Maybe not, but I got a notion to find out."

THE BLUE TWINKLE of dawn was lighting the sky when the cell door's lock turned over with a loud clank. Trace raised his head as the door swung inward, with the faintest of squeaks on its well-oiled hinges.

There was some muttered conversation in the corridor outside, and then Whistler stepped through the doorway, a tin cup in his hand. He surveyed the room with polite interest, as if visiting a neighbor's parlor.

The addict slept, bruised but still breathing, in the far corner. There were a couple spots of dried blood on the floor, and the puddle of spilled laudanum, which Trace had kicked some straw over.

Whistler glanced an order at the guards in the doorway. They came in, shook the addict awake, and ushered him out of the cell. "C'mon, boyo," one of them said. "Time to go."

Trace sat up on the edge of the bunk. Whistler drank from his tin cup. The smell of coffee wafted across the room.

"Rough night?" Whistler asked.

"Had worse," Trace said.

Whistler nodded. "The guards reported some kind of hullaballoo in here around midnight. Screaming and fighting and 'Holy rollin',' he described it. He also claimed there were flashes of lightning and some black smoke, but I don't see how that's possible."

"Doesn't sound likely," Trace agreed.

"You don't seem to be damaged."

"Not more than passing." Mostly he felt as though part of his brain had wrenched itself loose, and was looking back on the past thirty-eight years of his life with blatant incredulity. Something had *awoken* in him last night, and that detached part of him was clanging to take it out and let it run.

At the moment, however, his years of self-control were serving him in good stead.

Whistler sipped his coffee. "Your lawyer's here. He paid your fine. So you're free to go."

"Much obliged." Trace rolled to his feet, trying not to look too jaunty. His heel nudged the whiskey bottle on the floor, and it made a soft clink against the bench leg. He bent and swept it up.

"What's that there?" Whistler asked.

Trace tilted the bottle, which appeared to be full of liquid soot, or maybe ink that had spoiled. "Specimen," he said. "Thought my employer might be interested."

TRACE RECLAIMED HIS personal effects, including the embarrassing sheaf of letters, and then a guard led him out of the jail and into the receiving area between the jail and the courthouse, where a distinguished, silver-haired man in a fine suit was waiting for him.

"Marlin Clifford," he said, offering Trace his hand. "Miss Fair-weather hired me to take your case. There was a small fine incurred on the drunk and disorderly, which has been paid, and you are free to go. Miss Fairweather asked me to give you this."

The lawyer handed over one of the familiar sealed missives. "You may also be interested to know I am taking Miss Herschel's case, at Miss Fairweather's behest. I shall do everything in my power to pre-vent the case from going to trial, but if it does, you may be assured Miss Herschel will have a vigorous and thorough defense."

Trace thanked the man, shook his hand, and thanked him again. Then they parted ways—Marlin Clifford heading inside, and Trace exiting to the street. He blinked at the bright sunlight, gulped a dizzying lungful of fresh air. He was amazed to find the world still turning.

He'd let the power out, and it had not destroyed him. It had not destroyed the man in the cell, either. He'd been able to control it, more or less, and he had wrestled a demon to a standstill. Not a puny pale shade of a ghost—a *demon*.

He was pretty sure none of his priests or seminary teachers had ever done that.

He looked at the bottle in his hand, and Miss Fairweather's letter. *She* had known he could do it.

He broke the seal of the letter.

Mr. Tracy—

As Mr. Clifford has no doubt informed you, he will take the Anna Herschel case. You need now to concentrate on locating the Perpetrator of which we spoke. It may interest you to know that a reporter em-ployed by the Carondelet Citizen *hanged himself in that office some months ago. The reporter's name was Isaac Levy and prior to his death he shared a room with his brother, Daniel Levy, who is now employed by that same news office under an assumed name. Daniel Levy was previously enrolled at the B'nai El school for Torah studies on Cherry Street. I suggest you look into the Levy brothers' involvement with these events.*

S.F.

Trace stared at the page for a moment. He looked at the back of it. Foolish; of course there was nothing else. He felt strangely let down. She'd said he was hard to miss in the spirit world. She clearly was keeping an eye on him. She *must* have noticed what he'd done last night.

But what did he want, a pat on the head? She was *hiding* from something—he couldn't put his finger on what gave him that idea, but he was certain of it. She probably had better things to do than monitor his personal epiphanies.

And maybe—the thought came to him slowly, as common sense overruled the high of victory—no matter how tempting it was to pour his news into her interested ear, perhaps it was best if he didn't. After all, he knew nothing about the woman, except she wanted to use him.

But he hardly knew what to do with himself this morning. He'd let the power out, and God had not smitten him. The world was not as he had known it for thirty-eight years. Because *he* was different.

He didn't know yet if it was good or bad, but he was different.

CHAPTER FOURTEEN

". . . So I went to the lawyer Jameson said," Boz explained, "but the shyster didn't let me say, 'My partner's a white man,' he just shut the door in my face."

"Don't worry about it," Trace said, lathering soap on his shaving brush. "No sense you spendin our money on a lawyer. Was just a fine, anyway."

"And she paid it?"

"Yup." Trace glanced at Boz's sour expression. "Why not? Was workin her job got me arrested."

"And you're still workin her job, I take it?"

Trace met his eyes in the mirror. "I wanna find this thing, Boz. When it killed Herschel it got my dander up. When it tries to shoot my partner and gets me a night in jail, I tend to take it personal."

"You're awful chirked for somebody spent the night in jail."

Trace was spared the necessity of answering right away by the brush swirling over his jaw and neck. "You ever have a big worry on your shoulders, somethin you dreaded doin, and then when time came to do it, turned out it was no big thing? Maybe you even liked it?"

Boz sighed. "I'm not gonna like this story, am I?"

"There was a demon in the drunk tank," Trace said, with as much nonchalance as he could muster. "It had hold of this poor bastard in there, and I pulled it out of him and stuck it in that bottle there. Just like Miss Fairweather said."

Boz eyed the dirty corked bottle with its smudged label. "There's a demon in there."

"Uh-huh."

"You *put* it in there."

"Uh-huh."

"And you wanna go try it again with that thing at the newspaper office."

Trace looked him in the eye. Nodded.

"You told that rich witch yet? That you bottled her a demon?"

"Nope. Came straight here. Figured it was none of her business."

"Well that's somethin." Boz was quiet for a moment, while Trace whisked away the stubble from his neck. He could see Boz struggling with himself, trying to come to grips with this new knowledge of the world. Trace knew how he felt.

"You see the paper this morning?" Boz said at last.

"No. Which one?"

"Any of 'em. Most of the big ones are supposin you and Miss Anna were in it together, but the *Times* is sayin you were brought in for secret consults with the chief of police. Jameson gave it to me for you, along with a whole stack of letters that stink like a French whorehouse. Said there were at least five marriage proposals in there."

"Any of 'em rich?"

"Oh, and there's another piece in the *Times* says the Herschels were maybe *not* Jewish, they were good Protestant German folk, and sorta suggested the Jew undertakers came and took the bodies away to use 'em in some unholy ritual."

"Jesus Christ," Trace said, fervently if inapplicably. "That oughtta start a riot."

"You think maybe that's the idea?"

"How do you mean?"

"Well, this thing's been killin people one or two at a time, right? By gettin into 'em and turnin 'em on each other."

Trace wiped the soap off his face, looking at Boz curiously.

"It started out small and sneaky. A babe in its cradle, an old man in his house. Then a whole family at once."

"Yeah."

"And from what you said, all those folks who was killed was down in the German quarter. I had Jameson look up the names in his city directory. All of 'em Jews, or workin for Jewish businesses."

Trace turned away from the mirror to hide his smile. However much Boz was discomfited by this demon business, his natural inclination to *fix* things wouldn't allow him to let the puzzle alone. "Miss Fairweather said demons tend to keep to familiar ground."

"An' the Jewish folks in this town are a tight-knit bunch. There ain't very many of 'em, so they take care of each other. Same as the Irish and the blacks, but you don't hear so much about the Jews stealin, or loiterin, or gettin hauled in drunk. Or hackin up their kids with axes, for that matter."

"So you're thinkin such lofty and do-gooder behavior might stick in a demon's craw?"

"Or maybe they're easy pickin's. Like a snapping turtle in a barrel full o' minnows. An' maybe, the barrel ain't big enough to satisfy it anymore."

Trace chewed that over for a minute. "You think it's gettin stronger."

"Ayup."

"So where's Danny Levy fit in?"

"I ast myself the same question last night. Cuz clearly that kid wasn't sayin everything he knew, and a man with a dead brother and a pretend name has somethin to hide. So, while you were sleepin it off in the drunk tank, I went round to the Roth Funeral Home and had a chat with their parlormaid."

"Huh," Trace said. "And was she young, pretty, and colored?"

Boz grinned. "I'd say that was a fair description of Miss Deirdre."

"And what did Miss Deirdre have to say, that can be repeated in polite company?"

"That young Mr. Roth at the funeral home is good friends with Mr. Levy, and ever since Mr. Levy's brother died the two of them have been up to some mighty bad juju."

THE ROTHS' PARLORMAID had told Boz that Mr. Levy liked to come by and study with Mr. Roth after supper, them being of the same age and attending the same school, before Mr. Levy dropped out to support himself after the death of his brother. It was only the past few months,

Miss Deirdre said, that their after-supper meetings had turned sinister. The parlormaid had heard strange chanting, seen them packing and unpacking bits of clay, hair, feathers, gunpowder, and iron filings—all ingredients well known, to a girl from Mississippi, as ingredients in Black Magic. Once she had cleaned up blood off the floor. Very little, as if from a cut finger, but blood all the same.

Miss Deirdre let Trace and Boz into the house through the kitchen, just after seven in the evening. Mr. and Mrs. Roth were out visiting friends, she said, and the young misters were alone in the back laying-out room.

"Been there about half an hour," Deirdre said through disapproving lips. She had big pansy-brown eyes and a voice like dark honey. "Tole me to go away and close the door, not to bring 'em coffee or nothin. Mr. Levy brought more of his *photographs* with him." A grimace over the word made it sound sinister.

Trace and Boz exchanged glances. They had already discussed what Daniel Levy might be doing with those pictures he took—whether, for instance, he might be capturing the souls of the dead, the way the Indians suspected white men of doing with their cameras. Or taking them as trophies, instead of scalps.

Deirdre led them into the back servants' hall and pointed to a door at the end. "It ain't locked," she said. "Don't be breakin anything in there, or I'm in for it."

"Much obliged, Miss Deirdre." Boz gave her a melting look.

The girl tossed her head. "Oh, go on," she said, but there was a gleam of pleasure in her eye.

Trace waited until she was out of sight before laying a hand on the knob. He opened it quietly but not too slowly, the way Deirdre might if she had to enter unobtrusively. As he had hoped, the two young men were bent over their work, backs to the door. Danny Levy was reading aloud in Hebrew.

Boz slipped into the room behind him and Trace closed the door.

"Deidre, I told you we didn't want any—" The Roth boy turned around and squawked in alarm. "Who are you?"

Danny Levy twisted, a book in one hand and a smoldering twig in the other. He yelped and fell back against the table. "It's them—they're the ones—" He shook the smoking bundle of brush at them and proclaimed in Hebrew.

Trace advanced on them, digging in his pocket for the red pepper.

The Roth boy backed away behind Danny, his hands linked together into a lump of knuckles, which he shook at Trace.

Trace threw the pepper at them. They flinched and Danny waved the smelly fagot menacingly.

"Ana becho'ach," he sang in a high, ululating voice. "G'dulat yemincha, tatir tz'rura!"

He threw the bundle at Trace. It struck him in the chest and fell to the floor. Trace noticed that the carpet had been rolled back, and there was a circle drawn on the boards, surrounding the table where the boys worked.

"Is it working?" the Roth boy asked frantically.

"It can't cross over the circle," Danny Levy said. "Get the bowl and the candle."

"Are you boys trying to *exorcise* me?" Trace demanded.

ONCE TRACE GOT the boys calmed down enough to believe he wasn't a demon—and got Boz to quit laughing like a damn coyote—Solomon Roth rang for Deirdre to bring them all coffee and they sat down to trade stories.

Danny Levy looked like he hadn't slept in days. "I haven't been back to the print shop since you saw me there Wednesday. It drove me out. Or rather, Mr. Avery drove me out with a fire iron. I think it rearranged the type he was setting. That's how it possesses people—it makes messages to them with the ink."

"We know," Boz said.

Trace related the story of the boarding-house notice with the bad message on it. Danny started shaking his head halfway through. "When you showed up here I thought you were possessed, too. It *knows* I'm trying to trap it. And I guess it knows you are, too. I printed those notices myself, but I promise you, that type said nothing about you shooting anybody before I ran it through the press."

"Which press?" Trace asked. "If it's just in the machine, maybe we could destroy it."

"I thought of that, but I've taken apart every piece of both those presses in the last five months. I've purified, prayed over, replaced, done everything but burn the place down—"

"Maybe we should do that," Boz said.

Danny turned as green as cheese. "I tried that, too. I went there one night when I knew Mr. Avery wouldn't be there. I figured I could make it look like some sparks jumped out of the stove—there's so much paper and kerosene sitting around anyway. Next thing I knew I was pouring kerosene on myself. If Sol hadn't been standing watch I'd be dead, too."

"He was sick for days," Sol said. "It got all down his clothes."

"And I think," Danny said, "that's what happened to my brother. I think he tried to stop it, and it made him kill himself."

"Did he say anything to you about the demon before he died?"

Danny drew a short, hard breath. "He said he'd made a deal . . . to make the *Carondelet Citizen* the biggest paper in St. Louis." He looked Trace in the eye. "My brother wasn't the most righteous of fellows, Mr. Tracy. Our father said he was always looking for the quick way to do things."

"So how did you learn there was a demon in the shop?"

"I went to Mr. Avery first because I needed the job, and I knew a bit about the business. My father was a bookbinder. But as soon as I set foot in the place, I knew."

"How?" Trace asked.

"A feeling of evil," Danny said bluntly.

"Describe it to me."

"Cold. Stabbing into you. Like it wants to eat you and fu—er, fornicate with you at the same time. Like all the bad habits you ever had, all the wicked desires you'd never—" Danny shivered. "All these months, every time I was in there, I could feel it watching me. I don't think it could get to me directly, because I always wore this." He touched the star around his neck. "But it was always *whispering* to me. And watching the customers. That was how it picked new victims. People who came into the office for printing, or ads."

"And you're tryin to stop it," Boz said. "That's what the sage and the white wax is for, right? Voudou, for bindin evil spirits."

The boys looked sheepishly at each other. "We were running out of ideas," Danny admitted.

"It was Deirdre gave us the idea," Sol said. "She'd sprinkle salt in the doorway to keep out evil. Said her grandmother swore by it."

"And I had an old dybbuk bowl belonged to *my* grandmother," Danny added.

"So you just took a pinch of hoodoo from everybody," Boz said.

"Not as much as you'd think," Sol said earnestly. "The old Kabbalah texts contain a lot of writings about demons and how to banish them. Many of the principles are the same—making an image of the demon and then binding it in a vessel. And then Danny found that he could capture it in a photograph for a time—"

"Is *that* what you were doin?" Trace said, and Danny nodded. "Show me."

Danny fetched a stack of prints from under the bench. They were all about the size of a hand, and the contrast wasn't great, but Trace recognized the body of Judd Herschel as he'd seen it two days ago. There were strange white blotches, in the shape of tears or tadpoles, leaking from the face.

"They show up white on the photograph," Trace said, half to himself.

"You can see them, can't you?" Danny said. "I mean, you saw them on the body that day."

Trace nodded. "Do you?"

Danny shook his head. "Only through the camera. But sometimes in the shop, I've seen things, at the corner of my eye. It's getting worse, the longer I'm there. Sometimes I feel as if the platen press is waiting for me to slip, to get my hand or my head in there . . ." He spread out several more prints, of the pressroom. They were dark, having been taken indoors, but there was a strange cloudy white aura in all of them—around the iron joints of the job press, hovering over the longer cylinder press, clotting on the type in the cases.

"It's *everywhere*," Boz said.

"In all the empty spaces," Trace agreed. "So when you capture it in the image, does it hold it for a while?"

"At first, it did," Danny said. "These are the first pictures I took, when I was trying to see what I couldn't see with my eyes. Then I noticed the pictures would change if I stared at them too long. So I put them in a box, with some scrolls and white sage, and buried them. Things were quiet for a month or so, but then I guess it got out. I tried it a few more times, but every time it escaped faster and came back stronger."

"Have you tried to exorcise it?" Trace asked.

The two young men looked at each other.

"We don't know how, exactly," Sol said. "The texts that describe actual exorcisms are . . . well, Rabbi Ernst says they're not for foolish boys."

"*If* he even has them," Danny said. "He says they're deep mysteries that we're not ready for."

"Supposin you told him there was a demon in the print shop?" Boz said, half-seriously.

Danny's mouth soured. "I *told* him I thought there was an evil spirit in the place. He said it was the influence of worldly things and I should be spending more time on my Torah."

That speech sounded familiar to Trace, excepting the *Torah* part. Meanwhile this talk of mysteries and Hebrew had jogged his memory. He felt in his pockets and fetched out the creased page of Miss Fairweather's instructions. "Take a look at this. Does that mean anything to you?"

Sol craned his neck, then grabbed for it. "This is Kabbalah! Where'd you get this?"

"Can you read it?"

"Yes!" Sol's lips moved as he felt his way through the archaic words. "I've been looking for this rite for weeks!" He spread the page on the table so Danny could see it too, and read aloud, " 'Sprinkle salt or ash or earth into the vessel . . .' Did we bring that graveyard dirt?"

"Here." Trace threw his packets of salt and mummy on the table. "Use that."

" 'Make a trail of blood leading to the vessel,' " Sol muttered, still reading, " 'and half-fill with blood, and surround with lights to draw the spirit . . .' "

"Can you get us into the print shop?" Trace said to Danny.

"Sure," Danny said. "At least I got a key. But Mr. Avery will be working there and he may come after us with a fire iron."

"I reckon *I* can handle Mr. Avery," Boz said. "And no offense, Trace, but are you *sure* you wanna try this again?"

"Yup," Trace said.

"Just cuz you got lucky once—"

Danny and Sol looked at Trace in some surprise. "You've done this before?" Sol said.

In answer, Trace drew the wax-sealed whiskey bottle from his vest pocket. He hadn't dared leave it behind in the boarding-room.

Danny leaned close to the bottle and its clotted-looking contents. "What *is* that?"

"That's the demon I bottled last night," Trace said. "Why'n't you show me this dybbuk bowl of your grandmother's?"

CHAPTER FIFTEEN

Trace and Boż marched through the front door of the *Carondelet Citizen,* guns and crucifixes at the ready, to find the place quiet and still: a clock ticking on the wall, lamps burning warmly on the desk and counter.

Avery looked at them over his spectacles. "Office is closed, boys."

Trace walked up to him and threw a pinch of pepper at him. The old man's brows knit together. He set down the type fence, took off his spectacles and rubbed them, looking at Trace with faint contempt.

"It's not in him anymore." Danny came in with the dybbuk bowl in his hands, and Sol behind him carrying a whole parcel. "If he's looking at you like a bug, he's safe. When the demon's in him he'll come after you instead of talking."

"Mister, I'm gonna ask you to step away from the bench," Boz said. "Come stand over here," he indicated the rail that separated the customer entrance from the workspace, "and, uh—don't read anything."

Avery obeyed, without much urgency. "This is a waste of time if you think there's cash money in here. Danny should've told you that."

"Not after your money, mister," Trace said. "Just gonna have a little prayer service and then we'll be on our way." He pulled out a tangle of silver chains and tossed them to Boz. "Put one of those on him." He pointed at Avery and then at the two young Jews. "You still wearing yours?"

Danny popped his collar to show the Shield of Solomon he wore. Sol did the same.

"Good lads. Let's do this fast and get out of here."

"What is this, some kind of Jewish ceremony?" Avery asked, eyeing the pendant Boz gave him.

"Let's use the white cloth," Sol suggested, consulting his notes, "and the white sage, and the candles, and put the bowl in the middle."

Sol's notes were unclear on how exactly the bowl was supposed to work. Danny claimed it was to trap the demon; Sol argued it was more likely a place to "feed" the spirit in order to placate it, to keep it from harming people inside a dwelling. Privately, Trace reckoned whatever they got up to would hold the demon's attention long enough to let him grab it and stuff it in a bottle.

Danny unrolled a bundle of pale tallow candles and wedged them into holders. "There's a box of safety matches under the front counter there," he said to Trace.

Trace went around the rail and squatted, scanning the shelves. When he stood up again, Boz said quietly, "Trace," and nodded out the front window.

In the falling sunlight, a small parade was coming up the street: ten or twelve men with a determined slant to their walk. A larger group, mostly women, followed more slowly, but with their arms folded in that way women have when they are bolstering their menfolk to do the right thing.

Trace swore under his breath. "You think they read somethin in the paper disagreed with them?"

"I don't think they're the welcomin committee. Whatever you're doin, do it fast—I don't wanna be the darky with a gun in my hand when the neighborhood watch rolls around."

Trace locked the front door, then pointed at Avery. "Get him back behind the rail."

"Look, boys, this really is a waste of time," Avery said, but he ambled where Boz steered him, to his chair behind the type desk.

"Do you remember takin after that kid with a fire iron?" Boz asked him.

Avery looked nonplussed. "How do you know he didn't deserve it?"

"Where are we going to get the blood?" Danny asked, but abruptly his gaze shifted beyond Trace's shoulder and his mouth fell open.

Trace turned to see Rex Reynolds standing not two feet from him, as if he'd materialized behind the roller press, wearing that carrion-eating grin.

"Well, hey!" Reynolds said. "Looks like the gang's all here." The grin slipped as Trace started toward him. "Now take it easy, son—"

Trace grabbed him by the lapels and shoved him against the nearest cabinet. Things rattled and crashed inside.

"Whoa! Easy on the threads, there, young'un—"

"And here *you* are," Trace said, "come to feed off the trouble you stirred up."

Reynolds's mocking grin narrowed to something darker, more menacing. His eyes lit with sparks of red in their depths, and Trace felt the hairs on his neck stand up as the power in his brain came suddenly awake, throwing up a shield between himself and the reporter.

"Ah," Reynolds said quietly. "Getting smarter, are you?"

Avery got up from his chair. "I told you not to come in here again, mister."

Reynolds shook off Trace's hands and twitched his tweed back into place. "What kind of welcome is this? I thought I was bein' plumb considerate to come down here and tell you there was a mob on its way."

"Why?" Trace demanded. "What did you write about us?"

At that moment there was a loud banging on the front door. "Avery!" a voice bellowed. "We know you're in there! We wanna talk to you!"

"There's a rumor going around that the proprietors of this print shop are engaged in devil worship." Reynolds eyed the apparatus on the table. "So you might wanna wrap up your revival meeting before they break in here."

"Avery!" The banging became a crash, as if a boot heel had struck the door.

"You." Trace pointed at Avery. "Go out there and talk to them. Tell 'em whatever you have to, just don't let 'em in here."

Avery gave a beleaguered sigh and shambled toward the front rail. "All right, but my type isn't getting set. Don't blame me if the paper's late this week . . ."

Abruptly there was a crash and a bang from the type desk, followed by a patter of lead. The upper case had flipped upside down and fallen smack on the desk, scattering a hail of letters everywhere. The little bits of type stirred, as if in a wind, and began to align themselves in ragged rows.

"*Now* look at this mess," Avery grumbled. He bent over to the type and sank stiffly to one knee. "Every time you damn kids come in here, stuff starts flying off the walls. You whippersnappers think I've got nothing better to do than clean up after your tricks . . ." Abruptly he went still, hunched over the type, head hanging down. "'You will all die,'" he read in a hollow voice. "'I am born of the shadows and the hearts of men—'"

The lamps in the room dimmed noticeably. A moment later there was a scattered exclamation from the crowd outside. Trace glanced through the window and saw there were more men than before, some of them bearing torches. Then he spotted the silver star lying abandoned beside Avery's chair. "Wait—!"

"'Four men were killed,'" Avery intoned, "'when a mob attacked a local newspaper office—'"

Boz took a long step forward and kicked at the spread of letters. They went scattering, and Avery slumped to one side like a rag doll. His mouth and eyes were slack, empty.

A sound like angry bees began to build in the room. A cloud of ink lifted off every surface in the shop, rose into the air like black fog. It coalesced into a whirling funnel which swept across the room and toward the front door. There was a rattle and thunder as the door trembled, and the black cloud sucked through the mail slot, the transom, the keyhole.

The crowd outside fell ominously silent.

Then Boz said, "What are y'all *waitin* for? Do the damn exorcism!"

A cry went up from the crowd outside, and footsteps pounded onto the sidewalk, crowding the building. Something crashed through the plate glass window at the front. The men inside all crouched slightly, eyes following the brick as it skittered across the floor and struck the rail.

"Blood! Now!" Trace bawled at Danny and Sol. "Get to reading!"

Danny popped open his cuff and flicked out a jackknife. He held his arm over the bowl and applied the point of the blade to the back of his hand. Blood spurted and he turned his fist down over the bowl so the flow dripped off his knuckles. Trace grabbed the knife from him and cut the back of his own hand, adding to the pool in the bowl. Sol began to read, gabbling the words in a gutteral sing-song.

Boz, showing as usual more sense than anyone else, extinguished the lamps on the desk, then picked up the spilled type drawer from the floor. Holding it as a shield before his body, he hopped the customer rail and propped the drawer against the broken window. He snuffed the two lanterns on the front counter, darkening the front of the store and giving Trace a clear view of the mob outside for the first time. He caught a glimpse of torches and long gun barrels. Boz snaked out an arm to pull the wooden shutter nearest the desk, but as soon as he did a shotgun blast took out most of the shutter and the window. Danny and Sol cried out in alarm, and Boz dropped flat to the floor.

"You all right?" Trace demanded, from his own crouching position.

Boz rolled to one elbow and fired three quick shots through the hole in the window. Screams from outside. He knocked the shutter closed and dived over the rail to the back of the room.

"There's more of 'em," he said through his teeth. The sleeve of his shirt was turning dark and shiny.

"You're hit!"

"It ain't much," Boz insisted, but Trace grabbed the sleeve and tore it, and felt his heart start up again when he saw it was only glass cuts, not the raw meat of a buckshot wound.

Suddenly Danny yelled. Trace turned to see Avery advancing on the boys with the fire poker. Sol raised his hands, eyes wide, chanting frantically, and Avery laid the iron across his temple.

It made a sound like splitting kindling. Sol dropped like a feather pillow. Avery stepped over him, his drooling, vacant grin now fixed on Danny. He raised the iron for another stroke, but Danny grabbed for the poker and Trace seized Avery from behind.

It should have been no contest—Trace's size and Danny's youth against the old man—but the strength of the demon was incredible. It twisted the poker, smacking Danny across the ear with the butt of it. Then it stabbed back at Trace, who dodged and fell against the table.

Avery grinned, black slime oozing between his teeth. He raised the poker over his head and Trace stepped inside the swing, caught the old man around the chest and felt the poker fall past his arm, smashing the dybbuk bowl into smithereens.

"No!" Danny cried.

Now Trace was mad. He drove one fist into Avery's gut, felt the lungs give way with a bugle of escaping air, and punched the man in the jaw. Avery went down without further complaint. Trace swept his arm across the debris on the table, hurtling down broken crockery, ash, and salt. Avery writhed and howled, and Trace saw the black tadpoles oozing from the man's mouth and ears, trying to get away.

Danny dropped to Sol's side, hands fluttering around his friend's head. Sol's eyes were open and Trace could see from where he stood there was no hope. He snatched the scroll from the floor and picked up Danny by the scruff of the neck. "He's gone. You read."

"He's dead!"

"We're all gonna be if you don't read the goddamn ritual!"

Danny's eyes flickered wildly over the ruins of the table. "But the bowl—"

"Never mind the bowl! I'll find something else. Start reading!"

Danny gulped and began to read. " 'By all the holy names of the angels! I beseech you in this circle to tell me the name of the evil spirit herein! I beseech you Michael, Gabriel, Shuviel . . .' "

While Danny read the endless list of names, Trace ransacked the shelves below the customer counter, and then the cabinet against the wall, searching for an empty bottle or jar with a lid. He found papers, wooden boxes, broken type, broken clamps, tins full of lead bits, pencils, pens without nibs, and inkwells without stoppers. There was a battered cracker tin with a broken hinge. A couple of patent medicine bottles with the corks permanently hardened within.

"'Ahadriel, Yechutriel . . .'"

An idea occurred to him. He moved around the corner to the editor's type desk and yanked open the bottom drawer. Sure enough, there was a half-full bottle of whiskey wedged in between a collection of wooden spacer blocks.

Trace yanked it out, pulled the cork, and poured the contents onto the floor. The sweet sting of whiskey burned his nostrils. His mind flashed briefly on that other bottle, in the jail cell, and its foul contents, and how it had been delivered to him. He glanced around, knowing as he did that Reynolds had vanished. Again.

"'Zumtiel, Zumtziel . . .'"

The sound of gunfire outside made him tense, turn toward the front. Boz had wedged himself into the corner beside the broken window, peering out in the dark, gun in hand but pointed down. The crowd outside was screaming, and by the sound of it, scattering.

"Police are here!" Boz reported.

"Well, thank God for small favors," Trace muttered. The sounds of riot, screams and shouts, hoofbeats and police whistles wafted in from the street.

"'All you who were made on the eve of the Shabbat, tell me his name!'" Danny cried.

A hush fell over the room. There was a feeling of uplift, as though the air was sucked up in a vast inhalation.

Ergoth, said a voice near Trace's ears. It was thick and whispery, like the wind through rotten leaves. *Son of Mirsoggh and of Mygaroth.*

Big-eyed, Danny looked at Trace.

Trace looked at Boz.

"That a good thing?" Boz asked.

"That didn't happen before," Trace admitted.

Danny opened his mouth to say something, and at that moment the platen press behind him lurched to life. It shook itself and yawned, the iron knees flexing, the wide metal tongue on top opening wide. The front legs buckled and it lunged at Danny, jaws clanging together. Danny leapt away, and stumbled over Sol's inert form. He went down with a yelp and scuttled back like a crab as the machine crashed at his feet.

Trace grabbed the last candle from the table and threw it into the press's gaping maw. A great belch of flame shot up as the grease on the rollers ignited. Something screamed, like fingernails raked down the back of Trace's skull, the terror of the damned for fire.

A terrific crash took out most of the front window. A flaming barrel of tar smashed through the railing and fetched up against the long roller press. In seconds it was aflame.

Boz fired a series of quick shots through the new hole in the window, retreating as he did into the back of the shop.

"Get Avery!" Trace said to Danny. "Drag him to the back door. Make sure it's clear."

Danny obeyed, grabbing Avery's ankles and struggling manfully.

Boz holstered his right-hand pistol and cracked open the breech on the left, shucking the empty cartridges. "Is that it, then? We done?"

"About to be," Trace said. "Go clear the way for the kid."

Boz's hands never paused in their reloading. "Case you ain't noticed, the place is on fire and there's a mob comin through the front door."

"I'll be right there," Trace said. "I don't need you for this."

He could feel the thing, trapped in the nooks and crannies of the shop where it had built its nest, burning in torment and struggling to free itself. Its struggles called to that lightning-bright power in him, excited it, fed it.

In the drunk tank, he'd hardly had time to think about what he was doing; the thing had attacked him and he'd fought back. But he had known immediately *how* to fight it, just as Miss Fairweather had said. All those years of ignoring the power, pushing it down, had banked it and given him a measure of control.

Or maybe he was just doing what God had meant for him to do with it.

Trace held up the whiskey bottle and his free hand. "Ergoth!" he bellowed, using his cattle-range voice. "Son of Mirsoggh and of Mygaroth! You hear me, you sonuvabitch?"

A great wind blew through the pressroom, roaring across the flames and flinging paper into the air. Trace felt heat and icy cold swirl around him, felt the demon's impotent fury at being so addressed. "Ergoth son of Mirsoggh and of Mygaroth, I command you in God's holy name and by the names of all the angels and all your masters, *enter this vessel!*"

The roller press groaned and shuddered on its burning legs. Bits of lead type pelted Trace like hail. He shielded the whiskey bottle with his body. This thing might be limited in its powers, but it was old, and proud. It twined around him, cajoling, threatening, pleading. Trace felt for that ball of lightning in himself and let it out, a little at a time, feeding along his arms and up the back of his neck until he was sure his hair must be standing on end. He cast out with the power, let it twine through the cold dark presence of the demon, and then tightened it like a lasso. The thing squalled with fury.

"Last chance," Trace said. "Into the bottle or I let you burn."

It rushed at him, a gale force that nearly knocked the bottle from his hand. He clutched it to his chest, reeling under the impact, felt the cold stone weight of the thing punch him in the lungs and then coalesce, contained.

No sooner had he jammed the cork into place than hands landed on Trace's shoulders, dragging him backwards so he almost lost his feet. His lungs were burning, and his eyes, and he couldn't see who had hold of him, but he let himself be dragged over the threshold and down the back stoop, into the alley behind the print shop, where the sky was twinkling twilight and the air was the freshest he'd ever tasted.

He leaned into Boz's arms, stumbling to a grassy patch across the street, where Danny and Avery huddled. Danny had a blanket around his shoulders and his head in his hands, but he looked up when Trace fell to his knees. "Are you all right? Did you get it?"

Trace nodded, hacking and unable to speak. The cold of the bottle was burning his hands. He set it down, coughing, and gratefully accepted the tin cup someone held out to him.

It was Whistler. The detective dropped to a crouch in front of Trace. There were cinders of burned paper in his mutton-chops, but his pale gaze was as imperturbable as ever.

"More lightning and black smoke, I see," he said.

Trace laughed in spite of himself, and then had to cough some more.

CHAPTER SIXTEEN

On Friday morning he went to see Miss Fairweather. It was early enough he figured she'd still be abed, or at least not fit for callers, and was unsurprised when Min Chan left him to wait in the library.

He was more surprised when she swept into the room a few minutes later, wearing a loose dressing-gown and an agitated expression. "Are you all right?" she demanded. "You are unharmed?"

"Fine," he said, taken aback. "Why wouldn't I be?"

Her brows snapped down into a look that Trace recognized—that of a woman who had been up all night worrying, and now was gearing up to lay into the cause of her anxiety with the rough side of her tongue. They were all alike, he thought in amazement. Wives, nuns, mothers—and now this covetous little harpy, who had no claim on him at all. He didn't know whether to be flattered or furious.

"I understand there was a fire at the newspaper office last night," Miss Fairweather said, with jaw-clenching restraint. "One might be moved to concern for the welfare of those in one's employ."

"One might," Trace agreed. "But I doubt *you* were." He took the two corked, wax-sealed bottles from the pocket of his duster and set them on the map table.

She frowned at them, distracted from her ire. "Which is from the printer's office?"

"This one." He touched the larger bottle, the contents of which were gray, shot through with red.

"And the other is from the jail?"

"That's right." Trace picked that one up, looked at her. "Did you send me this bottle? To Four Courts? Full of laudanum?"

"Certainly not," she said indignantly. "Surely you don't think me cruel enough to tempt a recovered user with opiates."

"But you *did* know I got arrested," he said, ignoring the question of what she was capable of. "You sent your lawyer to bail me out."

"Oh, I beg your pardon. Did I violate some code of masculine self-sufficiency?"

Her sarcasm was biting. She sure had her dander up this morning.

"No ma'am," Trace said. "I'm grateful for the assistance. I guess I'm just wonderin how close an eye you're keepin on my goin's and doin's."

"Quite a close eye, these past few days. And a good thing, since you lack the basic courtesy to keep me appraised of your plans."

"Keep you—" Trace swallowed a bark of laughter. "Lady, *you're* the one with plans. I'm hangin on by the skin of my teeth, here. I got demons croppin up everywhere I turn, and this thing in my head all riled up—"

"What happened to your eye?" she asked. "That was not done last night."

"No. Boz hit me while I was possessed."

"You were *possessed*?"

Trace sighed, and relayed briefly the story of the boarding-house notice, and his arrest, and the night in the drunk tank. But she was not content with the bare bones of the story; she urged him into a seat and sent Min Chan for the coffee tray, and questioned him backward and forward until she had got it all. He was uncomfortable describing how he'd brought the power out, how he'd been unknowingly cultivating it over the years, but she grew more calm and clinical the longer he talked, and professed admiration at his resourcefulness.

"Dr. Hardinger spoke highly of your will to overcome the opium dependency," she said. "Though I don't think he understood fully how your psychic powers were aiding the process."

"Neither did I," Trace admitted. "I'm still not . . . Hold up, when did you talk to Hardinger?"

She touched the tip of her tongue to her upper lip, briefly. "Last autumn. Shortly before I moved here."

But Hardinger had been dead for sixteen years. "All right, *how*? If you don't talk to the spirits."

"I don't speak to them as *you* do. There are other ways."

Her tone was coolly superior, and Trace resented it. "Then what in blue blazes do you need me for?"

"I told you, I cannot leave this house—"

"Yeah, you said. Consumption, hysteria, neurasthenia," Trace scoffed, and Miss Fairweather's expression turned to anger.

"I assure you, it is no fashionable or trivial matter. You have seen yourself that there are predatory things in this world, and some of them are attracted to persons like yourself, with powers you don't understand. If you are half as clever as you seem, you must realize the danger of dabbling—"

"I *do* realize it. What I *don't* know is why you're so eager to feed me to those things."

Her head went back, a line of consternation appearing between her brows. "That is the third time you have implied I am either callous or careless about your well-being. Do you sincerely believe I mean you harm?"

Trace considered her—the sharp pale eyes, the too-thin arms and throat, the hollows at her temples and wrists. She looked like a ghost herself, but there was nothing weak or transparent about the will that drove her. "I don't think it would suit your purpose."

"Then forgive me for presuming, Mr. Tracy, but I have inferred, during this meeting, that *you* are not displeased with the developments of the past week. Indeed my first impression when you walked in an hour ago was that you appear quite . . . *virile* today, unlike your usual melancholy self."

Trace shook his head in amazement. "How do you *know*? You say you don't have powers like mine—How did you know the spirits had quieted down around me, since Sikeston? How'd you know I had it in me, to . . . That exorcism you wrote out for me—do those words mean anything at all? Or are they just Texas courage?"

"Texas courage? I'm not familiar with—"

"Snake oil. Somethin to make me brave enough to take a dare."

"You have a *talent,* Mr. Tracy," Miss Fairweather said, exasperated. "A very *large* talent, I suspect, but you have been keeping it suppressed for years and years. I thought you might be reassured to know that others before you have used such talents in doing the work of your God."

"The work of God," Trace agreed, and got to his feet. "Not the work of *you*."

She went very still. She slid a careful look up at him, from under her lashes. "I see no reason why the two must be exclusive. You wish to understand your power. I can supply you with opportunities to use it. And *knowledge,* Mr. Tracy. I may not possess your gifts, but I have known others who did. Think of the good work we might accomplish together."

She was cleverer than most women. No sentiment or tears or appeals to his sense of chivalry. And yet her fingers were clutching the arms of the chair so tightly the knuckles were white.

"Let us not be tedious," she said coldly, after a moment when he didn't answer. "Either accept my offer or take yourself off. I will not waste time wondering when you will next come begging for my help."

And you won't beg at all, he thought. He could almost admire her for that. "If I agree to work for you, there's got to be enough work for Boz, too. And regular-like. He doesn't like sittin around idle and neither do I."

"How much would you normally earn, in a season on the trail?"

Trace told her what they charged to outfit and lead a wagon train to Montana and she nodded immediately.

"I will pay you that *now,* as a retainer," she said, her shoulders relaxing a fraction. "And a per diem of ten dollars for each day that you are actually on assignment for me. In return I ask that you check with Mr. Jameson daily for messages, and call upon me the same day that I summon you."

"Shouldn't be a problem."

"Would you like to visit my solicitor, to draw up a contract?"

"No, I'll take a handshake on it."

She put her small hand into his as she rose to her feet, but she staggered a little when her chair caught on the rug. Trace lifted it with the other hand and moved it out of her way.

"Thank you." Miss Fairweather looked up at him. "I *do* value your assistance, Mr. Tracy. Aside from your psychic powers, I believe you are an honorable and intelligent man. I should not like to search for your replacement."

Trace bent forward slightly, using his height as he seldom did, to subtly intimidate. But she did not appear cowed. She looked . . . intrigued. She was not, to his mind, a handsome woman, but there was something compelling about being seen so clearly, and so openly admired. Her pale eyes seemed to see straight into him. And she was still clasping his hand.

"You know what it's like, don't you?" he said, almost against his will. "The power."

She knew she had him, then. He could see it in her eyes.

"Oh yes," she said softly. "Delicious, is it not?"

SOLOMON ROTH HAD been buried the Friday before, but Danny Levy was still red-eyed and mournful when he dropped by Jameson's store Monday morning. Jameson had gotten in a couple hundred bushels of seed on Saturday, and every farmer in the county was coming by for his share of it. Boz counted and loaded wagons and relayed the numbers to Trace, who jotted down the tally for Jameson's books.

Danny was pressed and spit-shined, with a skullcap on his head and his books under his arm.

"You're a little far downtown for school, ain't you?" Trace said, shaking his hand.

"On my way," Danny said. "Came to say . . . well. You know."

"Yeah. Sorry about your friend. And your job."

"I still got my camera," Danny said, with a quirk of a smile. "I think I'll open a studio."

"Better put your studies first," Trace said. "I left seminary when I was about your age, and look how I turned out."

The smile turned into a grin, but it quickly faded. "Thanks. For not thinking I was crazy."

Boz came up then, and Danny shook his hand, as well. There wasn't much to say, but they said it, and then Danny Levy took himself off.

"He's a good kid," Boz said.

"Yep," Trace agreed.

"Pure as the driven snow," said a nasal voice on the stoop above them. "Sweet as honey on the vine. Not like you two sour old campaigners, eh?"

"What the hell d'you want?" Boz said.

"Take it easy, Sambo. I'm just here to settle accounts." Reynolds slapped a folded copy of the *Times* against his palm. "Seeing as how you rid me of the competition and all." He sailed the paper at Trace, who caught it. "Right there at the top."

ANNA HERSCHEL INNOCENT—
FATHER SUFFERED BRAIN TUMOR

New information brought to light at the inquest of Miss Anna Herschel has proven conclusively that the young woman is innocent of the murders of her parents and sister. An autopsy of Judd Herschel revealed an abnormal growth in the front of the brain. According to expert medical testimony, pressure from the tumor upon the brain could produce sudden violent rages, such as Miss Herschel described her father exhibiting on the night of the murders.

A judge has declared Miss Herschel innocent of all charges.

"Is this true?" Trace demanded.

"Near enough," Reynolds said. "That's what you might call the useful parts of the truth, which is all people really want to hear, anyway. So, I reckon that makes us square. Unless of course you change your

mind about telling me *your* story. Folks can't get enough of this Spiritualist pap. Makes 'em think they're not all bound for Hell after all."

"Not a chance," Trace said. "I gotta live in this town, you know. I
see a word in the *Times* or any other paper sounds like a story about
me, I'll know who to come lookin for."

Reynolds grinned, viciously. "I reckon you might *try.* You're pretty
good, son. You might manage to run me down . . . but you'd wish you
hadn't."

"I already bottled two demons this week," Trace reminded him.

"True." Reynolds clacked his sharp-looking teeth. "But you don't
see me squatting in a printing press, do you?" He winked, slicked a
finger along the brim of his hat, and sidestepped through the back
door of Jameson's shop. "Be seeing you, young'un."

END OF THE LINE

CHAPTER SEVENTEEN

The couple who came into the store looked harmless enough, but there was something purposeful in their smiling, serene cheer that put Trace on his guard.

Jameson had gone to visit with his banker, so Trace had volunteered to mind the store for a couple hours, during the lull between sunup deliveries and midday rush. He'd been using the time to write to Emma. She sent him weekly letters, written on Sundays at the nuns' direction, full of schoolgirl chatter and usually voicing hope that he would visit soon. He tried to get around to see her every couple of weeks when he was in town, but the nuns frowned on more frequent visits.

Lately he'd been wondering if it was time to take her out of that school. Emma was the product of his father's second marriage, born while Trace was away recuperating from the war, but he'd had the care of her since she was seven. She was fifteen now, old enough she ought to spend some time out of the convent and learn about the world, and he didn't trust anyone else to teach her.

But if he meant to have Emma live with him, he'd have to know his curse was under control. And a few ghost-free weeks were hardly conclusive evidence. All the same, he found himself writing about his new job in town, and how he hoped it would lead to brighter prospects for both of them. And then frowning at the words, wondering if he was planting expectations that would never come to fruition.

Then the missionary couple came in, smiling and radiating aggressive benevolence.

"Pardon me," the man said. He was about fifty, with bright blue eyes and a round, sturdy look about him, like a little Mexican burro. "Is Mr. Jameson about?"

"He's out for a bit," Trace said. "Can I help you?"

"Well, I don't know." The man drew out a folded letter that bore Trace's own inelegant handwriting. "I was supposed to arrange a meeting with a Mr. Tracy, but I'm afraid I don't have his direction. Mr. Jameson had been our intermediary—"

"I'm Jake Tracy. Are you Kingsley?"

"Yes! Martin Kingsley." The Baptist put out his hand, and Trace shook it. "This is my sister, Miss Eliza Kingsley."

"Ma'am," Trace said.

"How do you do, Mr. Tracy." Miss Eliza had a lovely smile, warm and gracious, as if he were just the person she'd hoped to meet that day. Trace gave her a longer look: she was about his age, with the handsome oval face of a classical Madonna. There was a single streak of silver in her dark hair, in rebellious contrast to her placid demeanor.

"The thing is, Mr. Tracy," Kingsley rocked from heel to toe as he spoke, as if he had too much energy to remain still for long, "—and I hate to do this to you, after I told Mr. Jameson we'd be needing your services—but we've just this week received a love donation, from a sister in faith. She had her servant deliver it specially, because she's in poor health and can't travel. She purchased railway tickets for the entire party and our cargo, and even offered a generous portion for building our church in the wilderness—"

It was the words *in poor health* that roused Trace's suspicions. "This servant—was he Chinese, speaks real good English?"

"Why yes," Kingsley said. "Do you know Sister Fairweather?"

Why was he surprised? Was he surprised? No, but he was madly curious as to what her game might be. "As a matter of fact, I just took a job with her myself. In fact I might've mentioned I had some other folks waitin to hear back from me about a guide job, so I'm not surprised if she took it on herself to pay your way. That's just the kind of thing she'd do."

Kingsley beamed. "Well! Isn't it Providential how these things work out? One good soul doing a turn for another, and all for the grace of God!"

"Amen," Trace said solemnly, and was interested to see a twist of amusement on Miss Eliza's lips. She lowered her gaze and converted the smirk into a serene smile.

"Well, I won't keep you then," Kingsley said. "I'm just relieved to know you haven't been put in a state of privation by our change of plans. And I did take all of your cautions about rail travel into account. In fact I have some misgivings about acquiring supplies, once we reach Idaho, and I had half-hoped you might be persuaded to accompany us . . ."

Kingsley went on talking, but his voice grew dim in Trace's ears: at the word *Idaho* it was as if a cold fog had swarmed in around him, blotting out the comfortable clutter of Jameson's store, and the air gone thin, chill, like the atmosphere in the mountains. Darkness filled his senses, and fire, and the sounds of people screaming and the snarling of beasts, and Kingsley's face contorted before him, mouth full of blood—

Trace gripped the edge of the counter and bowed from the waist. He gave his head a violent shake, and the screaming and the fog cleared, let him go.

"Are you all right, Mr. Tracy?" Miss Eliza's voice was alarmed.

"Oh dear," Kingsley said. "Did I say something untoward? But then I am taking up far too much of your time—"

"No, no," Trace said. "Don't mind me. Just remembered . . . um, old battle memories. What route did you say you were takin, to Idaho?"

TRACE HAD NEVER before called at Miss Fairweather's house without being summoned, so he wasn't sure what kind of reception to expect, but Min Chan didn't bat an eye. He ushered Trace inside and led him up to the laboratory in the attic.

Miss Fairweather was wiping her hands on a towel as he breached the floor of the workroom, brows knit as she looked him over. She wore a bespeckled apron, and her sleeves were rolled up. He glanced at the table behind her; there was something bloody and flayed, stretched out in a cork-lined tray.

"You are quite well?" she asked, once the courtesies were exchanged. "No importunate spirits loitering about, no demon possessions?"

"No ma'am. Been pretty quiet, last couple weeks."

"No . . . unfamiliar persons attempting to make your acquaintance? Ingratiating themselves with you or Mr. Bosley?"

"Just the opposite. Had some people runnin away from my company."

"I beg your pardon?"

"I met with a man named Kingsley today," Trace said, watching her face.

"Oh?" Miss Fairweather's brows lifted politely. He would have suspected nothing except her pale eyes riveted to his—suddenly cool, and focused.

"Yes ma'am. In fact I'd been tryin to meet up with him for a couple weeks, but we kept missin each other." Trace found himself lapsing into the exaggerated drawl he used around other working men, in deliberate challenge to her well-spoken mendacity. "Kingsley's a missionary, wanted to hire me an' Boz to lead his people out to Montana. But when I saw him today, he tells me some wealthy spinster lady gave him a big donation to take his congregation by train, instead."

"How fortunate for them," Miss Fairweather said, as if butter wouldn't melt in her mouth. "Especially since you were already engaged elsewhere."

"Yes ma'am, I told them that. But then a strange thing happened. As he was tellin me the route they planned to take, I got this vision of Kingsley bloody and dyin, and somethin . . . attacking them, up there in the mountains." Trace felt his throat and chest tighten, as his annoyance with her was blotted out by a larger concern for the Baptists—and a certain exhilaration at what he had seen. "Somethin bad's gonna happen out there. I saw it. I *know* it."

She stared at him, big-eyed, and then inhaled swiftly. "You had a premonition." Her body swayed toward him, and for a heartbeat he thought she was going to throw her arms around him, but she controlled herself, pressing her hands beneath her bosom. "This is the first time? How long did it last? How clear was it?"

"Pretty clear," Trace said, as she spun away and crossed to the nearest trestle table. "I mean I couldn't see the terrain, it was dark, but it *felt* like the Rockies, the air and the sky looked like mountain country. And there was somethin attackin people, like animals—"

He broke off as he got close enough to see the map spread on the table, and her markings on it: long lines of railways, and an erratic march of red X's from Utah up into Idaho, to a point just south of the continental divide. Trace knew the area fairly well; he'd spent several years working cattle in southern Wyoming before his marriage.

"This is the proposed path of the Utah and Northern railway to Butte, Montana." Miss Fairweather's thin white finger tapped the map. "In the past five weeks there have been several mauling deaths in the workers' camps. The railroad managers blame it on Indians or wild animals, but the attacks are too random for the former, too well organized for the latter."

She thrust a newspaper toward him. The headline read ANIMAL ATTACKS THREATEN RAILROAD'S PROGRESS.

"According to this, the Chinese laborers have a superstitious fear of whatever is causing the attacks. The reporter was familiar enough with their language and customs to extract the term 'keung-si' from a survivor." She pursed her lips. "It means 'hopping corpse.'"

"Which means what, exactly?"

"I cannot say what, exactly, it means in this context. I have spent the last several days monitoring spirit activity in that area, and it does appear something supernatural is haunting that railway camp. But I don't believe the attacks are the result of demonic influence. I believe there is something corporeal hunting the workers."

"A hopping corpse?" Trace said dubiously.

"If one digs deeply enough into superstition and folklore, one tends to find kernels of truth. I believe your Christian mythology is full of stories about corpses being preserved, appearing lifelike long after death?"

"Those were *saints*."

"And they are not the only examples. Nearly every culture in the world has a myth about deceased persons returning to prey on the living. Some drink the blood of their kin. Others suck out their souls. And in every system of primitive magic, there are myriad rituals for deterring such creatures." She pulled toward her a stack of papers and pamphlets. "Only in so-called civilized areas, where our cities are increasingly well-lit, do we feel safe enough to make monsters into figures of comedy and entertainment."

The booklet she held out to him was yellowing and brittle. It showed a man in a greatcoat, the capes ruffled like crow's feathers, his face distorted in an animal grin as he menaced the young lady beside him. *Varney the Vampyre* was the title.

"A case in point," Miss Fairweather said. "That particular drivel was serialized for three years, widely read by the masses in London."

Trace flipped through the little book. The illustrations were lurid. "So what're you doin with it?"

"Merely being thorough. I have an interest in rare diseases, for reasons you might deduce—particularly those that resemble anemia, or malnutrition. In many cases a simple change of diet will effect a cure, but until one understands the missing nutrient, such an illness might well appear to be the result of evil spirits. Or hopping corpses."

Trace had the feeling she was hopping around the subject herself. "So you're interested in whatever's out there attackin the workers, because you think it's related to your . . . uh, condition?"

She hesitated. "Not directly related, no. However, my own illness has a mystical component, and there are precious few references in the current medical journals. I must therefore chase down every possible lead."

Aha, Trace thought. "So you were thinkin to send me out there, to fetch you back a specimen."

"No!" Miss Fairweather looked at him in alarm, and actually laid a hand on his sleeve, before jerking it back as if he were too hot to touch. "No, I do *not* advise you to go anywhere near that area or those creatures. I would not have you risk yourself like that, whatever you may think of me."

"But you don't mind sendin the *Baptists* out there to get slaughtered?"

"I did not *send* them anywhere. I only provided the financial means to go by rail. They chose the route, and it appears they chose poorly."

"But if you knew there was somethin nasty out there—"

"I did not know, until a few days ago."

"You know *now,*" Trace said.

That stopped her cold. She stared at him, big-eyed. "Is that why you came up here? To get my sanction on some foolish heroic venture?"

"Well I hadn't thought of it that way, but I *did* think maybe you had some insight on why I had this vision. And come to find out, you know more than you let on . . . as usual."

She licked her lips. "Mr. Tracy, I do not hold back information merely to be perverse. There are things . . . I believe you would find your ideologies incompatible with certain truths—"

"If that means I won't stand by knowin those people are ridin into danger, you're right. And what was that you told me a couple weeks ago, about the good work we could do together?"

Miss Fairweather's jaw clenched, and Trace felt a glint of satisfaction. He could see her struggling with herself—her plans for him, whatever they were, versus his unexpected volition.

"You are too valuable," she said, her voice strained. "I have been searching for someone—for a psychic like you, for so long . . ."

That needy—no, *hungry* look was back in her face. The intensity of it repelled him. It was in his nature to want to help people when he could, but the darkness in her was so vast and single-minded, he thought it might consume him, if he let himself get drawn into it.

"Well, I'm goin." It seemed safer, ironically. "So if you know somethin that can help, best hand it over now."

TRACE WAITED UNTIL noon to go see Boz at the slaughter yards. When the skinners and bung-hole men broke for dinner, Trace skirted the sea of blood and shit and sawdust, until he spied his partner's long lean frame at the edge of the kill-pits. Boz had leaned his sledgehammer against a rail of the cattle-chute, and was using the edge of one hand to slick some of the blood and brains from his face.

"Here," Trace said, holding out his handkerchief over the rail.

Boz turned, eyed Trace in his clean black suit, took the rag and wiped the lower half of his face in one hard gummy pass. "You been up to bow to Her Worship, I take it."

It had been a little more than a week since Trace had come home and announced he was taking Miss Fairweather's retainer. Boz had said little about it, then or since; he had merely disappeared one morning and come back that night covered in beef blood.

"Got a job at the stockyards," he'd announced: tit for tat. The stink in their rooms had been a more lingering retaliation.

"I met the Baptist this morning," Trace said now. "Kingsley."

"Oh yeah? Where's he been hidin?"

"Turns out they raised the funds to go by rail, after all."

"Good for them," Boz said, not sounding as if he meant it.

Trace chose his next words carefully. "Thing is, the route they're takin out past Ogden . . . there's been some kind of animal attacks along the line."

"What animal?"

"Dunno. Miss Fairweather thinks it's a kind of specimen she's never seen before, wants us to bring one back."

"Takes both of us to do that?"

"Might. Somethin big's been pickin off the workers. Railroad claims it's wolves. Papers blame Indians."

Boz snorted. "They always blame Indians."

"That's why I thought you'd be a help." Boz's years in the army had been spent hunting Cheyenne and Sioux in Kansas and Dakota Territory. Miss Fairweather had been adamant that he not undertake this fool's crusade without Mr. Bosley's assistance, at least, and Trace had no intention of doing so.

Boz was intrigued; Trace could tell by the way his head cocked, the deliberate far-gazing toward the horizon. And a hunting expedition to the mountains had to beat the slaughter yards all hollow.

"It's ten dollars a day, for each of us," Trace coaxed. "We'll make a hundred apiece, easy."

"You know, if *she's* interested in it, can't be somethin as simple as animals."

"You want simple, I reckon you got it, here. I'll be happy to leave you to your four bits a day."

Boz looked as if he was going to take issue, but at that moment the pit boss passed by and snapped, "Fifteen minutes for lunch, boy. No extra for standin 'round jawin.'"

Boz's face took on the non-expression he used to conceal contempt, in the interest of self-preservation. "How we gettin there?"

"Train. Take us about eight days, through Ogden. Got cash for the trip right here. And I'll *front* you four bits for a bath."

Boz gave his hands a last swipe with the handkerchief and tossed it into the bloody sawdust. "Let's go."

CHAPTER EIGHTEEN

The planks of the depot trembled under Trace's boots, as thirty tons of iron and steam shuddered and screamed to a halt along the platform. The crowd surged toward the train like cattle scenting water, but the conductor held up a hand and a clipboard, shouting orders no one could hear. Trace held back; he knew from experience the third-class car would be loaded first, as the most unruly cargo the railroad had to handle.

Boz nudged him with an elbow. "That them?"

Trace followed his line of sight down the platform, where Kingsley and his sister were driving a gaggle of drab-clad, smiling followers toward the second-class car. "That's them. Kingsley's the short bald one."

"That his wife?"

"Sister. Spinster."

Boz looked again, assessingly. "She ain't bad, for the strait-laced type."

Trace had to agree. Eliza Kingsley wore a plain, sensible dress and a plain, sensible coat, but they did fit her well. Where Kingsley was stocky and stout, Miss Eliza was round and shapely. And there was a dignified grace about her, even doing the thankless job of herding a score of well-meaning fools onto a train. She had her work cut out for her—Kingsley kept calling out platitudes and conflicting instructions, and some over-enthusiastic soul was trying to whip up a chorus of

"Onward Christian Soldiers," which only added to the general noise and chaos.

Gradually the gaggle of Baptists funneled into the car. Boz swept up his saddlebags with a stoic glance at Trace, and the two of them ambled toward the train.

The conductor punched their tickets without a word or a second glance, and they climbed aboard, bringing up the rear of the shuffle of passengers—everybody negotiating seats, juggling luggage, and the idiot in the broadcloth suit still singing battle hymns. Trace made for a pair of empty seats near the back, knowing there would be less fuss if everyone else was seated first.

It might've worked, except the man in the broadcloth suit chanced to turn in the aisle, militantly conducting his choir with both arms, and cut off mid-note in a squawk when his eye landed on Boz. "You can't be in here!"

"He's all right," Trace said, in the tone of bland nonchalance that usually could embarrass minor complainants into holding their tongues. "He's with me." He bullied the little man back in the aisle so Boz could move into the seat, but Boz stood where he was, wearing that blank expression that suggested he had nothing to do with the madness of the white folks around him.

The missionary went quite red in the face. "Young man, I can tell by your clothes you live a rough life, no doubt squandering your earnings on drink and vice, but even *you* must have some respect for the virtue of womanhood! Can you condone the mingling of an inferior race among the purity of Christian females?"

"Well I know he's a fine specimen and all, but I reckon I can hold them off him," Trace said.

This drew a horse-laugh from the gangly fellow across the aisle, and a splutter from the little missionary. But their hold-up had attracted attention from Miss Eliza, who came up behind the indignant Christian soldier.

"Brother Clark, perhaps we could let these gentlemen go about their business?" Miss Eliza said. "Mr. Tracy and his partner are respectable trail guides and we may be in need of their services when we reach Idaho."

"Sister Eliza, I have no doubt of their qualifications in the wild, but the conventions of civilization must be observed—"

"What's the matter here?" the conductor said, coming up behind Boz from the back of the car. "Take your seats, boys."

"Good sir!" Brother Clark pounced on him. "Is there not desig-nated seating for Negroes on this train?"

The conductor looked at him with dislike, and then at Boz. He jerked his chin toward the front of the train. "Smoking car is two cars forward. Or you can ride in the stock car with the drovers."

"Excuse me, but there's laws against that in this city," Trace argued. "We paid for second-class seats and this is the second-class car."

"Unless you want to *stay* in this city I suggest you find yourself a seat, son," the conductor snapped.

Miss Eliza and the gangly man tried to protest that they had seen nothing untoward in Boz's demeanor and they were quite certain he could behave himself, but Boz took the matter into his own hands. He shouldered past Brother Clark and continued toward the front of the car. Trace ground his teeth and followed, caught up to him on the balcony between the cars.

"Hey!" he said, and Boz stopped on the gangplank, one hand on the door of the emigrant car. The switchman working over the link-age below glanced up, but quickly decided it was none of his business. "Don't you take that from the likes of him. You paid for a second-class ticket—"

"Waddya gonna do, Trace?" Boz said. "You gonna fight the rail-road, the passengers, the whole world? That might make us late gettin out to Idaho, and I wouldn't count on Her Ladyship bailin you out of jail too many more times."

"Well what am I supposed to do, stand by and take it? I don't like seein you treated like that, it ain't right—" Trace broke off as the switchman finished his chore and stood upright, staring up at Trace as if to offer the full effect of his mangled torso—the dragging of the leg from the crushed pelvis, the chest pinched nearly in two when a foot had slipped, or the signal came too late, or the eye misjudged.

Trace looked away, suppressing a shudder. The spirits had been drawing close again the past few days, especially when he was dis-tracted by other things. He pushed the power down into the back of his mind, and the switchman vanished.

"What?" Boz demanded.

"Railroads," Trace said shortly. "Graveyards on wheels."

Boz inhaled and took a step forward, poked a finger in Trace's chest. "That's what *I* don't like—you flinchin at things I can't see. But if I can't do nothin about it, least I can keep my mouth shut while you deal with it." He backed up, groping for the door handle. "You picked your battle, Trace. Let me pick mine."

MARTIN KINGSLEY AND Miss Eliza both apologized to Trace about Brother Clark's behavior. And when the train stopped in St. Joseph the next morning, while Trace and Boz were grabbing biscuits and coffee at the back door of the depot kitchen, the Kingsleys sought them out, with Clark in tow, to assure them that both men were welcome to join their party in Idaho, should they find themselves in need of lodging or company. Brother Clark did his best to look penitent and forbearing, but it came out gassy.

Boz swallowed his bile and said he appreciated the hospitality. Trace concurred. The men went away, but Miss Eliza lingered a moment.

"The offer presumes, of course, that you are going to Butte," she said. "Martin assumed you were, but I don't remember you mentioning your destination, Mr. Tracy." Her eyes rested on him, warmly. "I would not, of course, pry into your business."

Boz lifted an eyebrow and became very interested in his coffee, turning discreetly away from the conversation.

"More speculation than business, ma'am," Trace said. "I'm not sure yet where we'll end up."

"Well, I hope you will consider joining us. Martin thinks highly of you, and we could use a man of your . . . ah, worldly experience. My brother means well but sometimes I think his zeal outweighs his good sense." Her lips pursed in amusement. "Now you mustn't tell him I said that."

"Your secret's safe with me, ma'am."

"Yes." Miss Eliza looked at him closely. "You're good at keeping secrets, aren't you?"

Trace smiled. "What are you, a mind-reader?"

"I used to know a man like you."

"You've got a few secrets of your own, then," he said, and she met his eyes for a brief, bold moment. Not so innocent as one might expect, he thought, and his opinion of her warmed a few degrees.

She lowered her gaze, retreating behind the serene missionary's smile. "Good morning, Mr. Tracy . . . Mr. Bosley?"

"Ma'am," Boz said, and they watched her walk off, to rejoin her flock. "Guess now you're glad I wasn't bunkin with you last night."

If only the sleeping arrangements had been quite that agreeable,

Trace thought. "I'd take you over that scarecrow across the way. Fella talks in his sleep."

"Which one's that?" Boz asked, and Trace pointed out the man who had stuck up for them the day before: gangling and concave, with ears that stuck out from his head, a nose like a lumpy potato, and skin rough as a Colorado creekbed.

Sylvane Ferris was the man's name, and he did love to talk. He had introduced himself to Trace—and everyone else in the car—as a life-long circus performer: "Ferris the Fire-Master! I don't expect you to have heard of me. I haven't performed in six years." He was between jobs at the moment, he said, and on his way to Sacramento in hopes of joining a new outfit. It was hard to imagine Ferris having any kind of charisma onstage, but he was gracious and intelligent as well as loquacious, and Trace found him curiously appealing.

By the time they reached Ogden he had figured out why.

The train was positively lousy with spirits—a dead brakeman at every exit; an old woman sitting forever silent and patient in the dining car; a black man who'd been knifed and left to bleed out on the floor of the smoking car. Three days into the journey, Trace was starting to have a hard time blocking them out. If he didn't pay attention to keeping that wall up around his thoughts, he knew they would start talking at him, pawing at him, wanting him to do things.

On the fourth day of the trip, Trace was in the smoking car, playing cards with Boz and a couple of young cowboys, when Ferris came on board. Ferris looked directly at the place where the knifed man lay, his lip curled with distaste, and made a surreptitious sidle around the invisible body before choosing a seat at Trace's elbow and asking to be dealt in. Trace tossed him five cards, meeting Ferris's eyes briefly; the scarecrow said nothing for once but the expression on his face was eloquent enough. And Trace noted the sensation in his own head— like passing a hand through a candle flame—and understood that his power, for the first time, had recognized another like himself.

It was also perhaps the first time he'd felt the power as a *part* of himself. Not some harness he carried around on his back, but something as integral and familiar as a muscle. He could remember passing through an awkward growth spurt at fourteen, feeling gawky and out of control for a while, but somewhere around his nineteenth birthday—it must've been after he'd enlisted, and saw himself in comparison to the other recruits—he'd realized he was taller and stronger than most of them, that this long lean body was *his,* and it was not a bad hand he'd been dealt, at all.

"I call," Boz said. "What you got?"

Trace laid down his cards. "Full house."

THE AIR GOT cooler and thinner as they passed into Utah, and Trace's power got pricklier with each passing mile. It wasn't just the ghosts gathering near; his curse was sending out those alarm-twinges, just as it had in the presence of Reynolds and the other demons. His dreams had turned sinister, full of weeping statues and dark, faceless monks. In one particularly lurid vision, the leathery, preserved corpses of saints and martyrs, stiff with bindings and ornamental robes, had left their sarcophagi to hop ludicrously and yet menacingly toward some dreadful purpose. Meanwhile Trace knelt before the altar, alongside his old classmates and not a few of his long-dead company mates—all of them oblivious to danger, and he unable to move or cry out a warning.

"You doin all right?" Boz asked, the first evening out of Ogden.

They were having a smoke on the balcony outside the smoking car. It was windy and loud out there, but it was the one spot on the train where there didn't seem to be a lingering ghost to muck up his psychic compass.

"We're gettin close," Trace said. "I can feel it." The words sounded vague and pompous even to himself, like something Miss Fairweather might say.

"You, ah, you got any better idea what we're lookin for?"

"No, sorry."

"Don't be sorry," Boz said. "Ain't like that woman gives you much to go on."

Trace didn't answer. He had not told Boz about the vision that had prompted this trip. There was no better source of information there, and hearing about it would just make Boz worry.

"That Miss Eliza," Boz said. "Kingsley's sister?"

As if he didn't know who she was. "Yeah?"

"Seems to have a good head on her shoulders."

"She's a good Christian woman. Even if she is a Baptist."

"Aw, when did that stop you? What about that Mrs. Robards, out to Santa Fe last season? *She* wasn't Catholic."

Trace half-grinned. "Not even sure she was a missus." The lady in question had claimed to be a widow, but he had not demanded the details. They'd had a discreet, friendly arrangement for a couple of months, and parted on amiable terms when the wagon party reached Santa Fe. "But Miss Eliza ain't the kind you dally with."

"I ain't talkin bout dallyin," Boz said, and Trace looked at him in surprise. "I'm just sayin, if you want to go on to Butte, I reckon either of us could find work out there, just as easy."

"Cripes, you must be eager to get rid of me."

"I'm just sayin, maybe it's time we move stakes. We both know we can't keep workin out of St. Louis, and you, ah, seem to be gettin a handle on this thing . . ."

If only that were true, Trace thought, but he turned the idea over in his head. For the first time in a long time, it seemed like a possibility: settling down, having a home of his own. Children, maybe.

But then his mind slipped backwards, to his last memory of Dorothea—sunken eyes half-closed, lips peeled back in the grimace of death, and the grotesque contrast of her swollen belly, a mockery of life and potential, distorting her stiffening body.

He shuddered, hard. "No, Boz. I ain't takin that chance again."

Boz was quiet for a while. When he spoke again, his voice was flat and businesslike. "We catch this killer, how you want to fetch it back to Her Worship?"

"Dunno. Figure on crossin that bridge when we come to it."

"You figure on walkin off a cliff if she points you that direction?"

Old grief and guilt made him tetchy. "I ain't out here cause she sent me, Boz."

"What, you tellin me there *ain't* any animal attackin folks?"

"Oh, there is. But she didn't want anything to do with it. Tried to talk me outta comin out here."

Boz turned his head sharply. There was an agitated quality to his next breath, but he just stared at the side of Trace's face, waiting.

"I had a vision. Of the Baptists, in danger. I went to ask her what it meant. She told me there was somethin bad out here, and to stay away from it. But it didn't seem right I should know these folks were headed for trouble, and not do somethin about it."

"Christ on a *crutch*." Boz stood back, pressing into a corner of the railing as if his partner's stupidity were catching. "D'you *wanna* die? Cuz if you do, there's quicker ways."

"No." Trace thought about it for a minute. "No, I don't think God's gonna let me off that easy."

"Shit." Boz ground out his cigar on the railing. "So now it ain't enough, bein able to control it? Now you gotta be tapped by the Almighty for some holy purpose?"

Trace swung his head from side to side, wearily. "That ain't what I'm sayin."

Boz's response was foul. He spat at the ground and went back inside.

TRACE'S PRICKLY FEELING intensified as the sun went down. Miss Eliza tried to draw him into conversation, but he found himself being short with her, almost surly. His argument with Boz had resurrected that feeling of being unclean, poisonous—set apart, like Cain. He resented Eliza Kingsley for representing what he couldn't have, and that was hardly fair to her.

Ferris seemed to sense Trace's mood, because he was unusually charming and gentle, engaging Miss Eliza's attention and leaving Trace to wallow in his brown study.

Around eight o'clock, the porters began to come around and let down the sleeping berths. Those passengers with children began the arduous rituals of putting the little ones to bed—a process that involved a lot of wailing and shushing from the back of the car. Miss Eliza said good night, and went away to her own bunk, above her brother's. Trace declined the porter's offer to let down his berth—he knew he wasn't going to sleep tonight, and if he did, he'd as soon doze upright in the seat, rather than cramped into a bunk that was head and foot too short for him.

He pulled the little *Varney the Vampyre* book from his vest pocket and doubled it inside out, to the page where Miss Fairweather had summed up her research on predatory corpses:

Commonalities~
Consmptn. of blood
Exceptional strength
Nocturnal; averse to sunlight
Diff. to kill; most often purifying methds—fire, water, pure metals/woods, medicnl garlic, salt

Not much help there. He had tried to get a description from her of what a Chinese keung-si looked like and acted like, but she had flatly refused, saying she didn't want to hamper him with any preconceived notions.

"If the spiritual signature of this creature is any indication," she'd said, "you may well encounter something that has never existed in this world before—a corruption of nature into some new . . . abomination."

Trace had looked at her hard. "What do you know that you're not tellin me?"

"Many things," Miss Fairweather said grimly. "None that would give you any comfort."

Now, Trace was aware of Ferris watching him, as the man pulled off his own coat and boots, and made ready for bed.

"If I may be so bold as to intrude, Mr. Tracy," Ferris said, "what is in that book that makes you frown so? I have seen you study it many times, but it never seems to bring you any comfort."

Trace smiled, humorlessly. "You believe in demons, Ferris?"

"Indeed I do," the other said. "In fact I have seen things—events in my own life—which might best be explained as the work of evil forces."

"What did you do?"

"I prayed. Until I thought my heart would break. And then it did break. And after that, I am ashamed to say, there was no more room in me for faith. And so I turned to . . . to darker forces, darker places inside myself, in search of answers. But there was no solace there. You know the story of Sisyphus, Mr. Tracy?" Trace nodded, and so did Ferris. "Truly, to offer hope, with no intent of fulfilling it, is the cruelest bargain imaginable."

Trace nodded again, thinking of Miss Fairweather, of that sense he'd had that getting involved with her was a bottomless pit of despair, but he couldn't put a finger on what it was about her that disturbed him so. *He* had been the one to turn up the last two jobs—though come to find out she already knew about them. Was she watching him that closely? Were they both in tune with the spirit world in such a way that they noticed the same disturbances? Or was some other force driving his choices? He knew there was something driving *her,* he just didn't know what it was, or what influence it might exert over him.

"Ferris," Trace said slowly, "do you ever think there's some . . . invisible web between folks? I ain't talkin about destiny, or God leadin our footsteps. I mean, I met two people this last month, and come to find out they met each other, maybe because of me, though I never introduced them, and somehow knowin the two of them prompted me to take this trip because of some fourth thing that involves all three of us. How can that be? How can the three of us have met because we have somethin in common that hasn't happened yet?"

Ferris appeared to be considering the question very seriously. "I do have the opinion that time operates in both directions, although most of us can only perceive it from one perspective. Perhaps . . . if you will forgive me, I have had the impression that your perceptions are broader than most?"

Trace nodded, after the barest hesitation.

"Perhaps you have the rare gift of seeing ahead. I have known a few who did, in my career. It is not an easy gift to bear. All men question their place in the world, the purpose for which they were designed. The sad truth is, most of us will only ever live a small and mundane existence." Ferris eyed Trace's face thoughtfully. "I do not think that will be your fate."

Trace wanted to ask what made him think so, but it felt like fishing for praise. "My bein on this train is no accident," he said instead, and handed the *Varney* pamphlet across the aisle. "I *did* see ahead— and I think there's somethin bad waitin for us."

Ferris looked at the little book slowly, examining Miss Fairweather's notes and then the cover. His brows drew together, his amiable face twisting in a smile of savage bitterness. "And so I know my place in this world," he said, and gave the book back to Trace.

"Beg pardon?"

"It would appear, Mr. Tracy, that I was sent here to protect *you*."

"You know what we're ridin into?" Trace said, shocked.

"I have heard rumors." Ferris's mouth was etched around with deep anger, though it was not directed at Trace. He leaned across the aisle, lowering his voice. "Tell me . . . who are the two persons you mentioned, whose future you share?"

"The Baptist, Kingsley. And a woman named Sabine Fairweather."

"Fairweather?" Ferris's brows lifted in surprise, and a series of calculations rippled across his animated features. "I have never met the lady," he said carefully. "So I cannot guess what her interest might be in these matters . . ."

"What's *your* interest?" Trace demanded, but Ferris only shook his head.

"I have even less volition in these machinations than you, my godly friend, and I am not free to speak of the forces that compel me. I will only say, I believe you are right to think another hand is guiding your steps . . . or soon will be, if my presence here is any indication."

"Somebody's keepin an eye on me, then?"

Ferris allowed a single nod, though his usually open manner was withdrawing, and Trace sensed he would not get much more out of him. "For good or ill?"

Ferris's smile twisted. "I suppose that depends upon one's perspective, does it not?"

The train whistle began to blow, making them both jump. The sound was eerie, nightmarish. It echoed off the valleys and bounced back at them, *whooo-whooo-whooo-whooo,* like a deep-voiced mechanical owl. Then a single short *whoop.*

"There's an obstruction on the tracks," Ferris said, his voice taut.

"Holy God." Trace instinctively looked toward the front of the train, but of course there was nothing to see except the bunks down and jostling . . . and Miss Eliza, standing in the aisle in her nightdress.

CHAPTER NINETEEN

Trace hurtled out of his seat and up the aisle. Miss Eliza looked up, startled, as he loomed over her. He seized her by both arms and tossed her into the lower bunk alongside Kingsley, just as there was an awful, screaming, squalling roar that started at the front of the train and progressed backward, shuddering through the car as if the tracks themselves were shaking off their burden.

Trace was sure, later, that the collision must've made one hell of a bang, when the second-class car struck the emigrant car in front of it. He just didn't remember hearing it. The back end of the car bucked like an ornery bronc and Trace was flung forward. He landed on his chin and slid down the smooth-polished length of the aisle to end up in a heap next to the wood stove.

He *did* hear the screaming then, and the tinkling of broken glass and luggage bouncing off bunks and shelves to the floor. A series of blows shook the car, accompanied by the deafening and then diminishing *BANGbangbang* of each car behind them colliding.

At last the tremors stopped. The children were wailing and no few of the adults. Trace lay where he was for a minute, gingerly checking to make sure he was still alive. The back end of the car was elevated, propped up on the first-class car behind it, so he was cradled in the join of the floor to the front door. All manner of trash, luggage, hats, toys, bottles, and thirty pairs of shoes had slid down to the front of the car and buried him alive. He heard a pop, felt a flash of heat, and looked up to see a woolen stocking had fallen on the stove and burst into flame.

He flipped the stocking into the ash bin, where it lay smoldering. Then he carefully sat up, shaking off bits of refuse and old luncheons. He could taste blood, his lower lip was mashed, but no teeth were missing. His jaw felt like he'd been punched.

He got to his knees. The floor sloped up away from him, not too steep to walk but barely; all the oil lamps swung precariously on their hooks. People were trying to get out of their bunks, finding it hard to stand, casting about for clothes and belongings, calling out as to the whereabouts and welfare of companions. The porter was telling everyone to be calm, in a high and panicky voice. Brother Clark was praying and braying like a donkey.

Trace put a hand on the wall behind him, used it for leverage to stand. The front door of the car was buckled inward, about halfway up. He tried the handle and it broke off in his hand.

That left the back door or the windows. Trace started up the slope of the floor, straddling the aisle to step up each alternating berth leg, gently but firmly pushing people out of his way. "Stay down," he advised. "Stay in your bunk. We'll get the conductor down here, get the car settled down again. You just stay put."

He walk-climbed as far as Kingsley's bunk; he and Miss Eliza were both unhurt and collected in wit.

"What a piece of bravery!" Kingsley exclaimed. "To risk your own safety for that of another—"

"Are *you* all right, Mr. Tracy?" Miss Eliza asked. "You were thrown some distance."

"Nothin broken," Trace reported. "Can you see to those that are hurt? Try to get them up, get them dressed. Might have to get everybody off this car."

"*Nobody's* leaving this car until the conductor says so," the porter piped up. "The safety and comfort of the passengers is the responsibility of—"

"That's what I said." Trace gripped the young man by his jacket and pointed him aft. "You and me are gonna go find the conductor, ain't we?"

"I'm not supposed to—"

"Come on, son." Trace pushed the porter ahead of him and they clambered up the aisle as far as Trace's own seat.

"Are you all right, my friend?" Ferris was grim-faced but appeared unhurt.

"I'll live." Trace ran a hand down inside his bedroll, pulled out his gunbelt, and wrapped it around his hips. "You got a gun on you, Ferris?"

"I can protect myself," Ferris said.

"You can't carry firearms on this train!" the porter protested. "Only the conductor and the engineer are allowed to—"

"Hush!" Trace held up a hand. Someone was knocking and rattling at the back door of the car. Trace climbed toward it, saw the handle move and the door buckle open a couple of inches. Several sets of human fingers curled into the opening. Trace added his to the effort, braced his feet against the wall of the gentlemen's privy, and shoved.

The door slammed back with a splintering of wood and screaming of metal. There was a whoop from outside, and five Negro faces clustered around the opening, Boz's foremost among them.

"Knew that'd be you," he said, though Trace saw the raw edges of relief rimming his eyes.

They handed him out, and Trace descended the crumpled iron railing, dropped to the gravel of the track bed.

They were on a fairly gentle mountain slope, shallowly studded with scrub pines and juniper. The first-class car had not suffered much damage: only its front end was crumpled. Trace's car was tipped up, as was the emigrant car in front of it, and the smoking car before that was wrenched nearly crosswise to the rails. Every window in that car had been shattered, and Trace looked appraisingly at the five black men clustered around him; they all had minor cuts and scrapes, and Boz's lip looked swollen.

The engine was still on the track, but its cabin had been crushed by the coal car, and the boiler was sending squalling jets of steam into the air. The third-class passengers were hanging out their windows and exclaiming.

"Folks behind you didn't get much more than a bump," Boz said, gesturing with a thumb toward the first-class car. "All behind that's freight."

Trace could hear the cattle bawling in the stock cars further back. And jogging up the track bed, the rhythmic crunch of boots on gravel. A dark human figure, jogging toward them in the moonlight.

"Ho there! Anyone hurt?" It was the conductor, in his short white collar and spectacles, carrying a rifle. "You're not my brakemen. What are you doing off the train?"

"I told them!" the porter protested, climbing down from the mangled balcony. "I told them not to—"

"Shut up, Willie," the conductor said. "Anyone hurt on your car?" he said to Trace, who replied in the negative. "Good, then get back on board and stay out of our way." He turned, scanning the top of the train for men who weren't there. He lifted a whistle, on a cord around his neck, and blew several short blasts.

They listened. Nothing answered, except a far-off crack, and a yelp that might have been a coyote.

"Gunshot," Boz said.

The conductor gave him a look of dislike. "Get back on your car, boy, I'm not telling you again. Willie, you come with me."

Willie gave Trace a triumphant look and trotted off after the conductor toward the smoking engine. Trace looked at Boz, and at the colored men who hunkered on the roof and railing of the car. "You men heeled, any of you?"

They all had revolvers. One man said there was a shotgun in his baggage.

"Get it," Trace said. "Stay watch up there." He turned and started up the grade after the conductor.

Boz followed. "What is it?"

"Not Indians," Trace said.

The wind was cold and the air thin. The sky was bright with stars and the moon coming and going behind clouds. Bare-headed and in shirt sleeves, Trace could feel the chill on his skin, but it wasn't getting through to his blood. His heart was thudding hard and slow, his senses alive with eerie clarity.

The engine cabin was flat as a flapjack and burning.

"Earl!" the conductor bawled into the dark. "Tommy?"

"They woulda jumped," Trace said, low. "Can't be far."

"What'd we hit?" Boz wanted to know.

They trotted to the front of the tracks, stepping over bits of coal and smoldering wood. A sizeable cairn of rocks had been piled across the tracks—from the depth and extent of the scattered debris, Trace guessed the pile must've been half as high as the engine.

Not a slide, either: there was plenty of stone on the ground, but they weren't in an area where it was likely to fall. And there was no telltale skid of gravel on the bed above. "These were put here by hand," Trace said.

"You hear that?" Boz asked, and started downslope, into the dark.

They found the fireman not ten yards from the train, trying to crawl back through the shale and juniper brush. He was sobbing in that broken, wheezy way Trace remembered from the battlefield. His shirt was wet and sticky when Trace touched his shoulder.

"Easy, fella, we got you." Trace turned the man onto his back in Boz's arms. The fireman began to scream immediately, and bat at them with his shredded hands. His face was dark and shiny in the moonlight. The rest of him was shaking and cold, the breath rattling in his throat. "Conductor! We got your man down here!"

There was a skidding and scuffling as the conductor and Willie scrambled down the grade. Willie's lantern threw shards of light over the ground and the chewed-up fellow between them.

"Tommy!" the conductor said, dropping to one knee. "Tommy, what happened? Where's Earl?"

The fireman gurgled, hands falling slack away from the conductor's coat. His sleeves had been torn off, and there was a big chunk of meat missing out of his forearm. In the lamplight they could see a flap of scalp dangling over his brow. It looked like a bear had bitten into his head.

Trace met Boz's eyes, read the question there, and stood up, looking back toward the train.

"What was it, Tommy?" the conductor asked. "Wolves? Did they get Earl?"

Trace squinted. The windows of the passenger cars glowed dimly from the lamps; he could just make out people moving inside. Two men paced the roof of the first-class car, dark silhouettes against the moon-drenched sky. One of them had a spark of fire in his hand, which he raised to his lips.

Something dark was slinking up the grade to the tracks. Something blacker than the train, darker than the shadows. It moved low to the ground, crawling like a frog but much faster, as big as a man. Another one, behind it. Two more, two cars down. Converging on the train.

Trace skinned his Colt and shot the nearest one.

He knew he hit it. It wasn't a long shot and he saw the thing flinch; worse than that, he *felt* it squeal, a metal-on-metal shriek that pierced his skull. But it jumped—all the black shapes did—and scattered like roaches. The men on the roof jumped, too, spun around and looked toward them.

"Back to the train," Trace said. "*Now.*"

"Son, I've got a man down here and at least five missing," the conductor snapped.

"Your train is under attack, mister, and that man's bled out." Trace thumbed another cartridge into the Colt's chamber as he spoke, backing away up the grade, Boz already running for the tracks. "Unless you want to lose more passengers you'd best—"

A scream from above. Cracks of gunfire followed, sounding thin and puny in the wind. Trace turned and hightailed it up the slope.

He saw the two men go down off the roof of the first-class car—one flipped out flat as if his legs had been pulled from under him, and the other jumped. More gunfire came from the other side of the train, and a high, terrified scream. He saw Boz ahead of him, leaping across the link between the first-class car and the one behind it. Trace angled his steps to follow but then saw one of those black shapes appear on top of the second-class car.

It perched on the upthrust edge of the roof for a moment, hunkered like a mountain cat or a circus monkey. Its shape was more or less human, but there was something bestial in its movements and the length of its back, the way it crouched on all fours. It swung its head to one side, and then there was another beside it, and another, and a fourth.

They pushed and jostled at each other, like a crowd of young toughs egging each other to take a dare. Suddenly one of them went over the edge of the roof—and twisted as it fell, swinging clean through the doorway. Trace shouted and ran toward the car, shooting at the three on the roof. They scattered into the darkness.

From inside the sleeper car came a rolling and screaming and crashing that sounded for all hell like a fox in a henhouse. A man in a nightshirt and boots clambered through the door, and was instantly snatched by a black shadow that hauled him down the grade to the underbrush. The lady behind him saw it and began to scream, but some panicked soul pushed her from behind and she fell, headfirst onto the gravel. A black shadow flung itself on her as if it meant to ravish her. She screamed and beat at it, but it caught her up in clawed arms and fastened its jaws on her throat, ending her scream in a choked gurgle.

Trace ran up to the thing and kicked it in the ribs. It turned on

him with a shriek of rage. All he saw was gaping mouth, filled with
teeth and blood, yellow eyes reflecting hate and fire. He shot it between the mouth and the eyes. It rolled over backwards and down the
grade—he had no idea whether it was dead or not. The woman was,
her throat was torn out, and the emigrant car was rocking with the
force of the battle going on inside.

He clambered up the end of the car, all but throwing people out
of his way. He shouted at them to get to the dining car, not knowing
if they heard—the ruckus inside was deafening. Trace fell into the car
and slid halfway down the aisle before he caught himself; for a moment he couldn't see the monster. All the berths were still down and
the oil lamps were swinging dangerously, people were falling over each
other trying to get out of the way, while the battle surged back and
forth across the front of the car, something dark and snarling in the
middle of it.

It resembled a man, but was gray and hairless, with the round flat
eyes of a fish and a gaping wound of a mouth. In one long, spidery
arm it held a child, limp and bloodied, while it used the other to grab
those nearest it and fling them across the car. The men were trying to
corner it, wielding chunks of firewood, walking sticks, and a fire-iron,
but the beast was laughing. It held up the child by its hair and slung
the lifeless body at them. The nearest man went down under the
weight of it, and the thing leapt over him, took two more down with
it and dashed their heads against the floor. One of the men brought
the fire iron down on its back, but it only squalled and whipped an
arm around, backhanded him into one of the berths.

Trace took the opening and fired. The first shot hit it high in the
shoulder, the second below the ribs. The sound it made was truly awful, a scream Trace had heard only in nightmares, but it crumpled, fell
back in the aisle, and slid down a few feet.

He dry-fired twice more at it, advancing by slow steps, while frantic people huddled on the berths and cowered in the aisle. It wasn't
moving, and neither were several of the passengers. Trace saw at least
six lying in pools of blood, and the little girl with her neck bent at a
terrible angle, and an old man with his chest torn open, as if the thing
had shoved a fist in and pulled out his heart—

It was Martin Kingsley. He had the fire-ax still clutched in his
hands, a surprised expression on his face. Miss Eliza huddled on the
berth behind him, her arms around his shoulders, looking at Trace
with a blank, lost expression.

"It was so strong," she said faintly. "It tried to get me."

"Miss Eliza, you just come here," Trace said.

"Martin's dead," she said.

"I see that, darlin, you just come here to me. That's a good girl."

She blinked, slowly, and then her face tightened like a fist. She rolled her brother's body off her lap and climbed over it to the aisle, taking Trace's hand. The front of her bed jacket and nightdress were soaked with blood.

"You hurt?" he said.

"I—I don't think so. Are there more of those things out there?"

Trace could still hear screaming and gunfire coming from outside. "There are, but we can't stay in here. We got to get to one of the other cars, isn't so damaged."

"I'm not going out there!" another woman cried.

"Don't like the idea myself, lady, but this car ain't safe." Trace flipped the Colt's gate open and shucked the spent brass onto the floor. He pulled a fresh cartridge from his belt and thumbed it into place.

"Look out!" Miss Eliza gasped, and he heard the snarl, the scuffle from the end of the aisle, and half-turned just before something heavy and stinking knocked him to the floor.

His head struck and the weight of the beast drove the air from his lungs. His vision was blotted out in red, but he felt its hot exhalation on his face and jabbed his hand up blindly, wedged the heel of his hand under its chin so it couldn't bite.

It was horribly, demonically strong, and its arms seemed to be ten feet long. It stabbed him low under the ribs, claws punching through shirt and flesh, a feeling of tearing in his side and pain rushing in like an express engine.

Trace hiked up a knee and got his heel wedged in the monster's hip, sat up and shoved with everything he had. It threw it back a foot or so; Trace brought both feet together and drove them into its midsection as it pounced, threw it over his head and up the aisle.

It landed hard on its head and Trace was up before it could turn around, snatched the fire-ax from Kingsley's stiffening fingers. The creature lunged at him, snarling, and Trace twisted aside at the last second, swung the ax down at an angle.

The blade sank into its side and it squalled, turned on that impossibly flexible spine, and swiped at him with its claws. He yanked the ax free and swung again, cutting up under the armpit this time, followed through with a kick to the chest. It somersaulted backward down the aisle with a hard grunt, as if he had winded it. Trace leapt after it with a yell and a wild swipe of the ax, buried the blade in the join of the neck and shoulder. The thing convulsed, unable to squeal with its throat mostly severed; one more fall of the ax and the job was done.

Panting, Trace turned and marched back up the aisle. Miss Eliza held his Colt out to him and he took it, handing the ax off to one of the men. He began shoving bullets into the breech again, faster this time. "Now," he said. "We got to get *out* of here. Get to the first-class car, ain't so damaged. Got it?"

Suddenly there was a crash from the front of the car. Trace wheeled to see two of the beasts knocking the glass out of the broken windows, beating the frames out of the walls, crawling through to the floor.

"Move!" Trace bellowed, as everyone began to scream and climb toward the exit. He backed up the aisle while the two things crouched over the dead one, sniffing it. For a moment the corpse appeared to be suffused with a faint blue glow, as another figure, the transparent shade of a man, separated itself from the monster and stood up, turning to look gravely at Trace.

A slight, neat Chinese man, with the front of his head shaved and wearing those baggy pajamas they all favored: he put his hands in his sleeves and bowed to Trace, as if in thanks, before the two living monsters brushed through his ghost and obliterated him from sight.

The keung-si grinned at Trace and started up the aisle toward him. They looked like the cartoons in Yellow Peril articles—flat faces; grinning, toothy mouths; abnormally wide foreheads. Their skins had a wet, transparent sheen, like slugs, and Trace could see where their bellies had been cut by crawling through the glass. The wounds were white-lipped, leaking blood like a punctured waterskin but closing up even as he watched.

It was hard to watch. There was something so human and yet so *not,* especially in their faces, that fought with his sense of reality and kept pulling him toward the detachment of nightmare. They had genitals, he saw with distant revulsion, like a man's might look after he'd pulled himself out of an icy creek.

Then one of them rushed him. Trace almost shot it, but it stopped short, grinning, taunting. He backpedaled harder, felt cold air on his neck, risked a look behind him to see the coast was clear. He boosted himself through the doorway and onto the railing, took a big step onto the roof of the first-class car.

The wind was acrid, searing the lungs and eyes. The engine cab was still burning and it looked like there was a fire in the third-class car, as well: bright light danced in the windows and smoke poured out. People staggered out of the car and ran, wavering and ghostlike in their white nightclothes. Some of them carried torches. Shapes that were not quite men oozed under and between the cars.

The two keung-si had climbed out after him and onto the high vantage point of the upended passenger car.

"That's fine," Trace said, backing away and trying to watch in all directions at once. "You just stay there."

One leapt onto the roof behind him.

He felt it more than he heard it—sensed something dark and silent looming in on him, as if death had materialized out of the night.

He twisted on the slippery roof, wrenched his knee but managed not to go down, whipped the Colt around. The thing leapt into the air, six feet up, pushing off with its knuckles and thrusting its legs forward. It sailed right over the slugs he fired at it and hit him feet-first in the chest. They skewed off the roof in a tangle and plummeted to the gravel.

Trace landed on the bottom, winded and brains clubbed half to mush. He raised the Colt groggily, but the beast slapped it from his hand. Its mouth was red and grinning, full of little sharp teeth like a pig's. He could hear the croaking of his own lungs as it bent over him, its breath hot and foul like rotting meat, like the kill pits at the slaughter yard, like a sunken road choked with the bloated bodies of comrades—

Trace's hand fell to his own throat, scrabbling for the fine chain under his shirt. *O Lord, not like this*—He closed his fist around his crucifix. *Bite on this, you bastard*—

He shoved the crucifix at its face and it reared back, snarling. Suddenly a stream of fire shot out of the darkness and struck it between the shoulder blades.

Its growl of anger turned to a howl of agony. It hurtled away, wallowing in the shale and shrubbery, but the flames would not be smothered: they rose and consumed, and in seconds the thing had collapsed into a pile of bone and ash.

"Trace!" Boz ran toward him, carrying a torch, followed closely by Ferris and two of the colored men. "Shit, Trace, I leave you alone two minutes and you're gettin yourself dead."

Trace sat up, holding the back of his skull with one hand, looking past him to Ferris. "Did you just spit fire at that thing?"

Ferris gave him a sardonic look, and a mock toast from the flask in his hand. "None of us is what we seem, Mr. Tracy."

"Come on." Boz wedged a hand under his armpit. "Get up, we gotta move fore they come back around—"

"This your gun?" One of the colored men was holding it out to him.

"Yeah." Trace looked down at his gun hand, saw the crucifix and its broken chain still wrapped around his fingers. He shoved it in a pocket and took the Colt. "They're eatin my Baptists," he growled.

They made for the first-class car, only to find the passengers had mostly escaped and made a run for the stock cars farther back. Every few yards, one of the monsters had caught a straggler, and three or four people had stopped to fight it, beating it off with cudgels or rocks. Trace descended on the nearest of these small battles, put two slugs in the thing's head and let someone else bash it aside. They picked up the victims that were still breathing and carried them along, collecting survivors as they went.

Trace could *feel* the black things gathering behind them. His power was wide awake and tracking them, like drafts in a warm room, as they converged on his retreating party.

"Get *down!*" he shouted, and shoved the two colored men to the ground. A black shadow hurtled off the top of the third-class car, right over their heads. That one missed, but the tumble delayed them long enough to let the three behind them catch up.

Trace and the two Negroes were hit at once. Trace shot his through the head, but the Negro's shotgun was spent and the thing plunged its fist into his chest, scything through bone and gristle with a sound like a gourd splitting open.

Ferris loomed up beside the other man, torchlight glinting off the amber bottle in his hand. He took a sharp pull from it and then spat. Fire streamed from his lips, engulfing the third monster and propelling it off the colored fellow. Boz helped the man up and they pelted after the last fleeing passengers, running up short against a blockade of cows—*cows?*—milling about beside the track, sleepy and bawling and jostling each other.

"Hee-*yaw!*" Boz screamed, and fired into the air. The cattle shifted and lurched, and Trace saw the yawning mouth of the first stock car, side door open, the conductor leaning down from the bed and helping to hoist up the last few refugees. Boz went next, then the colored man, then Ferris, and Trace last, while the men leaned on the sliding door from inside, propelling it closed.

A clawed hand closed around Trace's knee. He yelled, and Boz yelled, and grabbed him by the gun arm, which saved him falling but the Colt clattered to the floor and somebody kicked it into the dark corners of the car. The claws sank into Trace's thigh, hot as any branding iron, and another of the things leapt at the door, landed with one foot in the opening and the other on Trace's chest.

"Shoot it, goddamn it!" Trace hollered, but a shapely pale form thrust between the men, Miss Eliza coming with her arm extended, face drawn and serious as she pressed the cross in her hand against the brow of the demon in the doorway.

It shrieked, a high-pitched wail of mortal agony straight out of hell. The cross sank into its flesh. The yellow lamp of one eye winked out, and it pinwheeled out of the car, landed on the one that had Trace.

It let go. Boz heaved. The door slammed shut with an echoing thud, blotting out the night and boxing in the frightened cries of the passengers—emigrants, railroad employees, second class, first class, white, colored, Baptist, and ex-Catholic—packed into a stinking filthy stock car like so much meat for slaughter.

CHAPTER TWENTY

It had fallen quiet, except for the moaning of the injured. The few remaining children had lapsed into sleep, and some of the traumatized adults were sunk into fugues. Brother Clark was preaching to them—or rather *at* them—out of Revelation, with assorted Beasts and Plagues. Trace thought uncharitably that he would have sooner seen *Clark* with his chest ripped open, instead of Martin Kingsley, but he doubted Brother Clark had made any effort to put himself between the monster and its intended prey.

"How many did we leave Ogden with?" Trace asked, low.

"Seventy-three souls, plus twelve hands," the conductor said, rubbing Willie's dried blood off his face. He'd lost his spectacles during the massacre.

Trace did a quick head count; the combination of hay and cow manure they'd lit in one of the troughs gave a little light, but it made breathing a chore. The stock car was one of the modern ones—it was solid walls except for the top three feet or so, which were slatted. The breeze took some of the smoke out the top but swirled the rest of it around. From time to time Trace heard one of the creatures slither across the roof, and saw a black silhouette peer in through the slats, but it couldn't reach the people inside.

There were about forty of them in the stock car. More than half lost, then, unless some others were holed up elsewhere. At least they had water in this car: feed and water troughs kept the beef from shrinking on its way to sale.

"How long before they call us missin?" Boz asked.

"Few more hours," the conductor said. "We're not due in Eagle Rock until five A.M. They'll send an engine back after us. But it'll be sunup before they get here."

"After sunup, it won't matter," said Ferris, coming to join them. "If we can hold our position til then, we'll be all right."

"How d'you know that?" said Charles, the last of the colored men.

"Isn't it obvious?" said Ferris. "They're vampires. They don't like the daylight."

Miss Eliza, who was bandaging the wound in Trace's side, stopped what she was doing and stared at Ferris. So did everyone else.

"What makes you think these things are vampires?" Trace asked. He didn't need convincing, himself, but he could see the others did— except for Boz, who had his head down and was shaking it ominously.

"They were men," the conductor all but snarled. "Chinese, I should say, gone savage from living in the mountains."

"Never saw a man could jump like that," Boz murmured. "Not even a Chinese."

"I know it sounds incredible," said Ferris. "But in circus life you come to accept the incredible. Three-headed calves, pigs with two tails and no heads, men with women's parts and the other way round—"

"Anybody works on the range's seen cows with extra parts," Charles said.

"But have you ever seen a man with the teeth of a wolf, and a thirst for blood?" Ferris said. "A man, even a heathen Oriental, who recoiled in pain from the simple touch of a Christian cross? A man who burnt to ash as soon as he was touched by cleansing flame?" He looked at Trace. "A man who could not be slain by a bullet? Whose unnatural nature made him colder and blacker than an Idaho night?"

Trace stared at him, thinking if he survived this night he was going to shake some answers out of the Fire-Master.

Boz broke in. "I don't care what they are—they're hard to kill and they're hungry. They're still out there, in case you can't hear 'em."

They hushed for a moment, casting wary glances at the roof. Trace could have sworn he heard something chuckle. Brother Clark's sermon rose in volume slightly; he had moved on to the Whore of Babylon.

"How many are there?" Trace asked. "How many did we kill? I hacked the head off one in the emigrant car, and Ferris there burned at least two, that I saw."

"I reduced no less than three to ash, if I may be so boastful," Ferris said.

"That's four. Any others we know didn't get up?"

"The one I smote with the cross," Miss Eliza said. "Not the one you saw—one of them attacked me as I ran from the passenger car. I struck it in the mouth and it . . . melted."

There was a short silence. Trace remembered how her cross had sunk into the face of the beast; how the one that attacked him had shied from his crucifix. He fished it out of his pocket, found the broken ends of the chain and twisted them together, back around his neck.

"I blew the head off one," the conductor said.

"We burned up a couple with the torches," Boz said, nodding at Charles.

"Eight, then?" Trace looked around at them. "How many are left?"

"At least that many more," Boz guessed, "since they took half our numbers. They ain't dumb animals, either. They flushed the passengers out—shoved one of their own into the car, caught the ones who ran out."

"I saw that, too," Trace said. "And they built the blockade on the tracks."

"And they laugh," said Miss Eliza. "That one laughed when it . . . killed Martin."

"Then they're human," the conductor said.

"That is a fatal mistake to make, my friend," Ferris said.

"I'm not your friend, *friend,* I'm the conductor of this god-damned train and I'll not hear any more of this foolishness. Now we are gonna sit here until daybreak or until—"

The conductor was drowned out by the sudden bawling of cattle. It was frantic and loud, punctuated by the skidding and thrashing of hooves on the gravel. Everyone inside the stock car went still and stiff, listening to the sounds of butchery outside. Even Brother Clark's sermon faltered.

"Never heard a steer make that noise," Charles muttered.

It sounded like the cow was screaming. Then strangling. Then there was a long, agonized moan, and the sing-song gibbering of the beasts.

Miss Eliza was wide-eyed. "What on earth are they—"

"They're killin the cattle," Boz said, and then something huge struck the side of the car.

The stock car trembled on its rails. The passengers screamed and clutched at each other.

"What the devil—" the conductor said.

The impact came again, closer to the ceiling this time, and for an instant a large, dark shadow blotted the stars outside the ventilation slats. The slats cracked under the impact, buckling inward.

Boz leaped to his feet. "They're throwin that carcass at the—"

The third blow crashed through. The narrow slats, not built to withstand a half ton of beef, splintered to admit the front half of a steer. The passengers screamed and scattered from the spot, packing into the ends of the car, but the body stuck there and hung, head lolling, one horn broken off. One of its front legs cocked through at a grotesque angle. Blood and froth dripped from its mouth.

Then it began to saw back and forth in the opening. The things outside fluttered around it, climbing over the slats, trying to pull it out. The limp head rolled and bobbed.

"Oh, my Lord," Miss Eliza said sickly, and put her hand over her mouth.

But the beef was well and truly stuck. One of the keung-si shrieked in rage and drove a fist into the steer's side, then began to squeal and thrash when its hand became stuck. One of the others came to its assistance. The first one swatted it away, but the jerk freed its arm and they both toppled off. There was a thud and a yelp as they hit the gravel.

Somebody laughed, screamingly. It was an awful sound, choked and hysterical, and others in the car took it up, wailing mad laughter until it dissolved into crying. Brother Clark's voice rose shrill over the chorus.

"Brethren! Be not afraid! Though the hour of death may be upon you, trust in the Lord and you will be redeemed!"

"Hour of death, my ass," Boz said. "I don't mean to die in some box-car like a damn steer."

"Nor do I," said the conductor, hefting up his rifle.

"Though this darkness may surround us, and the minions of Satan try to tempt us to the path of unrighteousness—"

"I say we go out there and give those bastards a taste of lead," said Charles, brandishing his shotgun in one hand, a torch in the other.

"Don't go near that door," Trace snapped. "You open that and all these people are dead. We're not fightin them off a second time."

"You wanna wait here til they break in?" Charles demanded.

"Lead don't stop them, remember?" Boz said. "I didn't mean we should go rushin out there."

"Yet we must not falter! For we do not wrestle against flesh and blood, but against principalities, against powers, against the rulers of the darkness of this age—"

"They won't break in, and if they do we'll make our stand here," the conductor said. "Better to take one at a time than open up our flank to their numbers."

"Mr. Tracy?" Ferris said quietly. "Did you not have some insights on how to defeat these demons?"

Boz turned and gave Trace a long, hard look. "Yeah, partner—you have any *insights*?"

"I told you everything I knew for sure," Trace said.

"So what do you *not* know, for sure?" Boz demanded. "What else she tell you that you think I didn't need to know?"

"It ain't like that, Boz, I *told* you she didn't know much about it, she only gave me a half-assed list of ideas—"

"Which you never bothered to read to *me*—"

"What in blue blazes are you two carrying on about?" the conductor demanded. "Who is *she* and what do you know about these critters?"

Trace broke off, noticed the others staring at them. Ferris looked thoughtful; Miss Eliza's eyes were lowered, her lips pursed in disapproval. And in the sudden quiet, Trace heard something else.

"Listen," he said.

There was a soft, slithery sound under their feet, something sliding under the floor of the car. A series of gentle thumps, and something rattling.

"What's under us?" Trace asked.

"Feed boxes," the conductor said.

"Full o' hay and corn," Charles added.

"And the wheels and undercarriage, of course, the journal boxes."

"No doors?" Trace asked. "No access in here?"

"No. What was that you were saying about how to kill them?"

Trace glanced from Boz's accusing look to Ferris's encouraging one, and swiped a hand down his chin. "Fire kills them—we know that. Sunlight . . . I think Ferris the Fire-Master is right about that, but it doesn't do us any good. Pure metals, like silver and gold, maybe—"

"Lead's as pure as it gets," the conductor said, "and it only slows them down."

"Don't have any silver or gold, anyway," Charles said.

"Shut up, let him think," Boz muttered.

Trace ground his teeth: he'd looked at those notes often enough, he could see Miss Fairweather's spidery writing in his mind's eye, but not clear enough to recall the last item in the list. He scratched the back of his head and winced as his fingers raked over the goose-egg throbbing there. Whatever the word was, it made him think of food, of steak and potatoes—

Yum! said a voice.

Trace glanced warily at the waiting faces; he was pretty sure he'd heard that voice with his mind, not his ears. He felt the slight shiver of power along his arms and neck, but he couldn't fix on it coming from a particular point.

Yum! the voice said again, more insistently. *Yem!*

"Yim?" Trace repeated.

"What?" Boz said.

"Did somebody say *yum?* or *yim?*"

They all looked at each other, an exchange of glances Trace had seen many times, usually before somebody asked if he'd had too much sun, or too much whiskey. He turned, slowly, sweeping his gaze over the people huddled in the cattle-car.

The Chinaman's ghost stood in the corner, erect and still, while the emigrants around him cowered and wailed. His dark robe blended into the shadows, and when Trace looked directly at him he faded further, until only his face and his pointing hand showed pale in the flickering light.

Yim! said the dead Chinese, pointing under the feed trough. He raised his empty gaze to meet Trace's, and raised his pointing finger to his own throat. *Keung-si,* he said, and made an unmistakable slashing gesture.

Understanding rushed in on Trace, like a flash flood in a canyon. He dove for the space under the trough.

It was down there, a whole block of salt-lick for the steers. Trace hugged it to his chest with one arm and crawled out backwards. "Salt!" he crowed. "Salt! That was it!"

"Of course!" Ferris said. "Salt has powerful protective properties."

"Salt?" Charles repeated. "What, are you gonna pickle 'em?"

"I can't believe this," the conductor grumbled.

Trace gestured to Boz. "Gimme that ax."

Boz passed it over and Trace rose on his knees in the middle of the floor, lifted the ax handle up in two hands to bring the flat top of its head down square on the salt-lick.

But he checked it. His knees felt warm where they touched the floorboards. He bent over and put one palm flat against the floor. Not merely warm—hot enough he had to pull away after two breaths. The quality of the smoke in the air they were breathing had changed, too.

He looked at Miss Eliza, who was barefoot. "Your feet feel warm?"

"No," she said, and came closer to where he knelt, then quickly backed up. "Oh! It is there."

Trace beckoned to Charles. "Bring that torch over here."

There was smoke coming up through a knothole in the tightly-laid floorboards. He bent low, and got a whiff of hot metal, like a branding iron. "What did you say was under here?"

The conductor's face went slack, with terrible understanding. "The wheel journals," he said hollowly. "We've got us a hot box."

"I think they *made* us a hot box," Trace said.

"Ah yes! Lubricating grease burns quite well," Ferris said brightly. "They had only to light the animal fodder and let it spread."

"But they burn up if they touch fire," Charles protested.

"So do we, my friend," Ferris said, "but we still handle it every day."

"Maybe you do," Boz snapped. "These things are too damn smart to be animals."

"On the contrary, monkeys are quite clever," Ferris said. "They've been known to—"

"Will you shut up!" the conductor shouted. "There's a damn fire underneath us and this whole car's gonna go up in about five minutes!"

That, of course, started another panic. A number of people rushed for the door, but Boz and the conductor got in front of them, Boz with both guns out. Miss Eliza tried to calm them, her hands and voice soothing, pressing people back toward the edges of the car. Brother Clark called out for an angel with a fiery sword.

Trace got a leg up on one of the water troughs and stood, balancing against the wall to look out through the slats. Down the slope about five yards from the tracks, a half dozen of the black shapes crouched in a line, watching the car, firelight reflecting in their eyes. Smoke wafted up past the ventilation slats.

Trace hopped to the floor and caught up the ax handle in one hand. "Boz!"

"What?" Boz's eyes and guns were still on the passengers, but some of them had backed down, and Trace's words caught their desperate attention.

"Sponge this water out of here," Trace said, splashing his hand across the surface of the trough and trying to meet as many eyes as possible. "Soak the floorboards with it, where Mr. Railroad Conductor tells you to. Buy us some time."

"Sure will, boss," Boz said, but it was the passengers who surged toward the trough, taking off shawls and shirts to soak up the water. Charles and Ferris moved to help.

Trace caught Miss Eliza's elbow, drew her toward the back of the car where Brother Clark was standing and shouting before his glassy-eyed audience.

"Remember the prophet Elisha?" Trace said, kicking the block of salt before them. "How he cleansed the poisoned waters?"

She looked blank for a moment, then her eyes widened. "The salt?"

"Yes. It's one of the guards against evil I studied at seminary. Blessed Salt. Same use as Holy Water, more or less."

"Holy wa—" She blinked. "You're a papist? A *priest*?"

"Papist, yes. Never got as far as a priest. I know the words to say but we'll need Brother Clark to say them. You think his faith is true?"

"He's a believer, true enough," she said, her lips pinched. "But I don't think he'll agree to this, Jacob."

"Make him," Trace said, and put his hand on Brother Clark's shoulder. "Pastor, I think I'm ready to hear the error of my ways, now."

Brother Clark flung him off with a snarl. "Blasphemer! You brought this pestilence upon us!"

"I did not bring it," Trace said. "I came here to fight it, but I need a holy man."

"You know nothing of sanctity! You speak with a false tongue, and you bring judgment upon all of us!"

"You're right," Trace said. "I know I'm cursed. I've been this way for a long time, but I keep tryin, brother, and I need somebody to show me the right way." He got down on one knee, laid one hand on the block of salt. "I just need your help with this one thing. Just ask a blessing on this salt-lick and—"

Brother Clark sucked his breath in as if the suggestion were obscene. He whipped his right hand across Trace's cheek. "Blasphemer! Papist! I will not be led astray by your falsehoods! This is the hour we must stay true, and walk willingly into the fiery furnace! Those of the *true* faith will be saved!"

Trace's jaw had already taken some bad blows that night, and the slap was enough to make his eyes water. He clasped a hand to his chin, amazed that anyone could be that arrogant.

Brother Clark gave him a most un-Christlike look of triumph, and raised his hands. "Brethren! Though we are tested as Job, we must be ready as Job was, to go into that land of darkness, the place from which we shall not return, a land as dark as the shadow of death, where even the light is like dark—"

Trace swung and clipped him under the ear. His audience gasped. Brother Clark's head snapped back and he went down like a sack of potatoes, quiet at last.

"I always hated that passage," Trace said, flexing his hand.

"I've never been fond of it either," Miss Eliza said.

And that was a damn fool thing to do, Trace thought, looking down at Clark's slack mouth. He glanced at the huddled, shuddering congregation. "Anyone else here right with the Lord?"

They just stared at him—eyes wide and faces bland with terror. Like sheep, he thought with a contempt that shocked him, because he'd always resented that derogatory description of the faithful. But it certainly fit here—these folks sitting and waiting to die instead of—what was it Miss Fairweather had said? *Rather than accepting the truth, and learning to fight?*

"Jacob." Miss Eliza put her hand on his arm. "You do it."

"Ma'am, I can't," he said. "I was never ordained. It has to be a priest."

"Elisha was not a priest," she countered. "He was a prophet. And I know for a fact that you received a vision from God when Martin told you where we were going. I suspect your whole reason for following us here was to protect us from this evil."

Trace looked at her in surprise, but she only nodded, calm and sure. "My father used to say that the reluctant prophets were the only ones we could trust." She smiled her serene Madonna smile. "I trust you."

The hiss of steam caught his attention; Boz and Ferris had resorted to scooping water from the troughs with a feed bucket and flinging it on the floor. The wood was hot enough that the water just sizzled when it hit. The last few children were whimpering and trying to back away from the spot, but they were already crowded into the corner as hard as they could get. The air was beginning to get quite warm.

"Trace!" Boz hollered. "Whatever you're doin over there, you better do it fast!"

What the hell, Trace thought recklessly. Miss Fairweather had been right about the exorcism rite; maybe raw ability would serve him here, too. Or maybe God gave dispensation to folks who saddled up in a crisis.

He closed a fist around his crucifix and pulled it off over his head, kissed it, and crossed himself. He dropped to one knee and put his hand on the block of salt.

The words came to mind with frightening ease, bringing with them smells of incense, and old wood, and musty vestments. He shut his eyes, sucked into a memory so sweet and strong it blotted out the darkness around him—the younger boys whispering and fidgeting during Mass, the singing at Vespers, the simple feeling of being *good* that he had hugged to himself in those days.

"Almighty Lord, I beg you to bless this salt," he said, "as You blessed the salt scattered over the water by the prophet Elisha. Wherever this salt is sprinkled, drive from us all unclean spirits, all satanic powers, all infernal invaders, all wicked legions, assemblies and sects—" *Except the Baptists, we need them,* his mind added irreverently, and he nearly upset it all by laughing. That sense of exhilaration was building in him again, that sense of being exactly where he should be, doing what he was meant to do—of being *heard*. He made the Cross again. "In the Name and by the power of Our Lord Jesus Christ, drive away the power of evil, and protect us always by the presence of your Holy Spirit. In nomine Patris, et Filii, et Spiritus Sancti, Amen."

"Amen," said a chorus of voices, and he opened his eyes to see that a dozen of the passengers had joined him and Miss Eliza on their knees.

He saw something else, too. The block of salt was glowing white, faint but distinct in the smoky gloom. He lifted his hand from it with a quick startled inhalation, and a few grains clung to his fingers, like the luminescence of a firefly.

"It worked," he said stupidly.

"It did?" Miss Eliza said.

"Can't you see that?" he asked, but he could see she didn't. "Never mind. Step back."

He raised the ax like a tamping pole and smashed it down on the block. A big chunk split off and he hit it again, in short hard blows to break it up as much as possible. The glow never faded, but spread out across the floor wherever the salt touched. Trace bore down on the chunks with the flat of the ax blade until they subsided into powder.

Suddenly there was a fresh yelp and scurry around the edges of the car. Trace looked over his shoulder to see flames licking up through the floor, in a bull's-eye of rapidly spreading black.

"Trace!" Boz hollered again.

"I'm comin!" he said. "Everybody get over here and pick up some salt! Smash it up, grind it down so you can sprinkle it." Everyone's hands scrabbled for pieces of salt-lick. Trace scooped a handful of grains into his own pocket and hefted up the ax, moved toward the car door where Boz and the conductor were gathered.

"You really think that salt-lick's gonna hold them off?" the conductor demanded.

"We don't have a choice!" Trace shouted. "We can't stay in here. Try to corral them together, get them off in a body. I'll clear the way for you as much as I can."

"Excellent idea, my godly friend!" Ferris appeared at his elbow, saluted him with his booze flask. "I'll be right behind you!"

Trace glanced at Boz, who was showing some serious strain—his expression was determined, but his eyes were worried and Trace realized it was because Boz—for the first time in five years—didn't believe in him. "It's gonna be all right, Boz," he said. "Stay close to Miss Eliza."

He gave the door a yank.

It slid halfway and stopped, its track blocked by the dead steer hanging from the ceiling. But that was all right, as Trace had time to realize: the narrow opening meant only two of the beasts could attack at once.

And they did. Ferris spat fire at the one on the left. Trace swung his ax straight up and clove into the other's ribs. His wild swing threw it against the doorframe over his head; it collided and bounced back down, squalling and flailing. Trace shook it off and jumped out after it.

He landed solid and plunged his hand into his vest pocket, swept out his arm in a fanning gesture like sowing wheat. Glowing grains of salt arced out from his throw, and the five keung-si who had been converging on him suddenly leapt backwards, one of them falling right down and rolling over. It got up again, shaking its head, shrieking rage at him.

"Come on," Trace said, brandishing the ax. "Come on, you whore."

It pushed off on its knuckles and flew at him. He quick-drew the Colt and shot it out of the air, then buried the ax in its head before it could get up again. He wheeled at the sense of something behind him, but it was Ferris, who blew fire at the next one, missing but driving it away. Trace scattered another handful of salt and the creatures hissed and fell back further; he glanced over his shoulder and saw Boz and the conductor leap down from the car. Charles and Miss Eliza followed, and people were handing out the children, but Trace had no more time to look because they were circling him again. He and Ferris stayed back to back, while the beasts feinted and grabbed, shying back from the ever-widening lines he drew in salt.

There was a shout and a gunshot blast, and Boz hollering orders, and the crying of children, and Miss Eliza's voice rising calm over all. Trace saw their white nightshirts spreading at the edges of his vision, glimpsed Boz on his left and was glad, as they pushed their perimeter out further from the burning stock car.

It was almost light as day, now, and the heat was getting intense, as the treated lumber of the car began to flame in earnest. He spared a glance backward; two men were letting down the limp body of Brother Clark. All the passengers were out on the dicey shale slope, flinging salt around them as Miss Eliza directed, until they were all ringed in a shining white barrier, like a fence made of moonlight.

"It's workin," Boz said, relief in his voice.

"Yeah," Trace said, and laughed. The beast nearest him snarled at his mirth and Trace bared his teeth at it. "You like that? Huh? You want some of this?" He whipped out his Colt and shot it in its snarling face. It bowled over backwards and Trace leapt after it.

CHAPTER TWENTY-ONE

"I count fourteen," Charles said, flinging the last head into the smoldering remains of the stock car.

"Me too," Boz agreed. "Not countin the three or four piles of ash, can't tell what they were."

"I can account for five piles of ash, personally," Ferris said.

"That makes twenty even," Trace said, kicking the canvas-wrapped bundle at his feet. He yawned and cocked his right arm back behind his head to stretch the shoulder. He was going to be damn sore in those muscles for the next few days, although at the moment all he felt was limp and weary in a glad-to-be-alive way. The sun was coming over the rise, sending golden fingers of light over the ground and the sleeping pile of emigrants—those that could sleep, anyway. Some of them had just plain lapsed into senselessness.

Trace sobered, looking over at them, their clothes smeared with soot and blood. He saw the conductor looking, too. The man's gaze traveled from the little knot of survivors, over the butchered cattle, across the train standing like a gutted monument to the massacre. The conductor rubbed a hand across his face, paying extra attention to his eyes. He wiped away clean streaks on his cheeks.

Boz put a hand on his shoulder. "You did your duty, mister. You stayed with the train."

"Thank you," the conductor said in a shaky voice. He blinked several times, jabbed at his nose with a middle finger to push up spectacles that weren't there. He wiped his hand on his pants and offered it to Boz. "Thank you, Mr.—?"

"Bosley. John Bosley."

"Pleasure to meet you," the conductor said.

Trace felt a touch on his hand and looked down to see Miss Eliza smiling at him. She looked remarkably pretty and fresh, with a dressing-gown thrown over her soiled nightdress, and her dark hair hanging loose in the wind.

"Brother Clark is awake," she said, the corners of her lips twitching. "He doesn't seem to remember how he fell senseless. He thinks perhaps he breathed too much smoke."

"Funny, I would have said he was blowin it," Trace said, and they chuckled together, until her eyes suddenly brightened with tears. She put her fingers to her lips and looked away.

"I'm sorry about your brother," he said.

She managed a brave smile. "No greater love than this."

"Yes," he said gently.

She looked at her hands for a long moment, then gestured at the bundle under his boot. "You are taking that package back to St. Louis? To your employer?"

"Yeah."

"This Miss Fairweather you work for must be a remarkable woman, to concern herself so with the welfare of strangers."

"She's, ah, dedicated, for sure."

"Are you likewise . . . dedicated . . . to her cause?"

There were so many angles to that question that Trace looked at her, wondering if Eliza Kingsley was also more than she seemed.

But she was blushing. "I mean to say, with my brother gone . . . it would be a comfort to have a man like you in our number. At least until we reached Butte. Or if you needed to complete your business in St. Louis first, I daresay you might find a place with us, later . . ."

It was a flattering invitation, to be sure. It should have been exactly what he wanted. He braced himself for the onslaught of yearning, guilt, remorse—any of the caustic emotions that had gnawed at him for eighteen years.

He felt only a mild regret, like realizing a favorite pair of boots was worn beyond repair. "I'd like that, ma'am. But it's not possible."

"I see." Miss Eliza bowed her head again, then straightened and offered her hand. "God be with you, Mr. Tracy."

"And you, ma'am." He clasped her hand, warm, for a moment, and then let her go back to her flock.

Boz edged up on his flank a moment later. "Did that woman just *propose* to you?"

"Pretty much."

"You're a knucklehead."

Trace sighed from the bottom of his soul. "I know."

"Listen," Ferris called, and they all turned to look at him, standing poised with his head cocked northward. "I think our deliverance is at hand."

A moment later they all heard it: the long, echoing blasts of an approaching locomotive.

————

"YOU MIGHT HAVE sent word," Miss Fairweather said peevishly, as she led the way up the attic steps to the laboratory. "Surely there was a telegraph office *somewhere* between here and Eagle Rock."

"Look, lady, I had enough trouble gettin this thing on the train," Trace grunted, as he wrangled his burden up through the opening in the floor. "The brakeman thought I was carryin some kind of Indian corpse—I had to convince him it was sawdust and horsehide, like one of those patchwork critters in a carnival show. And you owe me another ten for the bribe I had to pay him."

"Oh very well." Miss Fairweather waved a hand toward one of the black-topped tables, and Trace rolled the bundle off his shoulder with a sigh and a thud. He took out his jackknife and cut through the twine, then peeled back the canvas until the thing was exposed to daylight.

It was even uglier dead than alive. She peered over it for a long moment, nostrils flared in distaste, and then summoned Min Chan, who peered into the sunken eyes, inspected the fearsome teeth, pinched and prodded the desiccated skin. Servant and mistress held a brief, murmured conversation, and Miss Fairweather's expression turned more dour, if that were possible.

"Is it what you thought?" Trace asked. "A kwang-see?"

"It is what I feared, and that is a false keung-si. Tell me, when you dispatched this creature, did you observe any spectral emissions from the body?"

"You mean the Chinaman's soul leaving it?"

"Is that what you saw?"

He had not quite doubted his own senses, but that night had been so chaotic and bizarre, he had hesitated to draw any conclusions. "The first one I killed, I saw the soul leavin it. He seemed thankful. And I think he stayed around to help me later. So you're sayin these were . . . men?"

"In some capacity, yes. I think they were infected with the corrupted essence of another creature, in an attempt to mingle and . . . manipulate their two spirits."

Trace felt his mouth curl in disgust. "Who would do that? Who *could* do that?"

Miss Fairweather hesitated for the briefest moment. "You recall the box you fetched for me, from Sikeston?"

He could hardly forget; he'd once dreamt it was trying to burrow its way into *his* guts. But he also remembered the erstwhile owner of that box. "You mean the Russian? Mereck?"

"Yes. I've seen his works in this vein before." She beckoned him to another table, on which rested a long glass cage. Inside was a small brown bat. "Are you familiar with this creature?"

"That's a bloodsucker." He'd seen plenty of them down near the Mexico border.

"Indeed. *Desmodus rotundus,* in the Latin. A torment to livestock in the southern parts of this country." She picked up a pair of pincers, dipped them into a crock, and drew out a bit of something red and dripping. She opened a door on top of the cage and dropped the morsel inside, leaving a smear of blood down the side of the glass.

In a flash, the bat leapt toward the treat, levering the tips of its wings on the floor and swinging its legs between, like a man on crutches. It covered an amazing amount of distance in a single stride and pounced on the dark tidbit, pale tongue lapping eagerly.

"Yeah," Trace said, trying to ignore the crawling flesh up his back. "That's what they did."

"While you were gone, I retraced the destructive path of these keung-si to a point north of Santa Fe. A month ago there was a rash of livestock being slaughtered by something larger than a bat, said to be almost human in appearance. A brief perusal of local newspapers reveals there was a carnival in the area at the same time."

"Wasn't Mereck travelin with a circus?"

"I believe he does, yes."

Trace thought of Ferris—his mysterious references to guiding forces, and his reluctance to say anything more about it. The Fire-Master had managed to disappear from the depot at Eagle Rock before Trace could collar him. Ferris had turned in his seat near the front of the rescue car, as they pulled into the station, and met Trace's eye over the heads of the thirty-odd survivors between them. He'd touched his hat in salute, slipped through the doors as soon as they were open, and vanished into Idaho Territory.

"I met a man on the train," Trace said slowly. "Said he was headin out west to meet up with a circus outfit. He knew your name."

Miss Fairweather frowned. "You were speaking of me to strangers?"

"Not to just anyone. This man . . . he was a bit like me. He saw the dead. And I think he could do a few other things, like conjure fire. He said he'd been put on that train to protect me."

Trace didn't recognize the next few words she spat out, but he knew cussing when he heard it.

"He was put there to *stalk* you, you fool! Ye gods! What else did you tell him?"

"He saved my *life*."

"Of course he did! His whole purpose—" She stopped, clenched her jaw, and began again in a more measured tone. "This sorcerer, this Mereck you have heard talk of, likes to prey on psychics like yourself—preferably those with little understanding of their powers. If this man you met was an agent of Mereck's, he was put in place to befriend you, to determine whether you were a likely mark. And if he saved your life, it was because his master would not want such a resource lost, before he could exploit it." She drew a deep breath. "Mr. Tracy, this haphazard approach to cultivating your abilities is putting you at unnecessary risk. I would have you live here, as my pupil, so that I may supervise your training and see that you are protected in the meantime."

It was too bad Boz wasn't there to hear this, Trace thought. Two proposals from two women in the same week.

But this time, God help him, he was tempted. Repulsed and fascinated, in stomach-churning succession. What *was* it about her that unsettled him so? Granted, he'd never met anyone like her—he'd known smart women and he'd known bossy, authoritative women, but the two traits seldom met in the same person, male or female.

"Well, forget it," he said. "If Ferris was there stalkin me—and I don't believe he was—I'd still sooner take my chances with his kind than—" He broke off, not wanting to stoop to outright insults. "Besides, it wouldn't be right, me livin here, with you unmarried and not another soul in the house."

"I could hire you as my groom," she said, without missing a beat. "There is a perfectly adequate apartment attached to the carriage house."

"Thank you, but no. And if you don't mind I'll be takin the rest of what's owed me for this trip."

She didn't like that answer, but she buttoned her lips and led him back downstairs to the front parlor, where she wrote out a bank cheque. "I shall expect a full report from you about this little excursion," she said as she tore out the page. "Everything you remember about those creatures *and* about the other psychic you met—"

She broke off as Trace tossed his packet of notes on the desk.

"Had to kill a few hours on the train, comin back," he said. "Figured you'd want the particulars. But you won't find much about Ferris in there. Whatever you think he is, he saved my life and he don't deserve you houndin him."

"*Hounding* him? I'm not sure *I* deserve such an accusation—"

"I know you ran down Kingsley to make sure I didn't take his employ," Trace said, and watched her face tighten in defiance. "And best I can figure, you did it more than a week after we'd shook on *our* deal."

She had the grace to lower her gaze. "I could not risk losing your services."

"But I'd already said I'd work for you."

"I could not risk it." She looked him in the eye, a pained expression on her face. "I do not mean to impugn your honor, Mr. Tracy, but I know you are not at ease with our arrangement, and you have this lamentable tendency toward heroic gestures. For all I knew you might have taken up the missionaries' cause and disappeared into the Wild West."

He twitched his shoulders, disturbed that she read him so clearly. "They're *Baptists*. I'm Catholic."

"Forgive me," she said. "I am not well versed in your American cults. I only remembered your *penchant* for the faithful and inept."

That did describe the Baptists, unfortunately. He thought of them cowering in the box-car, waiting sheeplike for their own slaughter, and met her eyes in a glance that was not exactly shared humor—more of a cynical rapport.

And he understood in a flash why Eliza Kingsley's invitation had held no appeal for him. She had glimpsed his power, yes, but she had immediately framed it in terms of submission to God and service to others. If he'd followed her to Butte he would have been putting himself right back into the situation of his marriage: keeping the power—and his real self—tamped down, constantly on his guard to maintain that illusion of mealy-mouthed piety.

The very idea made him feel smothered. Miss Fairweather might well be an imp of Satan, but she *admired* the darker parts of him. Since he'd met her he'd felt more at ease with himself than he could ever remember being, even around Boz.

It was a peculiar thought, and he shook it off, extending a hand to help her to her feet. "I gotta confess, these days I find myself inclined toward the worldly and sinister."

"Sinister?" she echoed, amusement in her voice. "Is that how you see me?"

"Well I know you ain't pious," he said, "and if you claimed to be helpless I'd be lookin for the knife in my ribs."

He could tell she took that as a compliment. "What a relief, then, to know I needn't play the damsel in distress. How tiresome that would be."

"Wouldn't suit you," he agreed, and won himself a wry gleam from those cool blue eyes. He put his hat back on with a half-cocky grin. "You just holler when you need me again."

PARLOR GAMES

While the breakfast sausages were cooking on their tiny boarding-room stove, Trace repeated what Miss Fairweather had said, about the keung-si being made with magic, and about Mereck being the likely maker, and about Ferris being sent to test Trace's mettle.

"I don't know," Boz said, when asked for his opinion. He scooped flour into a bowl, added salt and saleratus. "I don't know about none of it."

"Well, you met Ferris." Trace turned the sausages with a fork, rolling their pale bellies over in the grease. "What'd you think about him? You reckon he was a liar?"

"I didn't think so, but then I didn't think you was a liar, either."

"What'd *I* do?"

"You told me we was goin huntin for some animal!"

"Yeah, but that's about all she told me, too. And you said yourself it had to be somethin more, if she—"

"All I know is, you got all these new secrets with that woman, and it's got nothin to do with me." Boz's fingers swiped through the lard bucket and then mashed down into the flour. "Magic and religion, it's all the same—you in or you out."

"What're you talkin about?"

"Was the same thing with my wife." Boz jabbed at the dough as if he were mad at it. "Goin to visit with the Voudou woman next door, come back talkin bout dark futures. Wouldn't say what, or couldn't. Then one day she's up and gone."

"You said she was taken. Slave-stealers."

"Don't make her any less gone."

So Trace figured some of what was going on, at least. "Boz, if there's an inside and an outside, then I'm standin on the doorstep. I *have* to. Miss Fairweather's a liar if I ever saw one—"

"Hah!"

"—but I *need* her. And I need *you* to keep my head turned the right way." Trace forked the sausages out onto two plates. "I don't want to start thinkin everything has some sinister cause, or there's crazed Russians lurkin round every corner."

"Maybe better if you do." Boz elbowed Trace away from the stove and began to spoon out balls of dough, dropping them into the sausage grease. "The only thing I ever heard about all this spirit business that made sense is what some old Pawnee medicine man told me. He said you can't open your tepee to the sun and expect the wind to stay out."

That was unfortunately true. And there was no denying his power was growing—although to Trace it felt more like something *stretching*, uncoiling after a long slumber, hungry and eager to run. The buzzing in his head had never really quieted down since Eagle Rock. He felt as if he were constantly on his guard, listening for something that was not quite in range.

Worse, the spirits were growing bolder, more demanding. Twice in the last week he had been woken in the middle of the night—once to the sound of weeping, which proved to be an inconsolable Mexican girl, and the second time by a fellow who stood in the corner, ramrod-straight and screaming.

Trace had almost screamed himself, coming awake to that sudden panic. He was no longer merely seeing and hearing the ghosts, he was starting to feel them, to experience their last moments of despair or regret or terror. It had been that way in the old days, before he'd quit the morphine, but he thought he'd left that unpleasantness behind with the addiction.

He could still block them out when he was awake, and at night, if one managed to intrude on his sleeping mind, a quick, simple exorcism would send it away. But he had to wake up, and realize in time what was happening, to separate his logical mind from the spirits' hysterics. As it went on, night after night, it became harder to do.

Boz noticed he was acting frazzled, and demanded to know what was wrong. And God help him, Trace put him off with platitudes. He didn't know what else to do, because Boz wanted to hear that everything was fine, that Trace had it under control.

HE WAS LITERALLY shaken out of a sound sleep—came to in a spasm of disorientation, in the dark, thinking for a moment he was back at Sharpsburg, and artillery was tearing up the ground around him. But in the next breath he was groggily awake and there was a dead man at the foot of his bed, gripping the wrought-iron rails.

The heavy feet of the bed drummed on the floor like thunder. In another minute the whole boarding-house would be woken. Across the room, Boz sat up in a furor of quilts. "What the *hell*—"

"It's all right," Trace mumbled. Speech was a heavy thing, each word dragging a lead weight. "It's just a spirit. I'll take care of it."

"I dinna do it," the dead man gabbled. His face was swollen and dark, the eyes shiny and bulging. The tail end of a rotted noose hung around his neck, and his tongue protruded, dripping froth and obscuring his words. "Ye gotta tell 'em, I dinna touch that gel!"

"All right, all right, I'll tell 'em." Trace felt across his chest, and then the mattress beneath, for his crucifix. The chain must've come unknotted again. He had not had it repaired properly after Idaho.

"Listen to me!" the hanged man insisted, and suddenly Trace felt his wind cut off. He was jerked against the headboard of the bed, clawing at his neck, scrabbling for purchase with his heels on the mattress. Then, sickeningly, the bed was no longer there, he was dangling in midair, panicked at the relentless clutch around his throat, red flowers blooming in his vision, blotting out the faces of the watching crowd—

Hands closed around his wrists. He fought, kicking and thrashing, until a sudden, stinging flood of water filled his nose and mouth and dashed the vision from his senses.

He sat up coughing, the threads of the possession ebbing away as his shield came into place, throbbing and bright, so bright it made his head ache.

Boz's hands were rough in the darkness, patting over his wet shoulders and hair. Boz's voice was rough too as he demanded, "You all right?"

"Yeah," Trace croaked, and coughed again.

IT WAS STILL early when he got to Miss Fairweather's house. Min Chan left him cooling his heels in the library for so long that Trace wondered if he had caught her still abed, but then the servant came back, led him to the second floor and the back of the house, to a room plush with deep carpeting and heavy draperies.

Trace balked at the sight of the canopied bed and the light, feminine furnishings. The chamber was sweltering and smelled of menthol.

"Come sit, Mr. Tracy," Miss Fairweather said, from the chaise near the blazing hearth. Her voice was rough, and weak. "It isn't contagious, and I don't have the strength to speak loudly."

She *had* been in bed, he realized, and had gotten up to receive him. She looked smaller and more peaked than usual, swathed in a heavy velvet dressing-gown and a pile of quilts. Trace had a vicious memory of seeing his wife's face, just that drawn and drained of color, moments before he'd realized she was dead.

Miss Fairweather smiled grimly at his expression. "I told you it was no fashionable ailment."

"Ma'am, forgive me for sayin so, but you look like you got one foot in the grave already. Have you had a doctor up here?"

"Mr. Tracy, I expect you know how absurd that question is, so I will simply say, thank you for your concern. Please sit."

He sat, on the dainty upholstered chair near the foot of her chaise. "Is there anything I can do?"

"Your continued and diligent service is the best treatment for now," she said with a sigh, hitching the quilts higher over her arms. "But I am not sorry to have your company. I would have written to you earlier in the week, had I not suffered this attack. I expect the spirits have begun to present a nuisance, again? I must say you don't appear much hardier than I."

Once again her directness—and her insight—set him back. She had a knack for saying just the right thing, so as to divert him from the things she didn't say. Almost.

"Yes ma'am, they are. Becoming a nuisance, that is." Trace watched his hands shape the brim of his hat, and decided to match candor with candor. "Boz has a notion you're lettin me alone just long enough for them to become that, so I'll have a reason to come back and see you."

She lifted an eyebrow. "And do you share Mr. Bosley's . . . notion?"

"Well, let's see. After I went down to Sikeston, the power died down for a couple weeks—long enough you sent me a note askin if things had been quiet. Then after the print shop, things got *real* quiet, for maybe a week and a half. They were startin to draw close again just before we left for Idaho. And then after we got back to town, there were three or four days when it was . . . less, but never really quiet."

She nodded, once. "Your interval is becoming shorter."

"So you *have* been watchin." He tried not to feel so gratified about it.

"I wanted to know how long it took for your abilities to replenish themselves. I *had* noticed the spirits gathering in greater numbers, of late."

"They're gettin stronger, too."

"How so?"

"Wakin me in the middle of the night, throwin things around—"

"Moving material objects?"

"One last night picked up the bed and shook it. Blasted thing's made of iron, weighs more'n a steam locomotive. Shook it like a dog shakin a rat . . . And then he tried to hang me."

"To *hang* you?"

He pulled his collar down to show her the rope burn; she looked properly concerned. "I can keep 'em out when I'm awake, but when I'm asleep . . . I can't tell if I'm gettin more attuned to them, or if they—"

"Are feeding off your increasing strength?" she suggested, and he nodded. "I am certain it is both factors. That was one reason I proposed you take up residence here, so I could supervise your development. Have you noticed any other changes? Unusually lucid dreams? A sense of traveling through time or space? Any more premonitions?"

"No . . ." He thought of all the far-fetched claims he'd read in the Spiritualist journals: spirit-walking and far-seeing and the like. "You think *I* might—?"

"I am certain you will, and soon." She tapped her lips with a fingertip. "I must say, you are much more sanguine about these matters than I would have expected. You have shed your fear of these powers, have you not?"

Trace looked at the hat in his hands. "I guess I'm not worried they're a curse from Perdition, anymore. I'm not too easy about what else they might be."

"Meaning?"

Her intense scrutiny, combined with the intimate setting, was making him uneasy. He swung out of his chair and paced away in a circle, shrugging inside the tight wool coat. "You got it hotter than blazes in here."

"Then remove your coat. We needn't adhere to social niceties." She watched, frowning, as he peeled the coat from his shoulders. "I was under the impression, the last few times we spoke, that you had embraced the prospect of doing good with your power. Indeed you seemed to take pleasure in using it."

"I've taken pleasure in a lot of things weren't good for me," he retorted. She raised an eyebrow, and he sighed and tossed his coat over the back of the chair. "Look, lady, I spent five years in seminary, and the first thing they teach you is humility. *You* don't have any power; you wield the Lord's power for His glory. I don't know why this thing was put in me, but I'm not fool enough to think it was for my pleasure. So yeah, we probably saved most of those people on the train—even Boz says so—but on the other hand I've seen more folks die this spring than since the war. And I got to wonder if this work we've been doin is the right thing, or if we're makin excuses to do what we *want* to do."

Miss Fairweather considered him for a moment, fingers pressed to her lips. "Everyone you told of your curse died shortly thereafter, correct?"

"My sergeant. The company chaplain. Our priest back home. Dr. Hardinger." He took a deep breath. "My folks, and my . . . wife."

It felt overly personal, telling her that, and he saw the unease around her mouth, her fingers drawing awkward lines in the velvet lap-robe. "And how quickly did those deaths follow your revelation?"

"A month, at the outside. Most cases it was a week or less."

"Yet after nearly two months, Mr. Bosley and I remain unscathed."

He paused in his pacing. "What are you drivin at?"

"I am suggesting there may be factors more salient than the simple knowledge of your ability. Instead of asking why the others died, perhaps you should ask yourself why Mr. Bosley is still alive."

"The only difference *I* see is I've been workin for you."

"Precisely. Every fortnight or so, a purging of your power, thus rendering you less attractive to malicious spirits. Entities which, as you have seen, can destroy a family, prompt mysterious deaths in a secured cell overnight—"

"Don't." Trace felt he'd been punched in the chest. "Don't you dare—"

"I am not implying those deaths were your fault. I cannot even say to a certainty that the deaths surrounding your curse were correlated to it. But this power you have is not an inert thing you can simply bury and ignore. If it is not used, it *builds*. And while you have been surprisingly successful at keeping it suppressed all this time, I think it best you put it to use, rather than risk—"

"And ain't that just convenient for you," he snapped, testy because he knew she was right. "One more thing keepin me here, diggin me in deeper so I can't say no when you finally tell me what it is you're after."

That was *too* much candor, and he regretted it immediately.

Her face went slack with surprise, and then hardened into brittle disdain. "Oh, I see. And I suppose now we progress to the threats and extortion phase of the partnership? You're quicker than your philistine manner suggests, Mr. Tracy. I didn't expect this display of backbone for at least another month."

Her tone was pure acid, and Trace stared at her for a second, wondering what had so poisoned her against the world—or if it was something about *him* that rubbed her the wrong way. Because God knew she brought out his worst behavior. He raked a hand through his hair and tried for a placating tone. "I just think maybe we could *help* each other, instead of all this bickerin and leadin me around by the nose."

She gave a hostile little laugh. "Mr. Tracy, you have fought me at every turn. You disregard my warnings, you refused my offer to teach you—"

"Live here and be your house boy, you mean?"

"—and frankly I suspect you *prefer* to be led, so you can pretend not to notice the muck of the black arts in which you wade. You are perfectly willing to take my money and go running to help your fellow Christians, but gods forfend you expend any effort toward *my* goals!"

Trace ground his teeth. It was on the tip of his tongue to argue that he *had* asked what she wanted, more than once, and she had fobbed him off with that crap about finding a cure for her condition. Which might be true, but he was sure by now that small truth was connected to something larger, something shameful and probably dangerous, that she didn't want him to know. And he saw no advantage to begging and wheedling that ugliness out of her. His wife had been fond of that trick—wounded silences and accusations of indifference to her feelings, until he was apologizing for all kinds of things he didn't remember doing. But he wasn't a boy anymore and he'd be damned if he would play women's games with this conniving little harridan.

He drew a deep, controlled breath. "Is there anything you can tell me—any trick you know that will stop the spirits comin around in my sleep?"

"And so again, you come begging for my help—"

"I'm not beggin for anything," Trace said. "You said you had knowledge about my power, but all I've got from you is a lot of flimflam about bad men lookin to use me. *You're* the one who wants to use me, and *I'm* the one who goes out and bleeds while you sit up here and rub your hands together."

"I don't *have* your gifts," she said, as if explaining yet again to an imbecile. "Any knowledge I have would be secondhand—"

"Don't give me that. You know more than any so-called medium I've met. I think you hold back answers cause you like to keep me twistin on the line."

"If I hold back answers it's because *you* have not deigned to ask the questions—"

"I'm askin you *now*." Trace cut her off with a slash of his hand. "You said you found me by watchin the spirits gather round me. That means you been lookin awhile, and I'd bet fair money you know every half-talented medium and psychic this side of the Platte. So if you can't help me, send me to one of them."

He braced himself for more vitriol, but the look she gave him was slow and grim and deliberate.

"Very well," she muttered. "I suppose it will serve . . ." She pushed herself higher in the chaise and pointed at the hearth. "Fetch that desk here, if you please."

Trace circled the chaise and picked up the lap-desk on the hearth. It held a few books, papers, an inkwell. He settled it across her blanketed limbs; she reached to pull it closer, and in doing so one of her thin white hands lapped over his.

The contact spread through him like frost, as if he had plunged his hand into an icy mountain stream. Cold rushed up his arm, sucking greedily at his warmth and strength. Instantly his power reacted, throwing up that shield around his soul—but not only around himself: it spilled into her, too, like hot water into a bath, pushing back the cold.

The lap-desk clattered across her knees as they both dropped it. Pens and papers cascaded to the floor.

Trace stood back and stared at her. Miss Fairweather's eyes were wide and startled, her hand clasped to her bosom. He could still feel the tingle of contact up his arm and into his heart and throat, a queer, electric feeling, as if his power was still reaching out toward that connection.

"What did you do?" she said breathlessly.

"What did *I* do? What have you got in *you*?"

"What did you *feel*?"

Trace rubbed his tingling hand. "Cold." There was a gnawing in his belly, despite the breakfast he'd eaten an hour before. "Hunger. Whatever's in you—it's eatin you alive." He became aware of chill sweat on his brow, and running down his back. "No *wonder* you got it so hot in here."

"It's not I," she said quickly. "It draws through me. A sort of psychic leech."

"A demon?"

"No! Something I thought I could control, when I was young and foolish. The price of my knowledge, you might say." She looked him

over warily, as if he were something else she wasn't sure about controlling, but her eyes were clear of fever, and her color was a lot better
than when he'd entered the room. "Are *you* all right? Do you feel weak-
ened at all?"

"No. Just gave me a shock, I guess." The shield of his power was
relaxing in the absence of threat, and the feeling of drawing, of reaching toward her, was subsiding with it. "I think it *did* take off some of
the pressure."

"I should think so!" Even her *voice* sounded stronger, and the
bruised hollows were gone from under her eyes. Trace understood in
a flash that *he* had done that—that transfer of power through their
hands had beaten back whatever was harming her, at least temporarily.

She was trying to gather her cool, controlling manner around her,
but she was too flustered. "Names. Name. You wanted an address—"
She picked up a leather-bound journal from the floor where it had
fallen, flipped through it. "Yes. Herr Kieler."

She copied out a name and address onto a loose sheet of paper, held
it out, and then pulled it back when he reached for it. "Mr. Tracy. I
know you do not trust me, but I urge you to consider: my health, my
life may well depend upon your continued assistance. That alone
should convince you I do not wish you harm. And with that in mind,
I strongly urge you to consult with me before you take any action Herr
Kieler recommends to you."

"I'm touched by your concern," Trace said.

"I am not joking," Miss Fairweather said. "Franz Kieler will probably appear laughable to you, and he may in fact be harmless and well-
meaning. But dabbling in the spirit world is dangerous, especially for
someone like you. Your fears of damnation pale in comparison to what
is actually out there."

"Just let me worry about my own soul." Trace took the paper, careful not to touch her again. "Sounds like you got your hands full with
yours."

CHAPTER TWENTY-THREE

The address Miss Fairweather had given him was near the market district of St. Louis, in a neighborhood of shabby but respectable businesses and shops. It was an unassuming little storefront, with a plate glass window heavily curtained on the inside, dead houseplants and a pair of dusty chimney lamps on the sill. Flaking gold letters on the glass said BOOKSHOP, but a hand-drawn sign on the sash offered *Palmistry, Tea Leaves Read, Loved Ones Contacted. By Appointment.*

"What's it say?" Boz asked.

"It says 'Come in and get duped,'" Trace muttered, trying not to feel so disappointed.

"Aw, c'mon. Ain't like you tried *every* table-rapper in the Union."

"I just can't see anybody bona fide makin a livin off it."

"You got hired by *her* cause of it."

"You're not really makin me feel better."

Boz sucked his teeth. "You know, every time you go see that woman you come back tetchier than before."

"Well she ain't exactly a little ray of sunshine!"

"I don't got to live with *her*."

Trace scowled at himself. Met Boz's eyes briefly in apology. "Fair enough."

He pushed open the door. They found themselves in a space that had once been a storefront; the shelves and glass-front display cases were still in place, but instead of goods for sale they were now packed with mounds of rubbish: books, baby bonnets, hand tools, wallets, watches, old clothes, ladies' perfume bottles, jewel cases, and shoes. The contents of several attics, by the look of it, the kinds of things that one's relatives cleared out after a funeral.

And it was all *whispering*.

A prickle went up the back of Trace's neck. A thousand sighing voices, like the rustle of dry prairie grass in the wind, whispered around the fringes of his mind. Voices of the dead, imprinted in their cast-off belongings.

"Weird place," Boz said, surveying the clutter with a curl to his lip.

Even he can feel it, Trace thought. "There's been a lot of people—a lot of spirits congregatin here."

"That a good thing?"

"According to Miss Fairweather, it is. Means this Kieler is the real thing."

There was a narrow alley through the piles of junk and they picked their way through it, toward the murmur of voices and the smell of incense. The front room funneled into a short corridor that separated the back of the building from the storefront.

A woman stood in the corridor, her back to them, arms folded loosely around her waist while she watched some scene in the room beyond. By her casual pose and bare head, Trace guessed she was Kieler's wife or housekeeper.

"Excuse me, ma'am," he murmured. "We're here to see Mr. Franz Kieler?"

"He's in a reading," the lady whispered back, not looking at him. Trace edged into the doorway to see for himself.

The back room was more what he had expected of a charlatan's parlor: dark and womblike, with candles placed to create shadows rather than illuminate. Heavy drapes softened the walls and large gilt mirrors nestled among them, to fool the eye with illusions of movement. A thick, cloying scent caught at the throat and made the eyes feel heavy.

In the center of the room was a table, covered in velvet. The two ladies seated at it were middle-aged and respectable, judging by their stout figures and fine hats. Their faces were obscured in the shadows of the wing chairs.

The little man opposite them, however, was starkly and dramatically illuminated. He wore all black, so his pale face and hands appeared to float in the gloom. The lamp on the table threw his fine-boned face into sharp relief, making black pools of his eye sockets, except for a glitter of flame reflected from deep within.

He held a pair of ladies' gloves close to his chest, stroking them as if they were a small live creature. His gaze was blank and haunted, his jaw drawn long with concentration, an expression of tragic solemnity on his face.

"A Presence has come to me," he said in a sonorous tone. "My spirit guide brings one of the recently departed to this plane . . . Agatha, is that you?"

"Of course it is I," said the young woman beside Trace, at the same time as a sharp rap sounded in the room. The two matronly women jumped and clutched at each other's hands.

The girl beside Trace made a disgusted noise and folded her arms across her breast.

"That ain't you, makin that knockin sound?" Trace whispered.

She turned her head toward him and Trace flinched. Her eyes were shadowed as darkly as Kieler's but without the spark inside. When she turned them on Trace, he felt as if a shadow had moved between him and the sun.

"No, and I couldn't if I wished," she said. "I've tried."

"She is with us," Kieler said, and the elder of the two women gasped and pressed a handkerchief over her mouth. "She is trying to communicate . . . Agatha, your mother and your Aunt Sarah are here . . . Is there some message you wish us to hear?"

Rap! said the table.

"I keep telling you," the dead girl said peevishly. "Can you hear me or can't you?"

"Oh, Agatha!" the older woman wailed through her lace hanky. "Are you all right, darling?"

"Agatha," said Kieler in languid tones, "are you safe and happy, child?"

Rap! said the table.

"No thanks to you, Mother," Agatha said. "I told you that Walter Fitzsimmons had a cold look about him." She looked at Trace as if expecting him to sympathize. "He smothered me, you know. He made it look like a fit, and the examiner said I'd swallowed my tongue, but he put the pillow over my face." She sighed. "I never should have agreed to marry him."

"I reckon not," Trace said.

"Don't one rap mean yes?" Boz whispered.

"Yes, but—" Trace began, and decided Boz didn't really want to know he was standing six inches from a dead girl. "Never mind."

Kieler glanced their way, then extended his hands toward the two women. "We will join hands," he said, "and focus our thoughts on Agatha. If our concentration is strong, a doorway may be opened, and she will speak to us directly."

"I wouldn't count on it," Agatha said darkly. "This is the fourth time I've been here, and he hasn't managed it yet."

"Why do you keep comin, then?" Trace asked, ignoring Boz's questioning look.

"My aunt came first. She didn't like Walter, either, and she thought there was something suspicious about my death. She keeps trying to talk to me, but all this fool can do is knock on the table and speak in theatrical voices. The first time I came, I thought he heard me—really heard me. My aunt thought so, too, that's why she keeps coming back."

"Agatha Fitzsimmmons," Kieler crooned. "Come through the veil, child. See this light through my eyes, and speak with my tongue. Use this vessel to commune with your loved ones."

"Oh for pity's sake," Agatha said. "Open your eyes, old man!"

"Is there really a spirit here?" Boz whispered. "Or is he just talkin out his ass?"

"Little of both," Trace said.

"Is there someone with you?" Agatha said to Trace. "You were talking to someone, but I can't see . . ."

"It's my partner," Trace said. "He can't see you, either. So you, ah, you know you're . . . ?"

"Dead? I didn't, at first," Agatha admitted. "I thought I was dreaming. But then my aunt started visiting Spiritualists and calling to me—"

"What was it . . . what was the dreamin like?" Trace felt a weird quiver in his guts, a combination of thrill and dread. He'd never spoken to one of the spirits like this, never asked these sorts of questions. Wasn't sure he wanted to hear the answers.

Agatha shrugged. "Drifting. Pleasant. Warm, comfortable. Until I heard them calling me. Now I'm tired all the time, and they won't let me rest."

"And you can't see my partner standin here?" Trace gestured with his thumb toward Boz, standing wide-eyed and nervous behind him.

Agatha looked, but shook her head. "I see *you*. You're very clear. I see the room through there, but it shifts, grows lighter or darker depending upon Herr Kieler. He's bright and dim by turns, like a candle in a draft. But *you're* like a chimney lamp. You don't flicker. Since you've been standing here I can see the entire room." She looked him over, carefully. "You're not dead, are you?"

"No," Trace said. "You don't see other dead people, then?"

Agatha shook her head. "Do you?"

"Not here."

"Can you see my mother and aunt?"

Trace nodded, once.

"Would you speak to them for me?"

She made it sound so simple and sensible—the only polite thing to do, really. Trace felt within himself, cautiously—there was no fear, just a nervous sense of being in unfamiliar territory. "I reckon I could."

"Reckon you could what?" Boz interrupted.

"She wants me to talk to her mother," Trace said, and grimaced at his own stupidity when Boz looked alarmed. "She's just a girl, Boz. Just a poor dead girl, got a message to deliver."

"That's what you said about the last one." Boz's nostrils flared as he drew a short breath. "Well. That's what you came here for, ain't it?"

Trace wasn't so sure of that, but it was a sure-fire way of getting Kieler's attention. "Wait here a minute," he said, and glanced at Agatha. "What's your mother's name?"

"Ruth. Mrs. Ruth Walden."

He ventured into the room, measuring his pace like a pallbearer. Kieler was saying something about a place of rest and music in the clouds, but his voice trailed off as he and the two women became aware of a new presence in their midst.

Trace felt like a fool. "Pardon me, Mrs. Walden?" The elder of the ladies opened her mouth, glanced sideways at her sister, but did not answer. "Ma'am, you don't know me, but I, uh, I have a message from your daughter Agatha. She wanted me to tell you somethin."

Mrs. Walden's mouth was still open. Agatha's aunt looked confused and wary—this wasn't part of the show she had come to see.

"My son." Kieler's voice was tender, but it had been so long since Trace had been called that, he didn't realize he was being spoken to. Kieler stood up, all five feet of him, and gestured to his own chair. "Dear boy. The first visit from one of the departed can be strange and frightening."

Trace cocked an eyebrow at him.

"Providence has led you to us," Kieler said, signaling with his eyes. "Please, sit. Tell us how you were contacted by Agatha. Was it a dream?"

Trace blinked. "Yes, sir, a dream I had last night."

"And Agatha appeared to you in it?"

"She did." Trace took the seat that was offered to him, glancing at the women, the sudden hunger in their eyes. "She was . . . wearin a white dress . . . with a"—his mind raced futilely over all the things women wore—"um, cape . . . and she had flowers in her hair. She was sort of glowin, you know."

"The Celestial Aura," Kieler murmured, "that the residents of Heaven bring with them."

"The very same." Trace glanced toward the doorway. Agatha and Boz stood side by side, both with hands on hips. Neither of them was glowing.

"And how did Agatha appear to you?" Kieler asked.

Trace looked at him. "I just told you that part."

"But can you *describe* her?" Kieler suggested, inclining his eyes and head ever so slightly toward the women.

"Oh, right. Um . . . she was young and—not pretty, exactly." Had a face like a horse, now that he thought about it. And the mother looked just like her, but stouter and more horselike.

"Handsome?"

"Yeah—that's as good a word as any. Had a healthy look about her. Long and lean. Dark hair. Curly, I think." The two women frowned at him, not hearing what they wanted to hear. Trace drew a deep breath and dredged up phrases from the mollycoddling Spiritualist newspapers. "I remember the hair because it floated around her, like there was a spring breeze surroundin her. There was the smell of flowers in the air, and when I looked around I saw we were in a green field, standin in the sun, with bees and birds singin all around."

The mother was interested—more than that: hopeful. Her handkerchief was wrapped around white knuckles and she leaned forward slightly, eyes soaking him up like cornbread in bean soup. The aunt was more reserved; her gaze kept darting back and forth between Trace and Kieler.

"And when you awoke, you felt compelled to seek me out," Kieler said, his voice dreamy and soothing. "Forces you cannot explain led you to my door, though we have never before met."

"Somethin very like that," Trace said, lowering his own tone to a rumble. That was one thing common to preachers and confidence men—you had to know how to use your voice. "I walked around all day feelin like there was somethin I was supposed to do. I walked the streets like Saint Peter, wrestlin with my own unworthiness, and Agatha herself must've been leadin me, because next thing I knew, I was standin in front of Mr. Kieler's shop. And the moment I set eyes on you, ma'am," he let his eyes rest on Mrs. Walden's, "I recognized your daughter's features. And I knew I was sent here by a power greater than this poor soul."

"The Lord works in mysterious ways," Kieler said.

"Amen," Trace said, thinking he was surely going to hell.

Mrs. Walden's hand reached swiftly across the table and closed over Trace's. "Bless you," she said tearfully. "Bless you, sir."

"Tell us," Agatha's aunt urged. "Tell us what she said. It was Walter Fitzsimmons, wasn't it?"

"Sarah, don't." Mrs. Walden patted her sister's arm. "It's enough that she's safe and at peace."

"That man needs to be held accountable," Aunt Sarah protested. "Why else would she have appeared to this man?"

"She wanted me to tell you, she's happy where she is," Trace said. "And not to worry yourself about her. She said to remind you, the Lord takes care of his own, and judgment will come to us all, in good time."

CHAPTER TWENTY-FOUR

"That's all they want, really, is comfort," Kieler said, pouring draughts of beer from a jug into thick pottery goblets. He handed one to Boz, then to Trace, then took one for himself.

They were in the kitchen now, a homey and grubby bachelor's kitchen, around a simple plank table that grazed the stove at one end, and was piled with more of the same rubbish that filled the front room. This stack was mostly jewelry, and a few gold teeth. It looked as if Kieler had been making an attempt to sort out the pieces with any value.

In the daylight, the little German was slight and spry, almost childlike, with a sparse head of hair and a trim little mustache. He might have been thirty or sixty. His eyes were dark blue and sharp as a magpie's.

He offered them a plate of cold boiled beef, potatoes, and cabbage. "I must say, Mr. Tracy, for all your protestations of being a tyro, you handled those two women with a rare and fine control. Have you ever worked in show business?"

Boz snorted amusement and Trace aimed a good-natured slap at his head. He was in a much better humor than he had been an hour ago. Even that minor expenditure of his power at the séance table had left him feeling relaxed and relieved. "I was studyin to be a priest. I guess that's near enough. How did you know I wasn't fakin?"

Kieler chuckled and forked a bit of potato. "My dear boy, I am not entirely the fraud I must appear. I have the gift myself, though I am only a candle flame to your beacon. I knew there was a spirit in the room, but as to her name and message . . ." He shrugged, eloquently. "Sometimes I hear and see more. Sometimes less. It matters not to the bereaved. They want to be reassured, regardless. So we resort to the cruder methods." He gnawed at the potato and it crumbled off his fork. He caught it in the other hand.

"Trace wants to get rid of his," Boz said.

Kieler lifted an eyebrow at Trace. "This is true?"

Trace grimaced, remembering Miss Fairweather's admonition against wishing his power away. "I used to. Now I'd just like to control it better."

Kieler lifted both eyebrows. "You seem to me to have control. What is amiss?"

Trace told him about the spirits coming around and disturbing his sleep. "I got enough demands on me from the livin, I don't need the dead runnin me ragged, too." He showed Kieler the rope burn on his neck. "Used to be they were only a nuisance, but now they're actually attackin me . . . and Boz here can't get any sleep either."

"You are becoming more powerful?" Kieler said.

"It does seem that way, yes. And I can't . . . turn it off." It occurred to him, if this little man was not a complete fraud he might watch the spirit world the way Miss Fairweather did. Herr Kieler might've already marked Trace's power the way she had. In fact the two of them might be aware of each *other,* and that left him, Trace, once again at a disadvantage. "Anyway, I've been lookin for somebody else who might have more experience controllin it, and could tell me how."

Kieler nodded encouragingly, while his knife and fork were busy at work. "Tell me, your gift—were you born with it, or did it come to you?"

And so Trace related how he'd nearly died at Sharpsburg, and lain among the bodies of his comrades for almost three days before he was found. How he'd been sick and feverish for weeks afterward, out of his mind with pain and infection and morphine. And when he'd finally pulled out of the fever, he'd found he couldn't stop taking the dope without becoming sick all over again, and along with the nausea and cramps came visions worse than anything delivered by the drug.

He avoided Boz's eye as he talked. Boz had heard some of this, but not about the morphine. Trace told them it had taken him two years before he was free of the dope. He didn't mention he'd passed the second year in a Richmond sanitarium.

"And you have seen the spirits ever since?" Kieler asked. "But not before?"

"There on the battlefield was the first time." Trace hesitated. "I was lyin in that road, facin up at the sky . . . and I knew I was dyin. I could feel the blood leakin out of me, and it was gettin cold. My lungs were achin, like they do when you breathe cold air too deep. I couldn't feel my hands and feet anymore. And I was layin there with Jack Mallory's dead arm across my neck, cause he'd fallen on me, and all of a sudden he sits back on his heels and kind of shakes himself, like he'd fallen asleep. And he looks at me and says, 'Well, are you comin?' and I say, 'I don't think I can get up.' And he says, 'I'll give you a hand.' So I raise my hand up, but it doesn't feel like my arm, it's lighter and stronger and it doesn't feel like it's connected properly. But I watch it pull up, and the rest of me pulls up, and Jack's got hold of my hand but I don't feel it, either, but I feel somethin pullin at my feet, like they're stuck in mud. And I look back and I see . . ." Trace shuddered at the memory he'd let lie for so long, like grabbing for a stick of kindling and getting a handful of rot. "I see my body lyin there on the ground, with Jack's arm across my neck. And I look up at the sky and it's as though . . . all the color'd gone out of the world. The battle was still goin on all over, but I couldn't hardly hear it. I couldn't feel the ground shakin, or the men screamin—it was all faded out to gray. There was this light comin from the clouds, and it was shinin right through Jack and the rest of them. All around the battlefield there were men marchin up into the sky, and I turned to go with them, but my feet were stuck." He gave a bark of humorless laughter. "Feet of clay, I suppose."

"Then what?" Kieler asked.

"Then nothin. I was damn near bled out. Don't remember nothin more until the hospital, the surgeons." Except parts of him *did* remember, in nightmares. The dead dragging him down. The earth opening and sucking him down to hell. The sensation of worms and beetles tunneling through his flesh.

"So you were ready to go but something stopped you, eh?" Kieler said. "Some purpose you have remaining here?"

"Maybe," Trace said. "But that was eighteen years ago, and I haven't found it yet." His mind touched on Miss Fairweather—that big-eyed way she had stared at him after his power leapt into her—and he pushed her down ruthlessly.

"Perhaps you use the power to help others?" Kieler suggested. "To . . . free those souls who are caught?"

"I'd surely be glad to do it, if I knew how," Trace said.

Kieler laid his fork and knife on the table and folded his hands over them. He looked at Trace for a long moment, his expression unreadable.

"I'd be glad to pay you for your time," Trace said. "Or if you need some work in trade, I guess we could figure out somethin."

Kieler shook his head, appeared to come to some decision. "I will tell you a story." He lifted a finger in a staying gesture. "One moment, please."

He went away, back through the séance parlor, and they heard his footsteps climbing the stairs to the second floor, to the back of the building, and then doors opening and closing. The footsteps came back, and Kieler came into the kitchen with a framed tintype in his hand.

It was of himself, looking a good deal younger, wearing an evening suit and with a top hat on his arm. His other hand rested on a show placard that read THE TEUTONIC PSYCHIC.

Standing behind the placard, with a possessive hand on Kieler's shoulder, was a striking dark-haired gentleman, with sharp handsome features and a neat vandyke beard. His eyes were deep and black, magnetic, even in the monochromatic image.

"My mother had the gift," Kieler said, smiling fondly at the photo. "As did her mother. It tends to run in families, as you no doubt know . . . Your father or mother were not gifted with the Sight?"

"If they were, nobody told me."

"Someday, perhaps, you have a child of your own, and you then will know. There is a bond between families who have it, even after death. My mother's spirit was always there to guide me, after I became a young man. It was she who led me to that great gentleman you see in the image. Yosef Mereck, he was called. The Russian Mesmerist. From the great circus of the Czar, he came to this country . . . and he called to me."

Boz looked over sharply, but Trace shook his head, warning him to silence.

"Seldom have I encountered such a soul." Kieler's eyes had gone misty, faraway. "Such strength, such passion for life. He drew the gifted to him, and he loved us like children. We toured for heads of state, for the wealthy, the powerful. We made him wealthy, and he made us famous."

"What happened?" Boz asked. "Why ain't you workin for him now?"

Kieler's face darkened as if a candle had been blown out. "My gift left me," he muttered, and his gaze slid toward Trace with such sudden and naked avarice that a prickle went down Trace's spine.

Then abruptly the predatory look was gone and Kieler was all smiles and cordiality again. "But my life is unimportant. I am a *has-been*. Your friend here is the *now is*. Tell me, Mr. Tracy, have you any experience with spirit-walking?"

"Like the Indians do?" Boz asked.

"Perhaps," Kieler said. "Many faiths, many peoples have similar practices. It is a letting-go of the body, a freeing of the soul to venture into the spirit realm. The more gifted of our kind may see visions there, and thus uncover the mysteries of the universe."

That phrase again. Trace and Boz exchanged glances. "Can't say I've tried it," Trace said cautiously.

"It should be a simple thing for one such as yourself," Kieler said. "I should be glad to instruct you. The first few times can be strange and frightening, but—"

"Why do it, then?" Boz asked.

Kieler looked at him as if not comprehending the question.

"I don't know what the spirit realm is," Trace said. "I mean, the Spiritualists talk about the Summerland as if it were some kind of heaven—"

"No, no, no," Kieler said. "I am speaking of the reality that lies over and around and between ours. The space between all material objects, where the spirits move. The world where time and distance are without meaning."

"Then how do I get there?" Trace asked.

Kieler smiled and reached out to tap him on the forehead. "You already have the means, my friend. Shall I show you?"

Boz gave a slight shake of his head, but Trace hardly needed the warning.

"I might take you up on that," he said, checking his watch, "but the fact is we've got an early day tomorrow—"

"Missus Laufer's likely to lock us out if we get in late again," Boz added, scraping back his chair.

"Nonsense, it is still early." Kieler's eyes widened in dismay. "I would welcome you to stay here, in fact. There is plenty of room—"

"Thanks, but we've got stock to take care of." Trace stood and swung up his hat. "S'pose it'd be all right if I came back by, say, tomorrow night? Boz here's steppin out with his girl tomorrow, so he won't be around, but I could come."

As he'd guessed, Kieler pounced on that. He sized up the two of them, each standing a head taller than he in the dingy little kitchen, and agreed it would be far better if the first lesson included only himself and Mr. Tracy.

"Sweet Mother Mary," Trace muttered once they were clear of the building. "Was he a coyote wearin wool or what?"

"You shoulda seen his face when you first went up to those women," Boz said. "I thought he was gonna take a bite outta you."

"Mad?"

"Greedy." Boz sidestepped a puddle on the sidewalk. "And that business about Mereck. That ain't the first time we've heard that name."

It wasn't the second time Trace had heard it, either. Miss Fairweather had suggested the Russian was responsible for creating the keung-si, but then she had sidetracked him with that business about coming to study with her. Though her urgency about the latter had seemed prompted by her concerns about the former.

"You ever ask *her* who Mereck was?"

"Asked if she knew him. She said, yes, he was a real bad egg and I should stay away from him. That was it."

"You don't ask enough questions," Boz grunted.

Trace gave a bark of laughter. "You know, she told me just the same thing today, actin all offended cuz I hadn't got down on my knees and begged to know all her terrible dark secrets. But I'll tell you somethin, Boz, I could ask that woman questions til doomsday and she wouldn't tell me half the truth. She *wants* to tell me, she wants my help, but she's scared I'll say no. So she's tryin to get me in deep enough I can't refuse."

"Then why the hell do you keep goin back there?"

"You *know* why—"

"Yeah, you told me all your good reasons why, but I know *you*, Trace, and this woman's got her hooks in you like nothin I ever saw." Boz drew a short, hard breath. "You gone soft on her?"

"No!" Trace recoiled at the thought. "Lord, no."

Boz looked as if he doubted it. "Well, if she sent you to Kieler, it's a sure bet she knows *he* used to work for Mereck."

"True enough," Trace said, "but you maybe noticed how *he* managed not to tell us anything about it?"

Boz fell into surly silence, and they walked that way for half a block. The sky was streaked with indigo, and the narrow streets were heavily shadowed. "So I guess you're goin back up there to wait on her in the mornin."

"Well I sure I ain't comin back here without her say-so," Trace said, feeling nettled.

"You trust her more than him?"

"Yes," Trace said baldly, and then drew a breath, considering his answer. He didn't *distrust* her, exactly, he just knew she wasn't telling him the whole truth. And he guessed her reticence had as much to do with her own pride as with the darkness of her secrets. Perhaps because he'd carried his own secrets around so long, and at such cost, he could understand her need to keep quiet. "If nothin else, she wants to keep me breathin a while longer."

"She tell you that?"

"Didn't have to." Trace described how ill she had appeared that morning, and how his power had leapt into her when he touched her hand. How she had been shocked to find herself improved by it.

"So what . . . you healed her? Layin on hands and all that?"

"Don't think so. Wasn't anything I did deliberately. But whatever's in me seems to be a remedy to whatever's eatin her." He hesitated. "And she *did* warn me not to trust anything Kieler said."

Boz was silent for a long moment. "I wanna meet her."

"What if I don't want you to?"

"Then you'd best find yourself a strap to chew," Boz said bluntly. "You're all *I* got in this world, too, and I won't see you carved up like a Christmas goose between a pair of scavengers. I got Kieler's measure, now I wanna take hers."

CHAPTER TWENTY-FIVE

Miss Fairweather hardly kept them waiting at all. In fact Min Chan had scarcely left the room when Trace heard her little shoes on the stairs, and the rustle of silk following after.

She came into the library looking much as she had on that first day, but healthier. There was a bright social smile on her face as she came toward him, hands extended in welcome—until her eye caught Boz, who had subtly cached himself to one side of the doorway.

Trace saw her startle, and drop her hands, and button up her lips in irritation.

"Miss Fairweather," Trace said. "My partner, John Bosley. Hope you don't mind his comin along."

"Not at all," she said, in her schoolmarm voice. "At last we meet, Mr. Bosley. Mr. Tracy speaks of nothing else."

"Likewise, ma'am." Boz clasped her hand and they looked daggers at one another. From the corner of his eye, Trace saw Min Chan reappear and take up guard just inside the door.

"Well, Mr. Tracy?" Miss Fairweather turned to him with an icy smile. "What news have you?"

So they all sat down, and Min Chan brought the coffee tray, while Trace rehashed his visit with Kieler. Miss Fairweather was as cool and clinical as ever, but Trace couldn't help noticing she was rather slicked-up this morning—her dress and earrings were more suited to receiving callers than working in the laboratory. Her hair was piled in curls instead of scraped back into its usual plain knot. And as he recounted his tale, her sharp, clever face became animated, her eyes bright with interest. And Trace knew that Boz, who sat still and said nothing, marked all of these things and drew the worst possible conclusions.

"And what was your impression of Herr Kieler, Mr. Bosley?" Miss Fairweather said.

"I think he's a coyote," Boz said. "He ain't big enough to be a wolf, but he ain't above stealin somebody else's kill."

"A scavenger. A trickster."

"Yes, ma'am. And I ain't too keen on his talk about that Mereck fella, neither."

"He mentioned Mereck to you?" Miss Fairweather arched her brows at Trace.

"Yes, ma'am, he did."

"He was right proud of it," Boz said. "Did you know Kieler was in Mereck's circus?"

"It was always a possibility, given Herr Kieler's abilities as a medium, and his history in show business," Miss Fairweather said. "But I am in agreement with you, Mr. Bosley, on the issue of Herr Kieler being an opportunist. His powers are minor compared to yours, Mr. Tracy. He may well be seeking to use you for his own benefit."

"And she's the only one drinks from that well," Boz said to Trace.

Miss Fairweather's lips quirked. Trace glared at Boz. Boz tilted his head back, gazing innocently at the ceiling.

"What do you suggest I do, then?" Trace asked her.

"I agree that your venturing into the spirit world is the next logical step." She tapped a finger against her cheek. "But such an exercise is usually performed with a more knowledgeable party standing watch."

"Meanin you?" Trace said.

"You have someone else in mind?" Miss Fairweather queried.

"When the Indians go on vision quests, they do it alone," Boz put in. "So nobody interferes and the warrior's vision is his alone."

Trace was starting to want to throttle them both. "What do *you* propose, then?" he asked her.

"That I invite Herr Kieler here, and we conduct the séance under the appropriate protective seals and countermeasures."

"Protective against what?"

She made an exasperated noise. "Mr. Tracy, you are a medium. That means you are a doorway between this world and the next—perhaps between *several* worlds. Does a door have any control over what passes through it?"

"I'm not a door, I'm a man," Trace said stiffly. "And I *was* a man of God—"

Boz and Miss Fairweather made identical *hmph* sounds.

"And there are other men *not* of God, and not of anything you would consider sacred, and all of them more experienced than you." Her icy blue gaze held his. "If Kieler proceeds as I expect, he will attempt to induce a trance in you. If he succeeds—and it should not be difficult, because most mediums can self-induce at will—he will effectively be putting you to sleep, and he can keep you in that state for as long as he wishes, regardless of what comes through the doorway and makes itself at home in your corpus."

Trace's revulsion at the idea must've shown on his face, because her voice and expression grew more earnest.

"Believe me when I say this, Mr. Tracy. *You need someone to stand guard over you while you experiment.* And it should be someone unhampered by your concerns of morality, knowledgeable about the dangers, and experienced at defending against them."

"And somebody with a gun wouldn't hurt, either," Boz added.

Her eyes shifted toward him, cynical and amused. "Mr. Bosley has a point. And we shall need a fourth for the séance, in any case."

MISS FAIRWEATHER PROMISED to arrange everything for that night. Before he and Boz left, she wrote a gushing letter to Herr Kieler, explaining how her employee, Mr. Jacob Tracy, had told her all about the wonderful experience he'd had in Kieler's parlor, and how honored she would be if Herr Kieler would grace *her* parlor with his presence. She added a lot of vague references to Patronage, and Connections, and Society Friends.

"That ought to fetch him," she said, handing the letter to Trace. "Now, deliver that to his door, but don't meet him face-to-face if you can help it."

"No," Trace agreed.

"Be back here—both of you—at eight o'clock this evening. And we shall see whether Herr Kieler's intentions are honorable or not." She extended a hand, smiling politely.

Trace looked at it, and at her, and put his hat back on his head, holding her eyes in a pointed way until she returned the hand to her waist and her smile tightened into resentment. "Ma'am," he said, and followed Boz out the door.

"Well?" he said, once they were riding away. "Did you get your measure?"

"She's a shrewd one," Boz said grudgingly, and after a pause added, "She sure got a shine on for you."

"She's got a shine for my *power*, is all."

"Oh, is that what you call it?"

"Jesus, Boz." Trace nudged his horse to pick up the pace, putting a few yards between himself and his partner, whom he dearly wanted to punch at the moment.

After a quarter mile or so Boz caught up again. "Look, I reckon you're right about her not wantin to do you harm, but you said yourself she's got somethin planned for you. She knows Kieler had some history with that Mereck polecat, and she pooh-poohed it like it were no big thing. Now you givin her exactly what she wants—you and Kieler in her house doin a séance."

He wanted to argue, but couldn't fault the logic. "What d'you reckon she has in mind?"

"I dunno. Teach you a lesson, maybe."

"You think I can't handle her?"

Boz didn't answer for a moment. "I think the one good thing that's come out of this is you ain't so scared no more. You almost quit actin like God is out to get you."

There was some truth to that, and Trace nodded.

"I just wish you'd . . . I dunno, get away from this woman and figure things out for yourself."

"Go on my own spirit quest," Trace suggested. "Like an Indian warrior."

"If that's what it takes. There's plenty empty space out in Wyoming."

Trace sucked his teeth. "Y'know, my father was kinda like her."

"Mean as flint?"

"He could be a sonuvabitch," Trace admitted. "But he was no hypocrite. Taught me to rely on myself, and not be swayed by the world. Some of the things he did seemed harsh at the time, but if he hadn't toughened me up I might not've made it through the war and those first years after."

"If you're sayin she's gettin you ready for somethin worse—"

"I'm sayin, I think there's worse ahead. I feel it." He tapped his breastbone with a loose fist. "I've *always* felt it, Boz, that's why I been so afraid of this power. I kept pushin it down, runnin away from it, just like Jonah did . . . and that's why God sent the fish to swallow him up, put him back on the right path."

"So you're sayin Miss Fairweather's a big fish."

Trace gave a bark of laughter. "She did say, usin this power regular-like is what keeps the spirits from comin round to pester me . . . Might also be what's kept 'em from killin *you*."

That shut him up for a while.

IT FELT STRANGE to be riding up to the swanky part of town at the supper hour. All the houses along Miss Fairweather's street were warmly lit, and several of them had carriages parked along the curb, well-dressed ladies and gentlemen swanning up the walks to be greeted by butlers at the front door.

"Ain't we livin the high life," Boz said, as they dismounted at Miss Fairweather's gate.

The front foyer was mysterious and romantic in the evening gloom, lit with gas lamps and pale beeswax candles, points of light reflecting off the polished woodwork and floor. Trace found his eye drawn upward, by instinct as much as architectural design—there was a sense of psychic updraft in the place he had never noticed before. He craned his neck up the stairwell, past the open balustrade of the second-floor landing, and saw the lamplights reflected in the skylight at the top of the house. The effect was of standing in the bottom of a well and looking up into the heavens, and he had the distinct feeling that if he could just let go of the floor, he would float upward—

"Trace?" Boz said. He and Min Chan had paused at the library door, looking back at him. Trace hastened to follow.

The library was likewise transformed. In the candlelight it looked less like a gentlemen's club and more like a medieval monastery. The stained-glass windows gave an ecclesiastical air. Most of the central floor area had been cleared, leaving only the large round table, with a black cover on, and four chairs.

But it was Miss Fairweather who caught his eye, and held it. She looked like a little piece of the night sky in dark blue velvet, exquisitely fitted to her tiny figure, glittering here and there with diamonds. Her cornsilk hair was swept up grandly, her neck and arms bare. She was too thin for his taste, but she had an ethereal quality that reminded him of something, that poem about the fairy queen . . .

"Mr. Bosley." Miss Fairweather clasped Boz's hand, took in his new frock coat with an approving eye. "Stalwart *and* stylish, I see."

"Ma'am." Boz bowed and continued into the library, leaving Trace to stand over her, fingering the brim of his hat, holding it between her and himself as if it were a shield.

"You look well," Trace said at last, and it was not a lie. The candlelight was kind to her pallor and the sharp lines of her face. *La Belle Dame Sans Merci,* he thought. That was the name of it.

"I *am* better, thanks to you," she said quietly.

"If I were to shake your hand now, would you suck me dry like a spider?"

"I would not." Her pale blue eyes measured him with a good deal more caution than usual. "You must know I had no control over what happened yesterday."

"I know it."

"And yet you think me a spider?"

"I think there's somethin about this house I can't get my feet unstuck from," Trace said, and that was not a lie, either. Her lips quirked in amusement, and Trace felt his own face lightening.

Boz was wrong, he thought. She had no romantic interest in him, any more than he had in her. But there *was* something between them. Fellow-feeling. Recognition of mutual need. Something that didn't fit neatly into the pigeonholes of male-female relationships, that was for sure. He just knew, somehow, his fate was tied up with this mean little Englishwoman's.

Trace put out a hand and Miss Fairweather slid hers into it. "You are not lacking in courage, are you, Mr. Tracy?"

"I like to think not," he said, and she took his arm to draw him toward the fireplace.

"Now we await only Herr Kieler." Miss Fairweather ushered them into the wing chairs by the fire, and took her own seat beside the tea tray. "Have you both dined? Would you care for a digestif? I hope you will be content with coffee, Mr. Tracy. I think alcohol would not be a good choice for you tonight."

"Coffee's fine," Trace said shortly. Courage or no, he was tight as a fiddle string with anticipation. "On second thought, I'll have some of that Scotch."

Miss Fairweather's brows lifted, but she signaled to Min Chan, who brought Trace and Boz each a tumbler of whiskey. Miss Fairweather took sherry, and they all drank silently, absorbed in their own dark thoughts.

Boz had been cocky and purposeful all afternoon, almost belligerent. Trace guessed he had ideas about "settling" things tonight, maybe putting Miss Fairweather in her place. And that sounded like Custer's plan to subdue the Sioux. He had tried to explain to Boz that pressuring her was a bad idea, that despite her outward coldness there was something vulnerable in her that she would defend to the death sooner than risk exposing.

As for himself . . . Trace could hardly define his own expectations. He only knew he wasn't afraid. Not of her, not of Kieler. This séance had him a little nervous, but he found he *did* trust Miss Fairweather—if only to protect him in her own interest. And in the past several weeks he'd gotten a feel for his own strength. He might not have total control over his ability, but he was fair sure the two of them combined were no match for him in terms of raw power.

Already it was pooling and thrumming at the back of his skull, as if in response to his heightened nerves. And when he paid attention to it, Trace noticed again that sense of upward-drawing, as if invisible telegraph wires ran through the library and up through the timbers of the house. The area around the séance table felt particularly charged, and he knew she had not been exaggerating about her protective measures. There was no rug under the table and he could see no obvious marks on the floor, but the currents in the room dodged and flowed around that area like water around a boulder.

There was a low rumble of thunder, off in the distance.

"I do believe it is going to rain," Miss Fairweather murmured.

"Trace tells me you're an educated woman," Boz said. "Does that include divinatin of the weather?"

Miss Fairweather smiled. "Divination is not among my skills, I am afraid. I do, however, watch patterns of winds and barometric pressure. The glass has been falling all day. The cool breeze entering from the north should combine with the warm humid air of the day, and precipitation is the likely result. Any worthy sailor could tell you the same."

"You do the same thing with live critters? Bloodsuckers? Mesmerists?"

"Boz," Trace said.

"What? I'm just makin conversation."

"Mr. Bosley has a curious mind," Miss Fairweather said, with deceptive mildness. "You mustn't begrudge him that. Tell me, Mr. Bosley, were you fortunate enough to locate your wife and daughter, after the war?"

Boz froze with the glass halfway to his lips.

"Perhaps I am being naïve, as a foreigner, but I should think the Bureau of Military Information would have exercised its resources on your behalf, in return for your years of service."

Boz swallowed audibly. "No, ma'am, they were not that generous."

"What a pity. Did you think to ask Mr. Tracy whether he had encountered your family's ghosts over the years?"

"No." The revulsion on Boz's face approached awe. *I warned you,* Trace thought. "Can't say it ever crossed my mind."

"Ah." She sipped her sherry. "So you are less curious about things pertaining to you." She smiled awfully. "We all have our tender points, do we not?"

"Herr Franz Kieler," Min Chan announced from the doorway, and they all stood, the atmosphere twanging with heightened tension. Miss Fairweather slid from her chair and glided across the carpet, hands outstretched.

"Herr Kieler." She took both his hands in hers and he bent low over them, obsequious in every line of his body. "What an honor you do me!"

"Dear lady, the honor is mine. I only hope I can reward your generosity by bringing enlightenment to you and your guests . . ." Kieler's bright little eyes darted to Trace and Boz, and a furrow appeared between his brows. "Mr. Tracy . . . Mr. Bosley. Such a pleasure to see you again."

"You can't imagine my delight," Miss Fairweather said, drawing him into the room, "when Mr. Tracy informed me of his visit to you. I saw you in London when I was a girl . . . at Mrs. Blanchard's salon? I was too young to attend, but I crept down the servants' stairs and listened behind the door. You were *brilliant* that night—so wise and compassionate. Mother talked about it for weeks afterward. I have *so* longed to meet you."

Trace watched, fascinated, as she pressed both his hands between hers, an enraptured expression on her face. Kieler swelled with pride, taking on dignity despite his shabby suit and diminutive bearing.

"My dear child, it is clear to me, the fates have drawn our paths together again. When Mr. Tracy appeared in my salon I felt at once the pull of familiarity, but my poor skills could not have divined his connection to you—" (*Whatever that might be,* Trace thought, exchanging a sardonic glance with Boz) "—nor the connection between us. For we are all connected, my dear. No one is ever completely lost or alone, that is the wisdom I have learned over the years."

"May I get you anything?" Miss Fairweather asked. "Brandy, or some tea?"

"Thank you, I will take nothing before the séance." Kieler shot a glance at Trace. "Er—were you wanting me to lead this session, or will Mr. Tracy—?"

"Oh, he merely works for me." She waved a hand airily. "I only agreed to let him sit in on this session because he likes to dabble, himself." She threw Trace a smile that would have been dazzling if it were the least bit sincere. "Min Chan, would you dim the lamps for us? What marvelous atmosphere we will have tonight! I could not have predicted a rainstorm for my first séance. Tell me, Herr Kieler, do you still perform for salons and house parties? I have not been very sociable since I came to America, but I think the better members of St. Louis society would be greatly amused by a Spiritualist dinner party, for all they are supposed to be *déclassé*."

"Indeed, you may be right, dear lady. Shall we begin, then?" There was sweat on Kieler's upper lip, despite the cool in the room.

Miss Fairweather, on the other hand, seemed flush with health and then some; the color in her cheeks was high and excited, her pale eyes and diamond earrings reflected gold from the candle flames.

"Herr Kieler, I want to look directly into your face." Her hand pressed down on Trace's sleeve as she brushed past: *Sit.* Obediently, he pulled out the chair and sat. "Mr. Bosley, that leaves you the seat across from Mr. Tracy . . . Now, have I arranged this correctly? We are all aligned to the compass directions, although I suppose it would be better if I had invited another lady . . ."

"We will manage quite well, I think," Kieler said, smiling at Trace. Some small signal of humor was in his eyes, perhaps amusement at the flightiness of his patroness. Trace wished he could share it, but the poor bastard was *her* pigeon, not the other way around, and Trace couldn't see how it would go well for him.

Miss Fairweather settled herself at Trace's right and flounced like an excited child, her fingertips pressed to the table. "Oh! Would you like a planchette? Or perhaps pen and ink? Do you practice automatic writing? Min Chan, will you—?"

The Chinese stepped forward from his attentive position behind Boz, but Kieler waved him away. "We will begin simply, I think. If you please to join hands?"

Trace met Boz's eyes across the table and tried to look reassuring, as Miss Fairweather's small, cool hand slid into his. He felt a faint tingle between their palms, an echo of whatever it was in her that complemented his power, but none of the hungry pulling of their last contact.

Until Kieler's right hand clasped over his left.

CHAPTER TWENTY-SIX

Years ago, a much younger Jacob Tracy had attended a party hosted by a fellow who ran the local telegraph office. Late in the evening, after the obligatory rounds of Charades and Blind Man's Bluff, the telegraph operator had suggested a new game. He'd crowded all the young people into his office and made them hold hands, and then sent a jolt of electricity through their clasped palms.

The shock Trace had felt then was minor compared to the one he got now, as if two opposing waves had collided around his heart. His power reacted to it, unfurling down the back of his neck, into his teeth, and down to the tips of his fingers, commingling and clashing with the foreign energies flowing into his hands. They pushed at him, Miss Fairweather and Kieler, testing each other through him, neither willing to relinquish an inch. Kieler's grip was cold and drawing, tasting of that same bottomless hunger Trace had felt in Miss Fairweather the day before.

He almost pulled away, but her hand tightened on his. "This is all so exciting!" Her voice was giddy but her gaze, locked on Trace's, was dead calm. "I confess I would be quite terrified if I were not in my own home, surrounded by the safe and familiar."

Trace relaxed, but not much. He looked across the table at Boz, wondering if he felt anything strange, but Boz was watching Kieler.

The German's eyes were half-shut, his chin high, his posture aristocratic. He looked suddenly older, and at the same time more substantial, his fine bones made bold by the shadows. "We vill focus on ze flames," he said, his accent thickening as his concentration turned to other purposes, "und we will clear our minds of all thoughts . . ."

Boz's eyes met Trace's across the table. Trace gave him a nod, as much reassurance as he could offer without words, and then lowered his gaze to the flickering candles.

Their pull was immediate, drawing his attention downward and filling in the outer edges of his vision with black. At the same time, he felt a slacking in his mind, a letting-go of awareness. The edge of the table against his forearms, the crackle of the fireplace in his ears, Miss Fairweather's grip on his hand—all became faint and far away, as his focus narrowed to the tiny heart of a candle flame.

"And we are very relaxed, at peace, and feeling ever-so-slightly drowsy. We haff the sensation of being wrapped in cotton wool, and it is very cozy . . ."

Kieler's voice was slowing and lowering in pitch, as if Trace was hearing him through a fever. The candlelight splintered in his vision and his head rocked back but he caught himself, teetering on the edge of sleep. He struggled to blink, to pull his vision into focus.

"And we are still focusing on the candles . . . They are the only things we see, now . . ."

The table was seesawing gently as a raft on the Mississippi, and Kieler was dragging him toward the edge; the fine cool grip on his right hand was the only thing keeping him afloat. He tried to pull away but she clung to him and he saw, as if through a telescope, the long hard road that lay that way, the depth of her need and the toll it was going to take on him if he didn't get free soon—

"And we give ourselves with perfect trust . . . and bid *willkommen* to those who come . . . We are bidding dem welcome . . ."

The table was tilting, the candles sliding, the faces around him drawing out long, mouths and eyes hollow, limbs stretching, reaching, grasping—

"So gently we slide into darkness . . ."

"Boz," he managed, "don't let me—"

"*Fall*," said Kieler, and Trace did.

It was like going underwater, or stepping off the edge of awake into the first floating stages of sleep. Nothingness poured into his senses and closed over him without a ripple. He went down and down and then up and then there was no direction anymore, all directions were one and he was in all of them.

From a dreamlike distance he felt his body crumple like an empty rucksack, but it was impossible to care. He didn't have time to struggle, and anyway there was nothing to struggle against. No sound, no color, no sensation. That great void was where the beating of his heart had gone unnoticed for thirty-eight years, that vacuum where air had swirled through his ears and lungs.

He was still in the room. But he was also *above* the room and *around* the room and *a part of* the room. All the normal directions and distinctions no longer applied. He was in the table and the flame, the velvet of Miss Fairweather's skirt and the sweat on Boz's brow.

"Trace?" Boz said, alarmed, as Trace's body crumpled. He rocked forward to stand, but a band of leather lassoed around his chest and cinched him tight against the chair back. The flat, hard hand of Min Chan encircled his throat, pulling his head back taut. "What the *hell*—"

"Do *not* move, Mr. Bosley." Miss Fairweather was out of her chair as well but she had not let go of Trace's hand. She seized the tablecloth with her free hand and yanked it to the floor, revealing an elaborate design painted on the table's polished face. From the velvet folds of her skirt she drew a slim, shining scalpel. Keeping her fingers laced with Trace's, she unfolded her hand enough to made a short, precise cut across her palm.

"What are you *doin*, woman?" Boz heaved in the Chinese's grip, but Miss Fairweather was undeterred. She dipped her ring finger in the pooling blood and touched it to various points on the tabletop diagram, murmuring as she did so: "*Sanguis hic meus hominen hunc mortalem mihi ligat; ei panacea, protegeum, defensio impenetrabilis est . . ."*

This my blood binds this mortal man to me; for him it is panacea, protection, impenetrable defense . . . It wasn't Church Latin, but Trace had no trouble grasping the meaning.

The lady is more than she reveals, ja? Kieler said, and Trace turned his attention toward the German. The little man's body was likewise slumped over the table, but his spirit was standing there next to Trace—insofar as either of them was standing, or in relative proximity.

Lot of that goin around. The speaking didn't involve using his mouth. Nor was it using words, exactly, but Kieler seemed to understand him well enough.

I must apologize for the deception. I feared I would not have another opportunity. This is your first time in the spirit realm?

Yeah, actually.

And how are you finding it?

It ain't bad.

It was as Agatha had said—there was no color, and little light, but he could see quite clearly. Most of the room was illuminated, but dull and flat, like contours in a fog. Kieler put out a little of his own light, but Trace outshone him like the sun did the moon. He could both see and feel the power emanating off himself and stealing toward Kieler. There was a sensation of cold, like a draft, the only thing he could really feel except for the anchoring tug of Miss Fairweather's grip.

"Sanguis hic meus hostem quisque ab nobis repellat; Isti intrusori venenum fatalis, contagii, clades inevitabilis est . . ."

This my blood repels the hostile foe; to any intruder it is poison, pestilence, inevitable ruin . . .

So I take it the two of you weren't in this together? Trace said.

Goodness, no. Her deception is a surprise to both of us. I only hope my Master arrives before she can complete her spell.

If you're tryin to recruit me for Mereck's sideshow I coulda saved you the trouble.

The Master only initiates the very best, dear boy, Kieler said, with gracious condescension. *You are far too crude to be chosen for his family, but your power should win me great favor with him.*

Miss Fairweather dabbed Trace's brows and mouth with her blood, while Boz watched in riveted horror.

Now what's she doin?

I do not know . . . sorcery is not my forte. Ah . . . here is one who can tell us.

Cold rushed into the nothing, making it a brittle and hostile place: one of the upper layers of hell. And suddenly Trace was afraid. His body in the chair jerked in reaction; he felt it but had no control.

Meister, Kieler said. *Mein meister. I have brought you a gift.*

Malignancy swirled around them, curious, aloof, ravenous. Trace tried to retreat from it, but when distance was immaterial, there was no place to escape to. It piled around him like a thundercloud.

He is young and strong as I was, Kieler said. *He will provide you better sustenance than I.*

Icy claws sank into Trace's soul. He screamed, but his agony made no sound, only rippled the nothingness around him.

"What are you doin to him?" Boz demanded, as Trace's body again jerked in the chair.

"It's not I," Miss Fairweather snapped. "He must have been watching already."

"Who?"

"Mereck!"

The claws withdrew, leaving Trace scattered and numb, shuddering with revulsion. The hungry swirling paused, to listen. *Sabine,* it said.

"Yes," Miss Fairweather said, her voice a vicious purr. "It is I, *Master*—but no longer the student." She drew the knife across Trace's palm and ground her own hand into the raw wound.

A shock of power snaked through him like a whip, reaming out his veins like acid. The coldness spasmed, stretching and ripping through Trace's soul in its effort to withdraw from him. Trace jerked away, collected the scattered parts of himself and pulled. For a moment he was free, but then Kieler seized hold of him, made strong by desperation.

Nein! Nein! He will have you! He will have you and let me go!

The black thing lunged. Trace dodged, and then Mereck and Kieler were tangled up and the German was screaming, *I did not know! I did not know her! She does not bear your mark!*

Miss Fairweather was shouting something he couldn't understand through the psychic din, but he felt her tether go taut on him, and Boz was calling his name. Slaps landed on his face, faint echoes out here in the fog. For a heartbeat he felt warmth and air on his skin, but then he was pulled down again—Kieler's soul was being consumed and its death created a vortex that threatened to drag him in.

Whack! "Trace! Wake up, dammit!"

"Fight him, Mr. Tracy! You are as strong as he!"

I know your name, he said to the swirling black appetite. *She calls you Mereck, but I name you Deceiver.*

It roared at him, and Trace kicked for the surface.

He breached with a great sucking of air, pushed through a tingling of sensation and a pop as his ears opened. He flailed, muscles spasming at the shock of connection, found himself on the floor beside the table, with Boz kneeling over him and Miss Fairweather still clinging to his hand. His ears rang, he tasted blood in his throat, and his skin seemed too tight and heavy, but he could feel Boz's arm about his shoulders and was grateful for it.

Miss Fairweather took Trace's face in both her hands. "Look at me, Mr. Tracy. What's my name?"

"Fairweather," he croaked. *Sabine,* that other voice had called her.

"And who is this man here?"

"Boz."

"Good. Very good," she muttered. "Better than I expected. Rest here a moment; the disorientation will pass."

She stood, staggered a bit, and circled his feet to the table. She gestured to Min Chan and the two of them bent over the designs she had drawn in her blood, conversing in low voices.

Neither of them saw Kieler's head lift from the tabletop.

He sat up with the boneless drag of a puppet on strings, head lolling on his shoulders, eyelids rolling back over glassy eyes. Blood ran down from his ears and nostrils.

Cold poured out of him, a hunger and malevolence that made Trace's guts cramp. The thing inside Kieler lurched upright, murderous gaze fixed on Miss Fairweather, and Trace scrambled to his own feet, knocking Boz aside.

He got to the table just as the German's body lunged and Miss Fairweather fell back with a startled squawk. His hand closed on Kieler's throat, but the black gleaming eyes fixed on him, the hands hooked into his shoulders and started to sink, searing, into his flesh.

"*Jesus,*" Trace gasped in pain, and the bloody lips parted in a grin. He plunged a hand into his shirt for his crucifix, yanked it out. "In nomine Patris, et Filii, et Spiritus Sancti, I adjure you to depart—"

"*Hit* him, Mr. Tracy!" Miss Fairweather cried.

Trace smashed Kieler between the eyes with the heel of his hand, driving the crucifix into the bony brow, which caved like a rotten gourd. He heard the blackness shrieking, rising up in clouds like steam around him, felt Kieler's body softening like wax in his hands.

He dropped it hurriedly and stepped back, almost stepped on Miss Fairweather, who caught at his coat. She raised her left arm and made a violent slash in the air.

"*Ukhodite*," she snarled.

The air seemed to crackle, as if lightning had tried to strike in the library and changed its mind. There was a fierce *snap* and then it was gone, leaving an afterimage on Trace's brain like the smell of burnt leather.

For a moment, the only sounds were the crackling of the fire and the ringing in Trace's ears. He drew a deep breath, which hurt, and another, which hurt more. Blood was running down his arms from the stab wounds in his shoulders.

"You're hurt," Miss Fairweather said, at the same moment he noticed it. "Min Chan, fetch my medical bag—"

Trace hit her.

He hadn't been aware he was going to, but his conscience must've retained some degree of control because he pulled it at the last; his full strength would have broken her neck.

Even so she fell, hit the edge of the table, and went to the floor in a pool of velvet. In the next instant Min Chan had him over the table with a knee in his back, there was a shout from Boz and the unmistakable ratchet of a hammer drawn back. The Chinese froze with his blade at Trace's throat and Boz's barrel at his temple.

"Stop it," Miss Fairweather said in a low voice, getting to her feet. "All of you, stop it this instant."

She backed away, put the table between herself and Trace without taking her eyes from him. Boz lifted the gun, Min Chan lifted his knee, and Trace stood, pressing a hand to the worst of the pain, at his left shoulder. She had a hand cupped to her cheek and the other fisted in her skirt. Her face was smeared with his blood and her own.

"I am sorry," she said, breathing hard, "that I did not warn you—"

"Bullshit," Trace spat. "You think everybody else is too stupid to be trusted, so you keep us in the dark and expect us to jump at orders like damned trained dogs."

"If you had been more receptive to instruction I might have included you in my plans. You're willing enough to consult *other* mediums, but you treat *my* every word with disdain and distrust—"

"You *knew* Kieler was gonna feed me to Mereck tonight. Didn't you? And you let him do it so you could teach me a lesson." Her jaw clenched but she did not deny it. "I asked you *twice* what Mereck was to you and you told me *nothing*."

"You asked if I *knew* him. I said I did. And that was the extent of the conversation, Mr. Tracy. For such an intelligent man you have a staggering will to remain ignorant."

"Well, I reckon you know enough for both of us," Trace said, and turned toward the door. Boz moved after him, keeping his guns trained on the room.

"You great lummox," she said furiously, trailing them into the hall. "You won't even ask *now*. Are you that prideful, or just that set on damnation?"

"You wanna talk pride, lady, you could've tried askin for my help, instead of pushin me around like an ox in the bow."

"You'll be defenseless, you fool! He's seen you now. You can't hide from him!"

"Can't I?" Trace stopped on the threshold and looked back at her, standing in the shadowy foyer with her hands clenched at her sides. "You said yourself I'm as strong as he is. Seems you're the one who needs protection." He saw by her eyes, the sudden naked fear, that he had it right, and felt abruptly the weight of all the punishment his body and soul had taken tonight. He wanted very badly to lie down, or weep, or both. "Damn it, woman, all you had to do was ask for my help. If you know me so god-damned well, you might've known I wouldn't refuse."

She lifted her chin a notch, stubborn pride that made her look like a petulant child.

Trace slammed the door on her.

CHAPTER TWENTY-SEVEN

In the hazy golden twilight of a prairie evening, they rode up on a shallow tributary of the Platte, with a wide, sandy bank and willow trees overhanging the deeper pools. The horses slowed their pace, knowing it was close to suppertime. When Boz reined to a halt, Trace drew up alongside, crossed his wrists over the saddle horn, and squinted into the sun that sprawled across the approaching mountain peaks.

"Thinkin we'll make Fort Riley tomorrow," Boz said. "Stay here to-night?"

Trace nodded. "Horses or dinner?"

"Tell you what"—Boz nodded toward the creek—"we'll both get the horses, then if you'll start the fire and coffee, I'm gonna reach down the bank there and see if I can pull up a flathead or two."

"Sounds like a deal," Trace said, and swung his leg over to the ground.

They were two weeks out of St. Louis. It was nearing summer now, and long days in the saddle had sweated most of the chill from Trace's bones. And as usual, getting away from civilization had gotten him clear of the dead folks, too. He'd seen nothing otherworldly since they'd passed through Kansas City, and if anything evil was following them, he was unaware of it. He was almost sleeping normal again.

Catfish, rolled in cornmeal and fried in fatback, was the kind of grub that never tasted as good in a saloon or public house as it did under the sky, over a fire. He and Boz talked about the weather, and the first trail they had worked together, up to Yankton, and the Bad-lands. They split the last of the coffee and scrubbed down the dishes with sand. Boz rolled a little of the cooked fish in greasy paper, for breakfast. Trace washed his spare socks.

For all his complaints about not asking questions, Boz had hardly said a word about the séance, outside of ascertaining that Trace would not perish or run mad from the effects. He'd doctored Trace's wounds with whiskey and horse liniment and held his peace.

Trace could see him thinking, though. Sooner or later he was go-ing to have to allow Boz a couple of told-you-so's.

It was funny, really. He'd tried to protect Boz from his curse and from Miss Fairweather's machinations, but all this strange, scary springtime, Boz had been the one to take care of *him*. When con-fronted with trouble in any form, Boz was the first to step up and see what could be done about it. He didn't waste time worrying about whether his actions or intentions were right and good, he just made sure everybody was alive and whole and fed catfish rolled in cornmeal.

"What're you smirkin about?" Boz asked.

Trace stretched out on his blanket, head against his saddle, and folded his hands across his stomach. "Just thinkin you remind me of my wife."

"Huh. Reckon I can live with that, so long as you stay in your own bedroll."

Trace chuckled, enjoying the heave of his chest under his laced-together fingers. The matted prairie grass under his back felt good. Not exactly the Rock of Gibraltar, but he was fair sure nothing would be shaking it in the middle of the night.

Boz rolled a cigarette before kicking back on his own blankets. "My wife was like *you*. Used to consult with the Voudou woman next door, every Tuesday, and every time come home cryin and moanin cuz she didn't like what the spirits had to say."

"I can't picture you married to a religious woman."

"I just never figured why anybody'd line up to hear bad news. But Sarah's mother was a Voudou queen, so she was raised to it, and hated it. Like you."

"What happened to your little girl? You never told me about her."

"Left her with the neighbor lady when I went lookin for Sarah. I went back for her after the war, but everybody moved around so much in that time . . ." He made a gesture that suggested smoke dissipating, and Trace winced. Watching Dorie die had been bad enough, but how much worse would it be, never knowing? "That neighbor was the Voudou queen. Used to tell Sarah our girl was touched, that she'd grow up to serve the spirits, too. I guess if she grew up in that house, she would."

There was a short silence, during which the frogs sang, and a whippoorwill answered back.

Then Boz said, very low, "You'd tell me, right? If you saw them? Out there?"

"I'd tell you," Trace said. "But I never have. Nor my own folks, either."

Another, longer silence. Boz rolled up on one elbow, flicked ash from his smoke. "So why'd she do it? Let Kieler run that séance, knowin he'd feed you to Mereck?"

Trace sighed. "I think she ran afoul of Mereck when she was young—same as Kieler and Miss Lisette. Only Miss Fairweather somehow slipped his leash, and now she's huntin him."

"Why?"

"Not sure. I had the impression she's sickly cause of somethin he did to her. And she did say she needed my help fixin a cure."

"Fair nuff, but that still don't explain—"

"After we got back from Idaho, she tried to get me to come live with her."

Boz made a gulping sound, as if holding back a laugh. "You're lyin."

"My hand to God." It *was* a little funny, on reflection.

"Well hell, son, I *told* you she had a shine for you! Shoot, you'd told me that sooner, I wouldn'a rode you so hard. You coulda proposed marriage and never had to work again."

That was *not* so funny. "It wasn't like *that*. She wanted me to study magic with her."

"Trace, that woman lit up like a candle round you. She bought you *clothes*. Woman don't dress a fellow up unless she intends to be seen on his arm."

"She was *hopin* to get me in her debt so I'd be her lackey. And when I kept sayin no, she set up that séance to give me a scare—to show me how dangerous Mereck was, and I needed her protection."

"Hunh." Boz pitched his cigarette into the fire and lay down with a sigh. "She'da been too smart for her bloomers if she'd got you killed."

"And you think I shoulda *proposed* to that?"

"Hey, you spent all spring at her beck and call anyway, why not get bed and board in return?"

"You're a jackass."

"Pleased to know you, brother donkey."

Trace lay there and fumed. Not even sure why he was so angry, except Boz seemed determined to misunderstand why Miss Fairweather was so important to him. He supposed it was easier for Boz to believe he was a love-struck sap than to accept the enormous changes Trace had undergone this spring . . . was still going through.

And damn it, he was still mad at her, too. And disappointed in her. And frustrated that she had forced him into an intolerable position just when he'd thought they were beginning to understand one another. He kept remembering how her head had snapped back when he'd hit her—wasn't proud of that, not by a long shot—and her look of bitter resignation as she'd dragged herself up from the floor, as if she'd fully expected him to betray her.

I know you do not trust me . . . gods forfend you expend any effort toward MY goals.

But how could he have done, when she wouldn't confide in him? How could she expect him to trust her when all she did was threaten and maneuver?

"So I guess you're not worried?" Boz said, breaking the silence. "About Mereck comin for you?"

"Naw," Trace said, with a confidence he did not feel. "No, I don't think he knows me from Adam. *She's* the one he'll go for—it's their feud."

"Just as well," Boz sighed. "Horses suit me better than spooks."

Their camp fell quiet, except for the frogs singing and the soft crackle of the fire. Trace listened until he heard Boz's breathing deepen and coarsen, then turned on his side, focused his gaze into the flames.

It was getting almost frighteningly easy. In the space of three breaths, no more than four, he felt himself pulling away from his senses, attention funneling through that small window that seemed to open in the middle of his forehead. His awareness split in two: part of him still lying on that creekbed, part of him rising into a vast gray space, where all directions were one and distance was immaterial, where thousands of voices whispered like the ocean.

Out here in the gray he could *see* the power licking over his skin, a bright white glow spilling off his hands and arms. The spirits were attracted to it, all right, drawn like moths to a lantern, but with one foot in that gray other-world, he could watch the power bleed off and dissipate into the mist, until he was no more bright than any other living thing.

And that was only the prophylactic part of the exercise. With a little effort he could look all the way back across Kansas to St. Louis. He could see Emma at classes, safe behind the walls of St. Mary's. He only tried once or twice to look in on Miss Fairweather—and despised himself for a hypocrite and a voyeur—but her house was oddly obscured, surrounded by fog and strange shifts of reality to keep prying eyes out.

He guessed he could have found a way inside, had he put his mind to it. He remembered what she had said, about far-seeing and premonitions, and he felt the odd flex-and-pull of time out here: he could watch spiders weave their webs in seconds, or watch a drop of rain hang suspended in midair. And he felt the tremendous vastness of the world and sky around him; he sensed there were other thresholds he had yet to approach, much less cross, with this power. But he was not eager to test fate. For the first time in eighteen years, he felt he had a rein on this thing, instead of the other way around. These nightly meditations were keeping the power at low ebb and the spirits at bay. They were keeping Boz safe.

Trace sank back into his skin, feeling his ears pop slightly as they always did. The stars and firelight seemed brighter, more real, as his focus came back to the physical world. But something snagged at him before he came all the way out—a fine cool strand of need, catching at his right hand. A plea unvoiced.

"*No,*" he whispered into the darkness. "You had your chance."

She was in quite a snit tonight. If she'd been there in front of him she would have stomped her foot.

"I said *no.* Ask me nicer and maybe I'll reconsider."

She dissipated like mist, managing to convey a flounce of temper. Trace smothered a chuckle and rolled on his back, pulled his hat down over his face.

Didn't even *dream.*

HORSEFLESH

CHAPTER TWENTY-EIGHT

Trace could not remember exactly the conversation in which he'd told his family about his curse. They'd been sitting in the living room that evening—the elder Tracy, Aloysius, and his younger, golden-haired wife, Rachel; and Jacob's own wife, Dorothea, pretty and plump with pregnancy, her auburn hair gleaming in the lamplight. Probably she had been making something for the baby, whose arrival lacked only a month or so. Probably Rachel had been doing her own sewing; no one's hands were idle in the evenings. Probably Jacob had been whittling or greasing tack or braiding rope, while Aloysius read aloud to them from one of his Catholic-interest newspapers or political tracts.

Jacob was thirty that summer, and finally felt like a man. He'd been married nearly eleven months. He'd mended fences with his father, been welcomed home like the prodigal son, and thrown himself willingly into the family farm. The years he'd spent on cattle ranches out west had taught him a few things about the new breeds and ways to improve stock, and Aloysius—perhaps as eager as his son to smooth over the years of ugliness between them—had been surprisingly receptive to Jacob's ideas.

In the past year, since meeting Dorie, he had not seen a single spirit. Not one. And while some deep, intuitive part of him attributed the miracle to her bright and intoxicating presence—she kept his head so turned around he hardly noticed where his feet were, much less any sinister goings-on—with his rational mind he chose to believe that he had finally grown up, put away childish things, overcome the weakness of mind and spirit that had needed to see death and horror all around him.

The old man had been right, the thirty-year-old Jacob Tracy told himself. He'd spent too many years with his head in the clouds, dreaming of some grand calling instead of settling to mundane reality. At least there was no more talk of his becoming a priest. Getting married had put paid to that idea. And his brother Warrick was twenty-two and already a corporal in the army. The irony of Aloysius's pride in his younger son's career was not lost on Jacob.

That was probably what had prompted the confession, now that he thought about it. Aloysius had been reading one of Warrick's letters, and boasting about the younger brother's achievements. Jacob had felt compelled to remind them that he, too, had been in the army and there was nothing distinguished about it, from an enlisted man's point of view. That had goaded Aloysius to declare that fighting in support of such wickedness as slavery and rebellion was bound to bring on God's judgment.

And then the familiar litany, delivered not in a scold but in a rational, triumphant tone, as if Aloysius was imparting some higher wisdom that his son was finally old enough to grasp: that defying one's elders and falling in with ungodly companions were the first steps on the road to vice, intemperance, and insanity. It was only through God's grace, Aloysius reminded them all, that Jacob had recovered from possession by the demons morphine and madness.

Dorothea had gasped at that, her eyes darting from her father-in-law's face to her husband's. Jacob felt frozen with shame and fury; he had told her little about the two years after he'd been wounded.

Rachel, alone of them, had the detachment and grace to turn the moment. "Now Al," she said—the only person Jacob had ever heard chide his father and get away with it. "You know Jacob was badly wounded. *Of course* he spent time in hospital. We should thank God he survived at all. And let's not discount his own character in maintaining his temperate ways. Why, you know even Father Gilham has a greater fondness for the bottle than he ought. It's the curse of the Irish, my grandmother always said."

"I was never mad," Jacob said, looking his father in the eye. "I was out of my head with pain and fever, and yes, with the medicine they gave me. But I know what was what. I saw things out there on the battlefield, and for years after."

Aloysius looked stony. Rachel seemed poised, as if to grab for a knickknack in harm's way. Dorie stared at Jacob, big-eyed. "What things?" she whispered.

And so he told them. About lying there on the battlefield and seeing the tear in the sky, and watching his fallen comrades march up through it. About the hospital, later, and noticing how some of the dead seemed to linger, confused, and how they began to congregate around his bed, asking him for directions, for explanations, to carry messages to loved ones. How he had argued with them and then raved at them in his pain and fever, until the nurses, not knowing what else to do, loaded him up with so much dope he could hardly move, and the ghosts mingled with his opiate dreams and began to seem like demons.

By the time he was healed enough to be moved he was already known as a derangement case (Dorie's eyes were growing bigger and bigger) and the dope had its hooks in him. They'd transferred him, along with a few other ravers and cataleptics, to the sanitarium at Richmond, where he eventually came to the attention of Dr. Hardinger.

But he knew it would do no good to tell Aloysius Tracy that his saving physician had been a devout Spiritualist, who had tried to persuade the younger Jacob that he'd been favored by God to bridge the worlds of the living and the dead. So the thirty-year-old Jacob caught his breath and summed up weakly, "He helped me stop seein them so often."

"But you still *see* them?" Dorie insisted, her eyes darting around the room, as if reconsidering all the shadowy corners.

"No," Jacob said, taking her hand. She was a delicate little thing, afraid of horses and lightning and overly large dogs. It was one of the things he loved about her—that she made him feel brave and strong. "Not for some time now. Certainly not since I met *you*. You think I'd let anything evil near you?"

"But you *did* see spirits," Aloysius persisted, "after leaving the hospital. I saw it in your eyes, when you came here. The Devil's curse was on you, and his imps pursuing you."

Anger boiled up in Jacob. "Yeah, Da, they were. And you gave me no respite from them. You threw me out of here like Cain—"

"Jacob," Rachel interrupted. "Let it be. Your father has long regretted his treatment of you. Don't undo the goodwill you've built between you. And this quarrelling isn't good for the baby."

Jacob glanced at Dorie, who had a hand spread over her belly and was white as a sheet. Instantly contrite, he helped her out of the chair and to their room, where he spent another hour or more assuring her there were no ghosts in the house, no demons coming to harm her or their baby.

But three weeks later they were all dead.

On the eight-year anniversary of those deaths, Trace was going over the books with Boss Miller when Red stuck his head around the office door and delivered the news that they'd found another dead horse.

"Well, hell," Miller said, and Trace asked, "Where?"

"Up at the creek," Red said, breathless, the freckles standing out on his cheeks from running in the cool air. "Me an' Hanky found 'er, riding the fence line first thing this morning, and Preacher, you said you wanted to see the next one so we hauled 'er back up here—"

"I wanted to see it where it *fell*," Trace said testily. "Go fetch Boz, he's down in the paddock."

Red ran off obediently and Trace and Miller grabbed their hats to go outside.

"What's that, four?" Trace said.

"Four since you got here," Miller grunted. "Seven this spring. That dad-blamed wolf-hunter better get his ass up here."

Trace said nothing. He was yet to be convinced that wolves were the culprit.

They crossed the ranch proper, past the cook-shack where the boys were queued up for breakfast, past the dairy barn and the corral for the remuda horses, toward the edge of the north pasture where Hanky sat astride his fidgety pony, still holding the tow-line of the dead filly they'd roped and hauled back. Which had been a damn fool waste of time and effort, but Trace had long ago learned that the young and eager could foul up instructions in ways so creative that the old and seasoned would just drive himself mad trying to forestall them all.

Trace dropped to his haunches to survey the carnage, grimacing at the smell and the waste of a good horse. Miller swore when he recognized her—the three-year-old filly had been one of several he'd marked for breeding, having the broad quarters and fine head he was looking for. Miller's stock wasn't yet of the lineage or reputation of some of the Texas breeders, but he was getting there, and this was a setback.

"Slashed the legs to bring her down," Miller said, pointing. "Just like the others."

Trace could see that, but he could see also that the flesh of the throat and belly had not been eaten, merely shredded. After viewing the last two corpses, Boz had opined that their killer was a mountain lion: cats were known to kill for the fun of it. But lions usually jumped a horse from above and bit its neck, forcing its head into the ground. None of the wounds Trace had seen were conclusive, and that was why he'd wanted to see the corpse *in situ*, to get a look at the surrounding ground.

"Where'd you find her?" Trace asked Hanky.

At nineteen, Hanky resembled a coiled whip—lean, brown, and tough, already a seasoned cowhand, with a light way of sitting in the saddle and a young man's disconcern toward life. He jerked a thumb back north, toward the creek. "By that pool at the waterfall. An' I saw somethin *big* out there last night, movin up the cliff. Horse didn't like it either. Big as a bear, walkin on two legs. I shot at it and it ran."

"Best not to shoot at a bear unless it's coming toward you, son," Miller said, and Hanky looked as if he would argue, but he was interrupted by the jingling of tack and the thud of hooves coming toward them—Boz's horse, Nate, with Blackjack on a lead behind him.

"Hanky, go put that horse away and get breakfast," Trace said. "Then after, you and Red can haul this carcass down to the gully and dump it. I won't be an hour," he added, to Miller.

The rancher waved dismissal, and started his trek back across the yard. Trace untied the tow-ropes from the carcass and tossed them up to Hanky, who looped them over his saddle-horn.

"It wasn't a bear, Preacher," Hanky said in an undertone to Trace. "It didn't *move* like a bear."

"How clear did you see it?" Trace asked.

"Pretty clear. Looked like a man—a big man, with a buffalo coat on. Or with a bundle of furs on his back."

"Maybe it was," Boz said. "Some trapper, poachin beaver out of the creek."

"I never saw a man jump like that," Hanky argued. "Musta cleared twenty feet up'n over that waterfall."

"Hunh," Boz said, but no more; Hanky frankly worshipped Boz—all the boys did, since Boz was the best horse-trainer on the place—and Boz was careful with their pride.

"Breakfast," Trace said. "Chores. Get to it."

Hanky scoffed, but lightly; he wheeled his horse around and headed back to the ranch proper. Trace guessed his silence would not last long once he was there—ranch work was frequently tedious, so any minor adventure or curiosity must be told and retold, embroidered and exaggerated to the limits of credulity and beyond.

"He'll have 'em sayin there's a wen-di-go out here by suppertime," Boz said, their thoughts running in tandem as usual.

"Don't let's joke about that," Trace said, and swung up into Blackjack's saddle.

They followed the drag-trail Hanky and Red had left, back across the north pasture three miles or so, to the creek that bisected Miller's land. Most of the valley was gently rolling and grassy, but if a body followed the creek back into the trees, the terrain got steep and rocky, fast. At one point land and water took a leap upwards, forming a ten-foot cascade with a pool at its base. It was no difficult thing to find the site of the murder, there on the round-washed rocks beside that pool.

Trace dismounted, handed Blackjack's reins to Boz, and crouched in the middle of that arterial spray, laid his hands on the bloody rocks. He'd tried a couple times to get an impression of the killer through the dead horses' eyes, but apparently equine minds were not open to his power the way men's were. He and Boz had debated whether this meant horses had no souls, or if their brains weren't clever enough to retain memories, or if Trace's brain was simply different enough from a beast's that the memories wouldn't translate. It didn't matter; he had discovered he could sometimes get brief visions from a *place,* as if the very earth and timbers trapped vestiges of time and emotion. He had read about psychics who could "read" the possessions of the dead, and he supposed this amounted to the same thing.

Boz leaned on his saddle-horn, eyes raking the ground and Trace with dispassionate interest. "Anything?"

There was, a little. Like a vibration, or a scent, very faint. "Just the horse, here . . ." He could see the animal, edgy but not alarmed, flicking its ears back in the knowledge that something was close. "Doesn't seem too shook up."

The attack came without warning, and Trace recoiled from it; he seldom felt anything so violent in the spirit world, where sensations were blunted and everything had a dreamlike quality. He couldn't get a look at the attacker, but he felt the poignancy of its rage, the hopelessness in its blood-lust. It had enough self-awareness to hate what it did, and hate itself for relishing the task.

Trace shook himself out of the trance and found all his muscles knotted with that frenzied fury. He looked at his hands and was almost surprised to find them muddy, rather than slick with blood.

"Well?" Boz said.

"Still can't get a look at it. But it was plenty mad."

"At the horse? For wanderin into its territory?"

"I don't think it's an animal."

Boz sucked his teeth. "A man, then. Tearin up the wounds to make 'em look like claws."

"Could be." Trace squatted to wash his hands at the edge of the pool.

"It ain't wolves, for damn sure." Boz swung down from Nate's saddle and paced carefully around the blood-spatter. "Wolves don't cut the hind legs like people say. Too much risk of gettin kicked. Whoever did this prob'ly *heard* that's what wolves do, and don't know any better . . . Look." Boz planted himself like a tree, pointing to the ground on either side of himself, where there was a gap in the blood-spray. "Horse was facin this way, first gusher of blood came *whsst.*" He drew a line in the air across his chest. "Killer was standin here, got splattered."

"Standing?" Trace repeated. "Taller than a wolf?"

"Have to be. Man-sized. Also explain why the horse didn't bolt."

Trace nodded. All of Miller's horses, even the unbroken ones, were well used to men and not shy around them. "Well, Hanky *did* say it looked like a man. Could be an Indian renegade, slipped off the Agency."

"Or somebody's got a beef with Miller," Boz said, which was more likely. Water and grazing rights were a constant bone of contention these days, and Miller had fired his last foreman, not long after Trace showed up to take his place.

Trace combed through the bruised foliage along the edge of the pool, and found a pair of tracks, deep and skewed, as if something big had pushed off in a leap toward the top of the waterfall. "Look at this."

Boz came and looked. He hunkered over the tracks a long time, and then stood up and nudged his hat back, scratched under the band with one thumb.

"Just say it," Trace taunted. "You don't know what it is, either."

"Looks like a cat, to me."

"With five toes?"

"I ain't sure that last one is a toe." Boz eyed the rock face above the pool. "You gonna go up there and check, or am I?"

So Trace scrambled up the slippery rocks on the downhill edge, until he was standing at the top and looking at some muddy smears where the killer had landed—on two feet. "Looks like Hanky was tellin the truth."

"Tracks any clearer?"

"Nope. Too wet."

"Can you see where it went?"

"Into the creek." Trace stood there a moment longer, measuring the distance by eye. Hanky had not exaggerated for once: it had to be twenty feet from where the thing had pushed off. "You remember those bloodsuckers on the train?"

"Aw, for the love o'—I *knew* you were gonna say that."

"You ever seen a *man* make a jump like that?"

"Those things were pack hunters," Boz argued. "And they weren't shy of men *or* guns. If Hanky ran up on one of those things, you think he'd be alive to tell us about it?"

"Probably not," Trace conceded. He climbed back down the rise, mounted up, and turned Blackjack's head toward home.

CHAPTER TWENTY-NINE

It was a cool, clear, bright morning, promising a gorgeous summer day. Today was the twentieth, Trace reminded himself, mentally going over all the chores that needed parceling out. They'd been up to Evanston on the Fourth of July—that was the summer's big horse-fair, with races and exhibitions and prizes, and the ranch had acquitted itself nicely—but Miller wanted another batch of animals ready for the first of August, and that meant ferrying, exercising, training checks on some of the four-year-olds. Plus there was fence and tack to be mended, the chicken coop to be moved, repairs done on the bunk-house roof . . . Seemed like there was something else he was supposed to remember, about today. Something unpleasant.

"You, ah, you ain't maybe *seen* somethin out there, nights?" Boz ventured after a while.

Trace had confessed some weeks ago about his nighttime meditations. He had been careful to give Boz credit for his idea about the Indians and their spirit quests.

Boz had been equally careful to take the news with equanimity. "I figured it was somethin like that," he'd said, after Trace explained why he still took a turn on the night watch, two or three times a week, and how he'd learned to meditate in the saddle. "You been a lot more even-keel since we been out here. I just thought maybe there weren't so many spirits around these parts."

There were a few—murdered Indians, lost soldiers, a family of settlers who'd been slaughtered down by the creek—but Trace was keeping the power at a low enough ebb that none of them made trouble. And so far he'd seen no demons loitering about, no visits from sinister Russians. He was starting to think he'd dodged that bullet.

"Nothin out of the ordinary," Trace said thoughtfully. "I guess I could take a turn tonight, see if there's anything new in the area."

"How much *do* you see? In the dark?"

"A lot," Trace admitted.

"Like what?"

"Like every live thing from here to the bunk-house." He nodded at the horizon, where the smoke from the cook-shack was just visible. "In the spirit world everything is sort of gray and still and quiet—like bein in the woods during a snow. All the live things show up like fireflies, but white. Every mouse, every screech-owl. I can tell every horse at a distance, tell you each one by name and where it is. The men, too."

"Is that how you caught Droopy asleep on his watch last week?"

"Yup," Trace said, smugly.

"Hunh. So how come you ain't seen this thing killin the horses? Or if it's a man, why ain't you noticed somebody where they ain't supposed to be?"

"Don't know. Maybe didn't look in the right place. Maybe happened while I was asleep and not payin attention. I ain't God, you know."

"I was wonderin when you'd notice," Boz said amiably.

They dismounted in the remuda corral and stripped down Nate and Blackjack to turn them loose for the day. The ranch was beginning to bustle with early-morning activities—cows lowing in the dairy barn, hands rattling milk pails and crooning to their charges. Chickens clucking over their feed, and Mrs. Miller clucking right back at them. Trace and Boz said, "Ma'am," to her as they passed by, and she smiled and asked Trace how he was enjoying that volume of Shakespeare she had loaned him; Trace said he was enjoying it mightily. Mrs. Miller had been a schoolteacher for twenty years before she'd married Miller. She liked children, but she had none of her own, so she mothered the ranch hands as best she could.

Meals, during the summer months, were cooked in an open-sided shack outside of the main bunk-house. The hands had constructed a fire-pit there, surrounded by rough benches, and during all but the wettest weather this was the hub of ranch social life. Hanky was there now, with his regular posse. By the sound of things, he had already spilled the beans about the savage horse-killer in their midst, and in typical cowboy fashion, his audience was raking him over the coals as a liar, a fool, and a tenderfoot.

"No, no!" Hanky insisted, pointing an accusing finger at Red. "*You're* the one who don't know from bears. What about that night you fell outta the saddle cuz you rode up on that tree stump and thought it was a bear?"

"That wasn't me," Red countered. "Hey Droopy! 'Member that time you fell asleep in the saddle and rode up on that old stump afore you knew what it was?"

"I didn't fall asleep," Droopy protested, and the boys all laughed, because Droopy was *named* for his ability to catch a nap wherever he sat. "Least I make it into the saddle. Unlike *some* people."

There was a brief, accusatory silence, such that even Trace looked up from pouring his coffee to see who they were staring at.

The Kid, as usual, sat a little away from the others, head down over his Bible—the Book of Mormon, to be strictly accurate—and it took a few seconds for the stares to penetrate his isolated attention. "I beg your pardon?"

"Surprised *you* didn't come runnin when I shot at that critter last night," Hanky said.

"I didn't hear any shot," the Kid said.

"Where was you?"

"I was out on the east boundary, where I was supposed to be." The Kid looked at Hanky coolly through his spectacles. "How do I know you fired a shot? How do we even know *you* rode your shift last night? Maybe you got up at dawn and used your story of finding the horse to cover your sloth."

Hanky was not a stupid young man, but to call him sophisticated would be a stretch. He might not completely understand the challenge that had been levied at him, but he knew it required answering, and he let the Kid have it with both barrels. "You sure talk fancy for one o' them inbreds, four-eyes. How many Prophets did your momma marry, to make you so high-and-mighty?"

Trace was aware of glances darting his direction, wondering if the top screw was going to wade in before fists were thrown, but Trace knew better than to interfere in the pecking order, and he was curious to see how the Kid would handle himself. At sixteen, the Mormon kid was the youngest hand on the ranch, and the least experienced. He could ride well enough, and was neat about handling the horses and their tack, but he couldn't herd worth a damn and he knew next to nothing about roping, doctoring, fence-building, or any of the myriad other skills a cowboy needed. He obviously had been raised to a different kind of life, and Trace wondered what had driven the boy to abandon Salt Lake in favor of this roughneck outfit that he clearly despised.

Beyond that, there was something about the Kid that nagged

Trace's psychic sense. It wasn't the nerve-jangling alarm he got from demons, nor the sense of familiarity he'd felt from Ferris. The feeling was faint but off-putting, like a rank odor. The Kid just plain rubbed everybody the wrong way, with his watchful attitude and his scorn. And there was a streak of disquiet in him, which Trace and Boz had marked but the younger cowboys had not the experience to recognize: one of them was going to push the Kid too far one day, and end up with a broken nose or worse.

For a moment Trace thought today would be the day. The Kid's head went down and his eyes were cold murder behind the spectacles. But he said flatly, "There's only one Prophet, you ignorant Gentile."

Hanky laughed. They all laughed, with varying degrees of meanness and sympathy. But the taunting had run into a box canyon—it was no fun tormenting a victim who didn't fight back—so the boys returned to their grub, turning their backs on the Kid, who got to his feet and made as if to head for the bunks.

"Hanky," Trace said, before the Kid was out of earshot, "you and Red drag that horse off like I told you?"

"You said after breakfast, Preacher," Hanky said, holding his tin cup aloft.

"From the way you were jawin I figured you were done chewin," Trace said. "The rest of y'all can move the chicken coop and the pens to a new patch of grass. And make sure you clean out all the boxes and put in new straw."

Groans all around. Herding chickens was no one's favorite chore.

"And after that," Trace said, adding the coup de grace, "you can help Missus Miller with the weeding."

Shrieks of agony this time. Protestations of unfairness. Negotiations of souls, future prospects, and firstborn sons.

Trace raised his voice. "Kid!"

The youngster stood poised on one foot. "Sir?"

"After you get your morning chores squared away come see me in the office."

Voices dropped to a speculative murmur. Being called to the office, when it wasn't payday, usually meant dismissal. The last time it had happened, Miller had called down his old foreman and told him to get his drunken ass off the property before noon.

The Kid's jaw clenched, but he said, "Yes, sir," before continuing on his way.

Trace took his plate of bacon and biscuits and seated himself across from Boz. The cowboys scarfed down their food, shooting wary glances in Trace's direction, before scattering to the day's work.

"You gonna fire him?" Boz asked, when they were alone.

"Prob'ly not today," Trace said.

"COME IN," TRACE said, when the Kid appeared on his doorstep an hour later. "Sit down."

The Kid sat. He was a good-looking boy—a tad on the short side but stocky, with broad, rosy cheeks and a shock of straw hair. Trace looked for a glare of defiance in him but couldn't find it; just a wary control in his face and posture. The Mormon boy showed more respect to Trace than he did anyone else, and Trace guessed it was because of the moniker "Preacher" that Miller had laid on him, fourteen years ago when he was a greenhorn himself.

"Are you really a preacher?" the Kid had asked once.

"I was readin to be, when I was your age," Trace told him.

"Why didn't you finish?"

"Guess the Lord had other plans for me," Trace answered, and the Kid had looked thoughtful at that, but said no more.

"Is there any truth to what Hanky said this mornin?" Trace asked the boy now. "About you skippin your turn on the watch last night?"

"No, sir," the Kid said stoutly. "I mounted up the same time he did, four o'clock. He saw me do it."

"What horse did you take?"

"Buttercup, sir."

Trace made a mental note to ask Old Walt, who minded the remuda horses, whether Buttercup had been back in the corral that morning at dawn. "Did you or did you not hear gunfire last night?"

"I did not, sir." The Kid's eyes were guarded.

"Why not? Where were you?"

"Well I don't know, do I? Somewhere along the east boundary. I guess I maybe heard a crack during the round, but I didn't know what it was. Could've been a branch breaking."

Trace wasn't sure he believed that. The east boundary *was* full of pines and scrub, but a breaking branch made a much sharper sound than the pop of gunfire, and a gun report would have echoed like the dickens, back by the waterfall where Hanky had seen his monster.

"I want you," Trace took a clean sheet of paper and turned it toward the Kid, "to write for me," he passed over the ledger pen, " 'I, Karl Oscarson Smith, do solemnly avow that I rode my watch last night.' "

The Kid glanced at him mistrustfully, dipped the pen and wrote, with only a slight hesitation over the last part. He signed it with a flourish.

As Trace had suspected, the boy had a fine hand, regular and highly legible. "You like book-work, son?"

"I took the Prophet's dictation at the Temple for two years," the Kid said, with a hint of pride. "I wrote all his letters and declarations."

"I thought the Prophet passed on some years ago."

"Prophet Joseph Smith was martyred thirty-six years ago. Prophet Taylor is the President of the Quorum of Apostles."

"My mistake," Trace said. "Your pa must've been pretty close to the Prophet, then, if he saw your writing and offered you the job."

That seemed to touch a nerve. The Kid's poker face was smooth, but not that smooth. "Yes, sir," he said, without elaborating.

"Fine. You like hand work, you can help me out here, mornings." Trace pulled out a bill of sale and slapped it down on the blotter. "I need twenty-five of these copied out. Leave blank lines where it says the date, the name of the buyer, and the animal's description. You do those right and maybe I'll find somethin else for you to do."

The Kid looked stunned, but recovered quickly. "Yes, sir. Thank you, sir."

Trace got up, taking the boy's affidavit with him. "I'll be at the smithy, if anybody asks."

"Yes, sir." The Kid rearranged the inkwell and the blotter to suit him, and fell to.

Once out on the porch, Trace glanced at the paper in his hand. *I, Karl Oscarson Smith, do solemnly avow I was in the east pasture last night.*

A subtle distinction. Signifying what, Trace didn't know. But the Kid was lying about something more important to him than missing his turn on watch. Trace had done enough prevaricating of his own to recognize the signs.

THE REST OF the day was uneventful. There were only two branding accidents, and one broken finger, when Sam's grip slipped on a buggy-axle while Davy was putting a new wheel on. A horse stepped on Old Walt's foot, but it was only bruised, not broken. While Trace bound up the foot, Walt confirmed that Buttercup had been taken out last night; he'd saddled her after supper, and she'd been stripped and her tack stowed before six, when he'd arrived at the corral. The Kid's bunk mates also confirmed that he had been up and gone when they awoke at dawn.

Boz spent the day in the training paddock, putting the four-year-olds through their paces. He gave particular attention to his favorite pinto mare—too gaudy for a driving horse, but the animal had sense and fire, a deep chest and massive hindquarters that promised a hell of a jumper. There was a crowd of Englishmen up in Denver who organized fox-hunting clubs, just as if they were back on their country estates in Surrey. They were some of Miller's best customers.

Trace never tired of watching Boz work with a horse. The paint darted from one end of the barrel-lane to the other, stopping and backing on a dime, putting down every foot as pretty as a dance. Boz had acquired a certain prestige during their brief time here; the other trainers accepted him and even consulted him occasionally. Miller trusted him with the best of the stock.

"Put that one down for the market," Miller said, when Trace met up with him outside the paddock. Trace made a note of it, and then told the rancher he'd put the Kid to work in the office.

"Just as well," the old rancher said. "He's useless with the cattle."

"You hire him?" Trace asked.

"Sullivan did," Miller said, naming Trace's predecessor. "Found him in Evanston back in May. I think he just wanted somebody to record sales cause he was too drunk to do it."

That explained the strangely neat handwriting in the books. Trace knew Sullivan had stepped into the foreman's role when *his* predecessor had gotten married and pulled up stakes for San Francisco. Sullivan had been a good cowboy and popular with the men, but the higher foreman's pay had let him overindulge his fondness for whiskey.

"Kid causing trouble again?" Miller asked. "Martha overheard some of the boys saying they were going to 'fix' him."

"They're rough," Trace said. "He's not. He lets 'em know it. Have to wonder why he came up here, if he hates it so much."

"Prob'ly got nowhere else to go. The Elders tend to run off the young men—not enough women to go around, you know."

Trace nodded. He'd heard the stories about Mormons taking multiple wives. He'd always wondered how they meant to make that work in future generations.

"If a boy takes a shine to a girl his own age, but her pa wants to wed her to one of the church Elders, well, the boy's got to go. They tell him he's a wicked sinner and run him out of town. I get one or two of 'em every year. They all work hard, but some of 'em don't rest easy among the low-down sinner crowd." Miller gave a brief, mocking smile. "Seems I remember another young missionating-type who got his flint fixed for passing judgment."

"So do I," Trace said, "and he was a mush-headed young gull."

"Aw, you were young, that's all. Younger than your years, I used to think." Miller gave him the critical once-over he used to gauge horseflesh. "You grew into your legs all right."

CHAPTER THIRTY

It got dark early in the valley, shadows drawing long across the ranch even while the western sky was still amber with sunset. The evening milking was done by lantern light, and the hands built a fire in the center of their outdoor dining hall, to linger and socialize after dinner. Faint laughter and conversation carried across the yard to the porch of the foreman's house, where Trace and Boz were having a nip of whiskey before bed.

"You're quiet tonight," Boz said, tucking tobacco into a fresh rolling paper.

Trace contemplated the ash on the end of his own smoke. "You know what today is?"

"Twentieth, ain't it?"

"That's right. I marked it down in the ledger this morning, but it wasn't til after noon . . . Miller said somethin about the old days, and that made me remember, today's the day my wife and folks died." The breeze fanned a spark in his cigarette and he turned his hand to protect it. His mind had done the same thing when the memory came, curled around to shield his heart, but the expected flare of guilt and grief had not come. "Almost got past without me noticin."

Boz's profile was illuminated briefly by matchlight. He shook the match out and settled his head back against the chair. "S'cause you ain't beatin yourself up about it no more."

That was true. In fact, before Boz had spoken, he'd been sitting there in a kind of peace—melancholy, but accepting. Of course he had to wonder, in light of new knowledge, whether there'd been any sign of demon activity in the house before they all took sick, but if there had been, he hadn't marked it. Mostly he remembered feeling relief, that he could let go his constant vigilance. And that had been his mistake—if, in fact, his family had been felled by malicious spirits, and not simple hateful cholera.

There was no way of knowing. Trace thought he would rather *not* know for sure. But he couldn't help thinking, if Aloysius hadn't been so insistent that everything strange was the work of the Devil, the younger Jacob might might've grasped Hardinger's lesson sooner. He might've broken the power to harness so it hadn't run away from him that time—if, in fact, it had.

He couldn't despise his father for doing what he'd believed to be right. For all his faults, the old man had never been a hypocrite. But there was a certain satisfaction in redistributing the blame.

Laughter carried over from the fire-pit, and Trace remembered the other matter that had dogged his thoughts all day. "Miller told me the Kid's been here since May. Also said the first of the horses slaughtered was around that time. And you remember that tin-peddler came through here last month, up from Salt Lake?"

"Yeah?"

"He said there was sheep getting tore up, south of here, earlier this spring."

"An' you suspect the Kid?" Boz sounded dubious.

"There's somethin bout him ain't natural. Somethin my power picks up on, but I don't know what, I never seen it before. And between what you said, about somethin man-sized cuttin down that horse, and him hedgin about ridin his shift last night, I got to wonder."

Boz thought for a while. "Still, that's a awful lot of damage for some boy to do with a knife. He'd need . . . a curved blade. Like a farrier's knife, but pointed. And there ain't no way to do it without gettin blood all over him."

"He could wash up in the creek."

"Blood don't wash out of clothes."

"Maybe he did it naked," Trace said, half-serious.

Boz chuckled. "As neat as that boy is? You see him runnin round buck-naked in the dark with a knife?"

The image was more chilling than humorous, in Trace's opinion. "I knew a man in the hospital, after the war . . . sweetest fella you ever did see, until the moon came full. Then they had to put him in restraints and throw him in a cell, or he'd chew your leg off. He *did* bite the ear off an orderly who got too close." He cocked a wry smile. "Thought he was a wolf, see?"

"A *shape*-changer?"

"Nah. He never changed his skin—not that I saw, anyway. But we've both seen demons get into people and make 'em murderin-mad. Maybe he's doin it and can't help it. Doesn't even know he's doin it, maybe."

Boz sipped from his glass. "So what d'you want to do?"

"I don't know," Trace admitted. "Watch him, I guess."

They fell quiet for a while. The sky overhead was blue velvet now, twinkling with diamond stars, and as the twilight deepened he began to feel the seductive slide toward trance, the urge to wander in the gray space for a while. He didn't need to do it every night, once or twice a week was enough to keep the spirits at bay, but there were other enticements, other tricks he was learning . . .

The scar in his right palm itched and he rubbed it irritably on his pants leg. He'd almost succeeded in not-thinking about her all day and he didn't want to start now.

"Did, ah . . . did Her Worship say aught to you about that sort of thing? Shape-changers and whatnot?"

It was uncanny, Trace thought, how Boz could track his moods like that. If he didn't know better he'd think *Boz* was a psychic.

"Not that I recall. We didn't talk much outside of the job at hand." And bicker over who was withholding the most from whom. "Why?"

"Just—it's funny how all manner of folks have stories of men changin into beasts. When I was a boy my mam used to tell me stories bout werewolves. Said they were bad witches who made a deal with the devil and would eat up little boys who stayed out after dark."

Trace chuckled. "I think all mothers know that story."

"Then in the army, I heard stories from our Crow scouts. Most of the Plains tribes see wolves as brothers, cuz they're smart and good hunters, and they look after the pack. Crow scouts put on wolf skins when they go out trackin the enemy ahead of a war party. But the Navajo have stories about a skinwalker, a bruja who can change his shape for real. That's powerful bad magic. He has to kill a brother or a father to get it."

"The Christian witch-hunters said much the same. That werewolves were the worst of blasphemers, eatin babies and matin with animals. Claimed that demons gave 'em power to change into beasts.

But Thomas Aquinas said it was all illusion, that the devil didn't have the power to manipulate the laws of nature."

"What do you think?"

"I . . . think after what I've seen this year, I'd be a fool to say anything was impossible."

Boz grunted assent. "Hearin you talk, it's like my mam was right—there's this whole other world I can't see, but it's waitin to pounce on me an' eat me up."

Trace huffed. "That's how I felt most of my life."

He tried to make light of it, but Boz's silence was serious. There was a long, pent-up breath, and then Boz said, so carefully he might have been handling a stick of dynamite, "You miss . . . you know, talkin to her bout this stuff?"

The question made him feel morose. And guilty. Because, of course, he did. He missed her cool, rational voice, laying out all the reasons there was nothing wrong with him. Her occasional scathing flashes of humor. Her frank admiration of his abilities, even as she scorned the faith that shaped and governed them.

And as much as he felt disloyal for thinking it, he missed her mind, and her refinement of manner. Those weeks of working with her had roused a hunger for learning he'd not known was still in him. Not only learning about his power, but just plain *study*. It had been a long time since he'd had the time or excuse to learn anything new. He did not think he was a snob, but he *had* been educated better than the average ranch hand, and sometimes he craved a little . . . well, erudition.

And there was the rub. If she had been merely hateful he could have banished her by now. But he had glimpsed the method behind her madness, and the desperation. Yes, she had manipulated him and hidden things from him and let Kieler serve him up to Mereck on a platter, but she had also gone to great lengths to ensure the Russian wouldn't have him.

(this my blood binds this man to me)

She'd *kept* her end of the bargain, dammit, and all he'd done was smack her and abandon her.

"I miss what I could have learned from her," Trace said wearily. "I'm just sorry she had to be such a bitch about it."

The voices around the fire-pit changed pitch, suddenly, swelled to a mocking whoop and then yips of alarm. Trace looked over to see cowboys falling out of the way, and two bodies grappling on the ground, dangerously close to the fire.

Trace sighed and rocked up out of the chair. "Got a minute?" he said to Boz, who made a *tsk* noise and got up as well.

By the time they reached the fire-pit the Kid was sitting on Hanky's shoulders and whaling on him with both hands. He could have done a lot more damage if he'd used his fists, but he fought like a bawdy-house harlot, slapping and clawing. Trace picked him up by the scruff of the neck and flung him at Boz, who put the boy in a full Nelson and let him thrash and kick both feet off the ground, squalling like a scalded cat.

Hanky got to his feet with a hand to his nose, staggering a little. "You are one crazy little pecker, you know that?" he yelled at the Kid, but Trace put a hand in his chest and held him back.

"Y'all done now?" Trace drawled. "Cause if you wanna go another round, I reckon it'll be your last."

"He started it!" Hanky protested.

"I don't give a damn," Trace said. "I warned you all about fightin on this outfit. Next one lays a finger on skin don't belong to 'em, is fired. Got it?"

"Yeah," Hanky said sullenly.

"What about you, Kid?"

"You're all godless cretins," he spat. He had lost his glasses and his eyes shone gold in the firelight, but he had stopped fighting Boz's hold, and his head hung low and baleful. In that moment he *did* look like the lycanthropy patient from the hospital, the same predatory intensity, freed of human reason.

"That's as may be, but if you wanna stay on here you've got to put up with us." Trace glanced at Boz, who loosened his grip.

The Kid slung off Boz's arm. "And *you* keep your hands off me, you filthy ape."

Trace stepped forward and slapped him, hard enough that he reeled. The boy clasped a hand to his face in hurt astonishment, violence flaring up in his eyes. Trace stood his ground, looming in the way that he saved for occasions like this, waiting until the lesson sank in.

"You wanna be real careful how you talk to people, Kid," he said quietly. "You ain't been alive long enough to know who's your betters. And you keep this up you won't live to find out. You got me?"

No answer.

"*Do* you?"

"Yes, sir." It was hard to know if he did. The Kid's face crumpled up and he hurtled off into the dark, not quite running, toward the dairy barn.

The others shuffled their feet, embarrassed. Pancho picked up the Kid's spectacles and offered them to Trace, who put them in a pocket. Hanky hung his head, ran a hand under his bleeding nose. "You hurt?" Trace asked him.

"No." Hanky snuffled and spat in the dirt. "Sorry, Preacher."

"Ain't me you should say that to," Trace said, and Hanky looked away. Trace shifted his gaze to the others. "Y'all got bunks—get to 'em."

The crowd cleared out pretty quickly after that. Someone kicked the logs apart in the fire so it would die faster.

Trace started back to the foreman's house. "Thanks for gettin my back," he said, as Boz fell into step beside him.

"Always do," the latter replied.

CHAPTER THIRTY-ONE

The landscape was foggy, indistinct, though he could see blue sky overhead, and fresh-cut grass under their feet. Miss Fairweather clasped his sleeve, dainty in white muslin, her eyes cool and challenging as they turned up to his.

She wanted to show him something. They strolled together across the mown field, other couples and families drifting along in the same general direction, no one in a hurry, no sense of any danger.

And yet he did not want to go. He dragged his feet like a small boy with a loose tooth, knowing it needed to come out but dreading the operation.

They passed a brightly colored sign, red and gilt looming out of the mist, promising wonders and miracles behind the curtain. A scantily clad acrobat danced by, snapping a banner of pink silk; a leering clown tumbled after her. A barker called from somewhere distant, *Laydees and gennlemen, who among you has the fortitude to witness the beast that walks like a man? All the writings of the ages cannot prepare you for the shocking truth! What about you, sir?*

A long striped cane jabbed at his chest, and Trace saw that the barker was Reynolds, grinning his death's-head grin beneath a straw hat. *How bout it, young'un?*

Go on, Miss Fairweather said to him. *I never expected you would stay.*

He ducked through the tent flaps and found himself in the ranch yard, just beside the remuda corral, with all the hands standing and sitting on the rails, whooping encouragements and insults to the combatants in the middle. Under and over their cheers Trace could hear the flat packing sounds of blows, the huffs of hard breathing, and a strange gasping whine like a frightened animal.

He elbowed his way to the rail, got a glimpse of the bare-trod ground and a stout pole driven into the earth, a thick black chain stretched taut by the weight of the body hanging from it.

The hands in those shackles were as familiar as his own—dark and square, attached to wiry wrists and corded arms. The woolly head bowed and lolled, as something huge and hairy crouched over him, tearing at his guts, battering his body against the pole.

No! Jesus no I don't want to see this!

Boz's head rolled back, eyes showing the glazed whites; his blood-filled mouth contorted with the effort to speak. *Trace—don't . . .*

But it was too late; the killer turned on him with lethal grace, muzzle wrinkled back to show fearsome teeth, yellow eyes blazing hate. Trace flung out an arm—

—and woke himself up.

The darkness of the foreman's house was thinned by a faint orange glow from the stove. His knuckles stung where he'd struck them on the wall. Through the blood pounding in his ears he could hear Boz snoring faintly.

Trace fell back with a shuddering gasp, easing the crush of terror on his chest. That had been a nasty one.

But some of it was still with him. An awareness, a compulsion he'd felt before: something was happening, or about to happen.

He felt for his clothes and boots, slipped out of the bedroom, through the office. Opened the front door as quietly as possible and stepped out onto the porch to dress. July nights were still chill at this altitude, and the wind prickled through his johnnies.

Sounds carried to his ears—the shuffling hooves and anxious calling of horses. Something was amiss in the remuda corral.

Later, Boz would call him a fool for walking out there alone, in the dark and without even the shotgun that hung over the office door, and Trace would not argue with him. But just then he wasn't thinking in practical terms—his power was insisting that he go over there and get a look at this thing *now*.

He jogged across the yard, fetched up against the corner of the dairy barn, where he could see into the corral. The wind was in his face, carrying the stink of blood and predator. The night-horses were clustered at the far north of the corral, shuffling and calling anxiously. And near the barn wall, something big thrashed and grunted.

Bear, he thought, but then it reared, tossing its head, with a grisly sound like tearing cloth. Trace saw a flap of ragged flesh sling out from its jaws, saw the angle of the head and shoulders above the haunches, and for one mad moment he thought it was a man.

But abruptly it went silent and motionless, and Trace felt a prickle of awareness go up the back of his neck. His power woke like a live thing, screeching *Danger*.

A low growl carried across the corral.

And *now* Trace realized he was standing coatless in the dark—alone, and absent any weapon but his spirit-talking power that seemed absurdly inadequate against this bone-and-sinew creature.

"Hiiii!" he shouted, and the thing crouched as if to spring. He didn't wait to see where it went—he ducked around the dairy barn and ran for the smithy, bellowing for all he was worth. The shotgun was in his office, but the woodpile was closer, and the ax was there—

His power warned him. He felt death loom out of the darkness and cut to the left, turning in time to see the thing land with a grunt in his path. It rolled with a predator's agility and turned back on him, snarling, bristling with coarse hair, muzzle wrinkling back over teeth as big as a grizzly's.

Not a bear. Nor a wolf—not entirely. There was something lupine in its elongated snout and gold-flashing eyes, but then it stood up, tall and taller, lethal grace uncoiling in its long spine and powerful thighs, long sinewy fingers flexing like a gunfighter's. Trace's mind fought with the vision before his eyes; he felt reality shift and reform itself into a world where such things existed. Neither Miss Fairweather nor Thomas Aquinas had prepared him for *this*.

It was *not* the Kid. Its aura was similar to the boy's, but smoother, more fluent. Not mindless. Not self-hating. Quite the opposite. He could have sworn it grinned, daring him to make a move.

Somebody yelled, from the bunk-house. Trace and the beast both twitched toward the sound, and then it leapt straight at him and threw him to the ground, knocking the wind from him. He grabbed at it, foolishly, felt the hot slide of skin over muscle before it wrenched free, vaulting into the darkness.

Men pounded up to him with lanterns and guns, Goliath and Boz in the lead. Trace sat up, wheezing, with a handful of greasy fur and the creature's stink in his nostrils.

"What happened? You all right?" Boz dropped to one knee, set his lantern in the grass to run a hand over Trace's shoulders and chest.

". . . m'fine," Trace croaked, and pointed. "Went that way . . ."

The others sprang up, alert to the hunt, more men coming out of the bunk-house, voices and lanterns lighting up the yard. Goliath took up the trail, ordering the men to split up and circle around. Trace caught Boz's arm and kept him there until there was space—and breath—to talk.

"Your mam was right," he said. "It's a werewolf."

Boz looked at him in dismay—but very little doubt. "What'd it look like?"

Trace held out the coarse black tuft in his fist. "Tall as me. Face like an ugly mutt's and big nasty teeth to match. And it ain't stupid. It coulda killed me just then, but didn't want to."

"You think it knew you?"

"I don't know. But it ain't the Kid."

"How do you know?"

"I just know." He got to his feet, painfully.

Boz turned his nose to the north, listening to the men yelping to each other across the dark pasture, sounding for all the world like a pack of wolves themselves. "If they catch it they'll be killin a man."

"They won't catch it." Trace picked up the lantern. "It killed another horse."

They went back to the remuda corral. Dark spatters fanned out from the darker mound of horseflesh on the ground. Boz made a hoarse, shocked sound as their lantern-light played over the hind legs, the distinctive white socks and the splash of white on the chest, now blackened by blood.

It was Boz's horse, Nate. The face had been peeled completely off the skull.

"Son of a bitch," Boz said, as if all the air had been knocked out of him. He clapped a hand over his eyes. Trace wrapped an arm around his shoulders, felt a shuddering breath go in and out of him. He put both arms around his friend, sorry for the loss, but glad as hell it hadn't been Boz himself.

CHAPTER THIRTY-TWO

Come sunrise, the mood on the ranch was an edgy combination of jubilant and spooked. The hunting party had come back empty-handed, but with a number of fantastic stories. Some of the boys claimed to have seen an enormous wolf, as big as a horse, that led them on a chase to the river, and then disappeared on its banks. Droopy even swore he had seen the beast rise on its hind legs and look back at its pursuers, but Goliath told him he was full of shit.

"T'was just a' ordinary buffalo wolf," Goliath mumbled around his bacon. "Prolly got the hydrophobia, is why it come so close to the ranch."

"That weren't no wolf did that butchery," Walt insisted. "That was a mountain lion."

"Oh, shut up, old man, you didn't see it."

"I seen enough to know what a wolf bite looks like."

"What was it, Preacher?" Hanky asked. "You saw it up close."

"Didn't," Trace said, spooning sugar in his coffee. "Knocked me down and all I saw was stars."

"You lucky it din't have yo' guts, too," Pancho informed him, and the others agreed wholeheartedly.

The Kid hunkered over his plate and said nothing. No one said anything to him, either, and the boy hardly mumbled a thank-you when Trace gave him his glasses back. The Kid looked paler than usual, but his face was notably unmarked, unlike Hanky, who was sporting a scratch over his eye and a swollen lip.

Boz had skipped breakfast. In fact he had not budged from the corral since midnight. Trace had pointed out the unlikelihood of the beast coming back, and Boz snapped that he knew what he was doing and to leave him the hell alone. But Trace could not do that, not after the premonition he'd had, so he'd spent an uncomfortable night sitting watch from his chair on the porch.

Boz was currently pacing the length and breadth of the corral, head down and chin thrust forward—reading the ground, no doubt. During the night Boz had roped off the end of the corral by the barn, to keep the remaining horses away from the murder scene and help preserve whatever tracks were there. At the moment he was this side of the barn, where Trace had tussled with the beast. He studied the ground and the roof, crouched to run a hand over the grass, stood up and walked back to the corral.

"Boz is a good tracker, huh?" the Kid said, interrupting Trace's scrutiny.

"One of the best I ever met," Trace agreed.

"My father always said Negroes and Indians made the best trackers because their animal natures were more attuned to the wild."

And the sad thing about that, Trace thought, was the boy actually believed he was paying Boz a compliment. "A man is a man, Kid. A beast is a beast. If it walks upright and uses words, everything else is just a matter of schoolin. And you shouldn't be lookin down on Hanky and the others just cause they were schooled different from you. If you were to get caught in a stampede or a blizzard, you'd be glad to have one of 'em with you. They might keep you alive."

"I'd rather die pure than take help from those heathens." The boy scowled at his plate, stirring the mush of cornbread and beans with his fork, and then burst out, "How do you *stand* it, Preacher? Doesn't it offend you, how ignorant and ungodly they are?"

Trace took his time about answering, both to consider the question and to dampen the Kid's ardor. "I suppose it did, when I was your age. But that's cause I hadn't seen anything outside of the seminary since I was fourteen. When the time came to make my own way in the world, I had to get along with all kinds of people. Came to find out there's good and bad in all camps, not just the ones who call themselves godly."

"Why'd you leave seminary?"

"My old man was set on me being a priest, but by the time I was your age I knew I didn't want to be. Then the war started up, and a friend of mine got a letter that his father was going off to fight." Jack Mallory had been from North Carolina, the son of a well-to-do farmholder, and chock-full of Confederate pride. "He decided to leave school and enlist, and I went with him."

"So you went to war?"

"Yeah. Served about a year before I was wounded, went into the hospital. After I got better, I went home, but my father told me I was a godless good-for-nothing, and threw me off his land. Said I wasn't his son anymore."

The Kid nodded, eyes intense behind the glasses. "What did you do?"

"Came out here. Worked cattle for a few years. Met a girl and got married. After we were wed I took her back home. My father was re-married by then and had a young daughter, and he'd softened up in his old age. He took us in and allowed as how he'd been too hard on me. So all you got to do, Kid, is meet a nice girl and settle down. I reckon your folks couldn't say no to a new convert, if you brought one home."

The Kid looked away, across the yard. "They're dead."

"Your folks are?"

Shrug.

"When did that happen?"

"Four months ago."

Trace looked at him for a long moment. "You wanna tell me about that?"

But the Kid had gone still, nose pointed into the wind, north to-ward the Big House. Miller was coming across the yard with a stranger, a rough-looking fellow in a shaggy black coat and top hat.

Fear suddenly rolled off the Kid—fear, and a whiff of that dark wildness that made Trace's alarms prickle.

"You know that man?" Trace asked.

"No, sir. I mean, I've seen him before. In Evanston, maybe. I don't remember." The Kid stood and slung his uneaten breakfast into the grass. "I better get to work."

He made for the ranch office. Trace thought about following, but Miller and the stranger were headed toward the corral, and Boz.

Trace decided to beat them there. He found Boz standing over poor Nate's scalped head, coiling a length of rope into a lasso, preparing to drag off the carcass. "Help you with that."

"No need," Boz grunted.

"You got company comin."

"I see 'em."

"You see anything worth tellin me, 'fore they get here?"

"Yeah," Boz said. "There's two of 'em."

He slid a wry look at Trace's startled expression, but there was no time to say more, as Miller and the stranger came through the gate.

"Preacher. Boz." Miller nodded a greeting. "This here's our wolf-hunter, Etienne Remy."

The man in the top hat ignored them both. He approached the dead horse and dropped to his heels in a squat, doffed the hat and set it upside-down in the dust. He scratched at his short black hair, loosening a shower of dandruff onto his shoulders. He hunkered for a long moment, neck craning as he surveyed the damage, taking in long sniffs as if he had a case of catarrh.

At length he stood up, rummaging in his pockets. He came out with a long machine-rolled cheroot and stuck it between his teeth. He struck a match on the seam of his trousers, cupped dirty hands around his smoke, and sucked in short, prissy puffs to get it going. Once this was accomplished, he put one hand behind his back in a curiously aristocratic pose, and turned to Miller.

"Eez wolves," he announced.

Miller gave a satisfied nod. "Figured as much."

"Dey cut de heels, there, bring 'im down, chew the rest."

"That's what I figured," Miller said, as Trace and Boz exchanged glances.

"Dis same big damn wolf as d'others. Been tracking him for months. Guess you have more kills round here dis week?"

"Last night," Miller said.

"Ah, oui. And more last month? Two-three in the same week?"

"That's right."

Remy nodded. "Is same damn thing south of here. Sheeps, down by Salt Lake."

"Is that where you been trackin him?" Trace asked. "Cause he's been doggin this ranch for weeks, but I haven't seen you round here."

Remy's gaze slid over Trace and then cocked toward Miller, inquiring why he was being importuned by this *cochon*.

"This is my foreman, Jacob Tracy," Miller said. "We call him Preacher."

"Prêtre, eh?" Remy exhaled more smoke than a steam engine. "You got un ange on your shoulder? Steer you from harm?"

The wolf-hunter's eyes were a queer, clear hazel, almost gold. His black brows nearly met in the middle, his teeth were long and startlingly white in the blackness of his beard. But more telling—to Trace, at least—was the shadow that seemed to cling to his skin, like a second aura. There was a hint of restless aggression in the man's gaze, as if he knew he could handle himself and was not averse to proving it.

"Sometime Remy not be seen when he don' wanna be seen, eh?" he said, with a slow, insolent smile. He thrust out a hand. "Plaisir, Prêtre."

Trace shook, but not with pleasure. The wolf-hunter's hand was rough as rawhide, nails black with filth. There was a fearsome strength behind that grip, and Remy held on just long enough to make the point.

Then he dropped Trace's hand, gestured languidly toward the dead horse. "Don' worry—You cut dat up for bait, Remy catch him two days, mebbe three."

"No," Boz said, the first word he had spoken during this exchange. "Nobody's butcherin this horse. You want meat, have Hanky show you where he dumped that mare yesterday."

Remy's eyebrows went up, but Miller said, "That'll do. Remy, whyn't you have yourself some breakfast, it's early yet."

The two men left the corral, Miller describing the animal attacks this spring, and Remy assuring the rancher he'd seen the same thing south of here, and he was getting close to catching the culprit.

Boz looked at Trace, mouth curled with distaste. "He's one of 'em, ain't he?"

"How could you tell?"

"Cuz you ain't got no poker face when you get one o' your hunches. *He* knew it, too, the sonuvabitch. He was laughin at us."

"Course he was. He figures even if we know, we can't do anything about it."

"We can catch him out on the range come nightfall and fill 'im full of lead," Boz said curtly. "*He* may not've killed my horse, but he helped the one who did."

Trace waved a hand at the blood-spatter. "Show me."

So Boz walked him through the story on the ground: how one of the beasts had come from the west and stalked the horses outside the fence, until he could separate out the one he wanted, and then jumped poor Nate beside the barn.

"But then you came upon him, there—" Boz pointed to the place outside the corral where Trace had spotted the killer "—and he jumped and ran. *You* went south, toward the smithy, and if you'd kept goin you woulda run into him. But the other one jumped you."

Boz led him to the spot where Trace had tussled with the man-beast. "Goliath and the boys took after that one, toward the creek. But the one that killed Nate, the little one, kept going toward the water mill."

They walked around the back of the bunk-house and the bath-house behind it, where there was a windmill to draw up water and a pump for accessing it. The well-cover was a five-foot-square platform, about twelve inches off the ground. Trace could see the clawed, five-toed tracks of the beast that had approached the pump; he could see a faint stain of blood at the edges of the boards. And he could see the bare human tracks walking away from the platform and disappearing into the grass.

"He came over here and washed up after I spooked him in the corral," Trace said.

"Ayup." Boz nodded toward the bath-house. "Then he goes in there, gets dressed. Boot-prints mixed in with everybody else's."

"Small feet," Trace observed.

"Reckon you were right about it bein the Kid. Any of the others would be smarter bout coverin their tracks."

Trace rubbed a hand over his face, tired and aware of an irrational anger building on his mental horizon. Because this bullshit was *not supposed to happen out here*. He'd thought things would be *quiet* in Wyoming.

Though he had not quite believed that, had he? He'd kept up with the meditation, pushing his boundaries in the gray space, testing himself. Because he'd feared Miss Fairweather's warnings about being followed. Because he knew his eyes were opened now, and he was bound to see things most people wouldn't. He supposed it was possible these monsters might've wandered onto Miller's ranch this summer whether he had been here or not, but it didn't feel that way. Not with the dream he'd had. Not with the alarms the Kid set off in his head.

"Boz, are you sure Nate was singled out, special? You think it was a message?"

"More like payback to the nigger for layin hands on his lily-white flesh."

"But if he really wanted payback, wouldn't he go for Hanky's horse? Or mine? You weren't hardly a part of it."

"I don't care *why* he did it," Boz snapped. "Little bastard killed my horse and that's a hanging offense in this territory, whether he's got a demon in him or not!"

Trace gestured for him to lower his voice. "Listen to me. We gotta tread careful here. Even if the Kid's the killer, I ain't sure he knows that he's doin it. If he's anything like those folks we've seen possessed, he may not be able to control it."

Boz opened his mouth, closed it, and looked contentious.

"*And* we don't know if the pair of these critters—whoever they are—are in cahoots, or even know each other."

"That's some pretty long odds if they don't!"

"Not necessarily. Last night's the first time we've found more than one set of tracks. And I know Remy was the one jumped down in front of me—"

"If you can tell it's him so clear, how come you can't tell who's the other one?"

"I don't know. I only got a good look at the big one last night. And Remy just now . . . Hell, *you* know well enough when people are lyin to you. And the feel I get from unnatural things, spirits and monsters, it's the same sort of—" He made a frustrated gesture. "I can't describe it. It just *is*. And whatever's in the Kid, it ain't so clear. It's confused. Like maybe it's new, and it don't have a good hold on him."

"So again . . . whaddya want to do about it?"

What he *wanted* to do was talk to Miss Fairweather, but he knew that saying so would only make things worse. He rubbed at the scar in his palm with the other thumb. "Last night when I came out here, it wasn't cause I heard noises. I had a dream. A vision, I think." Boz looked at him warily. "I saw the werewolf attackin *you*."

Boz stared at him for a second, and then dropped his head, shook it. A tight little smirk twisted his mouth. "I *knew* you were gonna say that. You god-damned son of a bitch."

"I didn't tell you that to spook you," Trace said, stung.

"Well what am I supposed to do with that?" Boz's voice rose. "Damn it, I *knew* you were gonna do that to me, sooner or later."

"You think I *choose* to get these visions?"

"And now I guess you wanna wire Her Worship and throw us both on her mercy."

"I didn't say a word about it!"

"You were thinkin it." Boz pointed with his chin. "You know every time you think about her, you start scratchin at that hand, where she cut you?"

Trace felt the back of his neck flush. He put both hands on his hips and struck a belligerent attitude.

"And if you go tellin her I'm in peril, she'll have the bit in your teeth again. That's how she does, first with the Jews, then with the Baptists—"

"Now hang on. *I* was the one went to her about the Baptists—"

"I know it. I know you gotta have some kinda holy mission weighin you down. But I'm damned if I'll be the next one. I'm not your picka-ninny to look after."

Trace was shocked cold. "*You* can go to hell, then!"

"You first," Boz shot back, and then retreated, turning in a half circle, raising one hand to crimp the bridge of his nose. "Look—if you wanna write to her about the Kid, fine. Tell her we got werewolf prob-lems. Just leave me out of it."

"Boz—"

"I ain't *doin* this again, Trace. I can't keep thinkin this time I won't be quick enough, or smart enough, or there's somethin you ain't told me. I just . . . can't."

He made a throw-down gesture and stalked away toward the corral.

CHAPTER THIRTY-THREE

The rest of the morning was busy. A hundred and twelve calves had to be branded and wormed. Twenty-two horses needed their feet shod or trimmed before the trip to town next week. One of the men work-ing on the barn roof fell off and dislocated his shoulder.

Trace hardly stopped moving all day. And yet he could not, as he had done all the weeks previous, lose himself in the busyness. He was constantly aware of that nether-world moving just at the edges of his senses. Part of him was keeping an ear tuned toward Boz, and the Kid, and Remy. And another part of him was thinking about St. Louis, and the telegraph office in Evanston.

He'd been a fool to come out here. And a fool to run from Miss Fairweather, when all she'd done was show him the truth he'd asked for. It was the same old tired altar-boy reflex: anything new or inexpli-cable must be evil, and therefore avoided.

Is it so threatening to your tiny Christian mind, that you must deny the possibility, rather than accept it, and learn to fight it?

It was hard to think of himself as a coward. Miss Fairweather had said he was not, and he did not think he behaved like one when faced with a clear and immediate threat—like the keung-si. But he had to be honest with himself: he'd been pulling away from Miss Fairweather all spring, half-fascinated and half-fearful, because he was afraid of what she wanted from him. Because he was afraid of the *something worse* he'd always known was out there. Because he dreaded the gulf he could see widening between himself and Boz.

Boz kept to the training paddock most of the day. He turned up for dinner at noon with a nod and a nonchalant attitude, as if the quarrel had never happened. "Saw our wolf-hunter down at the bath-house this morning," he said in a low voice, sopping up bean juice with a bit of rye'n'injun bread. "He was markin out those tracks around the pump."

"You say anything to him?"

"Nope. Saw all I needed to see. But he don't know that." Boz jerked his chin. "Watch out."

Trace glanced over to see Remy ambling toward the fire-pit, a bloody mare's leg slung across his shoulders, and a burlap bag dangling from one hand.

The Kid was sitting alone; he too had lain low all morning, sequestering himself in the office, diligently completing every task Trace set him to. The others ignored him as if he had ceased to exist.

Remy straddled the bench across from the Kid, dropped his burdens on the ground. He upended the burlap sack and shook out a tangle of heavy steel traps, which scattered in the dirt like a giant's game of knucklebones. Remy leaned the mare's leg against his knee, drew a skinning-knife from his boot, and peeled off a fatty strip of hide. He began to grease the springs and hinges of the traps with the bloody rag.

The wolf-hunter whistled as he worked. The ranch hands, though hardly sensitive to blood and dead meat, cast puckered-up glances at Remy's breach of etiquette and turned away to their own meals.

Remy exhausted the greasy scrap, tossed it aside, and used the knife to peel off another flap of skin, then a bit of meat, which he stuffed in his mouth.

"Eez good for the blood, raw," the wolf-hunter said, to the Kid's stare. "Make you strong, so you never catch la grippe."

The Kid got up, dumped his plate for the second time that day, and stalked off toward the office. Remy's eyes followed him, as he took a cheroot from his pocket and lit it. The smell was like damp socks, rot under a log. Remy fished in the other pocket and pulled out an old, smudged bottle, full of something that resembled the specimens Trace had fetched for Miss Fairweather: dark amber, cloudy, and clotted.

Remy took a much-stained handkerchief, uncorked the bottle, and upended it over the cloth.

The waft of scent nearly made Trace gag, even from ten feet away. Boz made a low sound of disgust and the wolf-hunter looked up, smirking.

"Remy's secret receet," he said. "Wolf piss an' beaver-musk. Let it brew a few weeks. Wolfs come from a mile away, thinking they on the trail of some love-ly lady wolf. *Aroo!*" He howled lasciviously, and then laughed.

That was enough for the rest of the diners. The remaining cowboys vacated the fire-pit, some of them grumbling under their breath. Trace got up and went over to the wolf-hunter, stood there with plate in hand, and made an effort to speak without breathing.

"Listen, friend," he said. "I don't mean to get in the way of your work, but the rest of us'd take it as a kindness if you did it somewhere else."

"Oh-oh. Do that parfum de loup offend your nose, Prêtre?" Remy took the cheroot from his teeth and tapped the ash onto Trace's boot. It might've been an accident, since the wolf-hunter's sly golden gaze never left Trace's. "Remy *hate* to think he make a bad step in dis salle de bal." He made a sweeping gesture across the ranch proper.

"Just keep your traps and your bait outside the yard, hear?" Trace dumped his dishes in the wash-bin and headed for the office.

He expected to find the Kid quietly at work. He'd seen no one else go into the foreman's house, and so was surprised to hear the Kid's voice coming from within—arguing with someone, in a petulant, protesting tone.

Trace stepped onto the porch and the voice cut off abruptly. The Kid turned toward the door with a spooky, animal reflex. His cheeks were flushed, his eyes red and watery.

"Who you talkin to, Kid?"

The boy's chin wobbled furiously. "You better keep that animal away from me, Preacher, or something bad's gonna happen!"

"Who?"

"That Cajun trash! He followed me up from Salt Lake and now he's tracked me here from Evanston."

Even though Trace had considered the possibility himself, it still sounded unlikely. "Why would he be trackin you, Kid?"

"Because he's a devil! Or a deviant. I don't know! I just want him to leave me the hell alone!" The boy seemed manic, desperate. "You see things, don't you, Preacher? I mean they don't just call you that because you were at seminary. God talks to you."

"Sometimes," Trace said cautiously. "What're you gettin at, Kid?"

The Kid reached into his vest pocket and pulled out a folded page of newsprint, offered it up with a challenging look.

It was a page from the Salt Lake *Clarion*, dated mid-April. And there in the first column was a reprint of the original story about the Herschel murders. Trace read the words with a feeling of recurring nightmare—*intimations made by one Jacob Tracy . . . adamant in his assertions of Miss Herschel's innocence . . . Could some otherworldly knowledge be the source of his certainty?*

"That's you, isn't it?" the Kid said. "I heard you and Boz talk about St. Louis."

"Where'd you get this?"

"I read it. Back in Salt Lake, just before . . . I left."

"So who's followin who, huh?" Trace's skin felt taut, as all his senses groped for the lie, the trap. He couldn't remember the last time he'd met a man he couldn't get a read on, and that in itself was worrisome. "No—you can't expect me to believe you came up here lookin for me. *I* didn't even know I was gonna be here in April."

"I didn't," the Kid said. "It wasn't til you got here, and I overheard you tell Boz how you needed to take a turn on the night watch—"

"What do you do, Kid, listen at doors?"

"No! I wasn't trying to listen. But *everybody* knows you talk to God on your watches. The others make jokes about it, but not too loud, cause they all know you got eyes in the back of your head. And I thought I remembered your name from the paper, so when we were in Evanston on the Fourth, I went by the printer's office, and they had an old copy with the story in it."

It was possible—just. Given the sensationalism of the Herschel murders, and small papers' tendency to reuse any and all interesting content that came across the wire . . . it was appalling to think how far his fame might have spread. And what interested parties might have seen it.

"Look, Kid." Trace threw the paper on the desk, and sat. "You gotta realize reporters will take a little bit of a thing and twist it til it sounds like somethin entirely different."

"But you *are* a man of God, I *know* it! Please, Preacher, I don't know what else to do—"

"What's the matter, son? What is it you think I can help you with?"

The Kid wrapped his arms hard around his shoulders. "I *hear* things. Voices, telling me to do things. Making me *want* to do things."

"Like what?"

"Tear everything *apart*." He raked his nails down his arms hard enough to make threads pop in his shirt sleeves. "Last night I dreamt I was standing in the horse corral—*you* saw me there, with blood on my hands. But when I woke up, I was in the bath-house, and I was all muddy. I don't know how I got there."

Rather convenient, don't you think? Miss Fairweather's voice echoed in Trace's head. "Have you walked in your sleep before?"

"I did when I was a kid, but not like this. I didn't wake up in strange places. And I didn't have these dreams."

"How long has this been goin on?"

Some dark memory crossed the Kid's face. "Since April."

"Before or after your folks died?"

"I don't remember. Before."

There was something *hazy* about the boy's aura, as if a cloud of mosquitoes swarmed around him. The nearest thing Trace had seen to it was the demon in the drunk tank, but this didn't have the grasping, territorial feel of a demon. It was aloof, distant. He thought he might've been able to force his way through the veil, get a look at it from that side, but he didn't want to tip his hand. The Kid's distress seemed real enough, and if there was a demon in him—particularly one with a taste for blood—Trace didn't want to back it into a corner yet.

"So what do you want me to do, son?"

"I thought maybe you'd know how to . . . I always heard that Catholics had special prayers, to drive out demons—"

"You think you've got a demon?"

"What else could it be?"

"Well, did you talk to anybody else about it? I'd think the Prophet might know a thing or two—"

"My father knew," the Kid said curtly. "He said I'd brought it on myself for having . . . bestial thoughts."

In spite of himself, Trace winced. The Kid was watching him too closely for comfort—trembling downy chin and cold, old eyes. He didn't think the boy was wily enough to have contrived this scene, but maybe the thing inside him was.

Or he might be genuinely insane. Trace had heard similar

accounts of sinister voices, from fellow patients in the asylum. Not the lycanthrope—*that* fellow had been quite jolly and up-front about his affliction.

"All right," Trace said at last. "I know somebody who might know somethin. But I'll have to send 'em a telegram when we go into town next week."

The Kid's face lit up. "You mean I get to go to the horse-fair with you?"

"I don't see why not. You been enough of a help here, and I gotta take somebody." *And I'd rather not let you out of my sight while we're gone.* "But I was figuring on takin Hanky along too, so you might wanna bury the hatchet with him before we go."

The Kid's elation deflated like a pig's bladder. "What do you expect me to say?"

"Tell him you're sorry you hit him, for a start. And I expect you to treat Boz with respect from here on out, too. He's my partner and your elder, besides."

The sullen look did not alter, but the Kid's eyes shifted away. Trace had the impression he was listening to something—a whisper that Trace sensed only as an insectile whine.

But: "All right, Preacher," he said, and put on a meek good-boy face.

CHAPTER THIRTY-FOUR

TO: SABINE FAIRWEATHER, HYDE PARK, ST. LOUIS.
SUSPECTED LYCANTHROPE IN AREA PLEASE ADVISE RE INDENTIFICATION
SUBJUGATION OR IF SPIRIT SIGNATURE POINTS TO OTHER KNOWN
CULPRITS PORTENTS OMINOUS
J. TRACY

"Will you want that sent today, sir?" the telegraph clerk asked, rousing Trace from his scowl at the page.

He took the pencil out of his teeth and pushed the telegraph form across the counter, his arm stiff with the dual effort of moving forward and holding back. He wished he could *talk* to her. It was hard to know what to say in a telegram, or whether he was asking the right questions, even.

In the nine days between the slaughter of Boz's horse and their departure for town, the ranch had been quiet. No slaughtered stock, no mysterious tracks, no disturbances in the night.

"Dey not hungry after a big kill," Remy explained, when somebody asked why he hadn't caught anything. "He lay quiet for a while til he get hungry again." The wolf-hunter was making a batch of his cheroots on a little rolling machine, filling the papers with pinches of dried material that looked like no tobacco Trace had ever seen. "Besides, dey smell Remy nearby, dey know eez danger. Wolfs is smarter than you think." He offered the cheroot to the Kid, who gave him a look of contempt, so Remy shrugged and smoked it himself.

The wolf-hunter made a show of poisoning bait and setting traps, but as far as Trace could tell he was only there to collect three squares a day and get under everyone's feet. Twice he had left a pile of traps on the steps below the bunk-house door, right where somebody was likely to break an ankle if they came stumbling out in the dark.

"How well do you know that scalawag?" Trace asked Miller, just before they left for Evanston.

"Remy?" The rancher chuckled. "He's a rare one, ain't he? He's a good trapper, though, don't let him fool you. Just leave him be, he'll prob'ly be gone by the time you get back."

The fact that Miller had known Remy for several years made the Kid's claim of having been followed even less likely, which reinforced Trace's suspicion that the thing possessing the boy was trying to cover its tracks. Despite his unsavory habits, Remy did not seem inclined to provoke trouble. Other than mealtimes he never went near the Kid—or any of the rest of them, for that matter. The wolf-hunter's nature was as solitary as the critters he hunted.

Meanwhile the Kid, whether by contrivance or some remission of his condition, had been remarkably sweet-tempered for the past week. He made peace with Hanky—whether there had been actual apologies issued Trace didn't know, but soon after their talk he had seen Hanky teaching the Kid how to lasso, a glaring gap in the Mormon boy's knowledge that had cost him considerable skin from the others. Letting himself be taught was a gesture of tremendous condescension on the Kid's part, though Hanky was too open-hearted and blunt to realize it.

On July thirtieth they set out for Evanston—Trace and Boz, Hanky and the Kid—with twenty-two horses in tow. It was two days' ride at an easy pace along the Sweetwater River, and they stopped to camp at the halfway point on the first night. They staked out the horses, cooked and ate supper, bickered amiably about who would take the first watch. Boz drew the short straw, and everyone else stretched out to sleep.

Trace had not had the chance to meditate for several days, and although he'd planned to do so during his own watch, apparently his power—or something else—couldn't wait that long. As soon as his eyes were closed the vision began to lap over him, soft as velvet and enticing as perfume.

It was clearly and specifically a dream. The massive banquet hall, which might've been suspended in the cosmos, for all he could see; the walls were lost in darkness. The table groaning under its bounty of flowing wine, sculpted pastries, and quivering golden aspics. The laughter and indistinct conversations—that sense of important things being discussed just out of earshot.

He sat at the end of the table, his view of the other guests mostly obscured by a massive bouquet of fruit and flowers, but he could see the dusky-hued lady to his left, her tangled black curls falling over her decaying finery, and beside her a round, jolly Irishman, making merry with the wine despite the gaping wound in his chest. To Trace's right sat Kieler, dressed in rich robes and a ridiculous turban that did not quite disguise the misshapen concavity of his brow. While Trace watched, Kieler lifted his napkin and dabbed at the trickle of blood that ran down his temple.

"Do excuse me," he said to Trace. "My mental powers aren't what they used to be."

"More wine, Mr. Tracy?" said Reynolds, at his elbow. The reporter wore a waiter's uniform and his usual feral grin. He held out a bottle with a smudged label. "With the lady's compliments."

Trace followed his glance down the table, to where Miss Fairweather sat, regal in scarlet velvet, her face as white as wax. One frail arm lay stretched across the white tablecloth, and some awful wormlike creature, like an oversized leech, was fastened onto her wrist, pulsing as it sucked the life out of her.

All the diners had leeches, their long tails coiling and throbbing across the tabletop, weaving over and around plates and goblets, feeding into the towering, bubbling fountain in the center of the table. Trace could smell the iron reek of blood from where he sat.

The man beside Miss Fairweather took her hand, raised it to his lips, but she made no sign she appreciated or even noticed the gesture. She reached for her glass, turned it so Trace could see the skull and cross-bones marked on it, and held his eye as she took a deliberate swallow.

"You really should try some of this, young'un," Reynolds said, holding out the bottle. "It's the lady's own vintage."

Fairweather '71, said the label on the bottle, in her familiar handwriting. *Panacea, Protegeum, Defensio.*

"I had some of that." He held up his hand, to show the scar. "Didn't care for it."

"Didn't you?" Reynolds said. "Oh, look, here come the entrees."

All the guests were cooing and applauding, and the man beside Miss Fairweather stood, lifting his goblet, smiling benevolently and accepting the accolades, as a whole platoon of servants marched into the room, bearing masterpieces of cooking and chicanery: cockatrices, mermaids, phoenixes; homunculii with apples in their mouths; a whole roasted keung-si, charred black around the edges . . .

"You might wanna wake up now, young'un," Reynolds advised. "You won't want to see this."

The last salver was as big as a coffin, carried on the shoulders of six enormous wolves, and on it lay Boz, naked and hog-tied, gagged with a bit in his teeth. The wolves set the tray down before Trace, and Boz began to thrash, screaming against his gag. Trace saw all eyes turn toward him expectantly, found a carving knife and fork in his hands. The Russian held out his glass in salute, waiting, the promise of threat in that cruel smile.

Venenum Fatalis, Contagii, Clades Inevitabilis. He heard her voice as if she were whispering in his ear. He looked down the table again, saw her raise her left hand and pantomime thrusting a knife into it, at the same time as the Russian glanced down at her and fury crossed his face—

Trace was thrust away from the table, yanked away as if by a river current, awash in cold and tumbling confusion. He felt her hand clawing for his, trying to hang on, but she slid away like candle smoke—

—and he thrashed awake in a swaddle of blankets, cold night air bearing down on his lungs, neck and shoulders aching with the strain of reaching, trying to understand.

He fell back with a hard sigh, panic cooling in his blood and condensing to the weight of guilt.

"You all right?" Boz said, low, from across the fire.

To Trace's left, Hanky was snoring and senseless. To the right, the Kid whimpered softly, twitching in his sleep. The sky spread out above them, vast and black, with a band of stars across its middle. A few yards away, the horses stood patiently on their tethers.

Trace rolled on his elbows, rubbed his eyes with thumb and forefinger. "Just dreams."

"Was I in 'em?"

Trace shook his head. He got his knees under him and stood, wincing at the stiffness in his joints. "You might as well turn in. I ain't sleepin any more tonight."

That had been two nights ago. He had not slept much since, though he had spent long hours meditating while the others were asleep, searching in ever-widening circles around the river valley and through the wilds of Wyoming, for disturbances, portents, signs of any kind . . . but there was nothing. Or at least nothing he could recognize as threatening.

He didn't know what he was looking for, was the problem. This dream had been more pointed and cryptic than the others, full of things he recognized—the wine, the leeches, the words of Miss Fairweather's protection spell—but didn't know how to interpret.

Had she been trying to send him a message? But if she could do that, why didn't she come closer in the gray space? If he was such a powerful psychic then why couldn't he talk to her?

Their first day in Evanston was Sunday, but there was still plenty to do: renting a corral from the stockyards manager, arranging lodgings for himself and the boys, getting the horses settled. Boz handled the customers at the corral with thorough competence, and Hanky leapt like a frog to do anything Boz told him. Even the Kid was lickspittle diligent, although he was edgy and had twice reminded Trace of his promise to telegraph his friend.

So here he was, on the second of August, almost three months after he'd stormed out of her library, sending a telegram to St. Louis and praying to God she'd forgiven him enough to answer.

"Is this . . . Latin?" the telegraph clerk asked, frowning at Trace's handwriting.

"She's European," Trace said. He'd composed the message in a mishmash of Latin and French, in hopes the sending and receiving offices would not grasp its meaning and assume it was written by a lunatic. "Just send it as written."

"What service do you want?" the clerk asked, counting letters.

"The quicker the better."

"You want to wait for a reply?"

"No, I'll come back in the morning." He didn't allow himself to suppose she might not answer.

TRACE LEFT THE telegraph office and made his way along the crowded sidewalk, dodging ladies in fishtail skirts and cowboys in batwing chaps; the cowboys gave him berth and the ladies looked him over from the corners of their eyes. He felt awkward about that, particularly since he was wearing the suit Miss Fairweather had bought for him. He had to turn out respectable for his duties as Miller's agent in town. Hanky had made appreciative noises about his fine duds; Boz cocked a knowing eyebrow and said nothing.

He passed a mercantile and a café, the feed store and the pharmacy, stepped down into the street and headed toward the livestock yards. The air smelled of burning coal. Evanston was a mining town, supplier to the railroad that had birthed it, and the air was constantly full of smut and smoke from the charcoal kilns. A dozen trains a day passed through town, carrying beef back east and horses to San Francisco, quality folk from Denver to California, military to and from Fort Laramie, and Chinamen out to the head of the line. There was a sizable Chinese population in Evanston, crowded into ramshackle slums where the streets were rife with strange smells and stranger speech.

As Trace got closer to the stockyards, the earthy bleating and surging of men and animals swelled to drown out the rhythmic clang and clatter of the rail yard. He skirted a flock of sheep, along with their shaggy Basque tenders, and sauntered over to join Hanky and the Kid at the rail of their rented corral.

"Where'd you get off to?" Hanky said.

"Bank," Trace said. "What's happening here?"

In the corral, Boz was putting a palomino mare through her paces before a well-dressed lady and gentleman. The man was a slicked-up dude in striped pants and a beaver hat; the girl was dolled up in virginal white and blue ribbons, though the rouge on her cheeks and the hardness in her eyes suggested she was not as fresh as advertised. Nevertheless, the Kid was eyeing her as if she were a steak dinner at the end of the trail. She had noticed his interest and kept darting glances over her shoulder, while her protector spoke to Boz.

Trace could tell by Boz's posture that he was running out of patience.

"Lady wants the horse," Hanky explained. "Gent don't wanna pay for it. Keeps tryin to talk Boz down on the price."

"You don't say," Trace murmured, as the slicked-up dude noticed his arrival.

"Sir! You must be Mr. Miller." The man strode toward Trace with his hand out. He was affecting an English accent, Trace guessed, though his flat, nasal tones bore little resemblance to Miss Fairweather's cultured speech. "Sir Ashley Ravens, newly arrived from London, to rusticate in your fine mountain air."

"Pleased to meet you," Trace said, "but I'm just a visitor like you. That fella there is Miller's chief trainer, he's the one you wanna talk to. Hey, Boz!" he hailed, as if they hadn't clapped eyes on each other in a year. "Miller ain't fired you yet, you old so-and-so?"

Boz picked up the cue right away. "Why, Jake Tracy, ain't the law caught up with you?" He came over and they shook hands and clapped each other on the shoulders. "Here for your new racers?"

"Yeah, you set me back the number we agreed on?"

"Sure did, six of Miller's best with your name on 'em." Boz glanced at Ravens. "Just let me finish up with Mr. Ravens, here, and we'll talk."

Trace said that was fine, and turned to lean against the rail while Boz led Ravens back toward the two or three horses they had been discussing. Ravens' ladybird, meanwhile, sidled over to the Kid, all bold eyes and tossing curls. The Mormon boy, interestingly, seemed to get taller, more relaxed, more *there* under her attention. It was like watching the mismatched images of a stereoscope slide into focus, as the Kid focused in on the girl. He bent his head close to hers and said something Trace couldn't hear, but her eyes lit with a dark heat that he could read as easily as a scent.

"What was *that* about?" Hanky said, dragging Trace's attention back to Boz and Mr. Ravens.

"Fella's a four-flusher and a screw," Trace explained, "tryin to get as much as he can by claimin the stock ain't up to scratch."

"So why'd you act like you were buyin—?"

"Cause swindlers are the easiest to swindle. My guess is, he don't have a feather to fly with, but he's tryin to start a game here in town, showin folks he's got money with a prime fancy and a flash horse. So Boz gave him the idea *I'm* in a dishonest business, too, and that makes Ravens figure, if Boz'll do some under-the-table dealings with me, he'll be likely to knock down his prices for Ravens."

"Oh," Hanky said, chewing his tongue. "But you don't *want* Boz to knock down his prices—"

"Just watch," Trace said.

Sure enough, Boz called out, "Kid? Go bring Black Iron out here from the stable."

Black Iron was a five-year-old gelding that belonged to the ranch remuda, and he was the laziest, most contrary thing on four legs. He would lie down if anyone tried to saddle him. He would fall asleep if left to stand for even a few minutes. He had a tendency to lag when harnessed in tandem. The only thing he showed any interest in was food, and he would nip at the mares and other geldings to steal their grain.

Despite all that, Black Iron was a handsome brute, gleaming black with an undercurrent of red in his coat and a fine arch to his neck. Trace had brought him to town in hopes of meeting a buyer like Mr. Ravens.

When the Kid returned from the stable it was obvious he had taken a moment to run a brush over the animal's hide: Black Iron usually had a smudge on one side where he had been lying, but that was gone, and he wore one of the better halters. He looked very much like a pampered show-horse.

The girl cooed and exclaimed over him, and cooed and exclaimed over the Kid, too—how skilled he was, how kind and patient he must be, how brave—horses quite terrified her, they were so big—despite the fact that Black Iron had snuffled once over her hands and then stood there, lock-kneed and dozing. The Kid took her fawning with surprising aplomb, watching her with an intense, low-lidded expression that would have credited an experienced lady-killer.

Mr. Ravens made a show of examining Black Iron's teeth and feet, while Boz helpfully lifted the horse's hooves and opened his mouth.

"He is truly a beauty," Ravens said. "What do you think, my dear?"

"Oh, he's a beauty all right," the girl purred, without taking her eyes off the Kid.

"Is he what you want?"

"He's *exactly* what I want," the girl said in a throbbing voice.

"Very well, Mr. Bosley, I'll give you fifty-five dollars for him."

Boz shook his head. "I dunno . . ."

"Sixty-five."

"Really, Mr. Ravens, I don't—"

"Seventy, and not a penny more."

Boz exhaled hard, his hands on his hips. He gave Black Iron a pat—the horse snorted and opened his eyes—and then extended the hand toward Ravens. "All right, you convinced me. Seventy it is."

Which was not bad at all for a twenty-five-dollar horse, and Hanky gave a soft whistle of admiration through his teeth.

CHAPTER THIRTY-FIVE

"I been thinkin," Boz said several hours later, over their pushed-back plates.

They were in the hotel's saloon. The place was a roundhouse for cowboys and railroad workers, spare and utilitarian, but the food was decent and the owner didn't allow brawling or whoring on the premises. There *were* a few local girls hanging around the piano, trying to get the men to dance or buy them drinks, and Hanky had coaxed and bullied the Kid into joining him there, once they'd finished supper.

Trace had no objection to that, since it kept them out of his hair but still in sighting distance. He was writing up the day's sales for Miller's records, and Boz had his own personal bank book out. He'd been doing some deep and mysterious tallying in that thing for several days now, so Trace figured there was something portentous behind Boz's casual tone.

"You gonna tell me about it, or I have to guess?" Trace said. "I *know* we're not broke, this time."

Boz tapped his pencil on the table. "No, we're doin all right, for a wonder. Matter of fact, I been thinkin, why don't we go into the horse business for ourselves."

"We can't be doin *that* well?"

"We still got eight hundred seventeen dollars from what's-her-name, plus Miller'll owe us another eight hundred at the end of the season. That's enough for ten or twelve decent mares and a stud. Or eight really good mares and a stud. We can take our pay in horseflesh from Miller, or we can take the cash and hit the auctions ourselves."

"I don't like the idea of competin with him."

"Me neither, but we know his markets. We can go someplace else. It'd only take a dozen head to get us started."

"What're we gonna do for land?"

"We can bid for a homestead."

"Out here?"

"Why not?"

"Well, Emma, for one." Trace's half-sister was still at school, in St. Louis.

"You could bring her out to live with us. Be good help to have a woman around. Hell, you'd probably have her married off before she could unpack."

"She's fifteen!"

"All right, all right—But you been sayin it's time she got out and saw somethin of the world. She might meet somebody. Or I might. Or *you* might."

"I ain't lookin."

"No, I guess not." Boz cut a glance toward Trace's right hand.

Trace realized he was rubbing that scar again. He flattened both palms on the table and fixed his partner with a glare, daring him to say anything about it.

Boz smiled slightly. "What'd she say?"

"What?"

"What'd the witch say? Ain't she answered you yet?"

Trace ground his teeth. "I just wired her today."

"Well hell, Trace, we been in town two days. Surprised you ain't gone into a decline by now."

Trace told him, explicitly and at length, where he could go and what he should do with himself when he got there. "And I don't know what you think is so damn funny—"

"You are," Boz said, still wearing that thin smirk. "You are, partner. So'd you tell her about the werewolf?"

Trace glowered at him. "I told her there was suspicious activity in the area and I wanted to know if it looked like anything she'd seen before—"

"Like Mereck?"

"Or the bloodsuckers. Or anything else she knew."

"Hunh." Boz looked away, across the room. "You was dreamin about me the other night, wasn't you?"

Trace's anger drained away, left him feeling tired. "Yeah."

"Worse?"

"More of the same. You in danger, Reynolds callin me out, and I can't figure out how to stop it."

Boz looked down at his ledger, rubbed a hand over his mouth. "Well. I guess I could work for Miller another year. Still work out, just take me longer."

Trace felt a curious cooling sensation in his chest. "You got somethin you wanna say to me, *partner*?"

Boz studied the length of his pencil. "Just been thinkin about stuff, lately."

"Like what?"

"Like, for all the worryin you do, that folks around you is bound to die . . . could be Miss Fairweather's one you don't have to worry about. Seems to me she might know how to stand up to a curse or two."

The words seemed to come at him slowly, pregnant with meaning. "Boz, if you're worried about those dreams, it ain't—"

Boz rolled his head back on his shoulders with a groan. "I'm *tired*, Trace. Get it? I'm tired of you havin one foot out the door, and I'm tired of you usin me for your excuse to run away from your life."

"I'm not—"

"You *are*. You the worst man I ever knew for bein afraid of what you want. An' I guess I can't blame you, all the spirits ridin you for years, and folks dyin, and now the first woman you wanted in a dog's age is a lyin hateful bitch—"

"Now hang on a min—"

"And I ain't sayin you're in love with her or nothin like that. I'm not sayin you ought to be. But the two of you got *gumption* together, Trace. She's like your . . ." He made a winding motion with one hand. "What're those Greek ladies who tell the hero where to go? Opticals?"

Trace stared at him. "*Oracles*?"

"Yeah. And I didn't get it til I saw the two of you together. That damn séance, from the moment you was in the room, her eye was on you. Just like she was trainin a horse. And you watchin her for the signs, puttin every foot where she wanted—"

"That was the deal we made," Trace said, rankled.

"I know it. And I ain't sayin it's a bad thing. It ain't so different from you helpin me steer that dude in the corral this mornin." Boz pursed his lips and looked moody. "Look, you and me . . . we like an old married couple. And nobody can say you ain't done right by us. But all the time I known you, Trace, it's like you been holdin yourself down. Like God's gonna strike you dead if you step outta line. And what I seen you do this spring . . ." He shook his head, awed and angry. "Ain't one man in a thousand could do what you did on that train.

Or in the print shop, even. But you woulda never done it if *she* hadn't been drivin and cussin you all the way. And you got no business turnin your back on that, *specially* if you're right about somethin worse comin down the pike. You need to be back there with her, figurin how you're gonna deal with it."

Trace hardly knew what to say. "You don't even *like* the woman."

"Nor do you, but it don't seem to make a difference. You spent the whole spring moonin over her, you turned down that Baptist woman's invite to Montana—"

"That wasn't the reason—"

"It's all part'n parcel of the same thing, Trace! I know you think I don't get it, but I do. She *likes* this thing in you, and you like that she likes it. And you can holler all you want, but *I* think she's the perfect woman for you, only you can't see it cuz your head's all full of that Catholic crap, says you ain't livin right unless you miserable." Boz's nostrils flared in distaste. "And I think *she's* even more kinked than you are, but since you met her it's like . . . you're *bigger*, somehow. It's like *I* finally see you, proper." Boz waved a disgusted hand toward Trace's neat black suit. "And you ain't no roughneck ranch hand, partner. You clean up better than that."

They had to look away from each other then—Boz scowling across the room as if he'd just bitten into a lemon, and Trace trying to absorb the sting of Boz's words.

He was not wrong, was the hell of it. Miss Fairweather *was* the first person in twenty years that he'd been able to tell about his curse, and not fear the repercussions. And he *did* crave the approval she so willingly spooned out, knowing it kept him coming back, to learn more, to understand better, to believe he wasn't irrevocably damned. He despised himself for it, but there it was.

But the idea of her as a lover was ludicrous. She was *English*. And rich. And too damned smart for her own good. And even if she was impervious to his curse, her feud with Mereck was sure to make for a short life expectancy. For both of them, if he got involved in it.

"She might not have me back," he said at length.

"Uh-huh."

"And anyway, I don't dare leave til this . . . wolf thing is settled."

"Whyn't you just pack up the Kid and take him back to her? You know she won't refuse a treat like that."

Trace felt his lips twitch, imagining the excited tremor beneath her cool demeanor . . . but then remembered his dream—the wolves bearing Boz on a platter, the familiar but faceless Russian toasting him across the table. "It ain't just the Kid, though. I can't help but think—" He glanced toward the piano, and sat up straighter. "Damn. Where'd they get to?"

Boz turned and looked, too. Hanky had moved against the wall, in close conversation with a flaxen-haired girl, but the Kid was no-where in sight.

Trace swore, got to his feet and gathered up the record book. He stuffed the loose pages inside and shoved the whole into the leather portfolio. Boz pocketed his bank-book and threw down coin to pay for their meals, while Trace went over to Hanky and asked him where the Kid had gone.

Hanky looked around, surprised. "He musta left with that girl."

"What girl?"

"The one he was mashing on this morning—remember? She came to the corral with the English swell."

"Alice," put in the flaxen-haired girl. "She's got a room over at the Yellow Rose."

"How long ago did they leave?" Trace asked her.

She shrugged. "Couple minutes."

"Hanky, I need you to take these up to the room." Trace handed over the portfolio. "Do it right now, hear? Put 'em with my saddle-bags and then you can come back down and buy this young lady a drink." He produced a two-dollar coin, to Hanky's astonishment.

"Where're *you* goin?"

"Me'n Boz got some business down the street. Don't *you* leave the hotel tonight, understand? I'm countin on you to keep those records safe."

"All right," Hanky said, concern knitting his brow, but he levered himself off the wall and waved an elbow toward his companion until she looped her hand through it.

Trace and Boz headed for the door without further discussion.

The evening was clear and cool, and there were a lot of people on the sidewalk and on the street, merry spectres drifting in and out of doorways and lamplight. Trace crossed the sidewalk and stepped down into the thoroughfare, throwing open his senses without half think-ing about it, feeling out through the morass of thoughts and emotions, searching for the the Kid's peculiar double aura—

Boz lengthened his stride to keep up. "Is somethin gonna happen?"

"I don't know. I hope not." Some of his worry was only practical—

the Kid was unpredictable, and the thing driving him even more so. It had lain quiet for almost two weeks, and Trace recalled what Miss Fairweather had said about intervals getting shorter with use.

But his power was pushing at him, as well. Not the sharp prickle of alarm he got from demons or ghosts, just a nagging, seasick feeling that something was astir.

The boy couldn't have gotten far. Trace knew he'd only been distracted for a few minutes. Now that he paid attention, hints and flickers of emotion came to him—furtive lust, sly excitement, and pure, predatory intent.

"This way," he said, and they headed east, along Front Street toward the charcoal yards and the rougher end of town. The streets became less crowded, and darker as there was more distance between the buildings. And gradually, as the interfering noise of other minds fell off, Trace realized he was following more than one person. Some of it felt like the Kid, but Trace had again that sense of a stereoscope image sliding in and out of focus, as if an obscuring film lay between his power and the Kid's soul. And there was a competing aura, over *that,* though this one was rank as bear-musk and almost familiar—

"There's somebody ahead of us," Boz said a moment later. "Half a block forward and to the left."

The male figure was moving along at an easy lope, head down and turning side to side like a hound casting for scent. He wore a long coat and was hatless—no, the hat was in his hand, Trace saw when the fellow passed a porch-lamp. He was carrying a top hat.

"Is that *Remy*?" Boz said under his breath.

There was no way the wolf-hunter should have heard. The wind was in their faces and there was a good fifty yards between them. But the jaunty, loose-jointed figure paused in his tracks, cast an unhurried glance over his shoulder, and then melted around the side of the nearest building.

Boz made as if to go after him but Trace caught his sleeve. "No— we find the Kid. Stay close to me."

"Do you know where he *is*?"

Trace did. The boy's aura was bright and eager now, less than a block ahead of them, and there was a cheap boarding-house at the end of the street, with a sign proclaiming it to be the Yellow Rose. Every window in the place was open and the sounds of music and laughter poured out into the street.

Several couples loitered on the sidewalk and the yard surrounding the place. Lanterns had been strung from the porch and around the low deck that served as a dance floor. A jug band and fiddler were playing a jig and there was a crowd of whirling, whooping figures in the lamplight.

"Watch for Remy," Trace said, and shifted into his spirit-sight, scanning the crowd for the Kid. It was difficult sorting through so many unfamiliar souls, especially with the heightened emotions running amuck.

Boz nudged his arm and pointed. Trace spotted Remy's shaggy black head at the corner of the dance floor, golden eyes flashing in the lantern light as he watched something off in the dark of the railyard.

The wolf-hunter wrinkled his nose and slipped out of sight. On instinct Trace plunged after him, straight through the dance floor, dodging skirts and knocking elbows with indignant cowboys. He leapt off the edge of the deck and found himself on a gravel stretch between the boarding-house and the outdoor kitchen. Smells of woodsmoke and charred flesh and sweat, shouting cooks and scurrying serving-girls. His head beginning to pound from the onslaught of foreign feelings and thoughts crowding his skull—

Fear kicked him hard in the guts—someone else's fear—hard and bright as blood in his mouth. Slashes of pain across his belly and arms and face, sudden and shocking, and a disbelieving horror that clawed up his throat—

The girl's shriek was choked and thin under the music, but Trace felt it in his bones, ragged as fingernails down a blackboard. Across the yard to the slope of the railroad embankment, and the pile of railroad ties there, where two shadows were fighting over the girl, her white dress glowing like a spectral shroud in the darkness. She went on screaming as she was buffeted back and forth between the men's bodies; the larger male seemed to be grasping the smaller one's wrists and holding the girl trapped within their arms. The Kid scratched and struck wildly at the man holding him, but the growls that emerged from his throat were enraged rather than frightened, and Remy let the girl drop and caught him by the collar. The girl sprawled in the dirt, crawling and crying out feebly. The Kid lashed with a hooked hand and Trace saw dark furrows open across Remy's face, but the wolf-hunter barely recoiled before he socked the Kid in the jaw.

The boy's knees buckled. Remy saw Trace coming and turned to meet him, his posture straightening and his hands moving out to the sides, whether in surrender or invitation Trace didn't have time to decide. At that moment Boz appeared from behind the pile of railroad ties and swung a long plank at Remy's head. Remy turned almost casually and flung up an arm so the board broke across his elbow instead of upside his skull. It knocked him staggering even so, and the Kid made a lunge as if to flee. Trace grabbed the boy by the back of his vest and the Kid turned right around inside his skin and sank his teeth into Trace's hand.

The pain that lanced up his arm was incredible—icy needles piercing his flesh, the sickening ache of frostbite. Trace's arm and shoulder went completely numb and he dropped the Kid, stared in shock at the boy. The Kid snarled at him, flashing teeth that had never belonged in a human mouth, contempt and triumph swelling his aura before fear flashed in his eyes and he ran.

A gunshot sounded, close, echoed by screams. Trace was dimly aware that the music had stopped. The frostbite was spreading with terrible swiftness down his legs and up his back, clawing its way along his veins, trying to eat through to the very core of him, where his power retreated and pulled him down into the well of his soul.

He sank down strengthless, his throat closing up so he couldn't answer Boz's urgent questions. His ears were roaring. He heard Remy's rough patois over the din, glimpsed a man flashing a gun and a deputy's badge. Skittering laughter touched Trace's mind, the mad glee of demons, of lunatics. The Kid's spirit fleeing in fright at his own audacity but looking back once and again to gloat over his little act of rebellion. The girl's frightened mind clinging to life, clawing at it, fearing that Hell would be all her grandmother promised and no respite for her, she'd always thought she'd have more time, she'd thought she would be famous, that someone would remember her and she'd be better than her mother had—

Then the girl was gone, borne away like a leaf on a current, and a new presence oozed into Trace's awareness, thick and cold as a constrictor snake, hungry and familiar and surprisingly cordial: *Why, hello again, Mr. Tracy! Herr Kieler was right. What a rough treasure you are . . .*

CHAPTER THIRTY-SIX

He'd had the measles as a boy—one of the few times in his life, aside from the long recuperation after Antietam, when he had been really sick. He remembered the disorientation of fever, of feeling that his bed was at the bottom of some deep cosmic well, of looking up into a vast and whirling nothingness and fearing he would fall into it, until he cried out and his mother put her cool hand on his head and stopped the world from spinning.

The hands that pawed at him now were spectral, icy. They burrowed through his blood like termites, digging and gnawing at the edges of that well-cap in his mind. They threw themselves against the shield of his power, burned up in it, fell back dead to build a buttress for their fellows to swarm over.

Voices clashed over his head. Boz jabbered fast and angry at the other shadows and they droned back at him, unbearably slow and low. Other voices—a snide Cajun drawl and a quick nasal retort—*Reynolds*, he thought, furious, and started to come up after him, but the termites surged forward and he ducked into the well again.

Then, in the dark, Miss Fairweather's hand slipped into his, cool and anchoring. Her voice was calm and practical: *You are as strong as he is, Mr. Tracy—you can fight this. Remember: my blood is panacea to you, protection against his poison—*

He saw again the banquet table, the leeches drawing blood from all the guests and leading to the fountain. The Russian drinking from the fountain, and Reynolds offering the bottle of Miss Fairweather's blood. Her drinking from the goblet marked poison—

You poisoned your own blood. Fed it through me, to fight him off.

In a manner of speaking. I told you, your power is a shield, but you must have realized it is a sword as well. A fiery sword—

You're feedin me snake oil again.

She seemed amused. *So long as you find nourishment in it, Mr. Tracy.*

And he did. After all, she hadn't been wrong yet. He pushed open the well-cover in his mind and the termites swarmed in but the bright flame of his power drove them back, burnt them to ash. In the light and the burning he saw them for what they were—malicious imps, nasty little shades of demons or something similar, mindless but somehow willful, that sought to burrow into his living flesh and corrupt it. They tried to hide in his bones, in his heart, in the dark recesses of his self-doubt, but he'd had enough of letting other forces tell him what he should be.

He chased them all out and made himself clean again. And then he was glad to feel her cool lips on his brow, and hear her approval: *Well done, Mr. Tracy. I knew you had it in you . . .*

TRACE OPENED HIS eyes. Saw rough walls and flat steel bars. Smell of coffee and putrid smoke, like damp logs burning.

He remembered the Kid turning on him, the sudden snarl of defiance and fear, and sat up quickly. Found himself on the edge of a narrow cot, at the back wall of a jail cell. Brick wall outside the bars, with a heavy oak door. Daylight through the single barred window.

"Thought you was a goner, Prêtre," said a languid voice.

Trace turned his head and met Remy's yellow gaze, through the smoke of his cheroot and the bars between them.

"Good thing Remy not take dat bet," the wolf-hunter added. "Mitchie Boz be takin some money from me bout now."

"Where is he?"

"Back where he come from, je présume. Dat doctor wan' fill you full o' morphine, but Mitchie Boz throw such a fit they shoo him out. Dey listen better to Remy when he say it a bad idea."

Trace inspected the angry-looking bite mark in his palm, the radiating lines of infection trailing up his forearm, to the injection bruise near his elbow. "What'd they give me, then?"

"Aconite." Remy exhaled. "Is better for wolf-fever."

"Does it stop people turnin into wolves?"

Remy paused with his cheroot halfway to his lips, gazing low-lidded through the haze of smoke. "*Non* . . . just slow it down some. But Remy think you don't worry bout dat, hunh? Maybe you do got un ange watch over you."

Trace remembered those cool hands and lips caressing his brow. "Somethin like that . . . What about you? Are you watchin over that Kid, or huntin him?"

"Remy hunt wolves," he said blandly. "Miller say he have a wolf problem."

"That don't explain what you're doin here in town. Or why you were tailin the Kid last night."

"Eh, oui? Why *you* tail dat Kid?"

"Because I knew somethin bad was gonna happen. And I was right, wasn't I? *You* knew somethin was up or you wouldn'ta been there. So what do you know about that boy that I don't?"

Remy took his time about answering, picking his long teeth with a grimy thumbnail while he thought about it. At last he said, "He kill five people down in Salt Lake fore he make track up here, en Avril. Make a big damn mess, make us all in danger."

"Others like you," Trace said. "*Les loups-garous.*"

"Oui," Remy said, in an offhand, what's-it-to-you? tone. He took a fresh cheroot from his pocket and lit it off the old one, asking through his teeth, "So what *you* be?"

"A medium," Trace said, after a hesitation. "A psychic."

A grunt from the wolf-hunter. "Remy think you more than dat."

"Yeah, so do a lot of people." Trace got up, stiff and a little shaky from hunger—he was *starving*—but otherwise fine. His shirt was damp and greasy with old sweat. His vest and coat hung outside the bars of the cell. "So what is it about the Kid, that ain't what you expected?"

"He don' smell right. He don' act right. Down in Salt Lake, he kill couple sheep round d'full moon—dat normal for the young ones, dey got no control. But then bout same time Remy catch his scent, dat boy have some big fit—kill his mama and papa, two sisters, some neighbor who come help pray the devil outta him. Is like he *do* got some devil in him. He—"

"What is it, then? If it's not a devil in you?"

"Who knows? Dese doctors prob'ly say is madness, or sickness. Some people get it from wolf bites, comme la hydrophobie. Some get it from dey eat wolf meat, or drink water with dey piss in it. But some men *invite* the wolf in, comprenez-vous?"

Trace nodded.

The wolf-hunter pursed his lips. "But Remy never see nobody have un réaction like you. You fight, tremor, turn hot like you burn up. Mitchie Boz, he scared but he tell the doctor, leave you 'lone, leave you 'lone, and you come out of it. So the deputy say, lock him up, jus' in case, and you spend the whole night talking bout demons and burning swords." Remy eyed him thoughtfully. "You not gonna change, je présume?"

"No." It wasn't even a fear in his mind.

"You know he kill dat girl, oui?"

"Yeah."

"Try to pin it on me, lil bastard."

"Maybe." But Trace had gotten a whiff of the dark lusts driving the Kid. He suspected killing the girl had been purely for fun; Remy had just chanced to interfere.

"So what *you* know bout dat Kid that Remy don't?"

Trace weighed his words for a moment. "There's a man named Mereck . . . calls himself the Russian Mesmerist—"

"Le Russe." Remy's brows drew together. "Avec le cirque?"

"You know him?"

For the first time, worry marked the wolf-hunter's brow. "Last two-three year Remy hear story of people in cages, les experiments, les vivisections. Hear say le Russe like strange animals, strange people. Two-three month back some monsters tear up a train by Eagle Rock—"

"I was at Eagle Rock. Me and Boz both. Those monsters cut down forty people in a half-hour."

Remy's brow furrowed deeper.

"I think the Kid's one of the Russian's experiments. I think the Russian polluted him somehow, turned him into Pestilence. There's a . . . a doctor I know, she gave me a potion to fight off the fever. But anybody else that Kid bites is gonna turn into a monster—not a true loup-garou, but some abomination. You think Eagle Rock was bad, imagine what a score of *your* kind could do to this town, if they were crazed and hungry."

"Sacre bleu." Remy's neglected cherroot had burned down to his fingers and he dropped it abruptly. "So what you think to do?"

"Save him if I can." Trace's first thought was to wonder whether Miss Fairweather knew a cure. His second was, if the Kid was one of Mereck's creations, he didn't want the boy anywhere near Miss Fairweather. "Put a bullet in his head, if I can't. I could use your help— you got to him first last night—"

Remy shook his head in flat refusal. "If dat boy what you say, he already lost. He got no control, he make trouble, he bring le Russe on us. You want him, Prêtre, you welcome."

"Wolves mate for life. They'll fight to the death for their cubs."

Remy gave a bark of laughter. "If le Russe make dat boy, he no blood of mine. Wolves is good hunters, Prêtre, but when men with guns come, wolves *hide*."

Trace would have argued further, but at that moment there were voices in the front of the sheriff's office.

Remy cocked his head toward the door of the lockup, listening. "Dat the sheriff . . . and Mitchie Boz."

He was right. Two minutes later the deputy came into the lockup, rattling his keys and apologizing as he opened Trace's cell door. "Sorry about the accommodations, Mr. Tracy. So you're feeling better? None of us knew what to make of that fit you had. Sorry it took us a while to figure out who you were and wire your boss . . ."

"That's quite all right." Trace could guess what boss that was, though it was anyone's guess what she'd told them. He lost no time in exiting the cell and retrieving his vest and coat, catching the wolf-hunter's eye as he dressed. "I can get you out of here."

Remy shook his head again. "Merci boucoup, Prêtre, but Remy think he look after himself."

Trace nodded, once, and went through the door the deputy held open, into the front office.

Boz was the first person he saw, but the worry on his partner's face abated only somewhat at the sight of Trace upright and whole. His eyes slid warningly toward the sheriff and the man beside him—a short, carrot-topped fellow with a narrow, weasely face and unnaturally bright black eyes.

It took everything Trace had not to flinch. He managed a stiff nod, not sure what degree of recognition was called for.

Reynolds jerked his chin in greeting. "Detective Tracy." He was not grinning, for once.

"Reynolds," Trace answered.

"So you pulled through after all," the sheriff said, looking Trace up and down. "You want to see Doc Dreyfuss? I can fetch him for you."

"That won't be necessary." Trace took his gun belt from Boz's hand and wrapped it around his hips.

"Doc Fairweather answered your telegram," Boz said, pointedly. "Reynolds brought it to our room this mornin, and when I told him you were in lockup, he brought it to the sheriff, so he knew who you were."

"Let me see that," Trace said, holding out a hand toward Reynolds, but it was the sheriff who picked up a telegram from his desk and handed it over. The mark of origin was St. Louis, and the signature at the bottom was S. Fairweather. The words in-between had the look of snakes, writhing and tumbling over each other. He had to unfocus his eyes slightly to read the false message Reynolds had put there:

EYEWITNESSES CONFIRM SUSPECT IN EAGLE ROCK BEFORE AND AFTER
TRAIN ATTACK STOP RARE HOMICIDAL MANIA CONTAGIOUS USE CAUTION

ALL RESOURCES AT YOUR DISPOSAL WIRE WHEN APPREHENDED MEDICAL
ARRANGEMENTS WILL BE MADE

"I hope you'll forgive the misunderstanding," the sheriff said. "I spoke with the Union Pacific's head of security just last week but he didn't tell me he had brought in Pinkerton agents."

Trace glanced at Reynolds and got a very subtle nod. "This is a delicate matter, Sheriff. The railroad's gone to some trouble to keep this incident quiet."

"Of course, Detective. I've always given your office every cooperation—"

"I don't suppose you've got a lead on that boy since sunup?"

"No sir, we haven't run him down yet, but I've got men out combing the rail yards and watching the depot—"

"Call 'em off," Trace said. "He's too smart to take the train out of town and too dangerous to confront around civilians. He's got a condition, makes him unpredictable and strong like a madman. You don't want your men goin anywhere near him."

The sheriff cleared his throat. "With respect to you and your employer, we had a murder here of our own—"

"The Eagle Rock killings take precedence," Reynolds said.

Trace nodded agreement. "That boy'll be brought to justice, one way or the other. If by some miracle he slips through the noose, I will personally bring him back here to face Territory justice."

The sheriff didn't look happy about that, but Trace shot down all his protestations and bullied his way out of the office, herding Boz in front of him and leaving Reynolds to follow.

Ten minutes later they were all standing in the alley behind the jail, Reynolds fidgeting on the balls of his feet, Boz looking worriedly between the two of them.

"So now I'm a Pinkerton, huh?" Trace said, shrugging into his coat.

"Okay, so it was a hack job," Reynolds snarled. "I was in a rush. And you're welcome, by the way."

"Why are you *here*?"

"Because you're too thick to take a hint," the reporter snapped. His dark eyes were showing sparks of red in their depths, and for the first time Trace felt a real fear of him. He had never seen the demon so agitated, or so careless about his disguise. "You think I *like* poking my fingers through your soupy brains at night? *The Boss is coming for you.*"

I know, Trace wanted to bite back, but that would get him nothing new. "Look, I got no part in the quarrel between him and the witch. That séance was all her and Kieler—"

Reynolds's laugh was dark and choked, as if he were gargling blood. "You *are* tender meat, ain't you boy? The Boss's had his eye on you since *March*. That fool McGillicuddy staked you out right away, which was pretty careless of Her Snootiness. I thought she had better sense than that."

"So you showed up at the Herschels' already knowin who he was," Boz put in. "And I guess you're the reason the little demon in the press suddenly went for bigger game."

"Well, look who just caught up," Reynolds sneered. "More to the point, Buck, I knew your buddy here's the tastiest morsel anybody's seen since . . . Well." He actually gnashed his teeth, and for a second Trace saw the thing within the meat-sack, bones straining at the flesh as if they would tear through. Trace's own face crawled, with the instinctive fear of prey for a predator. His power was screaming at him to get away from this thing, but he held firm.

Reynolds controlled himself as well, subsiding beneath the human façade. "Once the witch flushed you out, it was a matter of time til the buzzards came circling. And I figured you were too green to survive your own bad luck and her bungling, so I took a friendly interest. Kind of a shepherding hand, you might say."

"On Mereck's say-so?" Trace said, knowing the answer. "Or your own?"

"Let me put it this way," Reynolds said. "How would *you* like living in a bottle? Sound a bit constraining? Well it is. And if you don't wanna end up the same way, I suggest you get your holier-than-thou arse out of town. In fact, out of the western hemisphere might not be a bad idea."

"How long have I got?"

"Couldn't say. That blood-spell makes you hard to pin down in the gray space, which is why the Boss started recruiting Dickensian orphans to hunt you down." Reynolds turned his head suddenly, as if hearing a faraway call . . . which he might well be, Trace realized, feeling a twinge along his own internal telegraph lines. The scar in his palm stung and he clenched his fist.

"I gotta go. And you will too, if you know what's good for you." Reynolds drew a telegram envelope from his pocket and tossed it at Trace. "Take advantage of the witch's hospitality. If anybody knows how to hide from him, it's *her*." He began to back away down the street.

"And for blazes' sakes don't be taking any more jaunts in the gray space until she shows you how to do it properly. You might as well smear yourself in hog fat and throw yourself to the wolves."

Reynolds turned on his heel. And between one step and the next—Trace wasn't even sure he blinked—the reporter disappeared from view.

Boz's breath gushed out as if he'd been holding it. "Jesus Christ, Trace. Jesus *Christ*—"

"Breathe," Trace said sharply. He put a hand under Boz's armpit just as his knees buckled. He didn't faint, but he did turn awfully gray. Trace folded him onto a nearby hay bale, sat beside him, and kept a hand on the back of Boz's neck until he started breathing normally again.

"Sorry," Boz muttered at length. "Stupid . . ."

"No," Trace said. "He affects me the same way. I've just got more protection than you do."

"He just showed up this mornin with that telegram, and I didn't know what else to do—"

"Don't worry about it."

"You gonna tell me what the hell *happened* last night? That boy bit you, didn't he? And it did somethin to you."

"He tried. Miss Fairweather's spell is still protectin me." He turned the telegraph envelope over in his hand, but there was no note inside, just several pieces of paper money. Trace retrieved the telegram from his breast pocket and unfolded it. This time there was no blurring of the words, and despite the disjointed language of the telegram he heard her voice in his head as he read:

SPIRIT ACTIVITY IN AREA RESEMBLES KEUNG-SI STOP LYCANTHROPE
UNIMPORTANT REMOVE SELF FROM DANGER LYCANTHROPY HIGHLY
CONTAGIOUS AVOID SALIVA BLOOD EXCRETA STOP SILVER NITRATE OR
ACONITE MAY SLOW INFECTION BUT IF VICTIM INFLUENCED BY OUTSIDE
FORCES NO HOPE I IMPLORE YOU RETURN IMMEDIATELY
S. FAIRWEATHER.

Somehow he hadn't been frightened until he heard the fear in her words. *I implore you. Remove yourself from danger. I have been searching for someone like you, for so long*—He felt the power trying to well up, to put that shield between himself and his fear, but he pushed it down. If he took the fear away—gave in to that sense of invulnerability—he was liable to do something stupid. As if what he was contemplating wasn't bad enough.

"What did she say?" Boz demanded.

"To leave the Kid alone and come back."

Boz stared at him. "But you ain't gonna do that. Are you."

Trace shook his head. "Mereck picked out that Kid cause he was like me—religious family, power he couldn't control. Maybe just meant for him to get close to me, maybe thinkin he could make himself a pack of werewolves if I didn't cooperate. I don't know. But I don't think he was supposed to bite me and I'm pretty damn sure he wasn't supposed to kill that girl."

Boz stared at him for a longer moment. "You mean to hunt him down?"

"I don't see as how anyone else can . . . Where's Hanky? At the corral?"

"I sent him back to the ranch. Gave him the bank-books and a message for Miller—"

"Shit," Trace said, because as soon as Boz said it, Trace's mind grasped and pulled on some thread he had been unaware of—the Kid's aura, faint and skittish as a shooting star, headed north.

"Well, I didn't think he ought to be around here, askin questions—"

"No. But the Kid's headed that direction, too. We got horses?"

Boz's throat worked for a second as if he were going to throw up, but when he spoke, his voice was startlingly normal. "I kept back three. Told Hanky to tell Miller we was takin 'em in payment for the last two months. The paint for me and a couple o' spares for us to change out, in case we have to ride hard."

Trace shook his head, lurching off the hay bale even as the words were leaving Boz's mouth. "Take 'em, Boz. Take the rest of the money and go. Don't even tell me where—"

"*Shit* on that," Boz said harshly. "Shit all *over* that, partner. You don't get to choose for me."

Trace looked away, far down the street. He didn't know which was worse, the fear or the craven, selfish relief. After a minute he said, "Are we ready to go?"

"*I'm* ready. You maybe wanna change clothes."

"Yeah. And visit the druggist." Trace began to turn toward the stockyards, their hotel, raking a list together in his head: *Aconite. Silver nitrate. Riding clothes. Bullets. Rope . . .*

"Trace." Boz put out a hand and caught his lapel, forced him to meet his eyes. "Just tell me you ain't plannin to ride out there and die."

Trace looked at him—the wide weathered brow, the steady dark eyes, the one mouth that had never lied to him, nor asked him to be anything he wasn't. "It's not me I'm afraid for."

Their faces were inches apart. He couldn't miss the subtle tightening of Boz's face, the mist of fear that welled in his eyes. "If I ride away you'll go after him on your own. Won't you."

"Yeah." He paused. "I think I have to, Boz."

Boz nodded, once, and let go Trace's coat, smoothing the lapel with a caress so loving and bitter that Trace wished he would have just hit him, instead.

"All right," Boz said, not looking at him. "Go do your business. I'll wait for you at the corral."

CHAPTER THIRTY-SEVEN

It was eighty miles to the ranch. They had taken two days on the way into town, but it could be done in a day, by two good riders with a change of mounts. Boz guessed Hanky would stop at nightfall, in the same place they'd camped on the way south, if they didn't catch up to him first.

And it was important that they catch Hanky before nightfall. Because woven in and out of Hanky's easy-to-follow trail—the single pony with a light rider, and nine horses on a string behind him—was a set of barefoot tracks, those same peculiar five-toed prints they had seen outside the ranch bath-house. Except now Trace could see they were the front part of a man's foot, the big toe prominent, long claws like a dog's cutting through the soil with each step. No marks of heels, and spaced at a length and depth that suggested a speedy lope.

"That's him," Boz said, mouth curled in distaste. "Followin Hanky."

"Leadin us," Trace corrected. He was getting more frequent flashes of awareness from the Kid as the afternoon shadows lengthened—twinges of excitement and gloating contempt. Like a trail of feathers and blood, leading to the gnawed and discarded carcass.

"You know this's a trap, right?" Boz said.

"I expect he thinks it is. I aim to catch him before he can spring it."

"And then what?"

"Shoot him."

"Bullets didn't kill those bloodsuckers."

"I know it. But Miss Fairweather said silver nitrate might work. So I got some of that." He reached in his vest pocket and pulled out a small brown bottle, tightly corked.

"What is it?"

"An ointment. Doctors put it on wounds and burns." The lycanthropy patient had been deathly afraid of it—had screamed and swore the nurses were trying to poison him when they tried to apply it to the numerous wounds he inflicted on himself.

"So, what—you plan to throw it at him? Hold him down and pour it down his throat?"

"If it comes to that. Also got some aconite tincture. Remy said it's good for wolf-bites, and Miss Fairweather mentioned it, too, so I got some of that, against either of us gets bit again." Not that it would do much good, he suspected. But he wasn't going to tell Boz that.

They continued north as fast as they dared, talking little, following the Sweetwater's dry gorge. The little canyon was shallow and wide, carved by eons of spring runoff, but this time of year the water was low.

"We're catchin up on 'em," Boz said, the next time they changed horses.

Trace nodded, but he was wishing Hanky had stopped sooner. It was falling dusk by that time, and they were coming to a place where the trail led down into the canyon, a shortcut through the gorge that was quicker than riding around the long curve of the bluff. It was the same path they had taken on the trip out, but then they had been four men in broad daylight. The canyon was a bad place to be in the dark, full of crags and rocks and shadows to fool the eye.

Hanky, of course, had taken the shortcut. They followed his trail into the canyon along with the last of the daylight. The wind whistled over their heads in hymn chords and the horses' footsteps echoed in so many directions they sounded like a whole cavalry. Darkness settled over them like a goose-down comforter, and with it came the familiar dreamy caress of power up and down Trace's nerves—like being horny, but of the mind rather than the body. He began to hear voices murmuring to him, one high and one low, like an imp and a devil having a sniggering conversation behind his back. As if they were *taunting* him to come and investigate, like the demon in the drunk tank, urging him to take a drink . . .

"You see a light?" Boz said, low.

"Where?"

"Bit to your right."

The floodplain of the river had opened up to a wide place, flanked by bluffs ten or twelve feet high, bottomed with gravel that slid treacherously under the horses' feet. And after a second he saw the light—not the flicker of flame he'd been looking for, just a glow, and no smoke at all.

But it *was* a campfire, built back in a semi-sheltered curve of rock wall. Half smothered by the cooking pot that had been dropped into it, blackened remains of dinner slopped over the side. Nearby were lumpy shadows of a bedroll, rucksack, saddles.

Their horses didn't like that place. They shuffled and shied away from the fire, backing down the gravel to the ribbon of water.

Boz dismounted and approached the fire, kicked the pan out, and set a long branch of dried brush onto the embers. It quickly began to snap and pop, little licks of flame flaring up along the dead tinder. In the swelling light Boz inspected the tack alongside the bedrolls. "This is Hanky's saddle." He traced the ground with his eyes, turned in a circle and paced a few yards away, where he abruptly stopped and crouched. "Aw, hell . . ."

Trace dismounted, moved to Boz's side.

It was Hanky, dropped like a pile of old rags on the gravel. One arm was pinned under him, the other flung up and out. His gun was still in his hand. His guts were all over the creek bed.

"Holy Mother." Trace crossed himself, touched his fist to his lips for a moment, then reached out and pressed Hanky's eyes closed.

The jolt he got was a kick to the chest—like plunging out of a steam tent into a cold river. Darkness closed around him like a vise, the darkness of someone else's memories; the vision was coming at him like a freight train and it was going to hurt—

close, confined space, like a storm cellar or an old well—damp walls, aching back and stinging skin from the bite of the strap, indignity of his own stink and a hateful rage boiling in his blood, loosing hot tears of impotence and self-loathing, and then the quality of the darkness changed, became intimate, caressing—a voice whispering assurance, invitation, such a voice as God was supposed to have, but this was not the God of his father, demanding bowing-down and submission, this was a God of retribution, of blood-lust and hunger, it spoke to the rage inside him, stroked it and made it sweeten, and he opened himself to the darkness, welcomed it in, and it filled him up and made him strong, made him matter, and O those unbelievers were blind and puny in their ignorance, especially that one who had the gall to call himself Preacher, and now it was time to make restitution—

Trace was dimly aware of Boz's voice barking at him, Boz's hands gripping his shoulders and pushing him away from Hanky's body, rough gravel at his back, Boz's arms holding him down as he fought the sickening carnality of the Kid's soul, not wanting to feel the gloating anticipation in him nor see what was coming—

Hanky was a small shadow bent over a small fire, surrounded by the comfortable forms of horses, looking up startled as they snorted and shied, one hand going to the unfamiliar gun on his hip, feeling suddenly his smallness, his aloneness beneath the uncaring sky

hot surge of triumph at the fear on his face, the quick clumsy shot squeezed off, the single cry of shock before his jaws were on the unbeliever's throat, the ecstatic spurt of hot blood in his mouth, better than sugar, better than his father's false tongue when he had bitten it off, because he was doing the will of the Master, and finally he had the strength and the authority to wreak all the havoc he wanted—

Trace rolled on all fours and retched. Bile drowned out the tang of blood and the wracking spasms broke him free of the trance. He put a mental shoulder against that door in his mind and shoved it closed, pushed the power down so hard he felt his brain cramp with the sudden collapse into silence.

He sat back on his heels, panting and wiping a sleeve across his mouth. Boz kept a hand on his shoulder, not saying anything, just waiting for the verdict.

Trace turned his head and spat into the gravel.

"Kid?" Boz said.

"Yeah."

"Same as the horses?"

"Yeah."

Boz turned in his crouch, surveying the desolate place and the ruin of a young man barely out of boyhood. "This's worse than the bloodsuckers. Those things were hungry, but this . . . don't make no sense."

"It makes sense," Trace said. "This is what happens when you take a child with a power he doesn't understand, and tell him every day he's bad and evil for bein what he is. He becomes the thing you tell him he is, cause he doesn't know any better. And if somebody like Mereck gets ahold of a powder-keg like that, this is what you get."

"Yeah, but how much of this is Mereck's play and how much is just mad-dog crazy?"

Does it matter? Trace was about to say, when one of the horses snorted, loud.

They both froze, hands to guns, listening. Boz turned slowly around, back to the fire, squinting into the darkness. Trace got his feet under him, scanned the upper edge of the nearer riverbank, over Boz's head. The rock face of the bluff reflected some firelight, but above that all was blackness. The wind moaned over the mouth of the wash-out with a sound like blowing across a bottle. Everything else was quiet enough to make his skin crawl.

Trace slitted his eyes against the cold he knew was waiting and stepped into the gray space. Starlight and fire-glow splintered in the edges of his vision. Boz's form leapt out of the darkness, so bright he looked like a man-shaped moon against the dark rock face of the creek bed. The gray swirled around him, whistled with the wind around the horses and the scrub brush growing along the top of the bank—

And the dark shape hunkered there.

"Boz," Trace murmured, "get behind the fire."

Boz shot him one wary glance and then turned to follow his sight-line. He backed down the gravel bed, skirting the campfire, easing his guns clear of the holsters. The dark figure slunk along the top of the bank along with him, and Trace recognized the shadowy aura that clung to the inhuman shape.

"All right," he said into the darkness. "Come on down where we can see you, so Boz here don't have to start shootin."

There was a soft snort from the cliff above. "Dunno, Prêtre, he look kinda spooky to me."

Trace glanced at Boz, who had both guns trained on the ridge. "Then I suggest you move slow and keep your hands where he can see 'em."

A rustle of the brush above the cliff, and then a rush of motion. A lanky form dropped like an oversized spider onto the sand, grunting as it landed. It hunkered there for a moment, giving the look of some-thing bestial, demonic. But then it stood up, taller than the Kid, tall as Trace himself, buck naked and hairier than any man ought to be, but human.

Mostly.

Remy's eyes reflected the low flames between them. His neck and shoulders were thickened, his back unnaturally arched. His teeth and jaw were distorted enough that his speech came out more garbled than usual. "Guess you know dat Kid been here."

"I did work that out for myself, yes."

Remy jerked his chin to the north. "He bout two hour gone, head on to ranch. Mebbe catch 'im if we don't wait."

"What made you change your mind?" Boz said.

The loup-garou's shoulders hunched—*Sheepish,* Trace thought, and then wondered if he was finally losing his mind. "He one of my kind," Remy said, and looked at Boz. "You know bout dat, eh, Compair Lapin?"

Boz glanced at Trace and holstered his pistols. "Can you track him?"

"Better than you, Mitchie Boz. Specially in the dark."

Boz jerked his chin. "You lead."

The loup-garou's eyes glinted in amusement. "You try an' keep up."

Trace turned away and walked around the fire to where Blackjack was rolling his eyes and stamping his feet. He didn't like the proximity of the blood and the wolf-smell. And his ears laid back at the sound of something stretching and groaning and a long, yawning whine that ended in a yelp. Blackjack tossed his head and whinnied in alarm. Trace steadied him with a hand and a murmur, and turned at the sound of feet padding across the creek bed.

A black wolf the size of a small pony dance-stepped down the gravel toward them. The horses snorted and shied back. The wolf locked eyes with Trace, dipped his head regally, and then trotted away up the draw.

"Handy," Boz said sourly, and boosted into the saddle.

THE RIDE THROUGH the dark was slow and nerve-wracking. The horses didn't like following the wolf, and because the wolf could see better than the horses, he kept running ahead of them and circling back. Several times in the first hour Trace thought they had lost him, but then he would appear again at Blackjack's stirrup and cause the quarterhorse to shy and snort.

After a while Trace decided if he was riding into a trap he'd rather see it coming, and opened up the veil a crack, casting his spirit-sight ahead of them. He could keep track of the Remy-wolf that way, follow

the faint dark trail of its essence—whatever it was that was not human soul, that nevertheless clung to the flesh and bone.

After a longer interval Boz rode up close to his stirrup. "Why are
there no lights?"

Trace pulled himself a little closer to reality, looked around at the
landscape, and did not quite recognize it. "Are we that close?"

"We're not two miles out."

Trace squinted into the darkness. All he could see was a long stretch
of black horizon, with aeons of stars stretching away overhead.

"Stop," Boz said. "Just stop."

Trace reined back. Blackjack stopped gratefully, blowing out his
sides. Boz's paint pressed in close, as did their two reserve horses. They
were nervous, sniffing the air and twitching. The wind blew in their
faces, too strongly for Trace to hear much else.

"What is it?" Boz whispered. "What do you see?"

He couldn't see anything, that was the problem. Even through his
spirit-sight, the prairie was a disturbing blank—the little critters had
bolted for holes and crannies. There were horses out far away around
the edges of the pasture, but none of the familiar man-spirits he
should have recognized. And the loup-garou had vanished. "I think
Remy gave us the slip."

Suddenly there was the thud of rushing footfalls—no more than
three, at close range, and a large, growling body landed on the back
of the sorrel gelding at Trace's flank. The horse screamed and staggered, knocking into Blackjack. The snarling beast on its back tore at
the sorrel with claws and feet, head bent over the horse's neck, trying
to bite. Trace yanked at the slip knot binding the sorrel's lead to his
saddle horn, and Boz reached around Trace's back, fired his pistol at
the beast at nearly point-blank range.

The monster fell from the horse's back with a yowl and thudded
to the ground. Trace tried to untangle his stirrup from Boz's while Boz
fought to separate his reserve horse's lead from his saddle. Everything
seemed to come free at once, and Blackjack took off like a shot, racing
like the devil was at his heels.

Trace didn't try to fight him. He bent low over the quarterhorse's
neck, gave him his head but applied firm pressure with hands and
knees, trying to reassure the animal and slow his panic. They raced
over the hard-packed ground, Trace praying that Blackjack wouldn't
put his leg in a hole or run them both into a fence.

The thought had scarcely passed through his mind before Blackjack sailed up and over, landed with a grunt on the enclosed side of the south pasture, and then slowed to a trot, his sides heaving and his mouth fighting the bit. "Easy, easy," Trace muttered to him, and the big horse huffed his annoyance. He was *home* now, he might have said, and what was Trace thinking, taking him out in the dark amid monsters like that?

"Sorry, fella, sorry." Trace patted the horse's neck and wheeled him around to see what had become of Boz. He could hear hoofbeats coming fast, though not at the breakneck pace he had just ridden. There was a flash of white underbelly as Boz's paint cleared the fence and trotted daintily up to Trace's side.

"You all right?" Boz demanded. "What was that? That wasn't the Kid?"

"I don't think so. Let's don't sit here." Blackjack was still moving agitatedly in a circle—he knew the paddock was close and wanted to go there, now.

They let the horses set the pace, and they pushed to an agitated trot, as if being pursued. Trace kept looking behind them, but saw nothing, not with his eyes nor his spirit-sense. He hadn't felt this blind in months, and he didn't like it. Boz rode with a pistol in his right hand, head up and scanning the darkness.

"Shit," he said abruptly.

They were almost upon the ranch's yard, and it was dark. At this time of night, every bunk-house should have been aglow with lamp-light. On a clear mild night like this, the boys should have still been loitering around the fire-pit, but it was dark and deserted.

The only light Trace could see came from Miller's house. There was lamp-glow coming through the front door, because that door stood wide open. He could see no movement within.

Far off in the distance they heard yips and yelps, and the sound of gunfire.

"This ain't right," Boz said, in a tight, nervous voice. "Where is everybody?"

They rounded the corner of the dairy barn and came upon the remuda corral. The wind hit them fresh in the faces, and the smell of blood was like a slap.

At least a dozen horses had been torn to pieces within the corral. Blood had pooled in the ring like black tar. One of the young colts had jumped, or been dragged, over the top rail and gutted there so it hung from its back legs in an awkward jackknife.

"The Kid didn't do all this himself." Trace's chest was tight with horror and a sense of doom. "It's started to spread already. We need to get out of here."

"And go where?" Boz lifted the reins from his paint's drooping neck. "These horses are finished."

"You think anybody else is here alive?"

"You'd know better than me."

Trace brushed the veil aside and scanned the dark, still yard. He went deeper, felt further, into the bunks, the barns, the big house—

"Miller," he said.

A single glimmer of life, in the boss's house. They rode across the yard to the front porch, where Trace vaulted down and threw the reins to Boz.

Boss Miller lay in the front hall, splayed on his back, as if something had forced the door open and tore into him before he could retreat. His shotgun was still in his hand, both barrels spent. His eyes were closed and there was so much blood Trace couldn't even evaluate the damage.

"He alive?" Boz called.

"Barely." Trace wouldn't have guessed it, except he could feel the faint spark in him. He grabbed the carpet on which Miller lay and dragged the rancher's body down the hall, around the corner into the parlor. Mrs. Miller was strewn across the sofa in that room. Her corsets and heavy skirts had protected her body from scrabbling claws, but her face and shoulders were slashed to bone. Trace covered her with a shawl from the back of the sofa.

He went back to the front door and took Blackjack's reins from Boz. "Come on. Bring 'em inside."

Boz dismounted without a word. Trace led Blackjack through the front door and down the short hallway to the dining room. The big quarterhorse's sides scraped the walls, knocking down pictures and toppling knicknacks. He could barely squeeze the turn between the dining table and the sideboard, but once alongside the table he huffed in relief and began nibbling the daisies in the centerpiece.

Boz led the paint in along the other side of the dining table, and then had to step up on the table and walk across it, to get out of the room. He hopped to the floor and started toward the front. "I'm gonna block up the door."

Trace followed him, intending to check the house's second story, but as soon as they stepped into the front hall they heard yips and howls and footfalls, out in the yard and closing fast. Trace recognized the spirit racing toward them, as well as the snarling dark menace closing in behind. He shouldered Boz out of the way and slammed the door just behind the sleek black missile that hurtled across the threshold and skated, scrabbling on the polished floor, a good length down the hall before rolling head-over-tail.

Something heavy hit the door against Trace's shoulder, almost forcing it open. Trace kicked back, his boots slick on the boards, and thrust the latch closed. Boz was right behind him with the cross-bar, which they dropped into brackets on either side of the door. Miller was no fool—he'd made money in the horse business, and he'd built his house to be a fortress. Which begged the question, why had he opened the door in the first place? Had he heard the horses being slaughtered, and gone to investigate? Or had someone banged on the door, hollering for help?

Trace backed away from the door, aware of a scratching and snuffling along the threshold outside. More footsteps landed on the porch, some thumping like boots, others clicking like toenails. Something yipped out in the yard, to be answered by a sharp growl from the porch.

"What are they?" Boz whispered. "Jesus Christ, Trace—"

"Eez wolves," Remy's voice said.

They turned to see him, naked and bloody and panting, slumped against the parlor door, one hand clutching his bleeding neck. "But none like I never see."

CHAPTER THIRTY-EIGHT

Remy healed with astonishing speed. By the time Trace and Boz had pushed all the furniture up against the parlor windows, and tipped the dining room table up against the windows in that room—which required a complicated and infuriating game of backing the horses into the hall, then stacking chairs in the butler's pantry—Remy had licked all of his wounds he could reach and bathed the one on his neck with brandy and one of Mrs. Miller's doilies.

He also talked, in between lapping and gnawing at his hide. "I never see no'ting like dis. Remy track dat Kid to the yard, true nuff.

But then I find dead horse, smell of Kid, smell of man-blood. Now smell of *two* wolves. Kid and new wolf-smell go to bunks. More man-blood, much hullabaloo, suddenly more wolves. New wolves spread out, track all over yard—every bunk, every corral. But they not wolves."

"They're werewolves," Boz grunted, holding up the table while Trace drove nails through into the walls. "Like you."

"Non." Remy sucked at the bite mark on his bicep and spat onto the carpet. "*Remy* eez loup-garou, true nuff. Dat Kid one, too. These new ones something else. Change like dis take years, sometime. Not same night, and not like—" He paused, mouth skewed as he groped for the words. "Remy change little by little—sharper teeth, better ears, better nose. Get stronger. Heal quicker. First full moon change full wolf. *That* some scary experience, be damn sure. *Years* later, learn to half-change—use d'ears, d'eyes, d'nose, but still walk upright."

He shook his head, swabbing with the doily at the half-healed gash on his thigh. "Dees things outside, they like patch-up quilt—some ears, some tails, some paws, some walk like man. An' dey all change *immediatement* after bite. That not normal. Most folks take many bites, long time to get infection."

"Hey," Boz said, alarmed. "Miller was bit."

"He dead?" Remy asked.

"He wasn't," Trace said, and they all trooped into the parlor. Remy appeared to feel no shame at striding around naked, and indeed his loins were so hairy he hardly seemed more unclothed than a dog or a bronc stallion.

The loup-garou dropped to a crouch alongside Miller's body, drew in a long sniff, and peered at the wounds. "Eez not bites. Dis all claws. Somebody want him dead, don't want him changed, maybe." Remy leaned his ear closer to Miller's lips. "Don't matter, he dead anyway."

"Trace?" Boz said, his voice high and tight. "Where's *Mrs.* Miller?"

Trace switched toward the sofa. The shawl lay on the floor; the body was nowhere in sight.

Suddenly there was a chorus of yips and howls from the front yard, right beneath the parlor windows, echoing under the porch's roof.

"Oh, no," Trace said, and they all lunged for the hallway.

Mrs. Miller was on her knees before the front door, her shredded dress hanging off her shoulders, her furred paws just lifting the cross-bar clear of its brackets.

Trace hollered and rushed forward, but she turned on him with a snarl, teeth and bone flashing in the ruin of her face, one eye gleaming gold and feral. The cross-bar crashed to the floor as Trace leapt away from the slash of her claws. She gathered herself to spring at him, but was caught by Boz's bullet through her mangled jaw. She crumpled against the wall, but before Trace could collect himself to say thank you, a heavy body hit the front door and the latch gave way.

A phalanx of horrors surged into the hall—a riot of claws and teeth and fur. Boz got off three or four shots before they overwhelmed him. Trace managed to get his gun clear but the first shot went wild as teeth closed around his wrist. He punched at a yellow eye—Pancho's olive skin and mustaches above those teeth, he saw in a kind of nightmare— and heard Boz's shouts rise to a shriek of pain. Trace fought like a madman after that—shooting wildly, punching and kicking at ribs, throats, hindquarters, but they laughed like coyotes and pulled him down in a mass. Claws sank into him; boots and bare, hairy toes pinned him down. The creature on his chest had Red's face, carroty thatch spread over his brow and cheeks like rust, breath of whiskey and blood in Trace's nostrils. Its eyes were quite, quite mad.

Trace strained and gasped and in desperation, slipped out of himself, hovered above the carnage in the hall, heard Boz's screaming as if at a distance, felt the kicks and scratches and thumps to his own body as faint echoes, saw Remy's lean fierce shape slash and twist free of the snapping jaws and grasping claws, and bolt for the door, ears back, running for his life. Trace felt a weak relief as the loup-garou cleared the porch and vanished into the night, pursued by two or three of the others.

It was short-lived. Somebody seized his balls and squeezed. He came back to himself with a choked scream, and the devils all around him howled in amusement. Their laughter mutated into yips of excitement as a new figure, slight and tow-headed, appeared in the doorway.

Head hung low, face rough with more beard than he'd ever grown in his life, the Kid swaggered through the pack and snarled at Red to get off Trace's chest. Red slunk away with a submissive yip and the Kid dropped both knees into Trace's ribs.

There was blood on his lips, and a cold, cold smile. "Guess God didn't tell you about me, huh, Preacher?"

THE MOON HAD risen, and a cold light spilled over the yard as Trace and Boz were dragged out into it. The wolves who still had fingers tied Boz's arms to an old ox yoke, and hung it from the porch of the foreman's house, just high enough that Boz's bare toes dragged in the dust. It was plenty low enough that the pack could still torment him.

"I always heard crucifixion was an awful way to go," the Kid remarked. "My father used to say that Jesus and the thieves could've hung there three, four days if the soldiers hadn't pierced their sides. I don't reckon Boz'll last that long, do you?"

Trace had a bit wedged in his teeth and a number of check-reins looped around his arms and legs. He was trussed up like a country ham, propped across the cold fire pit from the cook-shack. He couldn't see how bad Boz was hurt, at this distance in the dark, but at least he was still healthy enough to jerk and grunt when they prodded him. The pack had worn out their blood-lust for the moment and were confining themselves to teasing.

"Listen, Kid," Trace said, speaking carefully around the metal bar across his tongue, "I dunno what Mereck told you, but this ain't gonna win you any favor with him—"

The boy gave a low laugh. Ironically, he was more human in shape than any of the others, but he had retained the hair on his jaw, the savage teeth, the slightly elongated ears. With his broad, flat face he looked fey and wild. "You're a fool, Preacher. A liar and a false prophet, like the rest of them. All your blather about men being equal, when you know perfectly well they aren't." He rolled his razor-clawed fingers before his face and grinned. "Some of us are special."

"Kid—the man you been talkin to—he ain't *God*—"

"Oh, how would *you* know?" the Kid sneered. "It was all I could do not to laugh when you told me that sob story about your old man. I couldn't *wait* to kill mine. The sonofabitch tried to exorcise me four times. The fourth time, Mr. Mereck found me. Let me out." The boy tapped his temple. "It was all in here, the whole time. He just showed me how to let it out."

Across the yard, Boz let out a scream. Trace jerked, his teeth clashing against the iron bit, and the Kid glanced over his shoulder with faint gratification. "Mr. Mereck says you're more than you seem. I guess you must be, if you're protected against His curse. But all I ever saw in you was weakness, *Preacher*. Always licking up to Miller, your second daddy. Hauling that nigger around like a cross on your back, to keep yourself down."

"Hell with you, Kid. You ain't half as smart as you think."

The Kid laughed and pounced, landed straddle-legged across Trace's knees, catching Trace's chin in his clawed hand, five needlepoints digging into his cheeks and the bit making his jaws cramp. "I caught *you*, didn't I? Led you right back here, just like one of those stupid traps the wolf-hunter left laying around. Couldn't wait to come save me from myself. Put me right back into the cage *you* can't get out of." He let go Trace's face with a spiteful wrench. "You're *weak*, Preacher, and the Master only picks the very best for His service."

Trace heard the fawning note in the Kid's voice, and it disgusted him as much as it was frightening. "Listen, Kid. I've seen what Mereck does to his followers. He uses 'em up like hack nags. There was a man named Kieler—"

"Oh, I know all about *him*. Master told me all about his traitors, the ones who failed him. I already did better than that fool Ferris." His face turned sly. "Yeah, I know about the Fire-Master. Lost his nerve, stupid prat. I imagine he's having a worse time than your boy, right now."

Across the yard, Boz made a low, guttural moan that built into a scream and Trace jerked in his bonds. "Goddammit, Kid!" His teeth clashed against the bit. "He didn't do nothin to you! Mereck ain't gonna want him so you may as well turn him loose!"

"Oh, no. The Master was real specific—find his weak point, he said. And that's your pet nigger. So I figure I soften you both up for him, before he gets here."

"And when's that supposed to be?"

A beatific smile crossed the Kid's face. "Soon."

"How's he gettin here? Where's he comin from?" Behind his back, Trace fought with the knots of his bindings. They were not tight, but the leather straps were stiff and difficult to move. Even if he got them loose he had no guns and no way to flee. The horses were still trapped in the house—at least the wolves had been too busy with their captives to indulge in further slaughter—and since he'd removed his coat while they were barricading the windows, he didn't even have the apothecary bottles on his person.

"It doesn't matter," the Kid said. "The Master has many ways of watching His faithful. He can listen on the wind. Not a sparrow falls without His notice. That's how he found *me*—my blood cried out to Him. He sees into a person's *soul*, and He only takes the pure at heart . . ."

Trace tuned him out. While the Kid went on eulogizing, Trace slipped out of his skull and into the gray, hoping to get a look at the wolves' spirit-selves—maybe count their numbers, look for holes in their defenses—and to see whether Mereck was as close as the Kid seemed to think.

He saw immediately how the Kid's aura had changed. He had shed whatever restraints of morality or self-control had held back the beast; the power had settled over him like a coat, merged with his skin and bones, embraced him. And with that interference removed, Trace easily recognized that other hovering echo: Mereck's cold, hungry presence, whispering to the boy, stroking him, holding him in thrall.

The wolves, by comparison, resembled the keung-si more than anything. In the gray space he saw them as an absence, dark places that seemed to eat the light around them. And yet within each black void Trace could sense the living sparks of the men he had known, writhing and tormented, trapped in the nightmares of their own minds.

The pack suddenly roared in excitement, and the Kid broke off his monologue to snarl in their direction. "Hey! None of that!" Two of the wolves had turned on each other, snapping and tussling on the ground. "I said stop!" the Kid shouted, and started over that way.

Hot, rough hands closed over Trace's wrists, and he jolted back into his skin, which felt tight and breathless.

"Jus' keep still," Remy's voice muttered, his fingers fumbling at the bonds. There was a slither and a snap, and the leather immediately loosed around Trace's forearms. "Your guns is here behind you. Can you track Remy in the dark?"

"Yeah."

The loup-garou moved around and tugged at the straps around his ankles. Trace shrugged out of the remaining bonds and spat the bit into the dust.

"In a minute Remy gonna move upwind. They gonna chase him. You get to your man, get 'im down, get to ranch office. Is shotgun in dere, oui?"

"Yes." It was maybe forty feet from the fire-pit to the foreman's house. Trace thought of the thin door, the heavy desk, the shotgun on the wall.

"You wanna shoot after dem when dey run, is good, but don't shoot Remy, d'accord?"

"Bien sûr," Trace said, and Remy grinned, his teeth flashing in the moonlight, before slipping away into the darkness.

Trace felt on the ground and located the cool, smooth handles of two pistols: Boz's top-break Scofields with their silver grips.

Twelve shots. One for each of the wretches. He hoped Mereck felt every one of them.

Abruptly Boz hollered, and the pack howled for blood. Two of the wolves had seized his legs and were pulling, until abruptly the yoke slipped off its post. Boz crashed to the ground, and then they were on him—nipping, clawing, kicking. One of their number shoved his way to the center, crouched over Boz's chest, and raised a clawed hand high.

Trace shot him through the head.

The man-wolf pitched into the midst of his brethren and they yelped and bounced in chorus around the body, over and across Boz, who flinched and thrashed under their churning feet. They seemed to have no idea where the shot had come from, except for the Kid, who turned in Trace's direction, his face contorted in a snarl.

A long howl echoed across the yard, bouncing eerily off the close-set buildings. All heads turned; Trace spotted Remy at the same time as the pack—five paces beyond the lean-to, standing in the open ground between it and the office. He was in his half-human state—as tall as Trace and twice as heavy. His muscular thighs and shoulders crouched in an unmistakable invitation, his snout wrinkled back in a brawler's grin.

The pack broke. The first four or five took off like shots, melting lower to the ground, becoming sleeker and more lupine as they ran. They moved almost as one, merging into a V-formation like geese, intent on their target, who turned and fled.

The acquisition of grace might've been beautiful to watch except that one by one the pursuers were yanked short and bowled over with a yelp. Steel *snaps* echoed back across the yard as the wolf-hunter's traps triggered. Three, four, five of them were caught, in a double row of bone-breaking jaws, placed in strategic formation like the wolves' own hunting pattern.

Some of the others, less fleet and thus luckier, leapt over their fallen comrades and continued in pursuit of Remy while the Kid stomped his feet and screamed for them to come back. Three or four circled around, two-footed and less agile, and Trace walked steadily toward them, toward where the Kid stood and Boz lay still on the ground, and when they noticed him coming he started shooting.

Two fell; the others scattered. The Kid ran like his tail was on fire. Trace shoved one pistol in his pants and grabbed the lead ring of Boz's yoke with his left hand. He backed up swiftly toward the foreman's house, gun hand covering the yard ahead of him. He shot the wolf that leapt out of the darkness, kicked the door open with his heel and wrestled the heavy yoke and his partner's limp weight into the office. His limbs were trembling, his back running with cold sweat. A werewolf tried to charge the door and he shot it back. He dragged Boz out of the way, closed the door and ran around the heavy desk to push it into place.

It wouldn't budge; the legs were nailed to the floor. *"Jesus Savior sweet Mary PLEASE!"* Trace put his feet against the wall and shoved with all his might. There was a mighty *crack* as the legs split off the front end of the desk and its awkward weight toppled and skidded across the floor. He wheelbarrowed it against the door and dropped it face down by the wall.

He slid down beside it, panting, exhausted. Gradually Boz's ragged breathing intruded on his fog and he pulled himself up, crawled over to his partner's side. He clawed loose the ropes holding Boz's arms to the yoke and kicked it away.

It was very dark in the office. The sliver of moonlight coming through the single high window was little help. Even his spirit-vision could not help him see the damage that had been done—it showed him only how dim Boz's aura had become. The lightest touch of his fingers found only sticky blood and lacerated flesh, and made Boz's breath hitch in pain. Trace gathered him up in his arms as carefully as he could and held him propped against his own chest, leaning them both against the wall so Boz could breathe more easily.

Things became quiet outside. Far off in the distance he heard two shots, but that was all. He sat with one arm across Boz's shoulders and a revolver in his other hand, expecting at any moment the wolves would start throwing themselves against the door. That desk wouldn't keep them out. They were too strong.

He had five shots left. He'd seen three wolves left outside—at least two of those he'd shot had seemed to stay down. So maybe bullets *could* finish them off. But he only had five shots left, and Trace figured on saving the last bullet for himself. He'd be damned before he'd let himself be served up to Mereck.

Boz was dying, anyway. His life was soaking Trace's pants and the floorboards where they sat. Maybe they'd end up haunting this place together—an eternity of telling each other *I told you so.* Trace wondered if his power would render him different from the usual lost souls; if he would retain a sense of himself, maybe end up a spirit familiar for some half-baked medium like Kieler. Or find himself enslaved to someone like Mereck, or Miss Fairweather.

Maybe suicide wasn't the best option after all.

A foot landed softly on the stoop outside, making his every nerve twitch. He pointed the gun at the door.

There was a polite knock. "Mr. Tracy?"

It was a young man's voice. It sounded like the Kid, but the cadence, the diction were wrong.

"Mr. Tracy, I hope you will excuse my addressing you in this manner." The voice was cultured, with a slight foreign accent, full of gentlemanly chagrin. "I believe my servant has been acting rashly, and I have temporarily taken possession of his body. I thought you might feel more at ease if we were to converse in this manner."

"And who the hell are you?" Trace demanded.

"I think you know of me, Mr. Tracy. My name is Yosef Mereck."

CHAPTER THIRTY-NINE

That name, spoken aloud in the darkness, chilled the breath in his lungs. He became aware of a stealthy enmity sniffing around the edges of his brain and shrank into himself, pulling up his shields like a child pulling quilts over his head. "I got nothin to say to you."

"Will you do me the courtesy of listening, then?"

Trace could think of no dignified answer to such a request. The gun, still pointed at the door, began to weigh on his shaking hand.

"Mr. Tracy, I expect you will find this incredible, but I did not instruct this young werewolf to harm you and your friend. I asked him only to seek you out and report your whereabouts to me, until such time as I could arrive and meet with you in person. I am dismayed to find this young man's mind is far less stable than I supposed it to be. Religious fervor can . . . warp a youth's perceptions of the world, don't you agree?"

Of course he agreed. But he was repulsed by the implication they had anything in common. "So you just set him to spy on me. That makes it all right, then."

"Mr. Tracy, I do not wish to engage in an exchange of accusations and counter-accusations, but I have reason to believe *you* have been investigating *my* activities for some months now. Under the aegis of Sabine Fairweather? I cannot know what, precisely, she has told you of me, but I doubt she had any praise for my name. Will you give me the chance to speak in my own defense?"

The voice was warm, calm, reasonable. And the presence stroking his mind had turned curious, friendly. The hunger was still there— like a blind, grasping maw underneath—but Trace felt it had been leashed, scolded into the background.

"Mr. Tracy, I want you to know it was not my intent to infect all of your comrades with this plague." Mereck's voice sounded as if he were very close to the door, breathing on it.

"Why'd you make it, then?" Trace demanded. "What possible purpose did that serve?"

"It is an unfortunate side-effect of my research. My aim is to *help* people like your young friend, and like yourself. Herr Kieler told me you detested your power, and wished to be freed of it—"

"Was this before or after you killed him?"

There was a slight pause. "Herr Kieler's fault was always pride." The cultured voice was regretful, but resigned. "He undertook a dangerous venture into the spirit world, that he was in no way equipped to control, and summoned up forces beyond his comprehension. *You,* I believe, are more circumspect. You have been hiding yourself with fine control for almost half your life, but now I fear my former pupil has pushed you into extending yourself too far, too fast." That probing sensation lapped at Trace's mind again, as if it were tasting him, and he cringed away from it. Immediately other tendrils began to creep closer, like the leeches at the dinner table, inching toward the meat of his brain while he retreated, smaller and smaller within himself.

But mention of Miss Fairweather had distracted him from his fear. He remembered her cool, sensible voice saying, *Protection to you, defeat to him. A sword and a shield, if you would use it.*

He remembered the banquet table, with all of the leeches leading away from the diners and toward the fount that Mereck drank from— a painfully obvious metaphor, now he thought about it. Miss Fairweather poisoning her own blood and feeding it into that fount.

The circle of their clasped hands around the séance table, that clash of power as Kieler and Miss Fairweather both touched him.

That same jolt of connection when she had ground her bloody palm into his, and Mereck's sudden recoiling from it.

Her blood and her spell had protected him twice—once in the library and again when the Kid bit him. Though both times she had been merely the catalyst, showing him how to use the power he already had.

You are as strong as he, Mr. Tracy. You can fight him.

Trace wasn't so sure about that. The Russian was sneaky, and far older than Trace—he wasn't sure what gave him that impression but he knew it to be true. And anybody who could keep a thing like Reynolds on a leash—even if he slipped it now and then—was bound to be a real curly wolf.

But wolves got hungry. And the scent of fresh blood would bring 'em every time.

Never will your power away. Do you hear me?

"Mr. Tracy?"

"I'm thinkin." He eased out from under Boz's weight and settled him gently on the floor. Boz's aura was very dim, now, his breathing fast and shallow. Trace touched his lips to Boz's forehead, felt how cool his skin had become, the greasy chill of his sweat.

Then he sidled across the floor, to the clutter that had slid off the desk, and began to feel through it, searching.

"Mr. Tracy?"

"I guess I'm wonderin what you might teach me, that I couldn't figure out for myself."

"My dear fellow, that very question conveys to me the inadequacy of Sabine's instruction. She possesses a fine mind, but she has always felt herself slighted by her male colleagues. It makes her suspicious and miserly. Whereas a partnership between you and me could be one of equals."

Trace's hand closed on the paper knife. He tested the edge with his thumb. Sharp enough. "So what kinda partnership are we talkin about? Fairweather may be a mean stingy bitch, but she pays well, and I got mouths to feed."

A friendly chuckle from the porch: ripples of contempt through the gray space. "Mr. Tracy, I am proposing to reveal all the mysteries of the universe to you. The minds of men, the future of investments—the very bowels of the earth will yield up their treasures for your retrieval. I assure you, after a few weeks of my tutelage, money will never again be a concern of yours."

Trace did not doubt it. He ground his teeth and drew the knife across his palm, reopening the old scar and the half-healed bite mark. It hurt less than he might have expected. The gush of blood was warm and slippery down his wrist. He smeared the blade and then cupped the hilt in that same hand, holding the point flat against his forearm. He felt for the pistol he had set aside and tucked it into his waist as he stood up.

"All right, I'm comin out," Trace called. "But I'm still packin lead, and if any of those wolves try this door I'll blow their heads off."

"I have sent them away," Mereck assured him. "I give you my word, I want only to talk with you."

Trace tugged and shoved the desk away from the door, just enough to open it a crack. Nobody was in sight except the Kid, standing quietly a few paces away.

But it wasn't the Kid. His posture, his expression, his aura—the dark rage of his wolf-spirit was almost completely suppressed, cowed by that active, hungry nothingness.

Mereck stood with one hand clasping his lapel, the other behind his back. He inclined his head politely as Trace squeezed through the doorway, the gun in his left hand. "I hope you will forgive my appearance," he said, indicating the Kid's torn clothes. He made the gesture grand and gracious, like a prince in disguise. "I had hoped to meet you in more dignified circumstances than these."

"Ain't none of us at our best right now." Trace sidled onto the porch, right hand pressed against his side as if he were wounded there, holding the knife pressed between his hand and his body. His shirt was soaked on that side with Boz's blood, and Trace feigned a limp as he crossed the porch. "Fact is, my friend's bleedin to death in there, so it'd be a real goodwill gesture to our new partnership if you'd let me get some help for him."

"I quite understand," Mereck said, with the Kid's mouth. "You may know, I have some medical expertise. Perhaps I could—"

Trace pulled the pistol from his waist. "You just stay there. First of all I want to know the terms. Fairweather offered to have me come live with her and study with her. If I agree to the same with you, will you save Boz?"

"I will show you how to restore him to the fullness of health," Mereck said. "It is within your power, you know. And I will extract no promises from you, either. You must come to me of your own free will, uncoerced by obligation."

The worms caressing Trace's soul had crowded closer, sensing capitulation. The blind maw was poised, alert, listening for the signal.

O Holy Mary, help me out, here. Saint Michael, guide my arm. Boz, I'm sorry.

"All right, then." Trace shoved the gun into his trousers and held out his left hand. "You've got a deal."

The Kid's small, smooth hand closed around Trace's, and Mereck's expression smoothed out into cold contempt. His power lashed through the contact and knocked Trace right out of his skull.

Almost.

He caught on by spiritual fingernails, dug in grimly, refused to be sucked away into gray nothingness. Mereck's soul coiled around his like a bullsnake, trying to crush him and rip him apart at the same time. But the past weeks of spirit-walking served Trace in good stead. He slipped and twisted and fought like a cornered cat, writhing through Mereck's grasp, keeping him engaged in the gray space while, with his last thread of bodily control, he turned his fist and plunged the knife into the Kid's belly.

There was a crack, like lightning, but soundless. The boy staggered and bright silver fissures of pain lanced through Mereck's connection. Trace pushed back with all his power, and when Mereck faltered, he stabbed the Kid again. He felt warm blood gush over his hand and dropped the knife, pushed two fingers into the wound and ripped.

The Kid howled. Mereck did, too, as the blood-contact spread up his arm and into his head. Trace felt himself caught in a tug-of-war, between the boy trying to tear himself away from the pain and Mereck trying to tear his soul away from Trace's. But Trace had a strangle-hold on both of them and he twisted as hard as he could, no finesse, just a hard bright determination tempered by four decades of self-doubt.

I don't NEED your instruction, Trace told him. *Sabine and I are both doin just fine without you.*

Mereck made a last grab at Trace's mind: *You can't kill me this way.*

"Come on back sometime," Trace said, and thrust him away.

Mereck vanished, leaving the taste of hate and outrage in Trace's mouth. Trace let go the Kid, as well, who folded to the ground, writhing and clasping his belly and letting out mewls of outrage that were quickly turning to pain and panic.

"What'd you do, Preacher? What'd you *do* to me? You sonofabitch, you *stuck* me! Why'd you *do* that? You're supposed to *help* me! Mereck was supposed to *take* you! O Jesus God father—No! Master, Master, it's You I believe in! I brought him to You, You're supposed to save me now!"

Trace dropped to one knee and put his bloody hand on the boy's throat, bore down just hard enough to cut off his wind. "Stop that. Shut your yap."

The Kid stopped blubbering with a croak, wide-eyed and shocked—though whether it was the cold tone of command in Trace's voice or the light hum of power through their skin, Trace didn't know—he hardly recognized himself, tonight. The Kid's face contorted with fearful indecision, eyes darting around the sky and the yard, widening as Trace drew Boz's pistol from his waist.

"Aw, c'mon, Preacher, this ain't you." The Kid suddenly reverted to his aw-shucks put-on voice, and he attempted an awkward smile, despite Trace's grip on his jaw. Trace let go, stood up, and tucked his hand under his armpit, bore down to stop the bleeding. The wound was beginning to throb. "You're a *true* man of God. That's the difference between you and my pa. He never really believed, and so *I* never believed. But you know the truth, don't you? People like you and me, we're *proof* there's a God. Why else would He make people like us, if He didn't have some greater purpose? If it wasn't to show how merciful He could be?"

The groveling tone and self-serving logic would have turned Trace's stomach, if he'd had any sensibilities left to offend. He backed away from the little bastard, cracked open the pistol's breech to make sure there was a live round under the hammer. He sensed movement at the edge of the yard and glanced up to see Remy slowly approaching, in the path of moonlight beside the office: buck naked, favoring his left leg, and with a shotgun leveled at the Kid's head.

Trace pulled back the hammer on the revolver with his left thumb; his right hand was really beginning to hurt. "You got anything to say?" he asked Remy, over the Kid's yelp of protest, and the loup-garou shook his head once: left, right, center.

The Kid sat half-upright, grimacing in pain, blood darkening his teeth. "You don't wanna do this, Preacher. Think about your immortal soul. You ain't done nothing unforgivable yet *this is murder you son of a bitch the Master's gonna eat your SOUL AND SPIT OUT THE BONES YOU IGNORANT PIECE OF—*"

Trace shot him between the eyes. He'd heard enough of that talk for one lifetime.

CHAPTER FORTY

It had been several years since Trace had set foot in St. Louis during August. He had forgotten just how miserable it was. The heat and humidity had increased steadily throughout the four-day train trip down from Evanston, through Colorado, across Kansas and finally Missouri.

It beat riding all that way back. He'd have had too much time to think if he'd spent a month in the saddle. Besides, he hadn't dared stay out in the open that long.

He rode Blackjack from the station to Hyde Park, and when they reached Miss Fairweather's street the big quarterhorse turned onto her drive without any prompting.

"Back into harness, hey boy?" Trace murmured.

He had forgotten how the house had a presence of its own. Maybe it had gotten stronger, or maybe his senses had sharpened over the summer, but as he stood on her stoop and pulled the bell, he felt watched, prodded, sniffed over. Recognized. Min Chan answered the door as always, but Trace was not surprised to see Miss Fairweather hurrying down the stairs as he walked into the foyer.

What did surprise him was the wash of relief that rolled over him at the sight of her. Though that was probably the house itself—he felt its protective web close around him as he stepped across the threshold, and despite the weariness and grief and guilt, he drew his first deep breath in a week. All the way back on the train, he'd been afraid to meditate, afraid even to sleep.

Here, at last, he felt safe. And he saw a similar relief in her eyes as she halted on the bottom step and took in his dirty, disheveled self.

"Are you all right?" she said softly.

He cleared his throat. "I've been better, ma'am, and that's the truth."

She came down the last stair and crossed the floor to him, reaching up with one hand. He found himself leaning into her cool palm as she cupped his cheek, then his forehead. "I know you have just come in from the heat, but I believe you have a fever." She caught his wrist and turned his hand up, frowning at the dirty bandage and the red-flushed skin on either side of it. "Does this need cleaning?"

"I expect it does, yes ma'am."

"You have only just arrived in town?"

"Yes, ma'am."

"Then . . . will you allow me to extend you hospitality, until you can make other arrangements?"

The thought of staying—of being allowed to sleep—in this safe, quiet cloister was so welcome he could have wept. "I'd be grateful for that kindness, ma'am, thank you."

"Come along, then. Min Chan will bring your bags."

"I gotta tend to my horse."

"Of course." She had better sense than to suggest the Chinese could do that, too. "The stable should be well stocked. And then perhaps you will join me in the laboratory, and we might talk while I treat that hand?"

"I reckon I'll take you up on that," Trace said.

An hour later, he watched her nostrils flare as she peeled the bandage away from his oozing palm. His skin was stained black from the silver nitrate but the flesh was swollen and shiny, making a clear display of the ring of teeth marks.

Miss Fairweather made a *tsking* noise. "This looks human, almost. It isn't—"

"It is. Human. Almost."

She lifted her head, a line between her brows. "*Please* tell me you weren't bitten by the lycanthrope."

"That's exactly what it was. But you don't have to worry about me catchin it, like the others." She looked a question at him, and he drew a deep breath and said what he'd come to say. "You were right. About Mereck followin me. He found us out in Wyoming. Found himself a new lackey—the werewolf I wired you about. Set to makin himself a whole pack of werewolves and turned 'em loose on us. Just like the bloodsuckers in Idaho. Spread it among 'em like a fever."

Her eyes widened in dismay. "They attacked you and Mr. Bosley?"

"Us, and a wolf-hunter we met out there. Three of us fought 'em off, but it was a bloody mess." He'd decided, on the train, that he would tell her everything, that he had nothing left to lose, but it still felt like betrayal. "Boz got chewed up pretty bad."

REMY HELPED HIM move Boz to the Millers' upstairs bedroom. They stripped him down and washed his wounds and stitched him up as best they could, but the fever came on before dawn. Boz shook and sweated, and his bandages seeped through with foul-smelling ichor.

"He need medicine," Remy said in the pale morning, and Trace's exhausted brain remembered the bottles in his coat pocket. He went downstairs to fetch them, smelled the barnyard stink in the dining room, and thought he'd better lead the horses out of the house. He could not, at that point, feel grateful that Blackjack had survived the slaughter, but he had later, and ever since.

When he showed the silver ointment to Remy, the loup-garou winced.

"Will it hurt him?" Trace asked.

"Yeah, it gonna hurt like hell, but it mebbe save his life." Remy shook his head, and helped hold the patient down while Trace swabbed the worst of the infected places with the innocuously clear solution.

The reaction was immediate, and awful. Boz's skin erupted in a foam of blisters and roiling flesh. It looked as though rats were fighting under his skin. He shook and shrieked and fought them. He kicked Trace clear off the bed, and Trace would have stopped the torture, but Remy insisted on fetching the ropes and leather traces from the yard and securing Boz to the bed. Trace cleaned the rest of Boz's wounds with tears running down his face, and when they were done, Remy clapped a hand on his arm and told him to get some sleep.

"He gonna be out for a while. I stay with him."

Trace had stumbled downstairs, past Mrs. Miller's shrouded corpse in the hall, past Miller's body in the parlor, went into the kitchen, and dropped himself into a chair at the table. He put his head down on his arms and grayed out for a while. His dreams, not surprisingly, were full of teeth and blood and Miss Fairweather lecturing him on the nature of demons.

Around noon, the call of nature woke him to an overcast sky and a headache. He went outside to piss, and was leaning against the back wall of the house, gazing slow and stupid at the shapeless heaps of fur and clothing in the yard, when it suddenly struck him that those heaps were his friends. Men he had worked with and lived with for two months—most of whom he liked, some he even respected—reduced to mad beasts and put down like dogs.

He put his face into the crook of his arm, against the side of the house, and wept—great exhausted sobs of grief and rage. He wept for the men, and for Miller, whose trust in Trace had brought this evil to his doorstep. He wept for Boz, whose loyalty had led him full-knowing into the jaws of doom. And he wept out of guilt, that he hadn't been strong enough, selfless enough, to sever ties with the person he loved most, even to save his life.

At length he got himself under control. He wiped his eyes, buttoned up, went to the water pump and got a good chill flow started. His hands and arms were still creased with blood. He stripped to the waist, washed until his skin was numb and glowing red. Then he filled the bucket with water and took it back to the house.

He started a fire in Mrs. Miller's cookstove and put a kettle on to boil. Then he went to the dining room to lead the horses out of the house. They shied at the smell of blood in the yard, but he led them around to the pump, let them drink while he shucked their saddles and tack. He staked them to graze on the west side of the yard, where the battle had not spilled over.

The flies were starting to gather, and the warmth of the day was hastening the stink. The bodies had been horrifying by night, but by day they were just confusing—bits of men and fur patched together like carnival curiosities.

For a moment it was 1862 and he was standing on a battlefield, looking around at the ruin of men blown apart by cannon fire. He felt the weight of his own flesh and bone, this human machine into which some Almighty whim had installed a curious engine, which simultaneously protected him from and connected him to all this mortality. And he felt a terrible certainty—an old suspicion given voice for the first time—that all these untimely deaths were balancing some vast cosmic scale. Maybe all these other people had to die so he could live.

And he had to live. Because he knew now what he had to do.

"Hey Preacher," said Red's voice, and Trace startled, looked around to see the young cowboy standing there, saddle over his shoulder, rope in hand. He was as transparent as stained glass in the dull sunlight. "Where is everybody? Aren't we gonna round up the yearlings this morning?"

Trace swallowed around the ache in his throat. "No, son, we're not doin any roundups today. What're you doin here anyway? Thought you'd be with Hanky and the others."

"Couldn't find 'em," Red said. "Figured Hanky was playing one of his tricks."

"No, it's no trick, son. He just figured you'd catch up, is all."

"Where'd he go?"

Trace beckoned the boy toward him, laid a hand on Red's nape, and turned him toward the morning sun. His hand tingled at the contact of that phantom flesh, and his power welled up and enfolded both of them, transforming the overcast summer morning into a flat, fog-banked landscape, devoid of landmarks, restful in its lack of time or urgency. Where the weak coin of the sun had been, there was another kind of light—steady-shining and somehow *aware*. Trace was unable to look at it directly, but Red stared for a good long moment, head cocked to one side as if listening to a far-off call.

"Golly," he said. "I guess I oughtta go, then, huh?"

"I guess you ought," Trace said. "Give my best to the others."

"I will." Red shifted his saddle higher on his shoulder and stuck out a hand. "See ya, Preacher."

"Hope I will," Trace said.

They shook once and the boy gave him a cheery grin before turning toward the horizon. He had only taken a step or two before he was gone completely, and the spirit-sight faded out of Trace's vision, leaving him facing a mild summer day, and a yard full of corpses.

Trace turned and went back to the house. He was straining the coffee when Remy came down into the kitchen. He folded his arms in the doorway, wearing some of Miller's oversized clothes, and a thoughtful expression.

"Well?" Trace said.

"He gonna live," Remy said slowly. "It too soon to know if he gonna change."

"YE GODS," MISS Fairweather interrupted, her voice soft with horror. "Mr. Bosley survived?"

"He was feverish most of a week. Remy knew what to do. We dosed him with silver nitrate."

She winced, much as Remy had. "But that would only treat the wounds . . . I never heard of it fighting off the infection. You *do* understand that lycanthropy is communicated through saliva, like hydrophobia?"

"I knew," Trace said. "We all did."

TRACE KNEW THEY couldn't stay at the ranch any longer. Even if he'd had any doubts about Mereck's ability to regroup, it was only a matter of time until someone came to call on Miller, or some territorial marshal came looking for the Kid.

He took Blackjack and rounded up six extra horses, while Remy

vanished into the trees on the north boundary and came back dragging two ash saplings about twenty feet long. Between these two
poles Trace lashed the buffalo-hide robe from the Millers' bedroom,
to make a long stretcher. He lined it with a couple of wool blankets
from Boz's bed.

They raided the house and the cook-shack for supplies, and loaded
up the spare horses. Trace cleared the foreman's house of his and Boz's
personal possessions, and though it made him sick to do it, he rifled
through the bunk-houses and the Millers' house, took what money
and valuables he could find. As bizarre as the carnage at the ranch
would appear to any investigators, robbery would at least provide a
motive. If there was any justice in the world, roving bushwhackers
would be blamed, rather than the nearest Indian scapegoats.

As a last balm to his conscience, while Remy was pouring laudanum down Boz's throat and making him ready to be moved, Trace
went around the yard and did last rites on all the bodies. He found
Old Walt's spirit still lingering in the remuda corral, and sent him on
toward the horizon.

At last they loaded Boz into the travois, slung between two pack
horses, and set out north. It was late afternoon by the time they did,
but Remy knew all the back-trails and game-trails, like any good
hunter, and they rode until well after dark, through streams and over
rough terrain, putting as much distance as possible between themselves and the ranch.

Along the way, Trace scattered the personal valuables he had taken
from the ranch, dropping them into holes, behind rocks, into fast-
moving streams.

For five days, they moved steadily north and east, keeping to the
wilds, avoiding fences and homesteaders. Sleeping in the saddle during the day, keeping one eye on the gray space, sitting up nights with
Boz, who writhed in fever and opium dreams.

Boz's bites and lacerations healed with alarming speed, but everywhere the silver nitrate had been applied, his skin broke out in pale
leprous patches, which split at a touch, revealing matted fur that fell
out in clumps. Pus and silver nitrate dribbled out of these cysts, leaving black-and-yellow stains on the blankets.

Trace and Remy took turns coaxing water and medicine down
Boz's throat. He wouldn't take any food, not even beef broth, until
Remy came back in the dusk with a freshly killed rabbit, and slit its
throat over a bowl. Boz's eyes cracked open for the first time in four

days, gleaming golden in the low light, nostrils flaring at the scent. Remy lifted the bowl to Boz's eager lips and Trace had to walk away from the camp.

On the morning of the sixth day, Trace woke to gray dawn and the sound of men's voices in low conversation. He sat up in his bedroll and saw that both Boz's and Remy's were empty.

He found them a few yards away, sitting on an outcropping of rock, facing into the wind and smoking. Boz had only pants on, the suspenders over his bare shoulders. Remy had his shirt rucked up, showing off one of the myriad scars that raked his stocky frame. Boz's dark skin was marred by scabby rashes and matted stubble the color of rust. As Trace watched, Boz shook his head and ran a hand over his hair, in a gesture of disgust and resignation that Trace knew well.

They both turned as Trace drew near, and he was struck by the similarity in their movements—a certain rippling tension of the shoulders that eased as soon as they recognized him. Then Boz turned his face away, scowling, and Remy got up and jumped down from the rock.

"Remy gonna let you vaqueros talk for a bit," he said, and swished away through the prairie grass.

Boz took a long draw on his smoke, and looked up through heavy-lidded eyes that had taken on an odd golden cast—almost copper-colored. "You don't look too much worse for wear."

Trace considered Boz's face and frame, upright for the first time in a week. He looked gaunt, with hollows under his eyes that had not been there before, but the cut above his brow had vanished without a scar. "You look a helluva lot better than you did. I thought you were a goner."

"Yeah, well. Joke's on both of us." Boz exhaled smoke, and held up his cheroot. "Y'know, these things taste a lot better than they smell."

"What is it?"

"Monkshood."

"Jesus, Boz, that stuff's poisonous."

"Not to werewolves, it ain't." Boz looked him in the eye, but slantwise, as if expecting an ambush. "Remy says it keeps the wolf asleep. Says the other name for the stuff is wolfsbane—just like in the stories. You know that?"

"No."

"Me either. I seen it up in the mountains plenty of times, never knew what it was. Just knew not to let my horse eat it." He ran his tongue over his gums, contemplatively, and curled his lip to reveal a flash of canine. "Remy says you got the Kid?"

"I got him."

"Good. You get Mereck?"

"I ran him off. I reckon it'll take more muscle than I got, to kill him."

"Well, I reckon she can teach you. Or she'll claim she can, at any rate." Boz gave him another of those side-eye looks, while Trace stood there, mute and miserable. "And I reckon now you're tryin to figure how to get me to come back with you, so she can fix me up. Right?"

"Boz . . ." He spread his hands helplessly. "I tried. Goddamn it, I tried to tell you—"

"Yeah. You did. And I reckon you got a right to say so." Boz threw down the stub of his smoke, ground it out with his heel. "You know, I figured *you'd* be the one losin a life over this. I figured she'd use you up, or Mereck would. But the fact is, you're the same as both of 'em. Your curse don't eat you up—it eats everyone around you, and you just get stronger for it." He slid down off the rock on bare feet. "Far as I can tell, you all deserve each other."

Boz walked away across the prairie. He bypassed their camp, side-stepping Remy's inquiry, and kept going until he crested a small rise in the earth and went down the other side of it, disappearing from view.

Trace trailed back to the camp, stood there looking at the cold fire, the packs and bedrolls, the horses standing patiently nearby. All the familiar things he and Boz had used for years. He had to strain to remember what belonged to whom, what he could take, what he should leave.

"He jus' . . . you know, he have a shock," Remy said, gesturing awkwardly with his cheroot. "Is bad news to hear you gonna turn into monster next full moon. Be hunted rest of your life. Mebbe easier for a black man—they already hunted in this country." That sounded like a weak attempt at humor, but if anything it made Trace feel worse. "Mitchie Boz, he already good tracker, got good mountain sense. He figure how to control it, mebbe decide it not such a bad thing."

Trace lifted his head with a sigh. "Where will you go? When you leave here?"

Remy shrugged. "Got other ranches, other business. More pelts to find."

"You know where there are others like you?"

"Some. Mostly move round a lot."

Trace nodded. "Stay away from cities for a while. I'll make sure Boz has the bill of sale for those horses, but don't take risks. Don't make friends with any strangers."

"Bien sûr," Remy agreed. "You go to Saint Louie, n'est-ce pas?"

"Yeah." Trace hesitated, and offered a hand. "Thank you. You saved our lives out here."

Remy nodded, shook. Gestured toward the rise, where Boz had gone. "Don' worry bout him. He one of my kind, now."

THERE WAS A long silence when Trace had finished his recitation. He felt Miss Fairweather's gaze on him, her short, distressed breaths, her sympathy. He had not expected that, but he was grateful.

"And that was the end of it?" she said. "You didn't try to persuade him to return with you?"

"Couldn't see the point of it. Boz had his mind made up he wasn't comin back, even before he got bit. And he was right. My curse eats up the people I care about. I knew it, but I couldn't make myself—" He had to quit speaking, before he was completely unmanned in front of her. After a minute he added, "Besides, it made sense, if Mereck was still huntin me, to get as far away as I could. So I packed up and left that same hour. Caught the train in Cheyenne the next day. Came straight here."

Miss Fairweather made busy with the tools she had used to clean his hand, put away needles, swept away bits of catgut and cotton wadding. She had closed the wound with tiny black stitches, and applied a numbing ointment that was surely a mercy from heaven.

After a moment her hands came to rest, and her head bowed, over her tool kit. "I feel responsible," she said in a low voice. "I have had time to realize, these past weeks, that I should have been more forthcoming about the threat Mereck posed to you."

"Yeah. You should have," Trace said, and her head came up, lips compressed in annoyance. "But I guess that's what you meant with that séance—to let me see him with all his masks stripped away."

She looked down again, pale lashes fanning over paler cheeks, and he had the impression that most of *her* masks had been stripped away, as well. There was a softness, and an uncertainty, in her face that he'd never seen before. "You must know, it was never my intention to let him harm you. I took every precaution I knew to protect you during that séance, and it should have been enough. But Mereck has apparently been monitoring my activities more closely than I realized. And you proved more . . . aggressive than I anticipated."

Trace felt the back of his neck getting hot. "I'm sorry for that. It wasn't—I never in my life raised my hand to a woman. It won't happen again."

Her blue eyes lifted to his. "I believe you," she said quietly. "But I meant only, you have kept your power suppressed for so long, I never supposed you would embrace it so quickly, or have the strength of character to control it. You have surprised me, Mr. Tracy. Many times over."

Considering the source, that was probably the best compliment he'd ever had. He didn't know what to say.

"And now I must ask, have you seen any indication you were followed here? Any sign of Mereck or his minions since you left Wyoming?" Trace shook his head, and her shoulders relaxed a fraction. "Then may I assume your presence here indicates an acceptance of my offer? Will you remain here and allow me to tutor you? I'm sure you must realize, much of what I could teach you will offend both your faith and your sensibilities."

"You don't know much about my sensibilities," he said. "And my faith has got nothin to do with it."

"I wonder." Her lips pursed again as her cool gaze assessed him. She really did have fine eyes, he thought, they were her best feature. "I had a brother much like you."

That was a surprise, on several fronts. "A psychic? Or a trail guide?"

"Not psychic, no. He was a physician, which is not unlike shepherding fools through the wilderness. His crusade was in the London slums and charity wards, trying to educate the masses on the necessities of clean water and basic sanitation. Quite an uphill battle, considering half the doctors at his hospital didn't believe in those amenities, either." She gazed across the room, squinting slightly, as if the memory were too distant to make out. "He died, during a mysterious outbreak of fever at the hospital."

"Mereck's work?" Trace guessed.

"I have never been certain." She looked at her hands, wiped clean but still twisted in her apron. "After you insisted on that foolish mission to Idaho, I realized how like him you were—and I feared you would sacrifice yourself to the cause, as he did. He said once, the only thing that kept him from falling into despair was to bear in mind the people he *did* save, and how many more remained who could not save themselves." Her smile was bitter, ironic. "I cannot save myself, Mr. Tracy. I am asking you to help me."

The simple, humble words cut him to the quick. He could guess what that admission had cost her, and he had an urge to reach out, take her hands at least, but one didn't touch a lady uninvited. The idea made him uncomfortable, suddenly.

Maybe he did have a soft spot for her. But it wasn't a romantic poetry, courting-on-Sundays kind of feeling. It was the same protective instinct he had toward his sister Emma, and Boz, and the Baptists, and all the young cowboys who'd ever worked under him. She might be feeding him snake oil again, but if it was manipulation she had done it right this time. He could no more refuse a plea like that than he could cut off his own foot.

And since he meant to go after Mereck anyway, he'd be a fool not to take every advantage. So he said, "I want to kill that son of a bitch. Can you help me with that?"

Her gaze sharpened. "It is my sincere intention to try, Mr. Tracy."

"*Can* he be killed?"

"Everything has its antithesis. We have only to find the means." She pursed her lips, searching his face. "And I believe you are the means I've been looking for, for quite some time."

Trace put out his left hand, palm up. Miss Fairweather slid hers into it, cool and tingling with that strange affinity between them.

"Then I reckon I'm your man," he said.